A former au pair, bookseller, marketing manager and seafront trader, **Jessica Gilmore** now works for an environmental charity in York, England. Married with one daughter, one fluffy dog and two dog-loathing cats, she spends her time avoiding housework and can usually be found with her nose in a book. Jessica writes emotional romance with a hint of humour, a splash of sunshine and a great deal of delicious food—and equally delicious heroes!

Michelle Major grew up in Ohio but dreamed of living in the mountains. Soon after graduating with a degree in journalism, she pointed her car west and settled in Colorado. Her life and house are filled with one great husband, two beautiful kids, a few furry pets and several well-behaved reptiles. She's grateful to have found her passion writing stories with happy endings. Michelle loves to hear from her readers at michellemajor.com

Discover more at millsandboon.co.uk

MEDITERRANEAN FLING TO WEDDING RING

JESSICA GILMORE

HIS LAST-CHANCE CHRISTMAS FAMILY

MICHELLE MAJOR

MILLS & BOON

First Published in Great Britain 2020
by Mills & Boon, an imprint of HarperCollinsPublishers,
1 London Bridge Street, London, SE1 9GF

Mediterranean Fling To Wedding Ring © 2020 Jessica Gilmore
His Last-Chance Christmas Family © 2020 Michelle Major

ISBN: 978-0-263-27908-5

1220

MIX
Paper from
responsible sources
FSC® C007454

This book is produced from independently certified FSC™
paper to ensure responsible forest management.

For more information visit: www.harpercollins.co.uk/green

Printed and bound in Spain
by CPI, Barcelona

MEDITERRANEAN FLING TO WEDDING RING

JESSICA GILMORE

CHAPTER ONE

A GOLDEN SLANT of sunshine broke through a chink in the curtains to shine directly onto Lily's closed eyelids. She muttered, moving to escape the brightness, but with that movement came consciousness. She wasn't in her own bed, on her expensive sprung mattress, between her four hundred thread Egyptian cotton sheets, but on an old iron bedstead in a plain white walled room. Despite that she'd slept more deeply than she had for months.

Squinting a little against the sunlight, Lily slipped out of bed and padded across the cold tiled floor to throw open the curtains and to take her first proper look out of the wooden framed window. She inhaled sharply. Sky so blue it defined the colour greeted her, lit by an early morning silvery sun. For the first time in several months the pain inside Lily's chest eased. It felt as if it had done nothing but rain all year in England, and on the few dry days glowering cloud still greyed the sky. This vibrant, warm Croatian beauty was as foreign to her as the language and currency, but so very welcome.

She'd arrived late the evening before, a delayed plane meaning it was already dark by the time she'd cleared passport control, retrieved her bags and stumbled into a waiting taxi. The long day of delays and airports had left her so tired and wrung out she'd barely squinted out of the car window into the dark to try and get any idea of her surroundings. Even the night-time boat ride bringing her to the small island of Lokvar had failed to excite her, it was if she had brought the London gloom with her.

But the beauty of the early morning scene cleared the last remnants of that gloom, instead a hint of anticipation filled her. Reluctantly dragging herself away from the window, Lily darted into the small adjoining bathroom, jumping into the shower to clean the travel grime and sleep from her body, slipping into her comfiest jeans and a T-shirt and bundling her still-wet hair into a loose bun. Less than ten minutes later she was ready to go, running down the winding staircase that led to the main hallway of the large, empty villa.

Empty now, but in just a few weeks this villa would be filled to capacity with holidaymakers all relying on her and her team to ensure their stay ran smoothly. She looked over at the reception desk and her stomach clenched. It seemed impossible that just a week ago she had been Lily Woodhouse, lawyer, London dweller, city worker who routinely worked sixty-hour weeks and rarely saw daylight. What did she know about running a hotel, let alone a hotel in a country where she didn't speak the language, on an island with no cars and just three boats daily into Dubrovnik?

Fighting back the panic, Lily did her best to regulate her breathing, concentrating on inhaling and exhaling until the panic began to fade away, answering each of her panicked mind's questions as calmly as she could. She wouldn't be alone here, experienced help was on its way, and she still had time to find her feet before the tourist season really swung into action and the island welcomed the hordes of visitors who visited every summer. Today she was allowed to take time out and settle in. Today she was going to explore.

She'd bolted the villa's front door the night before, even though common sense had told her that on an island of barely three hundred residents and no way in or out other than by boat, she was safer with an unlocked door than she was behind the padlocks of her London apartment, but old habits died hard and over the last few months Lily had learned all about regret. Slipping her feet into her discarded trainers and grabbing her bag, she unlocked the door and wrenched it open before stepping outside, fumbling for her sunglasses as her eyes adjusted to the light.

The view from the window was nothing compared to the real thing. It might be early but the sun was already warm and she felt its welcome heat permeating through to her tired, tired bones whilst the vibrant colours—green, blue, turquoise—warmed her soul.

The villa faced onto a wide shallow cove, the beach sandy, unusual on this famously rocky coastline. The only building on this side of the island, it ran as a B&B and a beach café through the summer months, a reasonable part of its income derived by renting beach chairs, sunbeds and umbrellas to the day trippers escaping the heat and crowds of Dubrovnik. Lily had never visited Lokvar before, she hadn't even been to Croatia, but she'd seen so many pictures of the villa and Fire Cove, she felt like she'd come home.

Her stepfather, Josip, had described his boyhood home to her many times, and every autumn, after the season ended, his mother, Lily's *baka*, spent several months with them, full of stories about the season just gone, her guests and staff and her friends and neighbours who lived on Lokvar year-round. Josip would sometimes join in, but too often he would leave the room, jaw tight and eyes shuttered. He'd left Dubrovnik at the end of the Balkan conflict, never to return. Lily had never asked why, not knowing how to frame the question, but as she breathed in the fresh sea air and her eyes drank in the glorious scenery she knew his reasons must be deep and dark to prevent him from returning to such beauty.

As if on cue her phone buzzed and Josip's name filled the screen. She fumbled to answer the call, walking down the beach to watch the soft waves roll in as she did so. 'Hi. What time is it there?'

'Six, but your mother couldn't sleep until she knew you were okay.' Lily could hear the smile in his voice as her mother called out something she couldn't quite hear. Josip had lived in the UK for nearly thirty years now, his accent softened but still clear, and her heart filled with love for the man who had brought stability and peace to her turbulent childhood.

'I texted when I arrived last night,' she protested.

'I know that and you know that, but you know how your mother is.' Lily did know, just as she knew her mother would have liked to have accompanied Lily over to Lokvar and helped her ready the B&B for the season ahead, always trying to make up for the chaotic first decade of Lily's life. But she didn't like to travel anywhere without Josip, and he couldn't or wouldn't return to Croatia. Lily prided herself on her independence, but she had to admit that part of her would have liked her mother and her stepfather here as she negotiated her way through the start of her summer.

'Well, tell her I'm fine, at least I will be when I have found some coffee and breakfast.'

'And make sure you get your first grocery order in. Everything is delivered from the mainland, so you need to plan in advance. Ana will be with you tomorrow, she has worked at the villa for years, she will be able to help you with anything you need.'

'I know. I am so glad she has agreed to come early and help me prepare.' The truth was that Ana, Josip's cousin, could quite easily have run the villa without any of Lily's input, having assisted her aunt for the last decade or so. But Lily had needed a change of scene and direction and so when Marija, her step-grandmother, had announced her intention of taking a summer off while she visited cousins in America and New Zealand, Josip had persuaded Lily that the only way his mother would be able to fully enjoy her time away would be if she knew that Lily was keeping an eye on her home.

'She's not getting any younger and I think she needs to take the time to really rest and relax,' he had told Lily. 'I know she spends a couple of months with us every year, but London in late autumn and early winter is so damp and cold, she doesn't get out much. She deserves the chance to really enjoy her time off.'

There was just enough truth in that statement for Lily to agree without feeling too manipulated. It was becoming clear that running her beloved B&B was starting to take its toll on seventy-year-old Marija, and every November she arrived in London looking a little frailer than the year before.

She had confided in Lily that she had received a very lucrative offer for the villa at the end of the last season, but the buyer wanted the land and the access to the beach, not the graceful old villa that had been in her family for generations. 'I want my Josip to return one day, not sell his birthright out from under him,' she had said with a sigh.

Lily just wished she had actually spent a summer here with Marija, after all she'd been invited often enough. But then there were so many things she wished she'd done differently. Too many to name.

She wrenched her attention back to the here and now as her stepfather spoke. 'So what are your plans for today? After coffee, of course.' The jocularity in

Josip's voice didn't hide his worry, and Lily hated that she was responsible for it.

'Explore, start making lists of what we have to do,' she said as carelessly as she could, as if getting a small B&B ready for the start of a busy season was completely part of her skill set. 'Maybe a little sun-bathing while I have time. I know it'll be harder to relax once the tourists arrive.'

'Well, enjoy. And, Lily? Let me know if you need anything at all.'

'I will,' she promised. 'Love to Mum.' Lily swallowed as she disconnected the call, as if by doing so she had disconnected herself from her life. But then her life had already been disconnected three months ago when she'd received the phone call telling her that Izzy, her best friend and flatmate, had been knocked off her bike and was in a coma, and her world and everything she'd thought she knew about who she was and what she wanted had shattered irrevocably.

Inhaling deeply, Lily slipped her phone into her pocket. She was here to make a new start, to try and make some sense of her life. To try and live differently, to *be* different. More spontaneous, impulsive, to actually live her life, not plan her way through it. And she couldn't do that by dwelling on the past. '*Carpe diem,*' she said, her voice wavering as she said the words.

Her old motto, one she and Izzy had adopted at school as they'd competed for the top grades, the top prizes, the university places, had been an only semi-ironic *Veni, Vidi, Vici*. Young, bright and ambitious, they had been so sure that the world was theirs for the taking. And it had been, until a lorry had taken a reckless turn and in one screech of brakes had made a waste of all Izzy's talent and brains, her careful plans, her savings and dreams. So much time spent working and planning, so little time spent actually living. Lily had stood by Izzy's hospital bed and promised her comatose friend that she would do enough living for the both of them. Now she just had to figure out how.

Her new motto felt strange in her mouth. '*Carpe diem*,' she said again. Louder this time. 'Seize the day!' And then again and again until she was yelling it out to sea, hoping that by sending the words out across the waves and into the sea she could somehow make them true. Somehow.

Damir rounded the sandy path leading to Fire Cove and paused. Someone was shouting, calling out as if all the hounds of hell were after them. Adrenaline spiked. Lokvar was one of the safest places on the planet, especially out of season, but nowhere was completely safe. Croatians knew that all too well. He set off at a run, speeding down the slope and onto the beach, skidding to a halt as he looked out to sea, hoping not to see a drowning person, a boat in distress or any of the other scenarios that flashed through his mind as he heard the anguished cry.

His prayer was granted. The only person in view was a woman standing on the edge of the sea, shouting out her pain to the birds and fish. He paused, uncertain. Whoever she was she clearly thought she was alone. She would probably be mortified to know that she been witnessed, but at the same time just walking away and leaving a fellow human being in such a state felt wrong. Damir swore softly. He wasn't so good at the touchy-feely people stuff. His ex-wife had made that all too clear.

To his utter relief, the woman stopped shouting before he intervened. She still stood with her back to him so he had no idea if she was laughing or crying, but she didn't look as if she was in any imminent danger: she wasn't wading into the waves or pulling at her hair. She just stood, slumped, unhappiness radiating from her almost palpably. He should just leave her to it, whatever *it* was. Damir took a step backwards. And as he did so his gaze snagged on the graceful, white villa overlooking the sea. He narrowed his eyes, looking from the villa to the woman.

He didn't recognise her, knew no one with long, honey-blonde hair, currently falling out of its makeshift bun. He didn't know any woman of that exact height and build, tall, curvy and toned, with long lean legs. She could be a tourist as a few did visit out of season, lured by the quiet promised by the island. But she wasn't staying at his hotel, hadn't eaten in his restaurant, and none of his apartments had been let, which left her with very few possible places to stay. One of which was staring him in the face.

Damir retreated quietly until he was sure he was out of earshot of the beach. He pulled his phone from his pocket and found the contact he needed. Less than two rings and the phone call was answered.

'Damir?' The voice was sleepy, as if woken by the call. Damir smiled wryly. His cousin liked to take things easy. The only thing he worked hard at was partying.

'Goran, did you have any passengers yesterday?'

'No, at least nobody new. Just the usual Saturday marketeers. But I believe Igor had a late-night commission. An English girl, needed to be brought over from the mainland.'

Damir's pulse quickened. 'An English girl? Where is she staying?'

'You're best off speaking to Igor, but I think he had arranged a buggy to take her over to the villa at Fire Cove.'

'The villa?'

'Yeah, Marija's place. Igor said the girl is Josip's stepdaughter—he married an English woman a while back, that's why Marija always goes to England over Christmas. But he didn't get much more out of her. A looker he said, but pretty quiet. Why are you so interested anyway?'

'No reason,' Damir lied. He didn't want anyone, not even his cousin, to know how badly he wanted the villa. Not everyone on the island was happy with how much of the island's economy his family controlled. If word got out that he was trying to buy the villa—and with it the lucrative beach trade, he knew he would soon have competitors vying against him. They would be unlikely to be able to afford to outbid him, but they might put the price up. 'Like you say, she's a looker and it's not often pretty girls visit the island out of season.'

'If she's Josip's stepdaughter I guess that makes her one of us.'

'I guess that does. I'd better go make her welcome. Thanks.'

He pocketed his phone and stared back at the narrow sandy path leading to the beach. The one sandy beach on the whole of the island, one of the very few along this rocky coastline. Its perfect curve, fine white sand and gradual shelf made it a safe swimming spot, the tides predictable and gentle, a great place to learn to boat or paddle board or kayak. The sun hit early and continued to beam down until the spectacular sunset. No wonder it was a must-visit destination for the hundreds of thousands of visitors who visited the Dalmatian Riviera every year.

Most came as day trippers, but an increasing amount chose to stay on the island for a night or few, some for even a week, loving the feeling of exclusivity as the last boat pulled away. Damir owned the island's only hotel along with nearly all the apartments available for holiday lets, the island's best restaurant plus a harbourside café-bar, and he had a stake in several other businesses too. The ice-cream stall was his, the little local store and the bakery.

It was small fry compared to his investments in Dubrovnik itself and the rest of the Dalmatian Riviera, but Lokvar was where he was from, where his father and grandfather were from, and it was here that he had made his promise to make the Kozina name respected throughout the city, throughout the country. To achieve the dreams his father and grandfather had hatched throughout the years of repression and conflict. It was a promise that had cost him his marriage, but a promise he was well on the way to achieving.

If he could purchase the villa then his work here on Lokvar would be done. The owner of the villa—and more importantly, the land it stood on—owned the access to the beach, the land overlooking the famous bay, and had all the rights and means to capitalise on the tourists who visited there. Marija kept things simple; a modest B&B, a café-bar and a few sunbeds. Damir's plans were far more exciting. He could turn the bay into Croatia's premier resort. An island getaway. He just needed the villa and, with Josip, Marija's son, clearly settled in England, and Marija beginning to slow down, it had seemed that his time had come.

A grudging smile curved his lips. Trust Marija to make things complicated, saying she needed a year to think about it. With prices around Dubrovnik rocketing with every month and every film or TV series filmed in the scenic capital, a year could prove costly. Unless Damir could get the rest of her family onside…

He didn't know Josip himself. The older man had once been a close friend of Damir's own father, and with him had joined the volunteers tasked with defending Dubrovnik during the siege in the early nineties, but had left his island and country soon after, never to return, and the friendship had died. Any business with Josip would be impersonal, despite the age-old friendship between the families, conducted by lawyers. Unless he could get the step-daughter to look favourably upon his bid.

She might be here just for a night, checking in on the family's property or for a holiday before the season swung into place. Either way time was of the essence. Damir hesitated, picturing again the girl's defeated pose, the raw hurt in her cry, then set his jaw. He had a job to do, and she might just be the key he needed. It was time to show her just how friendly the locals could be.

CHAPTER TWO

LILY'S THROAT WAS RAW, but for the first time in months she felt, if not free, lighter at least. The heavy grief and anger that seemed to continually cloak her in misery and darkness had lifted a little, allowing her to not just notice the warm morning sun but to feel it, the view refreshing her sore eyes.

Wincing at the pain in her throat, she dashed away a tear and took a shaky breath. This fresh start was exactly what she needed. Josip was, as usual, right. A new place, a new challenge and the opportunity to figure out who she was when all she had planned to be seemed futile.

It was daunting, but for the first time Lily felt a tingle of excitement at the challenge. She'd promised Izzy that she would live enough for the two of them, and finally she was making a start. For the next few months this was her workplace and this her work wardrobe instead of the constricting power suits and crippling heels, early morning commute and endless billable hours.

Her stomach rumbled, reminding her she had

barely eaten the day before, but she couldn't bring herself to tear her gaze away from the beauty and tranquillity before her, feeling her battered soul start to repair with every rippling wave. She lingered, taking in strength from the sea, trying to summon up the resolve to walk the short but steep path to the tiny village, only to jump as a deep male voice spoke out from right behind her.

'Are you okay?'

Quickly spinning to face the speaker, Lily took a wary step back as she took in the man who had crept up so noiselessly behind her. Her hands tightened on her phone but whether she planned to use it to call for help or as an absurdly useless weapon she didn't yet know.

'I'm sorry,' the man continued in the same deep, gravelly voice, his Croatian accent as familiar to her as home. 'I didn't mean to frighten you, but you seem to be in distress. I just wanted to check that you're okay.'

Lily's panic ebbed as she noted that the expression in his dark eyes seemed sincere.

'Yes, thank you, I'm fine. Thank you,' she replied and did her best to summon a smile. 'It's very kind of you to check on me, but there's no need.' She held the rigid smile, expecting him to nod and move away, but he remained still, his dark eyes fixed on hers, his expression curious. How long had he been standing there? What had he heard? Enough to know to speak to her in English. Lily's cheeks heated and she tilted her chin, channelling as much poise and dignity as she could muster into her stance.

'I… Ah, I was just practising a healing ritual,' she said, semi-truthfully. Primal screaming was one of the many suggestions well-meaning friends and colleagues had suggested to her over the last three months: primal screaming, kickboxing, therapy, yoga both hot and cold, companion animals, poetry… Everyone seemed to know a way to heal her grief. But the truth was that Lily wasn't ready to heal. What if when the grief left her, Izzy went too? She wasn't ready to say goodbye. Not yet. Maybe not ever.

The man raised an eyebrow much to her reluctant admiration. She'd never been able to pull off that particular gesture although she had tried plenty of times in her teens. 'Healing ritual?'

'Apparently it gets rid of any negative toxins.'

His mouth quirked into a half-smile far more attractive than any smile had any right to be. 'And this is how you start every morning?'

'No, this was the first time. My home is in London and although Londoners are notorious for minding their own business, my neighbours would probably have something to say if I woke them up every morning in that fashion. But I thought I was alone here…' She put an emphasis on the word *alone* but the man didn't seem to notice. Instead, he held out a bronzed capable-looking hand.

'I'm Damir.'

Lily drew in a slow breath. Why couldn't he take the hint and just go away? But, she remembered, this was a small island, one with just three hundred full-time inhabitants. If she was going to spend the whole summer here, she would need to be civil to every one of those three hundred. After all, she was both a stranger and Marija's representative. Being civil, she supposed, included being polite to nosy men who seemingly couldn't take a hint.

Nosy and, if she was being honest, rather disturbingly attractive.

'Lily Woodhouse.' She made no move to take his hand and he casually dropped it to his side as if he hadn't even noticed her snub. Did nothing discombobulate him? Lily had never met anyone so seemingly at home in his own skin before. Tall, lean but with a quiet strength, Damir was just a few years older than she was, around thirty, she estimated. His jeans and short-sleeved white shirt were casual but exquisitely and expensively cut, showing off the breadth of his shoulders and muscled forearms and thighs. His dark hair was longer than she was used to, the alpha male city types she worked with favoured no-nonsense close crops and clean shaves, but Damir's chin was covered with dark morning stubble and his hair grazed his neck at the back, falling disarmingly onto his forehead, framing eyes so brown they were almost black. A firm chin, cheekbones cut sharper than a mountain ridge and a resolute mouth defined by a dangerously sexy dimple at the corner of his mouth, adding a boyishness to the handsome features, completed the undeniably appealing package.

Heat stirred low in her belly, as unwelcome as it was unexpected. The last thing Lily was interested in was dating, but there was an edgy attractiveness to him that even her tired body reluctantly responded to.

Damir's smile widened. 'Welcome to Lokvar, Lily Woodhouse. Will you be staying with us for long?'

Lily hesitated, but her job here was no secret and the sooner the word was out who she was and why she was here the better. 'For the summer,' she said. 'I'm looking after the villa over there. Marija's villa.'

'So you must be Josip's daughter?'

'Yes.' She didn't need to correct the assumption and add in the 'step'—she couldn't imagine loving any actual father more than she loved Josip.

'We all miss Marija, she is very respected. I hope she is okay?' The dark eyes glowed with sincerity.

Some of Lily's tension melted at the thought of her voluble grandmother. 'She had a wonderful few months in New Zealand. Her pictures are amazing, one minute she's in Hobbiton, the next whale watching. She's in the States now, planning a trip to Nashville.'

'And she's left you in charge? Quite a responsibility.' His gaze sharpened. 'Are you used to working in hospitality?'

'I'm a lawyer.' Lily said, bristling a little at the unwanted interrogation. 'But I waitressed a lot through school and university, I'm used to dealing with people.'

'A lawyer? Your firm must be very accommodating to allow you to take the summer off.'

What was with all the questions? Lily folded her arms and took a step back. 'I'm on a sabbatical.' That was what they were calling it anyway. Her boss had refused to accept the resignation she had sent in six weeks after Izzy's funeral. She was marked for partner one day, those fourteen-to sixteen-hour days leading her along a path she had thought she wanted. Had worked towards tirelessly, spending her life in the library while her peers were clubbing, determined not to make her mother's mistakes.

'Take some time,' Priya had said with uncharacteristic kindness. 'Think about it before you do anything irrevocable. Your job is open for six months. We'd hate to lose you, Lily, you are one of our brightest and best. I have great hopes for you.' Once those words were all Lily had wanted to hear. Now they were as meaningless as the glass and metal apartment with its views over London she'd been so excited to move into, or her wardrobe of expensive suits and designer shoes.

She glanced towards the villa, angling away from Damir in a clear gesture that she was ready to finish the conversation. 'It's nice meeting you, Damir, but I really need to find some breakfast before Ana arrives. I didn't get a chance to stock up yesterday as my flight was delayed.'

'In that case,' Damir said smoothly, 'you must allow me to buy you some breakfast. As a way to welcome you to the island. Please, it would be entirely my pleasure.'

* * *

Damir leaned back in his chair and surreptitiously surveyed Lily through his sunglasses as she dipped her bread in olive oil before topping it with creamy feta cheese. After her initial wariness she seemed to have started to relax, helped no doubt by the excellent coffee and platter of bread, cheese and olives along with the small pastries and homemade jam he'd presented her with after seating her at a table overlooking the harbour.

It had taken some of his best persuasive methods and all his charm to persuade the clearly suspicious English girl to accept his offer of breakfast. But once he'd mentioned that only one island café was open at this time of year, and that he just happened to be the owner, she had thawed a little and finally accepted his offer, although she had said little on the short but steep walk across the island to the village, clearly still preoccupied with whatever had provoked her distress on the beach.

He didn't mind her silence, it gave him time to work out how to turn this unexpected opportunity to his advantage. Marija had made it clear to him that she wouldn't consider his offer to buy the villa until she had spent a year away. He had planned to spend that time ensuring an irresistible proposal was ready for her return, and that everything was in place to start moving the second she signed the contract. Lily hadn't featured in his plans. After all, it was only a few days since he'd heard rumours that Josip's English daughter was coming to look after the villa.

But here she was, a pale, solemn girl with pain in her eyes and a smile that looked as if it was pasted on. There was a story there, but Damir wasn't interested in stories. What he *was* interested in was finding out just what Marija's long-term plans were and if this girl figured in them. If she did, he needed to make some readjustments. And if not, if she was only here for the summer, then maybe he could get her to see that his offer was the best thing for Marija. For the island. Which meant turning the charm up, breaking the silence and befriending her. After all, so far she knew no one here. He could show her around, make himself indispensable. It wouldn't exactly be a hardship, she was a pretty girl.

'How's your breakfast?' Not the most original of questions but he had to start a conversation somehow. Lily looked up, her expression a little confused as if she had forgotten where she was and who she was with. And then she smiled, her face transformed from pretty to extraordinarily beautiful by the gesture, and Damir felt a flickering of desire tighten his stomach. His clasp tightened on his cup. He didn't need or want feelings to complicate business. And this was all about business. What else was there?

'This coffee is the best coffee I've ever had in my entire life,' Lily said, taking another sip. 'I've been to so many hipster cafés with menus showcasing literally hundreds of coffees from all over the world, boasting about the origin and roasting process and the rarity of the beans, and not one cup has come close to this.'

'Croatians take their coffee very seriously.' Damir picked up his own cup and inhaled the satisfyingly bitter steam. 'If you're going to spend the summer here, then this is probably the most important thing you need to know.'

'Marija said that most of her guests are English or German or American, but she does get a fair number of Croatians as well. I hope Ana knows how to make coffee because I don't think my barista talents are up to scratch.'

'Just make it strong,' Damir advised her. 'That's the most important thing. Croatians may forgive a less than perfect cup, but they won't forgive a weak one.'

'I'll remember that, thank you.' Lily pushed her plate away with another of those breath-taking smiles. The flickering of desire intensified and this time Damir didn't rush to quench it, much as he knew he should. 'And thank you for breakfast. That was absolute delicious, I needed it much more than I realised. Yesterday was a very long day, and the last few months have been… Anyway, I feel much more ready to get started now.' She leaned back, looking around her, eyes wide. 'What an amazing view and right on the harbour. It's an incredible position. You must be the first port of call when the ferries and boats arrive.'

That was why his grandfather had chosen to situate the café here, of course, and Damir had learned the lesson well: his hotel and restaurant, like the café, were carefully positioned to ensure proximity to the small village whilst ensuring guests had the best views on the island—apart from Marija's villa. 'First and last port of call. There is no better spot to while away half an hour waiting for a boat.'

'Have your family always owned it?'

'My grandfather opened it—he was the village baker, but always wanted to own a restaurant. He passed it onto my father and then to me.'

'And what about the bakery?'

'I own that too.'

Lily raised her eyebrows. 'Quite the island monopoly you have there.'

'You could say that,' Damir said noncommittally. Of course, many people *did* say exactly that.

'What's it like?' Lily leaned forward, her hands clasped around the coffee cup. 'Living in such a small place, seeing the same faces every single day, with the sea between you and the next town? Does it get claustrophobic?' There was an intensity to the question Damir couldn't interpret. He got the impression that Lily Woodhouse was running away from something.

'Claustrophobic? How could it feel claustrophobic when the sky stretches all around, when you look out onto the endless sea? But, no, island life isn't for everyone. A few are born here and never leave, others return after time away and some go as soon as they can and never come back. But people here are like people anywhere, there are those who gossip, there are those who like to stir up trouble, those who don't pull their weight. But there's nowhere else like it. Of course, we all have our own boats so we can escape from each other when we need to.'

She laughed, but the shadows were back in her eyes. 'And do you? Escape?'

'Ah, well, I actually only live here part of the time. I have a villa in Dubrovnik, I run most of my business from there…'

'In Dubrovnik? There's more, then, than the café and bakery monopoly?'

'Some holiday lets,' he said smoothly. Damir wasn't sure why he was hiding the bulk of his business from Lily. After all, Marija had a very good idea of his situation, all the island did, it was hardly a secret. But he had a sense that it would be easier to get Lily to trust him, to advocate for him, if she saw him as a small-time businessman. Maybe, if she knew just how real his island monopoly actually was, with the hotels and restaurants and the apartments in Dubrovnik, the villas along the coastline, she would be as uneasy about his desire to also own the coveted access onto the beach as her grandmother was.

There was another reason behind his decision to downplay his wealth, although he barely liked to admit it even to himself. Money had changed how people saw him, changed his standing in the community, in the city. Since his divorce, he'd been the target of local socialites, interested not in him but in the wealth he'd accumulated and the covetable real estate he owned.

He had no problem with the unacknowledged chasm between himself and his former peers and he certainly didn't mind the attention of the city's wealthiest and most eligible young women. But there was a simple pleasure sitting in the morning sun, enjoying getting to know a pretty girl who had no preconceptions about him. A pleasure he hadn't enjoyed for a very long time. Not since Kata.

He pushed the memory of his ex-wife away, glad of the reminder that he should never mix business with pleasure. Attractive as she was, Lily clearly had secrets of her own and history had taught him that his dreams and complicated women did not mix. If he married again he would choose one of the socialites, a woman who understood how marriage at his level worked. Someone who in return for a lavish lifestyle would raise his family, be a consummate hostess and need nothing else from him.

'Thank you again for breakfast.' Lily pushed back her chair and stood up. 'You must let me repay you when we're open for business.'

'It was my pleasure, no repayment necessary.' Although he would take her up on the offer. It would be an excellent way to further the acquaintance. 'What are your plans for the rest of the day?'

'Explore a little and then I had better go and familiarise myself with the villa before Ana gets here so I don't look like too much of an idiot. I also need to put my first order together—Marija says if I email it to the supermarket they deliver it to the ferry and I just need to meet the ferry with a golf cart. Much cheaper than the local shop. Although maybe I shouldn't have said that.' She clapped a hand over her mouth, eyes bright with a laughing apology. 'You probably own the local shop too, don't you?'

'Everyone on the island orders off the mainland.' Damir neatly sidestepped the question of the shop's ownership. 'But they're very grateful for the shop when the weather is stormy or they've run out of milk for their morning coffee. It was nice to meet you, Lily. Let me know if you need any help with anything. I'd love to show you around sometime, you should take the opportunity to explore while you're here and I am a wonderful tour guide, or so I've been told.'

He also stood up and held out his hand, and after a tiny hesitation she took it, her clasp smooth and warm. His pulse jumped at the contact, electricity zinging up his arm, and it was all he could do not to drop her hand and jump back. What was that about?

True, he had been working ridiculous hours lately even by his standards so maybe this reaction was a sign he should indulge in one of the short, no-strings relationships he had occasionally embarked on since his divorce. He released her hand, his heart still hammering.

'That's very kind of you, but I'm not sure how much time I'll have for sightseeing. Thank you again—and I am sorry for this morning. I forgot how small the island actually is so no more morning rituals on the beach for me. Anyway, as it's a small island, I'm sure I'll see you again.' And with another quick smile she was off, hurrying back along the harbour-side to the narrow road that crisscrossed the island.

Frowning, Damir watched her go. She'd jumped back from his offer to take her out as if it were a marriage proposal. It was a long time since he'd been turned down by a woman. Still, it wasn't yet June and summer was a long season on Lokvar. He had plenty of time to befriend the English girl. By the end of the summer he'd have her exactly where he wanted her—on his side. After all, this was business and that was an area where he always won out in the end.

CHAPTER THREE

'I CAN'T BELIEVE that in a few days' time the villa will be full of guests.' Lily shook a pillow vigorously. 'I have no idea how we'll be ready on time. Thank goodness you already took care of hiring the staff and they'll be here tomorrow to help us.'

She placed the pillow with exaggerated care on the bed she was making up and grinned at Ana, Josip's cousin and Marija's right hand woman. Every summer Ana left her home in the capital, Zagreb, to return to the island of her birth and help run the B&B—and as Lily realised less than hour after meeting her she was a fount of all knowledge about everyone and everything on Lokvar.

Several times Lily had tried to get up the courage to ask her aunt about Damir but couldn't quite find the words. His offer to show her around was probably just common courtesy—but there had been something more than mere politeness in his eyes, a curious intentness she couldn't decipher.

Neither could she work out her own reaction to him. That jolting physical reaction, unlike anything she had ever felt before on a first meeting, unexpected—and not exactly unpleasant—heat coursing through her body. It wasn't like her. She always, always took relationships slowly; compatibility, then liking, then attraction. That was the safe, the sensible thing to do.

But, then again, wasn't she here to be a little less safe, a little less sensible? She picked up another pillow and pummelled it extra hard, glad to take out her uncertainty on the inanimate object.

'I had no idea just how much there was to do,' she continued, hoping to banish persistent thoughts of dark, dark eyes from her mind. 'All the floors to scrub and polish, the curtains to wash and iron, and that's not even considering outside. I've started the weeding, but all the paintwork still needs freshening. It's a good thing I didn't assume that spending the summer here on Lokvar was a chance to take things easy, imagine how disappointed I would be! I've barely had two minutes to sit in the sun, and I'm not sure that's going to change any time soon.'

What she didn't say, tried not to think, was that it suited her to keep so busy, it stopped her from thinking. Stopped her from missing Izzy, from remembering her promise, a promise she had no idea how to actually keep. How did she change the deeply ingrained habits of a lifetime, start living for today instead of planning for tomorrow? Yes, she had taken leave from her work to come here, but what next?

The way things were going she was going to be too busy to work out how to be spontaneous anyway. But if she didn't follow through then not only was she breaking a promise but she'd have failed. Only Izzy had known just how much Lily hated to fail. So somehow she was going to just get on with it. Be spontaneous. Have fun. Live enough for the lost years of hard work and planning, for Izzy's lost future.

'Don't worry about the paintwork. Luka can take care of that.' Ana took the battered pillow from Lily and placed it beside its fellow, straightening the sheet's edge as she did so. Immediately the room looked made up, crisp and clean. Ana had magic in her fingers, a way of making everything look just so. A talent Lily knew she didn't have a chance of emulating.

'We'd best make use of that lazy son of mine while we can. Once tourists start turning up and wanting to hire sunbeds and order drinks he'll be otherwise occupied. I hope I haven't made a mistake bringing him here this summer, I don't want him to waste his time lounging outside, flirting with pretty tourists.'

'I'm sure poor Luka will do nothing of the sort,' protested Lily. 'Look at how much help he's been yesterday and this morning.'

'When he looked up from his books, that was.' Ana might sound annoyed but she couldn't hide the proud glow in her eyes. Her other children had all grown up and moved out long ago. Luka, in his second year at the local university, had been a surprise baby, born once his siblings had reached teenhood and quite clearly the apple of his doting mother's eyes.

'You can't have it both ways,' Lily said. 'Either he's too studious or all he wants to do is ogle tourists, pick one.'

'I'm sure he is quite capable of doing both,' Ana said darkly, and picked up the pillow to give it another hard shake.

A warm glow filled Lily. It was nice, this comradely routine. At the high-powered corporate law firm she'd worked for since she'd left Oxford, there was no such thing as chitchat. Everyone was competitive, everybody out for the main advantage and every word a weapon. She hadn't enjoyed gossip at work like this since she and Izzy had worked together in a local café during sixth form.

She turned around to survey the bedroom, the first one readied for the expected guests. Marija's villa didn't labour under any boutique hotel pretensions. It was simple, clean and homely and Lily loved it. The floors were wooden and covered in brightly coloured rugs, the walls a bright fresh white, hung with Croatian seascapes. The furniture was unpretentious but well made: comfortable sofas heaped with cushions, iron bedsteads and soft white linen. There was no on-site gym, no pool, but there were stunning views from every window and it was less than two minutes from the front door to the edge of the sea.

A buzzing noise filled the room and Lily darted to the window to see a golf cart cresting the hill that led to the village. 'Ooh, I wonder what that is?' She couldn't get over the charming novelty of receiving her groceries by golf cart once they'd arrived on that morning's ferry.

'I thought we'd received today's order,' Ana said.

'We did but maybe we forgot something. I'll go check.' Lily sprang down the stairs, out of the open front door and down the small stone flight of stairs leading onto a wide paved terrace where she almost barrelled into the bronzed young man who delivered orders from the ferry.

'Sorry,' she gasped. 'I thought I'd save you a trip. Oh…' She stopped as she realised that, instead of the expected bag of groceries, he held a gorgeous bouquet of flowers. 'Are these for us? *Hvala.*' Thank you was of the very few words of Croatian she could manage.

She took the huge bouquet, barely able to see over the top of the colourful blooms and, much more carefully than she had exited the villa, returned to the hallway where Ana was waiting for her.

'Aren't they beautiful?' Lily carefully placed them on the perfectly polished reception desk. 'They must be from Mum and Josip. How thoughtful. That is, if they are for me?' She looked guiltily at the older woman. 'Of course, they could be for you.'

'For me?' Ana's laugh echoed melodiously around the hallway. 'Who would be sending me flowers like that? If it was my husband I'd be immediately suspicious about what he was up to.'

'I'm sure he still sends you flowers sometimes.

Let's see.' Lily extracted the envelope tucked into the side of the flowers and opened it, staring at the words in disbelief, heat infusing her cheeks as she did so. 'Oh! They're not from Mum after all. How peculiar.'

She read the card again, not sure she'd taken it in properly the first time, but there was no change in the words, written in decisive yet elegant script.

Dear Lily,
Good luck for the start of the season. I hope to see you at the island party tomorrow.
If you've changed your mind about that personal tour just let me know.
Damir

Lily's cheeks heated even further as she handed Ana the card and watched her read it, her thinly plucked eyebrows almost comically high. Ana whistled long and low as she gave the card back to Lily.

'Damir Kozina,' she said slowly, drawing out every syllable. Lily couldn't tell if her tone was admiring or admonishing. 'I didn't know you two were acquainted.'

'Hardly,' protested Lily. 'I ran into him just before you arrived and he bought me breakfast, nothing more exciting than that.' She looked again at the flowers, bright and cheerful and clearly expensive. 'Certainly nothing exciting enough to warrant flowers like these. Maybe he's just being nice…' she finished doubtfully.

'Damir? Nice?' Ana gave a snort of laughter. 'I've

never known him do anything if there isn't something in it for him. You must have made quite an impression.'

'I probably did,' Lily admitted. 'He caught me at a weak moment. These flowers are probably a pity gift more than anything else. I bet he thinks I'm not going to last the first week of having to deal with actual people.'

'If you say so,' Ana said. 'Be careful, though, he has quite a reputation.'

'Oh?' Here was the chance she'd been waiting for. So why wasn't she jumping straight in with questions? Luckily Ana continued before she could think of something that sounded suitably disinterested.

'He's been a bit of a playboy since his divorce. High-maintenance girls from the mainland if my sources are right, and they usually are. I wouldn't have said you were his type, I've never known him go after tourists or islanders before. I guess we'll see at the party. You'll be turning all the single girls green if Damir *is* interested in you. Half the seasonal staff only take jobs here in the hope of snaring him.'

Lily couldn't help but feel a twinge—well, more than a twinge if she was being honest—of curiosity at the information, but something more pressing had to be dealt with. This wasn't the first time the harbourside party that kicked off the season in Lokvar had been mentioned over the last few days. It was clearly quite an occasion, but the thought of spending an evening with a lot of strangers, bound to ask about why she was here, was a terrifying thought.

'Oh, yes.' Lily turned away, aiming for nonchalant. 'The party. I'm not sure that I'm going to go.'

'Not go?' Ana said, her voice incredulous. 'But, Lily, everybody goes. It's our last chance to relax and enjoy ourselves before the summer starts.'

'Parties aren't really my thing,' Lily said. 'Besides, this is the island's party, for the people who live here. I'm just as much a visitor as the tourists and I don't speak a word of Croatian. I'd probably just make people uncomfortable, hanging around not knowing anyone and not able to join in, needing everyone to translate all the time.'

'You may have noticed, everybody speaks English.' Ana put her hands on her hips. 'And you are Marija's granddaughter, which makes you one of us. Your grandmother never misses a party, in fact she is usually one of the last to leave. If you are here looking after things for her then it's your duty to represent her. We've got a long and busy season ahead of us, Lily, you have to grab your fun where you can.'

The protest died on Lily's lips. Hadn't she just been wondering where to start with her *live for the moment* project and here she was, failing at the first hurdle. Was it the thought of a whole party full of strangers that daunted her—or the knowledge that Damir would be there possibly looking for her? Or, worse, not looking for her and flirting with some heiress.

'Maybe you're right. I'll think about it,' Lily said. 'I promise.'

'Make sure you do. Don't shut yourself away,

Lily.' Ana gave her hand a quick squeeze before bustling away to berate Luka for taking a quick break.

Lily slowly made her way back upstairs, leaving the flowers on the reception desk. Beautiful as they were, they would dominate her small room, be a constant reminder of Damir and the way she'd reacted to him, the way a tingle had shot up her arm when he'd touched her, the way his half-smile had made her want to reach out and touch that unlikely dimple. She'd done her best to put him out of her mind, but when she'd walked to the shop yesterday and seen a tall, lean man in sunglasses and an expensive-looking shirt, an unequivocal quiver of expectation had rippled through her, only to turn to disappointment when he'd turned out to be a complete stranger.

She paused, torn between returning to work and taking some time out, before heading up another floor to her small attic bedroom. The room was sparsely furnished: a bed, a small wardrobe and a dressing table, a rug on the floor. She had brought little with her, and the room was almost devoid of anything personal except for a framed picture on the dressing table. Lily picked it up, swallowing as she did so.

She didn't really need to look at it, she knew exactly what she'd see, could have described every detail down to the flowers in the background and the colour of the subjects' brightly painted toenails. But she studied it, as if answers could be found in the laughing face of the two girls in the photo.

The girls were around sixteen, posing dramatically in the back garden of Lily's parents' small terraced house in Ealing. They were both dressed up, Lily in a floor-length dress of a deep blue that matched her eyes and made her blonde hair gleam golden in the sun, the neckline and waistline sparkling with tiny crystals, the same crystals studding her elaborate updo. Izzy, disdaining the traditional as usual, had gone for a vintage Fifties look in a vibrant red polka dot that suited her curves and wild, dark curls.

Lily couldn't look at the photo without remembering the intense concentration it had taken for Izzy to outline her eyes with a perfect cat flick, or the at least four coats of mascara it had taken her to achieve the big-eyed look she'd wanted. They looked so innocent, so full of life, convinced everything they wanted lay before them. If they'd known just how little time they really had, would they have changed everything? Spent more time living, less time planning? Been bolder?

'I can't remember the last time I went to a party without you,' Lily said out loud. 'Who will I talk to? Who will understand my signal when I've had enough and want to leave or want to ditch the guy who won't take a hint?' Or give her the thumbs up if she didn't want to ditch the guy but needed a second opinion?

Lily carefully placed the framed photo back onto the dressing table and started to turn away, but the sunlight fell on Izzy's face, and she stopped. 'What?' Lily asked. 'You think I should go? You were the brave one, not me. You led I followed, you know that.'

She waited, half expecting an answer, and dashed away a tear, angry at her foolishness. 'What more can I do? I know I promised it would all be different. I promised no more planning, no more existing. I promised I'd live enough for us both. Well, I'm here. Look. Not in an office, not in the apartment or the gym. I'm actually abroad. And, yes, I haven't seen much of abroad yet and, yes, I have been working since I got here but it's a start.'

Another pause then Lily heaved a sigh, one so deep it hurt her already weary heart. 'You're right. I should have said yes to the offer to explore. I should say yes more often, not hide behind, well, I'm not sure what I hide behind now you're not here. He was hot, don't you think he was hot? Not like those corporate finance guys I dated or even like the hipster Silicon Valley tycoon wannabes you used to meet. He didn't look like a treadmill pounder to me, more like someone who isn't afraid to get his hands dirty.'

She sat down on the bed, then flopped down onto her pillow, lying back to stare up at the ceiling fan, remembering the way Damir had held her gaze, the warmth in his eyes. He'd asked her out, sent her flowers and she was still planning to hide back at the villa?

Ana had said he was a playboy. That settled it. Lily was not a playboy's type. Too sensible, too busy, too boring.

But not here. Here she was new, different, trying

to be impulsive. And wouldn't a playboy be a good person to be impulsive with? Lily wasn't looking for love or marriage, but a summer away should include a little romance, surely? Armed with foreknowledge she'd be in no danger of falling for Damir's practised charms, but maybe she could enjoy a no-strings flirtation?

'Okay, you win. As usual. I will go to the party and I will try to flirt with the hot guy, and if he offers to take me to explore again I'll accept. Satisfied?'

Lily sat up and glared at the photo. Obviously it was a trick of the light, but for one moment she could have sworn Izzy gave her a nod of approval.

CHAPTER FOUR

D<small>AMIR DOUBLE-CHECKED THE</small> mooring ropes one last time before lightly springing off his boat onto the long wooden jetty, his chest clenching as he took in the carnival-like atmosphere.

The wide paved promenade that fronted Lokvar's small and only village hummed with a throng of excited, chattering people, many of whom were dressed up for the occasion. Fairy lights were strung around every available tree, sign or post and, although it was not yet dusk, shone brightly. The rich smells of grilled meat and vegetables permeated the air and the unmistakable heavy rock sounds of the island's one and only band rang out, a makeshift dance floor roped off to minimise the risk of one of the overexcited children already jumping up and down falling into the shallow sea.

Lokvar village spanned half of the island's wide main bay. The brightly coloured, thick-walled fishermen's cottages were now shops and apartments catering to tourists, the residents having moved inland to live in newer, more convenient villas and apartments. But for festivals everyone congregated here by the sea. Damir knew every single person drinking and laughing on the harbourside—and they all knew him.

His chest tightened further. Truth was he hadn't enjoyed an island party since the season end celebration seven years ago when his ex-wife Kata had turned and walked away, ending their marriage as she did so. No, before that, since his wealth had started to divide him from the people he had grown up with. He only attended because he sponsored it. Because it was expected.

He set his jaw grimly. He had only had two failures in his life. The death of his father and the collapse of his marriage. He would not tolerate a third. Tonight he would find, flatter and woo the English girl and find out Marija's long-term plans. Fulfilling his father's plan to develop Fire Cove would help assuage some of his guilt over how he had let him down in life.

But beneath the determination he was aware of an entirely different emotion—anticipation. Not the expected anticipation of long-awaited business success but anticipation of seeing the English girl— Lily—again.

He couldn't remember the last time such a short meeting had had such an effect on him—and he had no idea why. She was pretty enough, especially when she unleashed that breath-taking smile, but she hadn't said much during their one meeting, and of course when he had first seen her she had been

doing a fine impersonation of some kind of Bac-
chanal naiad, yelling out to sea. Not quite the cool,
poised, confidence displayed by the women he usually chose for the safe, short-term relationships he
preferred.

But the lurking sadness in her eyes, the sense of
regret and pain had called to him. After all, they mirrored his own. Hopefully tonight he'd be able to get
her out of his brain once and for all and concentrate
on what really mattered. The villa.

Damir squared his shoulders and strolled off the
jetty, joining the nearest gathering, radiating all the
confidence due to the owner of half the island. The
man who sponsored tonight's festivities and em-
ployed most of the guests.

'Damir, finally!'

'There's a drink here with your name on it, my
friend. Well, you did pay for it!'

Immediately friends and relatives, most of whom
worked for him, surrounded him, bombarding him
with the gossip from the evening so far, handing
him a gratefully received pint of beer. For a moment it was as if he had stepped back in time to
when his father had been alive, Kata by his side,
and he was still—just—one of the gang. Occasionally he missed this comradeship and ease, so different from the politely cut-throat friendships found in
the boardrooms, golf clubs and highbrow functions
attended by Dubrovnik's old aristocratic and new
moneyed classes to which he now belonged. Part of
him would have liked to stay right here, reverted to

being the old Damir for one night only. But as always he had work to do.

Work that would start once Lily arrived. The flowers were just the first step. Tonight he would dazzle her with attention, invite her out onto his boat, woo her. Play his cards right and the English girl would be putty in his hands, ready to be moulded into the perfect ally.

Taking a sip of beer, Damir looked around, hoping to glimpse a flash of honey-blonde hair. His earlier anticipation ramped up, humming through him, every nerve hyperaware of every smell, sound and taste, from the rhythm of the band to the salt permeating the air. He took a breath, willing the adrenaline to slow.

A hush fell over the group and Damir realised his friends were looking at something—or someone—behind him with a mixture of curiosity and admiration. Hair prickled on the back of his neck. She was here, he could feel it. Turning slowly, he inhaled, a long, deep breath of appreciation. Lily and Ana were walking slowly down the winding, hilly path that bisected the island, chatting casually as they did so.

Ana, like most of the islanders, had dressed up in a dress and heels but Lily was more simply dressed in jeans and a silky cream camisole top, her long blonde hair loose, cascading way past her shoulders and moving in time with her stride. She wore little makeup but her cheeks were pink, potentially with embarrassment as nearly everyone had stopped to look at the newcomer in their midst. She tilted her chin defiantly and her eyes blazed with purpose. Damir's pulse began to beat loudly. She looked magnificent.

Barely aware of his friends' comments and sniggers, Damir stepped away from the group and walked slowly over to greet her as she finally descended the last few steps of the path.

'I'm so glad you made it, Lily,' he said, and smiled at her companion. 'It's lovely to see you, Ana, welcome back to Lokvar. I hope your family are well.'

Ana looked from Damir to Lily, her smile knowing. 'Everyone is fine, thank you. How is your mother?'

'She's good. I'll tell her that you were asking after her.'

'I was hoping she'd be here. It's been a long time since I saw her.'

'Since she remarried she prefers to stay on the mainland.' His mother had always maintained that if his father had had his heart attack in Dubrovnik, he'd have reached the hospital on time. She hadn't returned to Lokvar since. Or forgiven Damir for not working that day as his father had wanted.

That was fine, he didn't want her forgiveness. After all, he couldn't forgive himself.

Ana nodded. 'Well, give her my best.'

'I will. Enjoy the party.' Damir turned to Lily. 'It's nice to see you again, Lily.'

For a brief second an entire reel of emotions passed over Lily's face. Damir saw uncertainty and worry flicker there, before they disappeared as if they'd never been as she tilted her chin and smiled at him. 'Thank you for the flowers. I should buy you a drink to say thank you.'

'Not necessary, the bar is free tonight. But, please, join me?'

He noted the barely perceptible hesitation before she answered. 'That would be lovely.'

'Great, the bar's this way. Have a good evening,' he added politely to Ana, before leading Lily over to one of the outdoor bars that had been set up for the evening. 'What would you like? Both the beer and wine are brewed locally, and I can recommend both.'

'In that case a glass of white wine, please.'

Damir was aware of being surreptitiously watched by at least half of the village as he procured a glass of white wine for Lily and a top-up of his own beer. He steered her towards an empty table, set aside from the rest, and placed the drinks on it.

'Thank you,' she said, as he pulled out her seat for her. 'And thank you again for the flowers, they're beautiful.'

'You're welcome. I wanted to mark the start of your first season. I know how hectic these weeks are even for people who do it year after year.'

'It has been crazy, although luckily I have Ana.' Lily shook her head ruefully. 'To be honest, she could run the whole place single-handedly. I'm pretty sure I'm more of a hindrance than a help.'

'I'm sure that's not true,' Damir protested, and Lily laughed.

'Oh, it is. I know she would deny it, she's far too nice, but she has to waste half her time showing me how to do things that are second nature to her.' She grimaced. 'In fact, the last couple of days have been a rude awakening. Quite a dent to my ego.'

'In what way?' Damir was, despite himself, intrigued. Lily was like a different woman. Last time they had sat here overlooking the sea she had been withdrawn, thoughtful, but tonight she sparkled with life. He'd been prepared to lead the conversation, to draw her out, not to find himself amused at her playful self-deprecation. Far from being wrong-footed, he found himself leaning in, fascinated.

'Okay, I appreciate how big-headed this sounds but I've always prided myself on being good at most things. I like to succeed. But it turns out being able to follow a recipe adequately does not equip me for a role in a commercial kitchen and my washing-up is not of a high enough standard for the chef. I only speak one language compared to Ana's four—four!—and so she will have to do most of the front of house and the bookings as well as manage the staff.

'And just when I think I've been really useful and cleaned something properly or made up a bedroom perfectly, I see her surreptitiously tidying up after me because I missed a corner.' Lily took a gulp of her wine. 'It's all been very lowering. My ambitions have shrunk to one thing only—to make a bed that Ana approves of. If only my manager could see me now.'

'Are you regretting choosing Lokvar for your sabbatical?'

It was a slightly flippant question, one in keeping with the lightness of the conversation. Damir

was expecting Lily to brush it away with a comment
about spending a summer abroad or the beauty of
the island but instead she sat back and sipped her
wine thoughtfully, clearly considering her answer.

'No,' she said at last. 'Obviously it's really lovely
to see Marija's home in person, I've heard so much
about it over the last few years. And it's been good
to be so busy, even if I am a little bit ineffectual. I'm
learning new skills and, more importantly, I'm learning how to get a sense of fulfilment from a small
job well done and that's good for me. I'm usually always ten steps ahead, I don't allow myself the time
to enjoy the moment and that's something I need to
change. But mostly it's been good to get away from
London and the office and start to think about what
it's all really about.'

'It?'

'Life.'

Damir wasn't sure he'd heard her properly. 'Life?'

She nodded, eyes focussed on something or someone far away, as if she were half somewhere else.
'Life. I made a vow, to start living properly. I came
here to get away from the sixteen-hour days and no
social life and the intensity, but I know me, it's easy
to fall back into bad habits, especially when there's
the B&B to run and there's always something to do.

'So I've promised myself that I must do one spontaneous thing a day to try and break the cycle. But
then I find that I am beginning to plan even that! I
find it so uncomfortable to try and go with the flow.
And then I feel like I'm failing and I'm back to where

I started. Promising myself I'll do better, be better.'
She stopped then, cheeks pink. 'I am so sorry. I am
so bad at this.'

'This?'

'Small talk. I am really out of practice—not that
I was ever really good at it. You must think I am utterly crazy, shouting at the sea one day, yakking on
about trying to be spontaneous the next.'

'I'm thinking,' Damir said slowly, 'that you're not
like anybody else I know.'

'I'm sure that's true. You must be dying to get
back to your friends and tell them all about the crazy
English girl. Honestly, please, there is no need to be
polite. I'll go find Ana. Thank you for the drink.'

'I'm not being polite,' Damir said, putting up a
hand to stay her as she half rose from her seat. 'I'm
right where I want to be.'

He would have said those exact words anyway,
but to his surprise he realised they were the truth.

'That's very kind of you, but I'm not sure I believe
you.' Lily covered her face with her hands for a second. 'What would Izzy say to me? No, I know exactly what she'd say, that I'm not fit to even conduct
a light flirtation unsupervised. And she'd be right.'

Damir stilled, all intent to laugh disappearing,
his whole body on high alert. He fought to keep his
tone light. 'A flirtation? Is that what we're doing?'

Lily could feel her cheeks get hotter and hotter. She
wanted to turn away, but was trapped by Damir's

dark gaze. She couldn't tell if he was amused or horrified by her gaucheness. Probably both.

But it wasn't amusement or horror she could see in his eyes. Instead there was a flash of something more primal, almost predatory. A shiver snaked down her spine as she finally looked away, grabbing her wine glass and focussing on it as if it held the elixir of life.

'I...'

Possible get-out clauses flashed through her mind. She could say she'd meant *hypothetically*, try to laugh the awkward words off or, preferred option, simply run away. *But*, she could hear Izzy say, *why not just own it?* Wasn't that what she was here to do? Flirt? Be spontaneous?

'Maybe not in any recognised sense of the word, but, yes, flirting with you was tonight's planned spontaneous decision.' She forced herself to sit back and sip her wine as if she were the confident woman she pretended to be. 'After all, you are the only person away from the B&B I have met so far and you *did* offer to show me around.'

'I did.' His gaze intensified. 'And I meant it.'

'Good.' She fought to keep her voice steady. 'Because I'd like to accept.'

'Good,' he echoed, and she could hear the smile in his voice. 'I wouldn't claim to be a master tour guide, but...' his smile turned wolfish and her insides molten '...I haven't had any complaints so far.'

Lily would bet a great deal he hadn't, not when he smiled with that particular intent, allowed his hair to fall broodingly across his brow, rolled up his sleeves to show bronzed, strong forearms, corded with muscle, folded his hands to show off his long, strong, capable fingers. She dragged her gaze up to meet his, lingering on the sensual tilt of his mouth as she did so.

'And what did you have in mind?' She tossed her hair back as she lounged back, glass in hand. 'I'm a lawyer, remember. I don't enter into any kind of agreement without clarity and a full perusal of the small print and sub-clauses.' Lawyer? Right now she was an actress. But she couldn't deny that now she'd started she was enjoying being someone else. Enjoying cutting loose from the confines of her rigid life.

'No small print. We spend time together. You set the limits. If you're uncomfortable say so and we stop.'

Why did she get the feeling he wasn't just talking about a walk around Dubrovnik?

'And when were you thinking?' Lily was aware that she was leaning towards him, that her gaze held his with coy challenge, that her voice was breathier than normal—and that hair toss was most unlike her. The atmosphere was charged, as if millions of pheromones were dancing around them, turning every word into a seduction, every look into a dance step.

'There's no time like the present.'

Lily swallowed, her throat dry. The game had got suddenly all too real and she had to decide whether she was really ready to play. What would be the harm in saying yes? She might make a fool of herself, even more than she already had, but she couldn't hide for ever. Not if she was going to keep her promise to Izzy and try living, not existing.

Lily didn't know what awaited her at the end of the summer, whether she would return to London, to her expensive sterile and lonely flat and her well paid soulless job and try for more balance, or whether she would make a more profound change. But she did know that if she didn't seize the chance to try living a different way, she would add to her already too heavy list of regrets.

'I guess not. So where do we start?'

'Have you properly explored the island yet? Why don't I show you around?'

Wordlessly Lily nodded, getting to her feet, almost hypnotised, starting slightly as he took her hand and led her away from the party. Appetising barbecue smells wafted over and Lily could see children dancing, young people eying each other up and friends joking and talking. The sun was setting and the fairy lights took on an otherworldly gleam in the dusk as they walked, still hand in hand, towards the path that led back to the villa.

Casually, slowly Damir began to draw small circles on the back of her hand as he held it. Languorous, light, almost casual touches that burned through her, sending licks of fire shooting up her arm and spreading throughout her body.

'I thought you were showing me around, I already know this way,' she said, and he laughed, low and deep and rumbling, vibrating deliciously through her.

'Trust me.'

* * *

His words hung in the air, then Lily nodded, her clasp tightening on his as Damir led her to the top of the steep path that bisected the narrow island. Instead of continuing straight on to Fire Cove and the villa, he turned left, leading her up a narrow, twisting path that climbed higher and higher through the trees until, after a couple of minutes, they emerged onto the hilltop, Lokvar spread out before them.

On one side the sun hung low over Fire Cove, on the other they could see and hear the lights and the sounds from the party. Before them lay the headland dominated by Damir's hotel, behind them the island tapered to a point, the end marked by the old medieval monastery, now just picturesque ruins. Beyond that was the mainland, barely visible in the rapidly darkening dusk.

'I used to come here when I was a boy,' he said. 'To look out at all this and swear…'

'Swear what?'

'That one day this would all be mine.'

'And is it?'

'Almost.'

'Quite the conqueror.'

'I try.'

'Oh, I bet you do. And I bet you succeed. Who could resist?'

Her words were teasing, but as she spoke the atmosphere became charged. Lily was so close, her hand still lay in his, her touch light yet searing through him. He could feel the slight movement as she breathed, smell the lemon of her shampoo, the sharp floral scent of her perfume and all thought of business disappeared, something more primal replacing it. She was warm, she was real and she was, oh, so desirable. He turned to look at her, at the sheet of golden hair falling down her back, her curves displayed by the silk vest top, at her long-lashed eyes, and he couldn't resist the urge to reach out and touch her cheek, one finger straying to caress the curve of her mouth.

Lily jolted, a small almost imperceptible move before she stilled under his touch. She wanted him, he knew it in every fibre. Despite their brief acquaintance, attraction burned between them, so tangible he could almost hear it sizzle. But this relationship wasn't about attraction, the stakes were far higher and wooing her was only supposed to go so far. Damir knew that the sensible thing to do would be to make a joke, lighten the atmosphere and head back to the party. He wanted Lily onside but that didn't mean seducing her. However, for once business wasn't the first thing on his mind. For once his need filled him, the air almost palpable with want.

And then all thought fled as Lily's hand tightened on his and she moved a little closer, turning a little more until she faced him fully, tilting her face to his, eyes half-closed as Damir traced the sweet lines of her face, his fingertips trailing down her cheek, the curve of her chin and down her long neck, lingering at the sweet spot where her pulse beat wildly, before moving onto her bare shoulder and coming to rest on her back. She swallowed, biting her lip as she looked at him, blue eyes full of shifting emotions. Damir paused, one hand splayed on her back, the other white-knuckled as he waited for permission or refusal.

'Is this part of the tour?' Her voice was a little hoarse, husking out the words as if her throat was full.

He smiled then, slow and full of intent. 'Not usually.'

Her eyes darkened to navy. 'But this evening?'

Damir didn't answer, he just stared at Lily steadily and she looked back, the questions and confusion ebbing away as she moved her hand up his arm, trailing it lightly over his skin until she reached his shoulder, further up until it was her turn to explore his face, each light touch like liquid flame. Sensation pulsed through him, hot and sweet and almost painful as she teased her way down his cheek, her fingers tracing the lines of his mouth, the sensitive skin behind his ears, her face intent as if she was learning him by heart.

'Lily?' It was both question and entreaty, begging her for permission, and she nodded, face solemn, lips half-parted in anticipation.

Primal need filled him. Damir wanted nothing more than to rush, to crush her to him, to explore her mouth, her body, to hear her moan and sigh and call his name, to tumble her onto the ground and cover her with his body. He wanted to tear at their clothes, for there to be no barriers between them. And he could do it, he knew it, sensed it as the air around them danced with the haze of desire; she wanted him as much as he wanted her. But he held himself back.

Slowly, every movement full of intent, he pulled her to him, one hand still on her back, the other clasping the curve of her waist. She was tall but still a head shorter than him and he had to dip his head to taste her. It was a light kiss, an exploratory kiss, an anticipatory promise of what could be, and it overwhelmed him like no kiss had for longer than he cared to remember. She tasted of salt, of sweetness, like sunshine and the sea, and he wanted to sink into her and never surface.

Lily made a small sound like a whimper as she stepped closer, crushing the curves of her body against him, and Damir groaned as he felt the softness of her breasts against his chest, her long legs tangling with his. 'Lily,' he said, this time in wonder, and she smiled against his mouth as she kissed him back. This second kiss was deeper, her mouth opening to his as she ran her hands along the planes of his back, setting him alight with every touch.

Still he held back, not allowing the flames to burn them, managing with a Herculean effort to not pick her up and lay her on the ground. They had all night, they could even have all summer, and anticipation would only make the coming together sweeter. But it still took all he had not to rush her, to allow her to set the pace.

Damir had no idea how long they stood there. The kiss deepened and intensified until he was consumed by her, every part of him aching to explore every part of her. He dragged his mouth from hers, ignoring her moan of protest, as he tasted her throat, her shoulder, as his fingers edged up her body, under her top, caressing every rib until he reached the underside of her breast, skin giving way to the lace of her bra.

Impatient, he slipped his thumb underneath the material, needing the warmth of flesh, and heard her gasp as his hand slid up to cup her, as she leaned into his touch. His need for her was evident, palpable, almost painful but still he stood, taking his time, letting her take hers, giving her every opportunity to walk away.

But she didn't walk away. Instead she pressed even closer so it was his turn to moan, the friction of her body against his torture. 'Lily,' he managed on a ragged breath. For a moment he didn't think she'd heard him as her mouth found his shoulder, and then she stood back. He was instantly cold, wanting to do nothing but to crush her against him, but he restrained himself, overwhelmed by how fast they'd ignited. It was nothing like the seductive games he was used to and the realisation of how close he'd veered to losing control scared him.

'I...' Her breath was as out of time as his, her chest heaving, pupils dilated, eyelids heavy. 'I guess I'm not as bad at flirting as I thought I was.'

He half closed his eyes, torn between a groan and a laugh. 'Oh, you're not bad at all.'

Was that all this was? Flirting? He needed to process what had happened, to figure out how his emotions, his body had escaped his usual iron-clad control. To figure out what happened next because that kind of desire, that kind of want was incompatible with the man he needed to be. The man he had to be. The man he was.

'Are you still up for showing me around some more?'

'If you want me to.'

'I'm only here for a short while. It would be a shame not to see a little bit more.' Her meaning was implicit. She had one summer. One summer for him to convince her that he was the best custodian for Fire Cove. Damir knew that mixing business with pleasure was a mistake but he also knew that it would be very hard to pull back now.

'It would,' he agreed. 'There's a lot to see and do. I'd hate for you miss out.'

'Great. I'm looking forward to the next part of the tour.' She looked around and shivered. 'It's getting dark.'

'We should head back.' To other people, the safety in numbers, to give his body time to recover and his mind the opportunity to regain control. Damir extracted his phone and handed it to her. 'Give me your number and I'll arrange a date. You don't get seasick, do you?'

'Not as far as I know.' She quickly pressed a few keys and handed it back. 'Damir...' She paused then took a deep breath. 'Look, I have never been the sneak out of parties to make out with a guy kind of girl, I was usually the hang out in a kitchen and then leave early to study type. But, like I said, I want this summer to be different. So thank you, for making me feel so welcome. For offering to show me around. I really appreciate it.'

'Really, there is no need to thank me, I'm enjoying getting to know you,' Damir said smoothly as he started to make his way down the path, realising that in just a few minutes it would be totally dark. He felt curiously flat. He should be congratulating himself on the perfect start to his campaign to get Lily onside—but instead for the first time in a long time he was conscious of doubt. Getting his hands on the villa was as important as ever. But was he really willing to deceive Lily to do it? Or, judging by his out-of-control response, was it really himself he was deceiving?

CHAPTER FIVE

IT WAS THE perfect day for a boat ride. Almost too perfect, the sun out in force, the sea flat enough to please all but the most sensitive sailor. The omens were good for the day ahead. A day in which Damir was going to stick to the plan: give Lily an unforgettable day but stay in control of both his reactions and the situation.

It all sounded so easy when he put it like that.

Damir checked his arrangements one last time, preparation being key to a successful campaign. All was in order with freshly laundered cushions and blankets heaped on the cabin seat and a delicious selection of food, wine and beer chilling in the fridge. Everything was perfect.

He just needed Lily to actually show up.

'Hi, sorry I'm late.' Lily panted up to the boat, a bag slung casually over her shoulder, hair scooped back into a loose ponytail. She looked ethereal in a blue sundress that floated down to mid-ankle, teamed with flat silver sandals, and Damir's stomach tightened in automatic reaction to her presence.

'Not at all,' he said, extending a hand to take her

surprisingly heavy bag before helping her into the boat, conscious of the feel of her hand in his. He hadn't seen her in the few days since the party. He'd thought the time apart sufficient to assert sense over emotions. It was possible he'd miscalculated as electricity zipped up his arm when she took his hand. 'I know it's an early start, but it gets very busy in the old town later on.'

'I don't mind early starts, at home I'm usually in the office around seven-thirty. Thank you.' She let go of his hand and looked around. 'Oh, this is beautiful! I didn't realise when you said boat ride that you meant anything this fancy. I would have done my hair and worn more make-up if I'd known. I'm going to let the boat down.'

'You look fine.' She looked a lot more than fine, honey-coloured hair falling around her face, her skin very lightly tanned, set off by the thin straps of the dress. Long and loose, the light fabric swirled around her body, showing off more of her curves than it hid. Damir realised that he was staring and with difficulty pulled his attention back to the conversation. 'The boat is mine. Glad you like her.' He tried for nonchalant, but couldn't hide his pride.

Like all island children Damir had been taught to sail before he could walk, but this boat was nothing like the small sailboats he'd grown up with. Teak and chrome, low in the water and speedy, it exuded class—and discreetly said money.

The deck included a large sunbathing platform and a table flanked by two padded benches, perfect for sunset drinks and intimate dinners. Below deck was a small sitting room and kitchenette, a shower room and a separate bedroom, just large enough to fit a small double bed. Despite its compact size the boat was fitted out to the highest specs and worthy of Lily's evident admiration.

'I don't just like it, I think I'm in love,' she said. 'Can I have a tour?'

'Of course.' He didn't need to be asked twice, showing off every cubbyhole, every beautifully carved finish, talking through the engine specifications in detail, until her responses became a little more formulaic, her expression more polite than enthused.

'Apologies,' he said, a little ruefully. 'My enthusiasm tends to run away with me where this beauty is concerned.'

Lily ran one caressing hand over the glossy teak finish and Damir watched her trailing fingers, envying his own boat. 'No, no, that's quite okay. Far be it from me to get between a man and his great passion.'

'It's true,' he admitted. 'There will always be three in any relationship I have.'

'At least you're up front about it. And I'm sure your girlfriends don't mind sharing you with someone so special.'

'I haven't had any trouble so far,' he told her teasingly. 'What do you think? Would you mind sharing?'

'Luckily I'm not the jealous type.' Colour edged her cheekbones as she spoke and she twisted round to look out to sea. The memory of the passionate kiss they'd shared hung in the air and Damir quickly changed the subject. Control was the theme of the day, and that kiss had been anything but.

'I hope you don't get seasick because I'm planning to take the scenic route today. It only takes forty-five minutes to sail into the City Port, but it's a taxi ride to the old city from there or a fairly hilly half-hour walk. So I'm planning to sail a longer route, past Sunset Bay and into the old harbour. We'll go right past the city walls so you can see them in all their glory from the sea—and get some understanding why Dubrovnik was so good at withstanding sieges. And why it's the go-to destination for historical film crews as well.'

'That all sounds amazing,' Lily said. 'Longer sail, view of the walls, all of it. Thank you for taking the time to do this for me. Is there anything I can do to help?'

'Have you ever been on a boat like this before?'

'Not as much as a dinghy. But I'm a quick learner.'

'In that case, get ready to catch this rope. You can coil it up and then hang it on that hook there. Ready?'

Damir issued a few quick instructions as he prepared to cast off and Lily was quick to catch his meaning, surefooted and steady as she helped him push the boat away from the mooring post. She stood next to him as he started the engine and began to guide the small boat away from the island, asking questions about what he was doing and why, seemingly genuinely interested in his answers.

Damir, normally possessive of his boat, insisted she take the wheel once they were clear of Lokvar and their course set, guiding and coaching her as she gingerly increased speed in order to drive the boat at a steady pace across the calm, blue sea.

'You've got a knack for this, good job,' he said as he took the tiller back and she grinned with unfeigned joy.

'Even I couldn't mess up on a straight line with no other boats within one hundred yards either side. I don't think I'd be comfortable gliding into the harbour and stopping alongside the platform the way you do. And I certainly don't think I could manage if there were any waves at all. Oh!' She scooped up her bag and held it up triumphantly.

'I forgot! I made some cakes last night. You wouldn't believe the way Antun watched me every second I was in the kitchen. He evidently did *not* trust me not to set something on fire or mess up his precious oven. But they came out okay and Ana gave me some of those amazing spinach pastries she makes as well. Don't tell anybody, but I also managed to snaffle some of that gorgeous home-made lemonade Antun makes. I don't know what his recipe is, he guards it with his life. I could get us some lemonade now. Do you have any cups or anything?'

'Look in the gallery. You'll find ice and glasses there.'

'Great, I'll be as quick as I can.'

And she was gone, bag over her shoulder, humming as she navigated the narrow ladder. Damir concentrated on the distant horizon, processing the conversation. He had invited a reasonable number of women out for a day—or an evening—sail over the last couple of years. They'd all arrived dressed in expensive teeny bikinis and luxurious wraps, expecting him to provide champagne and delicious, dainty food as a matter of course. Not one had baked before the trip, or had thought to pick up something to bring.

The unwritten assumption was that as the host, and a host who was known to be wealthy, he would treat them to the entire trip. And that was fine, he shared those expectations, knew what was required, and it had never been an issue. He just hadn't realised how good it would feel to have someone think about treating him as well.

Lily peered up eagerly as the boat finally rounded the curve of the coastline and the imposing walls finally came into sight.

'Oh! Oh, Damir!' She wasn't sure she could open her eyes any wider as she drank in the view, taking off her sunglasses so as not to miss a detail, even though the sun already reflected brightly off the water, the light bouncing dazzlingly off the old walls. 'It's magnificent. I've seen pictures, of course, and heard stories, many stories, but nothing could have prepared me for this. I can't believe you're lucky enough to live here.'

Neither could she believe that Josip had never returned here. If Dubrovnik had been her home city, nothing would keep her away, certainly not for years and years on end. If there was anything the last few months had taught her it was how important moving forward was, learning from the past and not being haunted by it. Maybe that was a lesson she should try and pass on to her stepfather as well.

This time Lily didn't offer to help as Damir deftly steered the boat into the already crowded old harbour, securing a mooring spot with a satisfied grin. She could barely contain her impatience as he securely fastened the boat before lightly jumping onto the wooden walkway and helping her out.

'This is why I told you to be ready so early,' he said, leading her towards the arched entrance into the fabled old city. 'As you can see, it's already pretty busy, but in less than an hour the cruise ship passengers will arrive and this street will be jostling room only. If you want to walk the walls, and I assume you do, then getting here as early as possible is essential.'

'I absolutely do want to walk the walls. In fact, I don't want to leave any tourist trap untouched. You are allowed to be my tour guide, but you can't be a local, dismissive of anything that's popular. I want to do all the tacky touristy bits. I'm going to consider it research, because otherwise I'll feel like a fool when I'm talking to the guests and they know more about Dubrovnik than I do.'

'Your wish is my command.' He smiled at her, sweet and slow, and Lily was conscious of her heart squeezing as he did so.

Don't get carried away, she told herself. Apart from helping her onto and off the boat, Damir had made no move to touch her, hadn't flirted with her, all morning, just as the texts they had exchanged to set this day up had been merely friendly, not flirtatious. It was almost as if the kiss just a few nights ago had never been.

But there was an acute consciousness between them, an awareness of each other's every move, a carefulness in their conversation that showed the kiss was very much on both of their minds. Whether that meant a repetition or not she didn't know. Part of her hoped so, wanted to allow the attraction to run its course, but she was also scared by the fierceness of her reaction to him. If Damir hadn't stopped, would they have ended up making love on the ground? Up against a tree? She couldn't say, hand on heart, that it was an impossibility.

Neither could she honestly say that she hadn't spent more than one idle moment wondering just what that lovemaking might have felt like…

She wrenched her mind back to the present as Damir guided her through the marble streets, Lily slowing to marvel at enticing alleyways running off on every side. Some were dead ends, others led to picturesque squares or to long, steep stone steps. But every time she slowed, Damir hustled her on, giving her no time to stop, stare, take pictures or set foot in any of the shops or restaurants. Instead, Damir marched her on until they'd secured tickets and ascended the stairs that led them to the top of the famous city walls.

Lily knew that in the heat of midday, once the city

was full of day trippers, cruise ship passengers and tourists pouring in from the hotels from all around Dubrovnik, it could be shuffling room only on the walls. Early as it was, there were still plenty of people walking along the wide turreted walkways, looking down on the one side into courtyards, windows and alleyways and on the other across the blue, blue sea. But there was plenty of room for everyone, and now Lily could stop as much she wanted, and take as many photos she wished, playfully pulling Damir in for a couple of selfies despite his protestations.

It was a surprisingly long way round, with some unexpectedly steep climbs as the sun grew hotter and hotter and the walls busier and busier. Lily wished she could take a slower walk round in the cool of an early spring or autumnal day, one when the tourists were few and the sun less intense. But despite the heat and hubbub, it was still one of the most awe-inspiring experiences of her life and when they finally descended, Lily's head was spinning with the history and the tales Damir had told her, her eyes and heart full of all she'd seen.

It seemed impossible that the old town itself could compare with its own defensive walls, but a place where the roads were literally made of marble, and every house was hundreds of years old, couldn't help but intrigue her and she explored every alley, stopping only for an ice cream and some much-needed water.

'Okay,' Damir said after a while. 'We've been

walking for hours and I for one am ready for a beer. Luckily I know the perfect place.'

'A beer?' Lily wasn't much of a beer drinker, happy with the odd glass of wine now and then. Her mother's struggles with alcohol and drugs had left Lily cautious about overindulging and daytime drinking really wasn't her thing.

'Or a soft drink of your choice, but the place I'm taking you to deserves to be toasted with a real libation.'

Intrigued, Lily accompanied Damir through yet another bewildering route of alleyways, small open squares and stairs. She should have brought breadcrumbs with her to scatter or a ball of thread as left to herself she would never find her way out again, but Damir was sure and certain of his route.

Finally they came to a small archway. A chalkboard by the archway simply said '*Bar*' with an arrow pointing through. Damir indicated that Lily should go first and, intrigued, she walked through, eyes widening in awe as she took in the scene before her.

The bar was perched on rocks that seemed to tumble down to the sea far below, tables positioned by railings that were all that stood between the bar's patrons and the rocks below. The rocks formed a kind of natural terrace, the bar on the top and tables on several levels beneath, each joined by a flat stone staircase. The fourth level was the largest and had no tables. On it a small group of young men congregated, talking noisily, all wearing just their swimming shorts.

As Lily watched one of them stepped up to the very edge and with no fanfare executed a perfect dive far down into the sea below. She gasped as she watched him go, his bronzed body momentarily gleaming in the sunlight before it fell. 'Fancy a swim?' Damir said with a grin.

'You must be kidding, there's no way I'm jumping off there.' Lily eyed the steep drop and shivered.

'That's one way into the water, but alternatively you could just climb down there.' And Damir pointed to a narrow ladder leading from the diving rock to a cluster of rocks just above sea level. A few groups were sunbathing on towels spread out over the hard surface, others had climbed into the water and were swimming out. This was no shallow, safe cove or cordoned-off area with land on both sides, these swimmers headed straight into the depths of the Adriatic, sharing the water with boats and kayaks. It looked exhilarating.

'You have your costume?' Damir asked, and she nodded.

'Yes, you told me to make sure I wore it.' Lily followed Damir carefully climbing down the steep ladder until she reached the rocks below. Unselfconsciously, Damir shed his clothes, standing there in just his trunks. Lily's gaze wandered appreciatively over his wide torso, narrow waist and strong legs, lust shooting through her with unexpected possessiveness.

'Come on,' he said with a boyish grin. 'What are you waiting for?'

Nobody was paying them any attention as Lily slipped off her long dress and her sandals. In her bag she had a pair of sea shoes, having been warned about the dangers of sea urchins on Croatia's rocky coast. She noticed that no local seem to wear them and Damir raised an eyebrow as she slightly defiantly slipped them on but she was glad of their protection as they walked over the rough rock until they reached one of the ubiquitous ladders that led into the Adriatic depths. Lily didn't allow herself time to stop and think about the cold. As soon as she was deep enough in she let go, straight into the bracing water, swimming fast until her limbs warmed up.

She didn't know how long they spent out there but she could have stayed there for ever, turning into a water nymph who lived in these turquoise waters. Bobbing in the water, she looked up at the walls rising far above her and felt a kinship with all the hundreds of generations of people who must've swum in this very spot.

They swam for at least half an hour, reluctantly returning to dry off on the rocks like a pair of merpeople, letting the sun dry them until they could put their clothes back over their swimsuits. Then, glowing with the warmth and the exercise, they clambered back up the ladder to the bar, where Damir procured a table right on the rocky outcrop, presenting Lily with a beer that she decided she did want after all.

'This place is amazing,' she said as she took an appreciative gulp of the bitter, amber liquid.

'It's a Dubrovnik institution,' Damir told her. 'It's one of those places that is in all the guidebooks, that everybody who has been here tells their friends is a must-visit and yet it always feels unspoilt, like you're the first person to have discovered it. Even at the height of the season, when it's at peak busyness, it feels as if there's space for everyone who needs to be here.'

'You come here a lot then?' Of course, she remembered, Damir didn't live on Lokvar but somewhere here in Dubrovnik.

'I haven't been here in over seven years.' His sunglasses hid his expression, but his voice was carefully emotionless.

'Oh?' Lily tried to match his lack of emotion, not wanting to show how curious she was.

'It's a favourite spot of my ex-wife's. We used to come here a lot. After she left, I found new places to go, ones without so many memories.'

And yet he had brought her here. Lily didn't know how to interpret that, but her stomach tumbled as she tried not to show her surprise—or how flattered she was.

'I'm sorry that your marriage didn't work out.' Seven years ago? He could only have been in his mid-twenties when they'd divorced.

He shrugged. 'It happens. In the end we wanted different things.'

'Such as?'

'Kata wanted a normal life. A family, a husband who was home for dinner with weekends off. She resented how much time I spent working. Meanwhile my father wanted to expand the business, needed me to step up, evenings, weekends, whatever it took. After he died the pressure intensified. We just stopped communicating and she left. She's remarried now, has a child.' He paused. 'I think she's happy.'

'I'm sorry,' she said softly, covering his hand with hers. 'For your father, your marriage, all of it.'

'We got together when we were at school, maybe we were too young when we married. Too busy living in the present to prepare for the future. How about you?' He turned his hand to clasp hers, his fingers folding around her palm, and Lily suddenly found it hard to concentrate, all of her being focussed on the sensations pulsing through her hand, zipping through her entire body.

'Me?' She managed to somehow answer his question. 'No, I've never been married. I've never even lived with a partner. Career first, my love life a very poor second.'

'It's hard to balance the two.'

'It is. Date someone with the same ethos and you run the risk of never seeing them, date someone with different priorities and they soon get bored with your limited availability. I was with this one guy, a lawyer in my firm, for a couple of years but when we broke up last year it didn't make any real difference to my life. I missed the convenience of him rather than Seb himself, and I'm sure he felt the same way.'

Lily looked straight ahead out at the almost over-whelming brightness of the sea and sighed. 'I look at my mum and Josip and they are so easy with each other, they really are two halves of the same whole, cheesy as that sounds. I've never felt like that about anybody. But then I haven't wanted to either, not while I was working towards being partner. It would be too distracting, having to factor in someone else's life and needs.'

Although that's not how her mum and Josip seemed. They just supported each other through all life's ups and downs, including her mother's decision to finally get a university degree and a career in her thirties. Sometimes Lily envied them, but she had no idea how to let someone get that close. How to be that vulnerable. The only person who she'd allowed in was Izzy—and now she was more alone than ever.

'That's it.' Damir nodded. 'You get it, to build something like a career or a business you have to be single-minded. And finding someone who under-stands, who isn't resentful of that is hard.'

'So you've been single since you divorced?' That didn't fit with Ana's playboy assessment, or with the easy charm he displayed with her.

'Single? No. But I'm not looking for anything se-rious and I am very clear about that. I don't want to break any hearts or raise any expectations. But if I like someone and they like me, and we want to spend some time together then great.' His hand tightened on hers and Lily's breath quickened. 'For instance, I like you, Lily, and I think you like me. I would very much enjoy getting to know you better while you're in Croatia.'

'Get to know me better? Is that code for a few trips out like this or for a no-strings, one-summer-only kind of deal?' She managed to sound nonchalant, as though she was always being propositioned by gorgeous, sun-bronzed men in idyllic locations, although her throat was thick, her ears buzzing and her pulse pounded.

'No code, simply getting to know each other better and seeing where it leads. If it leads nowhere, fine, otherwise we part when one of us has had enough or at the end of the summer with no hard feelings and some good memories. What do you think?'

What did she think? Lily was already overwhelmed by her physical reaction to Damir. She might not have put a lot of effort into her love life before, but she had also never had a fling. She was more of a few polite dates, gradually working up to formal couple status kind of girl. Was she emotionally able to cope with the kind of short-term relationship Damir was offering?

But she was supposed to be living spontaneously and trying new things, to be less sensible and have more fun. And she suspected she would have a lot of fun if she said yes.

She picked up her beer, willing her hand to steady, not to show any sign of nerves, and held her bottle up to his. 'I think we should drink to getting to know each other better. To the summer.'

'To the summer,' he echoed, his dark eyes opaque.

'I am very much looking forward to seeing how this turns out.'

'Me too.' And to her surprise Lily meant it. She wasn't going to plan or organise and schedule. She was going to wait and see and enjoy every moment of this unexpected summer romance.

CHAPTER SIX

'ARE YOU SURE you don't mind, Lily? You haven't had a day off for a week, and now you're cancelling your plans.' Ana looked worriedly at Lily, who gave the older woman a determined smile.

'Of course I don't mind. I can meet Damir any time.'

'But you have restaurant reservations—I heard there's a waiting list to get in there.'

'Well, Damir only suggested it a couple of days ago, so either he has a standing reservation or he can pull some strings. Either way, if I don't go it's not the end of the world. I'd be more than happy to go back to the seafood burger takeaway in the old town we visited last week. I've never eaten anything more delicious and I can do that any time.'

'But you've worked so hard. You deserve a break.'

'I'm fine, honestly. Ivona is no use to anyone until that swelling goes down. She's in a lot of pain. As are you, so go and lie down and stop worrying about me.'

Lily shooed Ana up the stairs, not allowing her smile to slip until the older woman was out of sight and then she leaned against the wall and let out a deep sigh. She would never have confessed it to Ana, but truthfully she was more than a little disappointed to cancel her much-anticipated afternoon and evening off. Damir been called away to a meeting in Zagreb earlier in the week, which meant she hadn't seen him since he'd sailed her back to Lokvar after their day out in Dubrovnik, receiving just a few texts in the week since.

What was the point of throwing a lifetime of caution to the wind and agreeing to a summer fling if you were both too busy to *do* any actual flinging?

Today was supposed to change all that. She had the afternoon and evening off and Damir, who was due to arrive back from Zagreb this morning, had offered to pick her up in the early afternoon and show her more of the coastline from his boat, before finishing the day off with a meal at an exclusive restaurant in Dubrovnik. The kind of restaurant Lily needed to dress up for. A real date restaurant.

But not today. Thanks to Ivona's sprained ankle and Ana's migraine they were two members of staff down. Lily had to step in. With a second heartfelt sigh, Lily pulled her phone out of her shorts pocket and quickly composed an apology to Damir. She stared at the message for a few minutes before pressing 'Send'. It was done. Hopefully he would be as understanding about her schedule as she had been about his—and if not, then, casual or not, this fledgling relationship was never going to take off.

Ignoring the disappointment that lay heavy on her chest, Lily tilted her chin and marched out to the beach café where she was needed to serve drinks and take payment for beach chairs.

Every table in the café-bar, every sun lounger was occupied. Lily couldn't believe the difference a couple of weeks made. Dubrovnik itself was busy all year round, a popular city break no matter what the weather, and the Dalmatian Riviera also enjoyed an extended season from late spring right the way through to Halloween, when the bustling resorts wound down for the winter break. Lokvar, however, like many of Croatia's many islands, enjoyed a much shorter season. But it made up for length with intensity. The B&B was fully booked for the weeks and months ahead, and every morning day trippers arrived early to enjoy Fire Cove and kept on coming throughout the day and into the evening—all happy to order drinks and food from the beach café. Unassuming as the café was, Marija was sitting on quite a little gold mine.

The rest of the morning and lunchtime passed quickly as Lily took orders and delivered drinks and snacks, keeping an eye on the sunbeds and beach chairs to make sure each occupant had paid for using them. Exhausting though it was, she found she enjoyed the constant buzz and dealing with such a variety of people from all over the world. Contract law was often solitary, just her, her computer and hundreds of lines of text to scrutinise. She'd thought she preferred life that way but maybe she'd been wrong.

Smiling at a happy, sand-covered family, Lily collected the empty plates and glasses from their table and began to manoeuvre her way back through to the kitchen, when she caught a glimpse of a figure waiting by the framed menu at the café entrance.

'I'll be with you in a minute,' she called over her shoulder, relieved that so far the vast majority of her customers spoke English no matter what their nationality and determined to spend some time with her language app that evening.

'Take your time,' the figure said in familiar tones, and Lily stopped stock still, almost dropping the heaped tray as she did so.

'Damir? Didn't you get my message? I am so sorry but I have had to cancel our plans. We're short-staffed and I'm needed here.'

'I know.' He sauntered towards her, quirking an eyebrow at the tray. 'Do you need a hand with that?' Before she could protest he took it from her.

'Thank you. But if you know I can't make it then why are you here?'

'We have a date.'

'Yes, but…'

'Maybe not the date we originally planned, but I thought we could improvise. What do you need me to do?'

'What do I…?' Lily blinked. Had she heard him correctly? 'What do you mean?'

'You said you were two people down? Luckily I was working in a café from the time I was old enough to collect glasses.' He held up the tray, effortlessly balanced in one hand. 'So put me to work.'

'I can't ask you to do that, you've been in meetings all week…' But she was torn. Luka was be-hind the bar, which meant she was covering both the café and the beach. Easy enough when it was quiet, almost impossible when it was as busy as this. Besides, she had been looking forward to spending time with Damir.

'You haven't asked, I offered. Lily, I've been in meetings all week and the only thing that kept me going was the thought of seeing you today. So if this is what I have to do…'

He didn't look like someone who had been in meetings all week and who had flown across the country this morning, he looked almost piratical with his dark windswept hair, the graze of stubble outlin-ing his jaw and rolled-up white sleeves showcasing strong capable wrists. 'Can you mix drinks? Make coffee?' she asked hopefully.

'Of course.'

'Because then Luka can manage the beach and I can stick to waitressing in here. You really don't mind giving up your Saturday afternoon?'

'I want to spend my Saturday afternoon with you,' he said, the heat in his gaze causing the rest of the busy café to fade away as she stood there, unable to move, unsure what to say.

'I don't know how to thank you,' she managed at last, and he winked.

'I'm sure I'll think of something suitable.'

'Two small beers, one large, a Shirley Temple, a lem-onade and an Irish coffee,' Lily panted as she passed

Damir the order note, scooping up the tray of coffees he'd just brewed with a quick smile. Her cheeks were flushed with the heat and exercise as she rushed around the terrace, her hair pulled back into a jaunty ponytail. She wore practical black shorts and a white T-shirt teamed with a small apron—not at all how he'd envisioned her looking when he picked her up for their date. Yet all he wanted to do was pull her into a corner and kiss her until they were both gasping for air.

'On it,' Damir promised, as he lined the glasses up before him, mentally running through the ingredients for a Shirley Temple. To his surprise he was enjoying the fast pace, even though spending his precious time making endless coffees, pouring endless beers and concocting endless sickly-sweet cocktails was not how Damir had planned to spend this afternoon. What he had planned was the next phase in the wooing Lily campaign after an unexpectedly excellent start.

He hadn't intended to mix business with pleasure quite as thoroughly as things had turned out, but the more he thought about it—and there were times when he could think about little else—the more sense it made. He was genuinely attracted to Lily and she was attracted to him. Why deny themselves an enjoyable few weeks or months just because he needed something from her?

And that was all this was. A few enjoyable weeks. So he had decided to come and help her out? It wasn't that uncharacteristic.

Only of course it was. Damir couldn't remember the last time he'd put himself out for another person, the last time he'd stood behind a bar rather than sat behind a desk, the last time he'd received orders rather than given them, but to his surprise the afternoon faded into evening long before he got bored.

'Okay, bartender, your shift is over.'

He looked up from the mojito he was garnishing to see Lily leaning on the bar, her hair now down and grazing her shoulders, her apron tossed over her arm.

'The night shift is here. It's time to collect your wages,' she said.

'Wages?'

'Payment in kind,' she amended. 'Dinner and whatever you want to drink. Antun is making us pizzas as I speak so get yourself a drink and come and sit down. You deserve it.'

The last ferry had departed and the café died down to a pleasant hum of regulars, those staying on the island and those with their own boats or charters, so they managed to grab a table at the end of the terrace, looking over Fire Cove. At this time of day it was easy to see where the bay had got its name from, the sun lying heavy and low, casting a golden path on the darkening sea, the sky a hundred different shades of red, orange and pink.

'It is so beautiful,' Lily said with a sigh. 'Every day I think that has to be the most beautiful sunset yet, and then the next day tops it. I can't believe I'm lucky enough to be here.'

'It's a gorgeous spot,' he agreed. 'So much potential.'

He hesitated, wondering whether to say more when Antun emerged from his kitchen in person to place pizza and salad on the table and for the next couple of minutes they were busy helping themselves to slices of hot, heaped pizza, forking the fresh salad onto their plates.

'Mmm, this is delicious,' Lily mumbled. 'I'm sure the place you had in mind was amazing too, but I'm not sure anything can beat this view and freshly made pizza with Antun's secret tomato sauce recipe.' She took a sip of her wine. 'What did you mean just now when you said potential?'

This was it. This was his moment. Damir did his best to sound nonchalant, as though he hadn't thought about nothing but this topic for years. 'Only that this is the best spot not just on Lokvar but possibly on the whole of the coast. The water is safe, the beach perfect, the view as you said is spectacular, and yet only a handful of people get to stay here. Don't you think it would be the perfect setting for a hotel complex? Rooms, sports facilities, a beach club, a five-star restaurant with floor-to-ceiling windows? I always think it's a shame that the tourist season is so short on Lokvar, especially when so many livelihoods depend on it. A resort here could change all that.' He sat back and picked up his beer bottle, every sense attuned to her reaction.

Lily looked around as if envisioning what he'd described. 'I can see what you mean, this place is blessed with everything and I guess the beach bar and villa are pretty basic, but don't you think that's part of the charm? I love how it's so democratic, anyone can come here for a swim or picnic, or rent a chair for just a few *kuna*, whether they're back-packers or own their own yachts. Besides, the villa has been in Marija's family for generations. I can't imagine her selling it and I don't see her wanting to do that kind of development at her age—or at all to be honest.'

'So will Josip come back one day, do you think?'

Her expression clouded. 'No, I don't think so. I don't know what will happen. Whether Ana will take over running it or Marija will sell it. To be honest, I think she's refusing to make plans, hoping Josip will change his mind.'

'And he won't?'

She shook her head slowly. 'I don't see it. He doesn't even talk about Lokvar much, but he must think about it all the time. How could you not miss this with all your soul? Don't you? I get it's more ex-citing in Dubrovnik, and it's beautiful there too, but there is something so special about Lokvar.'

'It's not really practical for me to live here. Once my father expanded onto the mainland we all moved. I do have a house here, but I don't use it. After Kata left I just wasn't here enough to justify running it so I converted it into a holiday let instead.'

Lily's eyes narrowed and she sat back. 'That re-minds me, you weren't entirely honest with me the first time we met.'

'Oh?' Guilt, unexpected and unwelcome, twisted

through his chest. It was so easy to forget his subterfuge while sitting out under the darkening sky. Every time he was with Lily, despite his vows to maintain the necessary emotional distance.

'A café, you said, a few apartments on the mainland. You didn't mention the hotel here, or the hotels and restaurants all around Dubrovnik. You practically own the whole island according to Ana.'

That lack of honesty. 'I didn't want to impress you for the wrong reasons. My grandfather had ambitions and started to fulfil them, my father carried them on and I have taken what they started and been very successful. I'm proud of that, but I don't want to be judged on it, especially by pretty strangers. I wanted to take you out because you liked me, not because you liked my portfolio.'

'I wouldn't have said yes because of what you have, it's who a person is that interests me.' She took another bite of pizza. 'So was it your dream as well to be a hotel tycoon or were you indoctrinated from a young age?'

A dream of his own? He'd never really allowed himself to consider such a thing. It was easier not to think about what could have been when what must be was so clear. 'I'm the only son of an only son. The Kozina ambition was pretty much instilled in me from birth. I told you I was collecting glasses as soon as I could carry them. By the time I was twenty there wasn't a job in the café or hotel I hadn't done, including working on the building crew. I studied business at university but my apprenticeship was here. With my grandfather and father.' Now he was the only one left. His failure to remarry, to father sons to carry on the business lay heavy on him. He knew his duty.

'But what if it hadn't been your family's dream? Take me, I knew I wanted to be a lawyer from a young age. Not because I had a passion for sub-clauses but because I knew it was a career that signified stability and success, respect. And that seemed enough. But since I came to Lokvar I've wondered who I might have been if I hadn't yearned for that stability. If I'd followed my heart.' She laughed, twisting the stem of her wine glass in her hands. 'Not that I have any answer to that yet. But I chose that, you didn't have a choice by the sound of it. Is there a part of you that wishes he'd been, oh, I don't know, a musician or an accountant or a teacher? Anything?'

'The only possible other profession my family would have been happy with is a professional footballer and I am nowhere near good enough. Lily, it's not as simple as wishes and wants. Around here, tourism pays the bills of nearly everyone, it has for a long time. And it's better to be the ones controlling that, profiting from it, than the ones losing out to it. This coastline has a long, bloody and difficult history, conquered over and over, annexed to too many empires.

'To be here, free, successful, respected? It's a luxury my ancestors could never have dreamed of. Even my father lived through a period of turmoil. Of uncertainty. He saw his country fall apart, saw war and devastation and hatred. No wonder he came out of that wanting control of his destiny, to own his land, to ensure our roots were so firmly planted we could never be torn out. He worked tirelessly, constantly to make that happen. I am honoured to carry on his dream.'

He looked out over the now-dark sea. His father's untimely death, the charge he had laid on Damir had only fired his ambition. Pushed him to be who he needed to be, whatever the cost. It was worth it. The late lonely nights in the office or at his desk at home, the risky deals and the falling away from his friends were all worth it.

It had to be.

Lily leaned forward and placed a hand on his arm, the warmth of her touch spreading through him. 'When your life falls apart, when everything you think you know disappears, it's hard to know how to make sense of it all.' Damir got the impression that she was speaking from experience. 'I don't know much about what happened here, about the war. I know that Josip left Croatia as soon as he could and has never returned. It makes sense that the war had a profound effect on your father as well, that it pushed him to take your grandfather's dream and do everything he could to make it happen. I'm sure he would be very proud of you.'

He shrugged. 'Maybe.' He'd never allowed himself to think about it. 'My grandfather died after we built the first hotel here, but he died knowing that we were on our way. And then my father was head of the family and he wanted more and more. One hotel wasn't enough, two wasn't enough. I don't know how many would have been, if there was a moment he would have thought, yes, we're here. I did it.'

'When did he die?'

'Eight years ago.' Now it was her turn to clasp his hand, her warmth offering comfort. 'I'd been married for a little over a year. Kata had her first teaching job, she liked me home in the evenings, liked to spend weekends with me…'

'That doesn't sound like too much to ask.'

'For someone else, maybe not. But she knew who I was when she married me, knew my family and our ambitions.' He looked out at the sea, remembering the pressure of those days, torn between two people he loved. 'It wasn't easy, balancing her expectations with my own. She always felt I put her last, my father that I was uncommitted. He doubled his workload to show me up, although his doctor had been advising him to take things easier.'

The conversation had taken an unexpected personal turn. Somehow Lily's soft questions got through his carefully built defences. First, back in Dubrovnik, he had opened up about Kata, now here he was talking his father. Topics he never discussed, not with anyone.

He hesitated, but the next words spilled out before he could stop them. 'He was here, overseeing the upgrade of the hotel, when he had a heart attack. Overseeing it because I had taken the day off to take Kata sailing.' Sometimes he thought that day out with

Kata had been the last day of peace he'd known. 'It took too long for the air ambulance to come. He was dead on arrival at the hospital. My mother blamed the hotel, blamed Lokvar, blamed me.'

'And do you blame yourself?'

How could he not? 'I should have been here.'

Her grip tightened as if she were trying to imprint her words onto him. 'It was the weekend. You were with your wife where you had every right to be and your father disregarded his doctor's instructions. It's very sad but no one's fault. Especially not yours.'

But he knew better. He was responsible and that knowledge was a burden he'd never be able to shed—neither did he deserve to. 'I knew what he was like. I just didn't want to let him win. He was a proud, stubborn bastard. I guess that's one thing I inherited from him. So I promised him I wouldn't let him down. Not again. And I haven't. I've achieved far more in the years since he died than he could ever have dreamed.' But it wasn't enough. He wasn't sure it ever would be. But developing this land, achieving his father's dearest dream here might just give him the closure he craved.

Lily looked at him keenly, and then got to her feet. 'Come on,' she said, pulling his hand. He didn't move and she tugged him again. 'Come on.'

'Where?'

'It's Saturday night, I've been working hard all day and I don't know about you but I feel like I deserve a treat. The island band are playing down at the harbour and although I would never have thought

I'd say this, I'm getting quite partial to their unique brand of rock covers of European pop. So let's go and dance.'

'Dance? Oh, no. I don't dance.'

'Sure you do, you just choose not to. I usually choose not to as well, but this evening I am planning to.' She smiled then, pleadingly. 'Don't make me dance alone, Damir.'

She wouldn't be alone for long. Not while she stood with big eyes blazing with hope, her hair falling silk-like down her back, long legs encased in shorts. Possessiveness seized him as he rose to his feet. 'You might regret this,' he warned her. 'No one has ever accused me of having rhythm before.'

'I won't judge you if you won't judge me,' she promised. 'Come on.'

He knew what she was doing. Trying to take his mind off the past, to lighten the mood, and it was working. Damir couldn't remember the last time he'd socialised on Lokvar, spent an evening in his own bar as a guest, not the manager, but to his surprise he realised he was actually looking forward to it. To spending the evening with Lily by his side. Just as if this was nothing but the summer affair he had offered her. And for a moment he wished that this was all it was. No business, no agenda, just attraction and fun.

Maybe it could be. For tonight at least.

CHAPTER SEVEN

THE MUSIC WAS LOUD, pounding through the bar, as the band added extra bass and percussion to last year's Europop breakout hit. Lily tossed her hair and twirled, any pretensions to rhythm and co-ordination long gone. Damir on the other hand hadn't been entirely honest when he had claimed to be no dancer, moving in a sinuous pattern that turned her whole body molten with lust.

He was an enigma, one she desperately wanted to puzzle out. Carelessly handsome, seemingly easygoing, the sheer scale of his success and the shortness of the timescale in which he'd achieved that success pointed to a man who was neither careless nor easygoing. And behind his flirtatious smile lay a man scarred by the failure of his marriage and his father's death. Scars she sensed he let very few if any people see.

Like her he seemed to be surrounded by acquaintances rather than friends, although he had grown up in this small tight-knit community. Only she had been lucky enough to have Izzy. Since his divorce she sensed that Damir had been almost entirely alone. Was that distance self-imposed or had it grown along with his success?

So why was he so open with her? Maybe because she was safe, leaving in just a couple of months. Or maybe because of the connection between them, unexpected but palpable.

A physical connection, a searing attraction, nothing more. Yet with every conversation, every touch, every glance she felt it sink further in, deeper and deeper, lodging within her. She wanted him, yes, more and more as the evening went on. But she wanted to know *him*, all of him. She'd never felt like this before, this out-of-control need. It terrified her and exhilarated her in equal measure. Control was so much part of her, built into her every thought and deed, her safety net and guidance. Yet here she was, dancing with no control at all with a man she barely knew, a man she wanted more and more with every passing moment. So much so that when she had gone upstairs to change her top and shoes and brush her hair before they had headed to the bar, she'd opened the pack of condoms she kept in her wash bag more out of habit—always sensible, always prepared—than any expectation of needing them. She could feel the outline of the foil packet in her back pocket, sure everyone could see it and know what she was thinking. Hoping. Wanting.

'Having fun?' Damir slipped an arm around her waist and pulled her close. No one took any notice. Their relationship seemed to be common knowledge already, thanks to the small island's extremely efficient grapevine, so Lily wound her arms around his neck and pressed closely against the hardness of his body, swaying in time with him.

'I am. Thank you for coming, it wouldn't have been so much fun on my own.'

'Thank you for asking me. It's been a long, long time since I spent a Saturday night here, but I'm having a good time.'

'As good a time as at a fancy restaurant in Dubrovnik?'

'It isn't the place that matters, it's the company. I'd still like to take you to that restaurant, though, show you my home.'

'Was that the plan? To invite me back for coffee?' she teased, pressing closer. He closed his eyes briefly as she moved against him, visibly swallowing, and the thrill of the effect she was having on him shuddered through her.

'Absolutely.' He bent his head and captured her mouth with his, a swift searing kiss that buckled her knees. 'Want to go for a walk?' His voice was ragged.

'I remember what happened last time you invited me for a walk,' she said, smiling up into his eyes and seeing heat flickering in their depths.

'Me too. Every second.'

'In that case let's go.'

Damir held her hand possessively as they slipped away from the bar and wandered back along the side of the harbour until they reached the path that bisected the island. This time Damir didn't take any diversions and fifteen minutes later they were back on the beach. The lights were still on at the beach bar and she could hear voices and music. Without speaking they turned the other way, making their way along the empty moonlit beach.

Lily took a long deep breath, inhaling the sweet sea air. 'There is nowhere like this, is there? I can't believe I get to live here, even if it's just for a while. I'm so glad I came, it wasn't an easy decision to make.'

'I'm glad you're here too.' Damir squeezed her hand and her whole body quivered. 'But I'm intrigued. What made a London lawyer decide to spend her summer serving beer and coffee to holidaymakers?'

'I make beds and dust too. Speak to demanding guests. I'm trying to arrange a wedding for a month's time and I have never had a client as difficult as this particular bride.'

'I don't pay my wedding planners enough for the problems they have to solve, I know that. It must be a reassurance for Marija to know you're looking after everything for her.'

'So Josip claims. But Ana can run the B&B perfectly well without me, we all know that.' She paused. He'd been honest with her, shared more than she'd expected. Could she do the same? Should she? 'But really I'm here under a pretext.'

'Oh?'

'It's a stitch-up between my mother, Josip and Marija to get me away from London, to give me some space. And I agreed because they were right, I needed to get away. And I agreed because I'd made a promise to start living differently and this seemed as good a place to start as any.' Lily took a deep breath. She could feel her heart pounding, her chest sore; her grief physically hurt, weighing her down, and she couldn't bear the solitude of it any longer. 'My best friend died four months ago.'

The words were out. Lily's eyes burned as she heard imagined echoes reverberating around the cove. Every time she said the words it was with disbelief. It was all so absurd. With a jolt she realised Damir had stopped, taken her other hand, his clasp strong and comforting. 'I'm so sorry.'

'Thank you.'

'Would you like to tell me about her?'

She stared up at him. His face was shadowed in the moonlight but his voice kind, filled with sympathy. She couldn't have handled either before today, getting by with practicality and a hefty dose of denial, but his comforting hands holding hers, the lack of platitudes gave her the strength to nod.

'I would, if you're sure.'

'She was important to you, of course I'm sure.'

They carried on walking until they reached the rocks clustered at the end of the beach. Damir let go of her hands and began to climb up, and Lily could see an easy path through them. 'There's more sand on the other side of here,' he said. 'Like a private little beach.' Sure enough, a brief scramble later and they were sitting on a tiny horseshoe of sand encircled by the rocks, the dunes and the sea. She could see the lights from the villa on the other side of the bay, a few boats moored further out to sea. Otherwise it was as if they were alone in the world.

Lily clasped her knees in one hand and stared out at the dark water for a long, long time, memories jostling for attention.

'Izzy and I were really close,' she said at last. 'We were more like sisters than friends. And in some ways we were alike, although she was a lot more outgoing than me. Everyone loved her. She was so funny, and she would do anything for the people she loved.'

'Sounds like a good friend to have. Where did you meet?'

'At school. When mum married Josip I had to start a new school. I was shy anyway, and all the friendship groups had already been formed so I hid in the library every lunch and break. I soon realised I wasn't the only lower school girl hiding out in there, mostly because Izzy insisted on sitting with me and asking me a hundred questions. She should have been the lawyer, she was always wanting to know about everything and everyone. She was insatiably curious.' She closed her eyes and saw them, two girls in too-big uniforms, side by side at the wooden table, books spread out in front of them.

'Izzy could have been in any friendship group she wanted, but she didn't care about popularity. She was determined to get the highest grades in the school, to go to Oxford or Cambridge, she had it all planned out. She'd grown up in care, you see, lived with eight different foster families by the time I met her. Mum and Josip adored her, she was in a stable home by then or I think they would have taken her in.

'Looking back, I realise I was probably too dependent on her, I didn't look for other friends, didn't need them. Izzy knew everyone, and I followed where she led. But although she enjoyed a party, usually had some besotted boy hanging around, her real focus was on her future. We drew up life plans that first year we met. Oxford for me, Cambridge for her. Law for me, computers for her. Then good jobs, sharing a flat in London, promotions. By thirty I would be partner and she would have got the investment for her first start-up.'

She laughed, hearing it all said aloud. 'It sounds ridiculous, doesn't it, but we had a whole timetable. And we stuck to it. Thought it was worth it, even though we missed out on a lot of rites of passage.'

'Success takes sacrifice,' Damir said, and she nodded.

'And we sacrificed. Especially after university. We never took the time to go to the beach on a sunny day, never travelled, barely took a full weekend off. We always thought we had all the time in the world once we'd got to where we needed to be. But we were wrong. Izzy didn't have all the time, her time was cut short.'

'Did she have a boyfriend?'

Lily laughed. 'Izzy attracted attention wherever she went, but when you're always cancelling plans to work, boyfriends don't tend to hang around too long. We were getting to the stage where we saw friends start to get engaged, a couple had babies, but neither of us wanted that kind of baggage, not yet. Izzy once said that she thought thirty-two was the right age to start thinking about marriage. It sounds silly, doesn't it? Our lives. All planned out and on track.

'But Izzy dying at twenty-eight wasn't in the plans, not at all. And then I realised we were so busy living for the future we'd forgotten to live at all.' Her voice faded to a whisper and Damir squeezed the hand he was still holding. She swallowed, the pain in her throat almost overwhelming.

'She always wanted children one day, a big family with a dog and a range cooker like in the adverts, she said, to make up for the family she didn't have. She wanted to foster herself, to give back. And she didn't get to do or have any of it. She was desperate to go to Costa Rica and see sloths, to travel up the Californian coast, to see Petra, but she never took the time and now she'll never go. So I promised her. I would start to live. For her as well as me. That's why I'm here. Trying to learn to be spontaneous, trying to have fun. To live.'

Lily's hand was warm and soft in his. Damir couldn't, wouldn't let it go. He'd never heard anyone sound so lonely, sound so desolate before and shame filled him for how he'd tried to probe to find out her family secrets, how he'd tried to use her. She deserved more than to be a pawn in his power games, she deserved to be loved and cherished. To be desired.

And, oh, how he desired her. That was no deceit.

'You must be the bravest woman I know,' he said, and she turned to face him, eyes wide with surprise.

'Brave? Me?'

'Coming to a place where you know nobody, where you don't speak the language, to do a job you have no idea how to do. To leave your family and job, your whole life behind. That's pretty brave.'

'Well,' she said a little shakily, 'when you put it like that, I guess it was a little brave. To be honest, none of it comes easily, I spend an awful lot of time thinking, *What would Izzy do?*'

'Do you speak to her?'

'All the time. Does that sound silly?'

'Not at all.' He paused. 'I speak to Dad, tell him my plans.'

'It's a way of keeping them with us,' Lily said softly. 'A way to carry on without them. There's a hole in my life, and it will always be there. I'll marry someone she will never meet, if I have children they will never know her. No one will ever know the me she knew. The insecurities she knew. No one will remember the way I cried over my first boyfriend even though I told everyone he was getting in the way of my studies, or how hard I worked for my A+ in maths. No one else was there when I got offered a place at my first-choice firm and danced around the kitchen.

'I told her everything. She was the most kindred

of kindred spirits and now she's not here. I can't just stop talking to her.' She smiled shakily. 'What do you say to your father? Do you ask his advice?'

'Advice, no. I tell him what is going on. Report in, I suppose.'

'Making sure you're on track?'

'Making sure I exceed expectations, keep my promise,' he corrected her, and she shifted a little so she faced him, her hand still warm in his. Anchoring him, grounding him.

'They hold a lot of weight, those promises to those who are no longer here. But believe me when I tell you that your promises are meaningless, your success meaningless if you don't take the time to just be occasionally. To live. To make memories. It took a lot for me to agree to sit with you at the party, to go to Dubrovnik. I wanted to hide behind my work at the villa, just as I always had. But I knew that I needed to make some memories.'

'Is that why you're here? Collecting memories?'

'I hope so. But at the moment I am trying to live in the moment, to be spontaneous. To feel.'

He had no idea who made the first move. One moment they were sitting side by side, their hands linked, the next she was in his arms and his mouth was on hers. This was no sweet, gentle exploratory kiss, this was an incendiary kiss full of urgency and need and pent-up frustration. There was no gentle exploration of bodies, no careful learning or touch.

Instead Lily impatiently pulled at his shirt, tugging it over his head still half-buttoned, her hands

immediately sliding down to unbutton his shorts. He
was no less busy, slipping her T-shirt off, inhaling
sharply at the touch of her silky bare skin under his
hands as he slid his hands across the back of her bra
until he found the clasp, undoing it and tossing the
garment to one side.

Damir hissed as Lily finally undid his trouser
button, beginning to push his trousers down around
his hips, all his blood rushing to that same spot with
deep, primal urgency. 'Not so fast,' he managed, cap-
turing her hands in his, stilling her progress.

'Why not?' she gasped, and Damir smiled, slowly
and with intent against the sweetness of her mouth,
edging back until he was leaning against the rocks
and pulling her onto his knees so she knelt astride
him, kissing her again, deep and hungry and so in-
toxicating he lost all knowledge of who and where
he was.

'Because we've barely got started,' he told her
after a moment, and chuckled at her whimper. With a
Herculean effort Damir slowed things down, grazing
his way down her neck, biting softly into the sweet
hollow there until she moaned, throwing her head
back to give him better access. He carried on exploring, his lips moving over the softness of her breasts
while he carefully, slowly undid her shorts, sliding
them down her thighs, stroking the soft skin beneath in slow, intent circles that mirrored his kisses,
his fingers gliding up by infinitesimal steps until he
found the very core of her.

She jolted as he touched her, then settled, moving in time with him. Damir's lips found hers as he continued to stroke her until, with a small cry, she came apart against him, falling into him with shuddering breaths. Damir held her close as her breathing settled, his own pulse beating wildly, the scent of her enveloping him until Lily pulled away, cupping his face with her hands.

'I haven't…' He managed to steady his voice. 'I wasn't expecting this, I'm not prepared.'

Lily smiled, reaching back into her shorts pocket and pulling out a small square package. 'Luckily for you, I am…unless you don't want to?'

It was hard to breathe, hard to function with his blood pulsing, with every instinct urging him forward. Damir reached out and took the packet from her unresisting fingers and drew Lily back towards him. 'Oh, I do want. I want very much. Would you like me to show you how much?'

'Yes please,' she breathed, and then she was kissing him again and everything and everyone disappeared. There was just her, and for now she was all that he needed or wanted. For the first time in a really long time tomorrow could take care of itself.

CHAPTER EIGHT

'Was it worth the wait?'

Lily waited until the waiter had finished clearing their plates and left the table before she answered. 'Honestly? I thought nothing would beat fresh pizza overlooking the sun setting on Fire Bay, but you have managed it. This place was *definitely* worth the wait. I just can't believe the setting.'

'There's a reason it's one of Dubrovnik's most sought-after restaurants.' A smug smile played around Damir's mouth but, she conceded, he had a right to be smug. She had never been anywhere like this in her life. The restaurant was actually *on* the old town's city walls, the intimate tables adjoining the parapets so that diners could sit and look out across the Adriatic whilst enjoying the exquisite tasting menu. Damir was on first-name terms with the waiters, and they had been steered to the very best table, in a private corner with stunning views all around.

'Thank you for the loveliest day, I feel very spoiled.'

To be fair Lily didn't just *feel* spoiled, she *was*

being spoiled. Damir had pulled out all the stops for their postponed date, sailing her across to Sunset Bay on the Lapad Peninsula, a bustling tourist resort just outside Dubrovnik. They'd walked around the beautiful headland, popping into a bar built into a cave for a coffee before enjoying a swim from the bar's bathing platform. Sunset Bay offered a very different holiday experience from Lokvar, with its myriad hotels catering for everyone from backpackers to luxury seekers.

A vibrant, café-filled boardwalk offered visitors a cornucopia of dining and drinking choices, with music pumping from several bars, screens showing sports and sales booths tempting visitors with various excursions along the coastline and out to the islands. By contrast, Lokvar was sleepy and slow, and Lily was only just beginning to realise just how much she loved the island and its laid-back pace.

'You deserve spoiling, especially after all those breakfast shifts,' Damir said, and she laughed.

'Breakfast, lunch and dinner. No wonder Marija is so fit, there is no gym programme that can burn as many calories as I have managed to burn over the last few days. The waitress work out with optional chambermaid cardio. I highly recommend it, I've never had such definition in my arms.' She flexed one for him to admire and he reached out to squeeze it, the caress softening as he ran a finger down her bare arm. Lily half closed her eyes as sensation rippled through her. How could one light touch leave her needing more in this way?

'Would you like to order coffee?' The waiter was back, and Damir looked enquiringly at Lily.

'Coffee? Or would you like to come back to my place for a nightcap?' The words were innocuous enough but the playful gleam in Damir's eyes told her he hadn't forgotten their conversation on the beach just before they had made love for the first time.

'A nightcap sounds nice,' she said as nonchalantly as she could, while every nerve fired up in anticipation. 'I'm happy to go back to your place if it's easier.'

A wolfish grin spread across his face and the anticipation intensified. 'Then let's go.'

It took less than five minutes for Damir to pay, waving away Lily's attempts to do so, before escorting her along the road. They'd travelled to Lapad by boat, then moored in the old harbour where they'd moored last time she'd visited the city, and Lily had expected that they would return there and sail to Damir's home. Instead they left the Old Town by a different gate and he led her along a wide promenade overlooking the sea. Villas and hotels were set back behind imposing gates and lush green gardens on either side, and he stopped at one gate, keying in a code so that it swung open.

'You live here?' She eyed the gracious stone building in some surprise. It was clearly old, at least a hundred years old, stately with its shuttered windows and pretty balustraded balconies fronted by neat lawns and cypress trees. She'd been expecting something modern and sleek and soulless, all glass and steel and cutting edge, not this beautiful piece of history.

'Do you approve?'

'I… On first impressions, yes, but I'll need to look around first,' she said. 'I have no idea about your taste in decor yet. You can't expect me to judge sight unseen.'

She needn't have worried. The villa more than lived up to its promise thanks to high ceilings, curving staircases and polished wooden floors. An enormous kitchen diner dominated the back of the house, sliding doors opening onto a huge flower-filled terrace furnished with a table and chairs and comfortable loungers. Steps led down to a swimming pool and hot tub nestled into the cliff side, the sea far below.

The decor was plain but clearly expensive, original pieces of modern art on the walls and some beautiful glass sculptures cleverly displayed. But there were no personal effects, no photos, no left-out books or notes, not even an unwashed mug in the sink. It was a beautiful house, but it wasn't a home. It could be one of his holiday lets, rather than the place in which he lived.

It wouldn't take much, she mused as she followed him around. Some family photos, a throw on the pristine, stylish sofa, a cosy armchair in the bay window, some bright rugs. And people. This was a house made for a family, not a man who spent most of his time elsewhere.

'You are so lucky to live in a beautiful place,'

she said, once they were sitting on the terrace with the promised coffee and a glass of Croatian walnut brandy. The terrace was lit by subtle lowlights all around, candles burning on the table in front of them. The air was sweet and flower scented, birds calling from the trees all around. It was so peaceful they might have been in the middle of the countryside, not the centre of a bustling city. 'Have you been here long?' Maybe he'd just moved in. That would explain the lack of personal effects.

'I bought it for Kata, she always wanted to live in one of these houses. But she left before we could move in.'

'You kept it?'

'Why not? It's central. Close to the harbour, to the business district, to the main road.' This was all true, but she still felt that this should be a family home with its large rooms and many bedrooms, not an austere bachelor pad. 'And I feel at peace here,' he added, his voice so low she barely heard him. 'Sitting here, looking out to sea at the horizon and the water. It renews me.'

'I think I understand,' Lily said softly, trying to reconcile this admission with the self-confessed workaholic he was. 'It is restorative, isn't it? Not just the view but the air, the silence—I can feel my soul reviving just sitting here. Although I suppose that could be the brandy.'

'What about you? Where is home for you? Where are you at peace?'

Home. There was a concept. Not in her apartment,

as soulless and modern as she had expected Damir's to be. Not even the small Ealing terrace where her mother and Josip lived.

The only place where she had ever felt anything like the peace Damir described was in Lokvar, and she was only a temporary resident there. 'In a way I've been looking for a home all my life, but in another way I think it's safer not to have one, because then you can't lose it.'

Where had *that* come from?

'Lose it?' Surprise flashed in his eyes as he turned to look at her.

'We moved around a lot when I was a kid,' she said as offhandedly as she could. 'My mother was a bit of a traveller. As soon as I was settled in one place we'd be on the move, until she met Josip, that is. They've stayed put since they got married. They don't even really go on holiday.'

'That must have been difficult.'

'It was all I knew, you know what kids are like. Adaptable.' She fixed a bright smile onto her face. 'It was a long time ago. Ancient history.'

'Not that ancient if you're still searching for a place where you feel safe,' he said gently.

'I do feel safe,' she protested. 'People make me feel safe, they make a home, not a place. Josip, Izzy… I guess that's why I am struggling so much. I haven't just lost my friend, I've lost part of me.'

'And your mother? Does she not make you feel safe?'

Lily bit her lip, old habits of loyalty making it

hard to be honest. 'That's a big question. I do love her, I love her a lot. But she was really young when she had me for a start, not yet eighteen, and totally not ready for a baby.'

'Just a child herself.'

'I understand that now. My goodness, when she was my age she had an eleven-year-old. It must have been hard. I do see that.'

'And your father?'

'Unknown. That's what it says on my birth certificate and that's what she's always said—that's the problem when you're conceived at a seven-day-long rave during the second summer of love. You try tracking down a man whose name she can't remember from thousands of attendees. My grandparents were kind of strict and Mum really rebelled against that, was always running away to raves and festivals. And then, once I was born, she just took me with her.

'Some of my earliest memories are of hanging out at a festival with anyone sober enough to take care of me. She lived in squats or travelled around in vans, we crashed with friends or lived in communes. Sometimes there were boyfriends, some more long term than others, a few better than others, but none that could be thought of as any kind of father figure. It was chaotic.'

Saying the words aloud brought it back. The constant change and uncertainty. The days or weeks when there was no money, the mornings her mother didn't wake up at all.

She took another sip, staring out to sea but not

seeing anything but the past. 'When I was ten my
grandparents took me away and I lived with them.
They were very keen to make sure I didn't turn out
like Mum. Very strict, it couldn't have been more
of a contrast.'

'That must have been really hard.' His voice was
gentle, the chill of his earlier words gone.

'Yes and no. I missed her so much, but all I wanted
to do was live in one place and have a normal life. No
more parties, no more changing schools or missing
school.' She paused, remembering the relief mixed
with the pain of missing a mother who had barely
noticed her absence. 'But my grandparents didn't really want me, I was a duty, and I knew it.'

'So what happened?'

'Mum overdosed. She nearly died. Josip was the
paramedic who saved her. A year later she was sober,
they were married and I went to live with them. She
went to university, became a social worker. She's
amazing, I am so proud of her. Josip changed her life
and he changed mine. I'll always be so grateful to
him. But I suppose part of me will always remember
what it's like not being able to depend on the people
who are supposed to look out for you. I look at Mum
and Josip, they are so happy, they have this perfect
partnership and I want that closeness and trust. But
I don't think it's in me.

'I don't trust people not to leave. Izzy did, she
didn't mean to but she did.' She stared at him in
horror, covering her mouth with her hands as if she
could push the words back. 'I didn't mean...'

'It's okay to mean it. Anger is part of grief. There's no one way to miss someone, one way to feel.'

'We were supposed to be friends all our lives,' she whispered. 'What if no one else ever knows me the way she did? What if I'm alone for ever?'

'Hey,' he rose to his feet in one graceful moment and walked around the table, pulling her to her feet and tilting her chin so she met his gaze. 'You are loyal and funny and kind and there are lots of people out there who would love to be part of your life if you let them.'

'You think?'

'I know,' he told her. His gaze darkened as it moved to her mouth and she was aware how close they were, every part of her pressed up against him. She looked up at him, lips parted, breathless, expectant, needing until he finally claimed her mouth with his. His kiss was gentle, weakening her with its sweetness as he explored her mouth unhurriedly, the tenderness in his kiss melting her. His arms slipped around her, keeping her close, but made no attempt to touch her further, to reach under her clothes, to move them onto the next stage in this particular age-old dance. This was a kiss for kissing's sake and all the more potent for it.

Lily rose onto her tiptoes, better to lean in, entwining her arms around his neck, pulling Damir closer, luxuriating in the feel of his mouth and hands, savouring every sensation. Time slid away, all she knew was him, the taste of him, the feel of him, his muscles under her hands, his light touch on her waist, those clever, sinful lips and the feelings they sparked shooting through her, weakening her.

'Damir…' Lily half moaned, wanting more, and yet at the same time not wanting this gentle seduction to end. He didn't answer in words but deepened the kiss, starting to demand, to taste, to make clear his want, and she responded in kind, wiggling closer, her body pressed against his. She tangled her hands in his hair, pulling him closer still, and Damir groaned against her mouth, his hands finally, finally beginning to move, sliding down to her hips to move her against him, backing her up until she hit the table.

'This isn't the most comfortable place to do this. We could take it inside.' He hesitated. 'If you want, you can stay. You're not working tomorrow morning, are you?'

'Is this your usual line?' Lily half joked, resorting to humour as she tried to process what had happened, her confession followed by the sweetest kiss she had ever experienced. 'Nightcap on the terrace then move it upstairs for a sleepover?'

Damir was silent, and she felt his body rigid against hers. 'No,' he said at last. 'I have dated many women since my divorce, yes. I've had sex with some of those women, always monogamously, always carefully. But I've never invited any of them to spend the night here. I sleep alone. You will be the first.'

She had no idea how to process that information. No idea what it meant. But Lily understood that the invitation was more than casual. That for Damir to ask her stay in a place that was obviously his sanctuary was a privilege. That for him to make himself vulnerable enough to ask her to stay was a gift, one she couldn't easily turn down. 'In that case I'd be honoured.'

'Are you sure?' The question seemed loaded. As if he was asking her about more than her agreement to stay the night, and she held his gaze as she answered. The next step Lily knew, was down to her and she thrilled with the power he entrusted in her.

'I'm sure,' she said. She leaned back and looked up at him fearlessly, her whole body tingling at the intensity in his dark gaze.

She led the way, wiggling out of their close embrace and walking as confidently, as provocatively as she could to the open doors that led into the villa. Damir stood by the table, one white-knuckled hand gripping it as he watched her, heat dancing in his eyes. Not breaking his gaze, Lily stepped inside, every nerve alight with trembling desire and need.

She walked through the kitchen diner to the tiled hall and slowly, purposefully up the curving staircase until she reached the wide landing and continued down it. Damir's room was at the far end, a corner suite overlooking the sea.

She didn't falter but turned the handle to open the door, pulling her dress above her head as she did so and discarding it on the floor. With one quick movement she unclasped her bra, discarding it likewise, and wiggled out of her underwear. Pulling the top sheet off the bed, she climbed in, resisting the temptation to cover herself. Instead she half turned to face the door, leaning up on one elbow, her legs curved behind her, and watched Damir stop at the door of the room.

With satisfaction she heard his intake of breath as he saw her waiting for him, his eyes travelling over her in excruciatingly slow detail, as if he were touching her remotely. Lily had never felt so powerful, never felt so beautiful, never felt wanted the way she felt wanted right now. The hunger in Damir's face was a gift, a homage to her, and she gloried in it.

He stood, holding her gaze as he disposed of his own clothes. Tall, powerful and, oh, so sexy it took less than two strides for him to join her.

'What took you so long?' she managed to say.

Damir cupped her face and stared at her for one long, endless moment. 'You're so beautiful,' he said hoarsely, before his mouth took hers in a searing kiss that made Lily forget who she was, where she was, forget everything but the sensations pulsing through her.

All she knew was the feel of this man under her hands as she tried to learn every part of him, the play of the muscles on his back, the strength in his arms, the delicious subtleness of his touch, the way he made her gasp, the way he made her yearn and want, teasing and giving until all she could do was call out his name, biting down on his shoulder, tasting him and knowing him, giving as she received.

But at the back of her mind, as with one delicious movement he joined them as one, Lily was aware of an extra intensity in her, an awareness that her response wasn't just provoked by the day they'd shared, by the chemistry between them, by the undoubted skill of his lovemaking. She could tell herself all she wanted that this was a summer fling, but her response to him was fuelled by emotion. She had no reason to trust him, every reason to remember that this was just a game they played, but as she held onto him and allowed the sensation to carry her away, Lily tried to block out the realisation that she might just be falling for him.

CHAPTER NINE

LILY FIDGETED NERVOUSLY as the boat sailed around the headland, Dubrovnik lit up in the distance, pulling her wrap more closely around her shoulders although the early evening air was warm. She felt a little uncomfortable, the only passenger on the charter boat Damir had sent to collect her, although she had insisted she would have been fine jumping on one of the open-topped passenger ferries that connected Lokvar with the mainland. The driver of the small speedy boat hadn't spoken to her beyond a few grunts, leaving her alone with her thoughts.

And she had a lot to think about, two emails that day jolting her from the contented haze that had enveloped her the last few weeks as she had spent her days either working or spending time with Damir—time that was becoming increasingly important to her. She pulled at her wrap impatiently. How she wished he had picked her up so she could discuss her news and thoughts through with him.

Damir had asked her to accompany him to the opening ceremony of the Summer Festival, a six-week celebration of arts and culture that encompassed the whole area—Lokvar would be hosting a theatre company who would perform several times a week in the small but idyllic botanical gardens. The opening ceremony, a concert, was by invitation only, followed by a champagne reception.

To be there with Damir felt like a huge jump from barbecuing at his villa or hanging out on Lokvar, where everyone knew them, and at the back of her mind she couldn't help wondering what this very public stepping out meant. Probably nothing as a quick internet search had shown her photos of Damir at lots of high society occasions, always with a perfectly groomed companion, rarely the same one twice.

Women who had agreed to the same caveat of short, sweet and finite as she had. But did they also find themselves forgetting those conditions, falling deeper with every conversation? Probably not, they seemed like the kind of women who didn't just know the rules but made the rules, while Lily was figuring it all out as she went.

It didn't help that the evening would also be a huge test of Lily's nerves. Big formal occasions always intimidated her, although she tried her best to hide it. Especially big formal occasions where she didn't know anyone. She knew Damir was there to be seen, to circulate. The opening ceremony was an important night in the Dubrovnik social calendar.

At least she had managed to find an appropriate outfit, a silver maxi dress and matching wrap that managed to look smart and feel comfortable. She'd left her hair loose but pulled back off her face and she wore the turquoise necklace and earrings Josip and her mother had given her for her twenty-first birthday.

This time, rather than the long sea journey round to the old harbour, she found herself taken to the much closer, but much less picturesque City Port, where several mid-size cruise ships were moored, along with hundreds of boats ranging from small dinghies to luxury ocean-going yachts. A car was waiting to whisk her to Pile, the entrance to the Old Town where Damir waited for her.

Lily's stomach fluttered as she took him in, sharply smart in a suit that had obviously been made for him, every line enhancing his tall, lean strength. His hair was slicked back and he was freshly shaved, smarter than she had ever seen him. Almost like a stranger, a reminder that for all their lovemaking, the confidences they had shared, she barely knew him at all.

'How was the journey?' His mouth grazed her cheek, lingering just a second too long for a polite greeting. 'Sorry I couldn't pick you up. My meeting overran.'

'That's okay, but I could have quite easily taken the ferry, you know.'

'I know.' He began to escort her through the now familiar gate that led into the Old Town, his hand proprietorial on her arm. Several other people, equally smartly dressed, called out greetings, looking curiously at Lily as they did so. 'But I promised to collect you and I always keep my word.'

'Good to know.'

The concert and ceremony were taking place in a square in the Old Town just outside St Blaise's church, the ancient building star of several films and television programmes. Seats had been erected in a square around a central stage and Damir escorted her to seats close to the front. The artists were beginning to tune up, the seats to fill, the whole square humming with excitement and anticipation. This concert would be broadcast live so the whole city could hear it, and would be followed by what she had been assured were spectacular fireworks.

'I'm sorry I didn't answer your call earlier,' Damir said once they were settled. 'Is everything okay?'

'Everything's fine, I just had a couple of emails today that I wanted to talk to you about. The first one was from the bride's family about the wedding later this month.'

Damir groaned. The whole B&B had been booked out the week after next for a wedding party. The wedding itself was due to take place in Dubrovnik, but all the guests would be staying at the B&B for a long weekend, arriving on the Thursday evening and leaving on the Monday. As the bride and groom's families were English, Lily had offered to deal with them, and as the wedding approached it seemed to take up a great deal of her time—and her conversation.

By now she was sure that Damir was as sick of them as she was.

The bride's demands had become increasingly onerous over the last few weeks, along with an ever-changing list of guest allergies and needs. Her demands had culminated in a sudden desire for separate dinners and entertainment for both the bride's and the groom's families and friends the evening before the wedding itself, both to be held at the B&B but not within sight of each other.

'Why can't one of them go over to the mainland?' Ana had grumbled when that particular request had come through, and although Lily had been too busy trying to work out just how they were going to accommodate it given the size of the villa to join in the grumbling, secretly she couldn't help but agree with her friend.

'No, what does she want now? For you to decorate the beach in her theme colours? An entire change of menu? Or does she want you to whip up several wedding dresses for her to choose from when she gets here?'

'No.' Lily laughed, though none of those suggestions would have surprised her. 'Much worse. They've split up, the wedding is off.'

'One of them has had a lucky escape, I can't help suspecting it's the groom.'

'I agree, but obviously they've cancelled completely and the bride's family are insisting on getting their deposit back. So that's been fun.'

'I take it you have told them just what they can do with that suggestion.'

'Several times. It hasn't stopped them trying,

though. I've had the bride's mother and father and even her aunt on the phone all telling me just how they'll ruin me with bad reviews.' She sighed. 'The annoying thing is that Marija wouldn't usually allow the villa to be booked out for one event at the height of summer, but the groom's family are regulars so we agreed as a favour.'

'Does that mean there was no contract?'

'You forget who you're talking to. I wrote that contract and they agreed to a completely non-refundable fifty per cent deposit. So they can huff and puff all they want but they won't get a penny. But this means we're going to be empty at the height of summer, to say nothing of all the orders we are now going to have to cancel, and the boxes of favours and decorations we'll have to send back to the UK. I've ten boxes of champagne arriving tomorrow, the rest of the wine later in the week, and Antun's food order needed its own delivery boat.'

'You won't be empty for long,' Damir said. 'At this time of year there are always last-minute bookings and walk-ins.'

'That's what Ana said.' Lily looked down at her hands. 'But, you see, that Thursday is Izzy's birthday. I was relieved we were going to be so busy that it meant I wouldn't have time to brood. I need to make sure I stay busy. Or celebrate her in some way. Because I had a second email today. One that is much bigger in the grand scheme of things, much more unexpected. I could really do with your thoughts on it, because I am all over the place.'

'What is it?' His voice was low, reassuring, and she leaned in gratefully.

'Izzy's lawyer, the one dealing with her estate, got in touch. I knew that Izzy had left everything to me, but I didn't realise just what that meant.' She could hear the pitch of her voice rising and took a deep breath. 'What am I supposed to do with it all? What was she thinking?'

'It was more than you expected?'

She nodded, biting her lip to keep back the threatened tears. 'So much more. You see, she was a computer genius, worked for a couple of the really big firms. More than once she was headhunted for roles in Silicon Valley but she always turned them down. She liked to be rooted, she said. I guess that's what happens when you grow up with no roots at all.

'Anyway, I knew she was well paid, but it turns out that she had well over a million saved up. A million pounds! She could have bought her own house rather than sharing with me, begun the start-up she was planning, done anything. Instead she just kept saving.' She stared unseeingly at the stage and the musicians still warming up. 'I wonder what she meant to do with it. All the things she could have done and never did…' Her voice trailed off.

'And now it's yours?'

'I suppose so. Legally, yes. But, Damir, it doesn't feel right. Her books, the couple of paintings she acquired, her clothes even, they are different. I can accept them and remember her every time I see them or wear them. But a sum of money like this? I can't take it! It doesn't seem right.'

There was a lot she could do with such a huge sum of money. Pay off her mortgage, go travelling and have a huge nest egg for when she returned. Start her own business or put it aside, as Izzy had done, for her own rainy day and hope hers would actually arrive. This money gave her freedom, but it also weighed her down. It didn't seem right to squander it, it didn't seem right to use it at all. She too was well paid, she had savings of her own. She turned to Damir.

'What do you think I should do?'

Before Damir could answer the audience hushed and a few moments later the strains of a violin filled the air. Usually music had the power to transport him, no matter if it was classical, rock or something in between, but tonight he barely heard a note. Instead he was all too aware of Lily, straight-backed next to him, absorbed in the music, her last words echoing round and round.

'What do you think I should do?'

Why did his opinion matter? They weren't friends or confidants, they were lovers, enjoying a brief amount of time together before going their separate ways. Lily's future was nothing to do with him. Spend the money, give it away, what did he care?

Only he did care. He wanted to help her make sense of this new development, just as he wanted to help her deal with the bridal party's cancellation. He wanted to take all her cares and concerns and shield her from them.

And that wasn't in their agreement at all.

He clapped politely, a second after the rest of the audience, relieved when a second piece started up, leaving him to his thoughts. There was no rhyme or reason to the way he felt. Their arrangement was, like all his arrangements, temporary. She was leaving at the end of the summer. And even if she wasn't, there would be an expiry date on their time together. She wasn't Croatian, she didn't come from an influential family, and although she shared his work ethic, she didn't have the background to help him expand, to move his business up to the next level. He sensed that Lily would never be happy with a role as hostess and facilitator. And that was the kind of wife he needed.

Hang on a second. Wife? Where on earth had *that* come from? True, he was in his early thirties, true, he'd always meant to remarry one day—he had to, had to father some heirs if the family business was to continue. But not yet. Not to a woman he had known for less than two months and slept with a handful of times. His marriage to Kata had been a failure, and he'd known her all his life. If and when he married again, guaranteeing the success of that marriage was one of his paramount considerations. And the only way to do that was through a mutual understanding of shared goals and benefits. A contract, not an emotional journey.

He knew all this, yet somehow, during the last

few weeks, he had relaxed his vigilance and this was the result, his mind wandering to forbidden places. Which meant he needed to take some action now. He could still see Lily while she was around, but maybe he'd better guard against getting any closer. Guard against saying too much, guard against showing too much, guard against feeling too much. Enjoyable dates and satisfactory lovemaking and no emotion. They were his established rules. It would be best not to deviate again.

Mind made up, he did his best to concentrate on the rest of the concert and to enjoy the fireworks that lit up the Old Town. He exerted himself, ensuring he was at his most charming and flirtatious, making Lily laugh and blush in equal measure, but he also made sure they didn't resume their earlier conversation. No more heartfelt confidences, no advice. Seduction and fun only. He'd been in danger of losing sight of the end game. Of the villa, of his plans for it. He needed to dazzle Lily, make her understand his vision, advocate for him, not allow her into his heart.

He refused to consider that maybe it was a little too late for that.

The following reception was an even more exclusive gathering in the Sponza Palace, just a short walk through the Old Town. Lily gasped as he ushered her into the candlelit room, with its stone arches and high ceiling. 'I just can't get over how old and beautiful everything is,' she said, turning slowly while Damir procured two glasses of champagne from a hovering waiter. 'Just look at those archways. It's so strange to be somewhere still so intact that makes you feel like you could be living any time in the last thousand years. London has a lot of history, but everything is being rebuilt at such a great rate it's impossible to imagine it in the nineteenth century, let alone the sixteenth.'

'Come on, I'll show you around.' He took her arm and started along the hallway, only to stop as an elegant woman in a fitted black cocktail dress turned to look at them speculatively, a flicker of disdain in her hooded gaze. His chest tightened as he took in the familiar eyes, so like his own, the immaculately coiled hair, the perfect make-up.

She nodded. 'Damir.'

'Majka,' he replied, then switched to English. 'May I introduce you to Lily Woodhouse. Marija's granddaughter,' he added meaningfully, and his mother's eyes widened. Was that an actual gleam of approval he saw in them? 'Lily, this is my mother.'

'How lovely to meet you,' his mother said in her careful English. 'How is Marija?'

'Very well, thank you.'

'Is she enjoying her travels?' So his mother knew all the island news, although she hadn't set foot there in eight years.

'Very much. She's now back in London with Mum and Josip.'

'Is she?' Damir asked. Did that mean her travels were over and she would return this season after all?

Lily turned to him with a smile. 'Didn't I tell you? She's never seen England in summer so they are planning a few weeks away to show her some of the country and to try and prove to her that it isn't always grey.'

'That sounds delightful,' his mother said in a voice that suggested it was anything but, and he could feel Lily stiffen beside him.

'I think so. It's nice to meet you,' she added. There was a dignity in her bearing, a cool politeness in tone that he had never seen or heard in Lily before. A memory flashed of just a few weeks ago, sitting eating pizza, telling Lily about his father's death. 'She blames me,' he had said.

Did Lily remember? Looking at the suddenly glacial woman beside him, he knew she did. She remembered and she cared. The tightness in his chest eased as she slipped her hand through his arm, tilting her chin a little more.

'Do pass on my best wishes to your family,' his mother said, her bearing as regal as Lily's, and Lily inclined her head.

'Of course. Thank you.'

'It was nice to see you, Damir. You and—Lily, is it?—must come over for dinner one night. Ask your PA to call mine and arrange it. Have a good evening.' And she was gone. Damir released a breath he hadn't even known he was holding.

'Get your PA to call hers? Seriously?' Lily was almost squeaking in indignation and to his surprise the last of his tension left him as he took in her reaction.

'She remarried into old money. Now she lives the kind of life she always wanted—charity committees, city functions. She keeps herself very busy. Those three homes don't run themselves, you know.' In fact, he realised, his mother lived exactly the kind of life he envisioned for his wife.

'Even so. I bet even the Queen doesn't expect her children to organise a family dinner through their PAs. Will you do it?'

'No,' he said slowly. 'There's no point. She has a new life, one that doesn't include me. She's only interested to hear what new deals I've made, where I'm expanding. To see if I can be of use.'

'I'm sorry.'

'Don't be. She's never been that family focussed. She married my father because she knew he was going places but she always felt she married beneath her—and never let him forget it. Life on Lokvar, as the wife of a man who liked to get stuck in and get his hands dirty, working behind his own bar or on the building sites, never really suited her. I think she's glad to have put it all behind her.'

'Well, she's the one missing out,' Lily said. 'She should be bursting with pride to have a son like you, she should be hounding you to be at every dinner so she can show you off, not fobbing you off without even an air kiss. Come on, you promised me a guided tour before we were interrupted.'

'Yes, I did. Come on, this way.' But as he showed Lily around the famous old building her words kept echoing through his mind, and he kept replaying the moment Lily had drawn herself up in coldly polite outrage. He didn't need defending, he was more than capable of looking after himself, but to know that someone else cared, someone thought him worthy of defending was something he hadn't felt in a very, very long time. One thing was becoming clear: he could tell himself to emotionally distance himself from Lily, he could tell himself that this was just an affair, but the truth was he was falling for her. Worst of all, he didn't want to change a thing.

CHAPTER TEN

DAMIR LOOKED UP from his laptop and grinned. 'Good morning,' he said appreciatively, looking Lily up and down, lingering on every curve and dimple. If there was anything sexier than a pretty girl, tousled with sleep and wearing a man's shirt, he had yet to see it.

'Good morning, I didn't mean to oversleep,' she said as she leaned over to bestow one sweetly chaste kiss on his cheek.

'You didn't, I was up early. Besides, this is the first time you've had more than a few hours off in weeks, you needed it.'

He, on the other hand, had been awake most of the night, all too aware of her slumbering beside him. All the reasons he should put some distance between them had rolled through his head over and over again, but he knew he wouldn't. More importantly, he couldn't. Luckily, Lily was still only here for the summer. The only thing really at risk was his heart. And until recently he had been pretty sure he no longer had one to risk.

'It was blissful.' She stretched, the shirt rising up

her thighs in a way that made concentrating on work almost impossible. 'No breakfast shift! No carrying coffee to tables, so desperate for a gulp it takes everything I have not to stop en route and finish the pot. No having to be perky and friendly first thing. Don't get me wrong, I love being there so much more than I could ever have imagined, but I was getting to the stage where I would have considered selling my soul for a lie-in.'

'No soul required and…' he jerked his head towards the kitchen counter '…there's a fresh pot of coffee over there.'

'You are a wonderful man, do you know that?' Lily padded over to the place he'd indicated to pour a cup, then returned to the kitchen table, pulling out a chair to sit opposite him. 'Mmm, this smells delectable.'

This was the first time they had spent a morning together like this. On the occasions Lily stayed over she usually got up bright and early and either Damir took her back to Lokvar or she caught the ferry home. Coffee was quickly gulped, breakfast snatched. This morning was unusually domestic.

And to his surprise he liked it that way.

'So what are your plans for the rest of your day off?' he asked, and she leaned back in her chair, pushing her unbrushed hair off her face.

'I think I might explore. There's a nice walk around the City Port, up towards Lapad, with plenty of beach clubs and swimming spots along the way.

Maybe a spot of shopping. What about you? Can you play hooky at all?'

'Not today,' he said, more regretfully than he would have imagined possible. 'I have several conference calls today, a site visit and a board meeting.'

'Fun, fun, fun,' she teased, and he laughed.

'I'd rather spend the day with you.' He meant it.

'To be honest, it might be good for me to spend some time alone. I had an idea last night and I need to mull it over.'

'What kind of idea?'

Lily sipped her coffee, her eyes bright with mingled emotions: excitement, happiness and a tinge of grief. 'I think I finally figured out what I want to do with Izzy's legacy. I know I only found out just how much money she left me yesterday, and the sensible, cautious part of me is warning me not to make such a huge decision on so little time and with so little research, so a day walking and swimming might help me figure out whether I want to explore it further. But it feels right, you know?'

Damir pushed his laptop away and reached for his own coffee. 'What feels right?'

'I want to help other children like Izzy.' Lily's words came tumbling out. 'Help foster carers like Janet, who looked after Izzy for her entire teen years. You know, literally dozens of children have passed through her hands. Some only stay a few nights, some like Izzy for much longer. Before Janet, Izzy lived in about eight homes, but Janet gave her the chance to stay at the same school for all her secondary education, to be settled. It was such a gift.'

'She sounds wonderful.' How could it be that some people had the capacity to care for so many children, when others, like his own mother, couldn't muster up enough affection for just one?

'She is! But it's not an easy life and it's hard to give the children she looks after things that other kids take for granted. Like holidays abroad, for instance.'

'I'd never thought of that before.' Damir donated liberally to several causes, some because it was expected, local hospitals and cultural centres, and a few secretly, ones closer to his heart, such as marine charities. But he had never thought about what he could do personally. The difference he could make with his money and influence.

'I am thinking of using Izzy's money to bring families like Janet's, foster families, on holiday to the B&B. I want to put three rooms aside in the school holidays for them to use free of charge and to pay for flights and transfers so there's no reason not to come. I want to make sure children like Izzy get the chance not just to have a beach holiday but to learn to swim, to sail, to paddle board. And more than that, I'd like to be able to offer summer jobs to kids who have turned eighteen, who aren't sure what to do next, to give them an opportunity to spend some time abroad and learn some skills. The villa is so magical, Fire Cove is so peaceful and so beautiful,

letting children like Izzy was experience it feels like
the best birthday gift I could give her.'

'What does Marija say?' Damir asked, trying to
process what Lily's plan meant for him and his plans,
his promises.

She looked down at her coffee and inhaled. 'I
haven't broached it with her yet. There's a lot to think
about, to plan and to figure out before I do, but I
would like to have an answer before Izzy's birthday.
I don't want to be sad on that day. I want to try and
celebrate her life the way we couldn't at her funeral.
If I knew that I could make this work that would
make a celebration so much easier.'

It was a great idea, Damir could see that, but to
fulfil it meant the villa staying as it was—and that
meant he would never make his father's dream come
true. There had to be a middle way. 'It's a great idea,
Lily, but you don't actually need the villa, do you?
It's Lokvar, not the B&B itself that's important, so
you could pay for these families to stay anywhere
on the island. In fact, I could donate rooms at my
hotel, it would be my privilege. And I could take on
a couple of summer workers. I'd be happy to support
you.' Why couldn't they both get what they wanted,
what they needed?

'That's very generous of you,' Lily said slowly,
the enthusiasm in her face dimming. 'And your hotels are lovely, but some of these children will have
never been abroad before, some have quite complex
needs, they'd probably prefer somewhere a little more
homely. I mean, I get intimidated by all those pristine

white walls and all that gleaming glass in your hotel. I'm not sure it would be the right environment. But I will give it some thought, of course. Thank you.'

Another thought occurred to him. 'Does this mean you're planning to stay on Lokvar?' He wanted her to say yes and no in equal measure. He hadn't planned for her to stay, the only way he could cope with his feelings for her was by knowing she would leave in just a few weeks. 'Marija is over seventy, she needed to take this year off. At some point she'll have to sell the villa if Josip doesn't want it. Like it or not, change is coming. Your plans are wonderful, but you need to think about the future. Accept my offer, that way you'll be able to help more people for as long as you need.'

'Well, I was thinking maybe I could buy the villa.' She peeped hopefully up at him. 'I feel at home there in a way I've never felt before. I don't even mind those breakfast shifts. What do you think?'

If he were a different man, if he was interested in a long-term relationship with Lily, if he was capable of one, then surely this would be fantastic news. But he wasn't that man. He was Damir Kozina with a promise to keep and a plan that didn't allow for a curveball like a bright-eyed English girl who set his pulse racing and his heart feeling emotions he couldn't afford to feel.

'But that would take all your money, surely, and then how would you pay for flights and everything else you want to provide? The season is short, re- member. Besides, would you want to stay here for the rest of your life? A summer, sure, but wait until you see the island in winter. Just you and three hundred other people who have known each other all their lives. It can be a lonely existence, Lily.'

'I know, I know. At the moment it's just an idea.' If she was disappointed at his lack of enthusiasm at her suggestion she stay, she hid it well.

'It's a good idea,' he said honestly. 'And I meant it when I said I wanted to help. I have other hotels, other villas that might be just as suitable. Fire Cove is special, but the whole coastline is full of beautiful spots that might serve you just as well. Why don't we discuss it tonight? After you've had the day to think about it?'

'Yes, you're probably right,' she said. 'Right now it's just ideas and dreams, maybe we can plan it all out this evening. I'm going to go and take a shower. I'll see you in a bit.'

Lily stepped out of the shower and swathed herself in the huge, sumptuously soft towel she'd found folded in the en suite bathroom. She felt more herself, with caffeine back in her system and freshly washed hair. Ready for the day that lay ahead.

She'd been a little deflated by Damir's lukewarm if helpful responses to her idea. But she had to admit he had a point. One perfect summer wasn't the same as making a life out here. Ana went back to Zagreb once autumn hit and the island quietened down, and it wasn't as if Damir had promised her anything more than a good time. She shivered, pulling the towel closer around her.

Was she basing her potential future on the hope of the connection between her and Damir being more than a one summer thing despite no indication from him that he was considering that? More fool her.

The irony didn't escape her. She, cautious Lily Woodhouse, considering giving up her hard fought for career to live on an island because she'd fallen in love. The very thought was laughable. After all, she'd considered herself incapable of falling hard and fast for any man. Turned out she'd just not met anyone capable of igniting that kind of desire before. It had been easy to think passion was beyond her when she'd never allowed herself to really relax with a potential lover. And she hadn't, her guard always up, even with the handful of boyfriends she'd had before. No wonder none of the relationships had lasted, she'd kept so much of herself locked away, all that was real and vibrant.

She pulled a face at herself in the mirror. No more dark introspective thoughts. She'd planned a fun day of leisure and exploring and she was going to enjoy every moment. Be a tourist, take selfies and live in the moment.

Lily dressed quickly in a pretty pink sundress before slathering herself in sun cream, adding the bare modicum of make-up, just some tinted moisturiser, lip salve and mascara and running the hairdryer over her thick hair to take the worst of the wetness out of it. She'd already prepared a tote bag with a bikini and towel, her phone, sunglasses and purse. She needed nothing else.

Grabbing her tote bag, she exited the bedroom and headed back down the landing and stairs into the kitchen diner where she had left Damir. He wasn't there, his laptop also missing. Neither was he in the shaded part of the terrace where he sometimes worked.

Lily stood irresolute. She didn't want to leave without saying goodbye, making plans to meet up later.

She wandered back through the kitchen, peeking into the large sitting room to see if he was there before trying the book-lined study at the front of the house. She had hardly set foot in this room, only peeped in that very first evening when he'd given her the grand tour. The laptop was here on the large desk set against the far wall, along with a tablet and Damir's phone, but no sign of the man himself.

She looked around, impressed by the large sunny room. It was exactly the kind of study she would like for herself, with its filled bookcases, cosy stove for winter days and a leather sofa in the bay window.

A large square table stood in the middle of the room, unrolled plans neatly laid out, an architect's impression, finely detailed in 3D. Lily glanced at them with idle curiosity and her heart thumped with painful recognition. The meticulously rendered plans showed a grand hotel curving round a gentle bay facing out to sea. It was lavish with rooftop swimming pools, grand terraces and lushly curved architecture. The sandy beach showed a swish-looking beach

club, small boats bobbing off a pier. It all looked extremely exclusive.

There were very few sandy beaches on this part
of the Dalmatian Riviera, and the size of the cove,
the hillside carefully rendered in what she assumed
was exact scale, was all too familiar. She took another look, trying to block out all the buildings and
concentrate on the topography instead. She could
swear that it was Fire Cove. That the heart of the
hotel was exactly where the B&B was...

'Lily, are you okay?'

She whirled round. Damir had obviously been
swimming. He stood there, wet hair slicked back,
drops still drying on his olive chest, a towel slung
low around his hips. His gaze quickly dropped to the
paper then back to her. 'Do you want some breakfast
before you head out?'

'Damir, what are these?' She gestured towards the
paper and he shrugged elegantly, but his expression
was wary—wary and a little sad.

'Plans my architect drew up.'

'Where for? Damir, I'm not a fool,' she said, proud
that her voice wasn't shaking because right now she
felt exactly like a fool. A fool who had been played.
More than played. Who had walked straight into a
set-up. 'This is Fire Bay isn't it? You're the businessman Marija mentioned. The one who offered to buy
the villa but only because he wanted to tear it down.
You still want it and that's why you've been so persistent. Wanting to get to know me, show me around,
buy me flowers, seduce me. Isn't it?'

Emotion flashed momentarily in his dark eyes and for one moment Lily could believe it was sorrow. 'Not seduce you,' he said levelly. 'That was never part of the plan, believe me.'

And just like that the rosy haze she'd been operating in evaporated. How could she believe him, even though sincerity rang in his voice? She couldn't believe anything he said, anything he'd done. The room swam as she took in exactly what this meant. Their entire relationship was an orchestrated lie. She had been used. Worse, she had allowed him in, confided in him, opened up in a way she'd never opened up to anyone. Not even Izzy. Nausea swirled as she fought to show some control, hide a hurt so deep she couldn't begin to contemplate it. 'I'm leaving. Please don't contact me again.'

Damir didn't say anything, but then again why would he? He'd been well and truly caught out and there was nothing he could say or do to change that. He had no need to try and make her stay, any use he had for her was at an end. All Lily could do was gather the scattered remains of her dignity and leave. Head held so high her chin ached, Lily marched out of the study, retrieved her bag and shoes, stuffing the silver dress and wrap on top of her bikini. She didn't look back once as she headed for the door, resisting the urge to slam out of the villa.

The lush front garden stretched out before her, the gates tightly closed. She forced herself to move forward, swallowing a half-hysterical sob as question after question tumbled through her mind. Was this what happened when she tried to be impulsive? To have fun? Was this what happened when she let down her guard? Had this all trying to be a new person, to live a different way been a terrible mistake? Should she have stayed home and stuck with what she knew, what she'd been working for her whole life? Wouldn't that have been a better tribute to Izzy, to achieve the dreams that they'd first made together?

She walked slowly to the gate, the sun hot on her bare skin, pain throbbing deep inside. Reaching the gate, she pushed it, but it was locked. 'Dammit,' she cursed, looking around to see if there was a release button. She couldn't go back inside, and it was too tall to climb over. She stood there, irresolute, when she heard a voice behind her.

'Lily!'

Damir stood stock-still in the study and stared at the treacherous plans. How could he have been so stupid as to leave them out? It was almost as if he had wanted to betray himself, to let Lily know who he really was before things went any further.

He laughed, short and bitter. Who was he kidding? How much further could they go? He was already in too deep whether he liked it or not. But wasn't this what he did? Break promises, let people down, betray them? His father, Kata, and now Lily. She was better off knowing who he was, better off without him. He hurt and he betrayed, it was in his DNA.

With a muttered curse he turned around, not wanting to look at the plans, and strode towards the

study door. He was ruthless, yes, he had to be. But
he wasn't an out and out bastard. Was he? Was that
who he'd become somewhere between his father's
heart attack and the day Kata had walked out?

A beep caught his attention as he reached the
door and Damir looked back, at the pile of paperwork lying on the table, at his phone flashing with
who knew how many unread and unheard messages.
There was always far more to do than any man could
fit into a day, even when his day started at dawn and
lasted long into the evening. He took a step towards
the phone, trying to drag his mind back to where it
needed to be, to the many things waiting for his attention, but all he could see was the anger blazing in
Lily's eyes, at the stricken look on her face. A look
he was responsible for.

He cursed again and then reeled around, making
for the door, not allowing himself to think about what
he was doing. Stepping out, he saw Lily standing by
the gate, her back to him, slumped as if she'd given
up. Shame shot through him. He'd seen her unhappiness that first day and disregarded it. He should
do the decent thing, let her out, apologise then walk
away and leave her alone. He didn't deserve to be
forgiven, didn't deserve any kind of absolution.

'Lily!'

She looked over and her gaze caught his. There
was no running away now. Holding her gaze as
calmly as he could, Damir crossed the short distance between them, stopping just beyond touching distance.

Lily was the first to look away. 'What do you want? Because unless it's the key code for the gate I'm not interested.'

'Lily, I...'

He took a deep breath. *Never apologise for who you are*, his father had told him many times. *Never apologise for your ambition, what it takes to do what you need to do.* Damir had never stopped to think about those words before, to wonder if perhaps there was another way.

'I'm sorry.'

'Sorry for lying to me? Sorry for seducing me? For listening to me as if you cared? For making me start to think I could fall in love with you? You're going to have to narrow it down, I'm afraid.'

Every word fell with skilled precision. He was guilty as charged. 'I'm sorry for misleading you. You're right. I guessed who you were that first day and thought that if we became friends, you might put a good word in for me with Marija. I thought that if I got close to you I might get to know what her plans were before anyone else. I deliberately be-friended you, that day on the beach just after you'd arrived, I sent you the flowers as part of a campaign to get you onside. But, Lily...' He stopped, trying to find the words. He didn't have any, but he had to say something.

'Lily, the rest of it, the spark between us, I didn't plan for that. How could I have? I don't understand it myself. I barely know you in many ways and yet I couldn't get you out of my head. I can't apologise for sleeping with you, because what we just shared was the one thing for a long, long time that felt real.'

Where on earth had all that come from? Damir had had no idea that he felt that way. But every word had been true. The vulnerability was terrifying, more terrifying than any leap of faith in business, than anything he'd ever done before.

Lily stopped walking, whirling round to glare at him. 'How dare you? How dare you say that to me?'

He shrugged. 'Because it's true.'

She stared at him for what felt like an eternity. 'Why?'

Damir's heart hammered harder than ever. He couldn't turn, couldn't look at her. 'What do you mean?'

When she spoke she sounded calmer, although sorrow laced her words. 'You have so much. Far more than I ever realised. When we first met, you gave me the impression that you owned a couple of businesses here in Lokvar, but actually you have quite the empire, don't you?'

'Yes.'

'And yet the villa is still so important you were prepared to do anything to get that as well?' She paused, but he didn't answer, the question clearly rhetorical. 'What happens next?'

'Lily, I—'

'You get your hands on the B&B, you tear it down, you replace half of that small but perfect coastline with another resort hotel, fill the beach with people who pay a fortune to stay there, change all that's special and unique about Fire Cove and then what? Will you be done? Or will you be onto the next project before the foundations are laid? Looking for the next person to charm and to help you on your way?'

Every word hit hard and accurately. His success had been as quick as it had been surprising in a country where connections still counted for everything, and talent and drive didn't always outweigh who you knew.

Throughout the last few years, Damir had managed to stay on the right side of the law, never venturing too far into the morally grey area, but he had had to be single-minded to do so. The price he'd paid, the price his ex-wife had paid, had been high. He told himself it was worth it. But Lily had struck to the heart of his doubt. When would it be enough? Would he ever feel that he had done enough or would he always keep striving to grow? To make more, be more?

'I don't know,' he said hoarsely. 'I just don't know.' But he did know. Whatever he achieved, it would never be enough.

'You told me once that you'd made a promise to your father. A promise to grow the business, to get the security he felt he'd never had. Is that what drives you? Is that how you justify what you do? If he were still here, would you still want to keep expanding so aggressively? Is that what he'd want?'

'It's all he ever wanted.'

'And would he think that the end always justifies the means? That what happened between us was okay?'

His laugh was bitter. 'Who do you think taught me, Lily? I am my father's son.'

Pain flashed in her eyes and Damir knew there was no coming back from this. He had no case to plead. He let everyone down, that was who he was. He might be falling in love with Lily—hell, there was no might about it—but she was worthy of far more than him. The best thing he could do, the only thing he could do was to let her go and ensure she didn't waste a single moment thinking about him.

Somehow he managed a twisted smile. 'Lily, I like you. I like you a lot, more than I should. But I never pretended this was, that this could be anything more than a summer fling. I don't have the time or the emotional freedom for a relationship. What we share physically is amazing, I think it's a shame to waste that kind of chemistry. But let's not pretend this is something it isn't. Like I said, I'm sorry I misled you, but this isn't some big betrayal. We're just two people with a spark. Sex is sex, business is business. Don't confuse the two. But there's no reason we can't keep having fun.'

Lily had her answer, now it was time for her to walk away. She'd already been hurt, humiliated, but she was strong, no lasting damage had been done. Damir was ruthless, wasting more time on him would truly make her the fool she'd thought she was.

Until his last comment she'd hoped that he was the man she'd thought he was, the kind and compas-

sionate man she glimpsed beyond the flirtatious fa-
çade. But she was wrong.

'Fun,' she repeated tonelessly. 'I see.' She did
manage a smile then, but there was no warmth, no
humour in it.

'Do you want to know what's ironic, Damir? Six
months ago you would have been my ideal man.
You're handsome and charming and a good lover,
and you're driven. You wouldn't have expected anything from me and I would have been free to work
as much as I wanted, to care as little as I needed.
Maybe we would have gone on not expecting or caring, sleepwalked into a convenient marriage. But I'm
not that woman any more. And you're no longer who
I think I need or want. Maybe that's why it feels like
you are. Maybe that's why somehow despite everything you have got under my skin, into my heart...'
She stopped, swallowing back tears she was damned
she'd shed in front of him.

'Don't worry, Damir. I'll put your case forward to
Marija alongside my own. I'll be fair. But it's prob-
ably for the best we don't see each other any more.
The fun is over.'

'If that's what you want.'

'I do.'

'Then goodbye, Lily. I'll open the gate.' And he
turned and walked away. She watched him enter the
house. He didn't look back once and so, as the gates
slowly swung open and she left the villa, neither
did she.

CHAPTER ELEVEN

DAMIR LOOKED AT his laptop, at the pile of documents waiting for him to read, to sign, to take action on and sighed. Despite burying himself in work for the last ten days, he was still nowhere near on top of it all. He'd let things slide over the last few weeks, taking days and evenings off. It was good to be back where he needed to be. Committed and focussed.

He leaned back in his chair and stared out of the window at his front gates. He could still see Lily standing there, tall and dignified and righteously angry. He saw her every time he looked at the gates, every time he entered his bedroom, or made a coffee, around every corner. He'd thought that the pain might have started to dim by now. It was only getting worse.

He missed her. Missed her laugh and her smile. Missed the way she got to the heart of the matter, the way she made him think, the way she made him feel. Her warmth and her wit. Her touch. The feel of her under his hands.

He'd been asleep for so long and she had woken

him. Was he really willing to drift back into that half-life again?

He jumped to his feet, prowling restlessly around the study, resisting the urge to text her, to call her, to hear her voice. Work had always, always helped in the past. Why wasn't it working now? No matter what he did, how many hours he put in, how many miles he travelled, he missed her. And now here he was, back where it had all started to unravel, and the pain of his loss was greater than ever.

Knowing that he had deliberately pushed her away was no help.

Walking over to the bookshelves, he pulled out a thin bound album and opened it. He hadn't looked at it for years. There he was. Much younger, much more naïve, much more hopeful, beaming in a suit, Kata beside him, his parents flanking them. They'd been only in their very early twenties when they'd married, still babies. Childhood sweethearts playing at being grown-ups. Would their marriage have survived if Damir hadn't checked out? Because although Kata had been the one to walk away, he had mentally left her long before, blaming her demands and his acquiescence for his father's death.

But there had been nothing wrong with her desire to spend time with her husband and he had been allowed to put his wife first. He could hear Lily telling him, 'It's very sad but no one's fault. Especially not yours.' She was right. He had to forgive himself and move on.

He flicked through the album, and to his surprise

he felt no sorrow, no regret. Their marriage had been brief, but they'd been happy for a time. The truth was that theirs had been a young love, a first love, sweet and innocent but not robust enough to stand any great tests. The only fault lay in the way he had handled the unravelling of their relationship, the way he had distanced himself from Kata, the way he had locked his heart away since.

The way he'd treated Lily.

That was all on him.

He put the book away.

The way he felt about Lily was still so new, but different from anything he had ever felt before. Deeper, stronger, wiser. He was no idealist, not any more, but she had filled him with a hope he barely recognised, the possibility of a different kind of future, not sterile and lonely but filled with laughter and love. She made him want to do better, be better, be more. He didn't deserve her forgiveness and even if she bestowed it on him he had to accept that she would be unlikely to trust him again.

But how could he not try? He'd never expected, never wanted, to feel again, but she had broken down his barriers and reached his heart. It was time to put that heart on the line.

But, first, to really move on he had to face his past, and put it behind him once and for all.

Damir guided his car smoothly around the hairpin bends. On one side houses blended into the rocky countryside, on the other the sea sparkled far below in the afternoon sun. Signposts pointed to the various resorts that served the hundreds and thousands of tourists who came to this part of the Dalmatian Riviera.

A different kind of resort could also be found along the coastline, a string of abandoned hotels, elite resorts from the communist era. His grandfather had once been a chef in one of these hotels, but after the war they had been left to crumble back into the cliffs and beaches, ghost buildings incongruous amongst the tourist-filled villages and towns. As youths they had sailed there, to party in the ruins, a rite of passage.

A sign directing traffic to the airport flashed by and then at last he saw the turning that led to Cavtat and he began the drive down to the pretty harbourside village. He found a parking spot at the top of town, locked the car and set off, checking his phone for directions. The house he sought was a pretty villa on the other side of town. Painted a fresh pink with white trim and glorious views, it felt prosperous and loved. The garden was neat and well tended and Damir noted children's toys lined up on the porch, a swing set in the garden. He swallowed, this was not going to be an easy visit.

He stood by the door for a moment, trying to summon up the courage, the resolve to knock but before he could do so the door opened. A petite, heavily pregnant woman, whose features he'd once known by heart, stared at him, arms crossed defensively. 'What are you doing here?'

'Hello, Kata.'

She glared for a moment longer before sighing. 'You'd better come in. I'm too big to stand at the door figuring out what you want.'

Ten minutes later he was sitting at her kitchen table, a coffee in front of him. The hallway and kitchen were as bright and cheery as the outside, this was clearly a well looked-after and happy family home. Looking around, he saw more signs of domesticity, a notice-board filled with appointments, letters and reminders, pinned-up children's drawings, and an open book lay face down on the table. A cat slunk around his ankles, purring loudly. Kata had always wanted a cat. He reached down to stroke the soft head and looked across at his ex-wife.

'When are you due?'

'Another six weeks.' She pulled a frustrated face. 'It's been much harder this time, being pregnant with a toddler and at the height of summer. Still, I shouldn't complain, it's what I always wanted.'

'You're happy then?'

She sank into the chair opposite him and stared searchingly into his face. 'Is that why you're here? Some kind of workaholic's twelve-step programme? You need absolution from everybody you hurt? Not that you deserve it, not from me.'

'I know.'

'But as you're asking, yes, I am happy. I'm married to a good man, a man who actually wants to be with me, who enjoys my company, who is satisfied with the life we lead. A man I love. I have a gor-

geous, healthy son and a second child on the way.
I've learned to appreciate every one of my blessings,
and I am blessed.'

'I'm glad.' He meant every word of it. 'You deserve it.'

Kata huffed, but after a while her face softened.
'Yes,' she said. 'I do. It took me a while to stop being
so very angry with you, to be able to trust again, but
I got there.'

'I am sorry,' he said softly. 'I'm not here for absolution, and probably don't deserve it, but I am sorry.'

'No, you don't. But it doesn't matter any more,
Damir. I moved on a long time ago, as you can see.
When I think about then, I don't feel angry or sad. I
just feel sorry for the young, naïve people we were.
I'm lucky I got to have a second chance, but I don't
take my happiness for granted, I know it needs work
and sacrifice and compromise on both sides.'

Kata drummed her fingers on the table, a gesture
he remembered her making when she was unsure
what her next step would be. 'How's your mother?
She remarried, didn't she?'

'Yes, several years ago.' He grimaced. 'She's exactly the same, only more so. I don't see much of her,
which is as much her choice as mine, more so maybe,
but she seems happy. Her new husband is a politi-
cian, she finally gets to sit on the fundraising boards
and attend the kind of events she always wanted to.'

He took a deep breath. 'I was wrong to allow her
words to poison our marriage, Kata. I know now
that I didn't cause my father's death, his heart did.

He'd been warned to take it easy and he chose not to. That was on him. It's a tragedy, one I live with every day. But it wasn't my fault—and it absolutely wasn't yours, and I am so sorry I ever put that on you. You had every right to want to spend time with me, I had every right to keep weekends free to be with you. We weren't being selfish. But putting all the blame on us, on you, freezing you out, pushing you away, that was selfish. That was wrong. I didn't mean to hurt you.'

'I know. But you still did.' She leaned back in her chair, hands on her belly. It was strange to see her like this. Pregnancy aside she hadn't changed, barely looking any older than the twenty-four she'd been the last time he'd seen her. 'Why now? It's all over and done with, ancient history. I appreciate you making the effort to apologise, but why?'

'You've moved on. And I thought I had too. But while you've been creating a family, what have I achieved? The business is a lot bigger, sure. But I spend my evenings working alone. Money isn't the only way of measuring wealth, I know that now. And when it comes to love, you are richer by far. I met someone, and in doing so I've had to confront a lot of things about myself I don't like. How I behaved towards you is at the top of that list. An apology isn't enough, I know that. But it's heartfelt.'

She didn't answer for a long time. 'You've met someone. So, what, you've come to ask for my blessing?'

'No. I don't need or expect that. And it may be

too late. I've hurt her too.' His short laugh was bitter. 'It's a pattern, isn't it? This time I'm going to learn from the past, I am going to try and fix things. But I couldn't do that without some closure from before, without telling you how much I wish I could have been a better husband, a better friend, been more honest with you, especially at the end.'

'In that case all I can say is good luck, Damir,' Kata said softly. 'Second chances don't come around all that often, don't mess this one up.'

'Thank you, Kata.' He pushed back his chair and got to his feet. 'For everything.'

'Goodbye, Damir.'

He stood for a moment, looking at the woman he no longer knew, content, happy, with a life in which he was just a footnote. And that was how it should be. He had many more chapters ahead of him, it was time to make sure they counted.

As always, the view was breath-taking, but Lily barely took it in, her eyes unfocussed and thoughts jumbled as she sat on the villa's porch, a coffee in her hand.

She had to stop wallowing, move on. It would be so easy to revert to her old self, go back to her office and her flat, her long days at her desk, her ambition and solitude, to tell herself that she'd tried and failed. Much harder to try and understand that being impulsive, being open to new experiences and new people was bound to lead her down the wrong path sometimes. After all, that was the very reason she'd avoided doing it her whole life.

One day she might look back and recognise that it was just bad luck that her first adventure had ended so badly. Damir had obviously recognised her emotional naïveté, her vulnerability. His decision to exploit that was on him, not on her.

But that reckoning was a long way off. First she had to get through the next few weeks, days, hours and minutes. Damir had hurt her. She'd liked him, or at least she'd liked the person she had thought he was, and she'd thought that he liked her too. More than liked. She had known she was falling for him, and had hoped that maybe he felt the same way. Thought he'd seen something in her that nobody else ever had, nobody apart from her family and Izzy.

'Oh, Izzy,' she whispered. 'You wouldn't have made such a stupid mistake, you were always better at reading people than me. What am I going to do? I finally fell in love, and it all went to pieces.'

In love. Not with the charming wooer or the tycoon but with the man she'd thought he was inside. A man with vulnerabilities and hurts, a thoughtful, funny man who made her body sing and her heart hope. Even now, she couldn't help but think that that man existed, if only Damir could trust himself to care, to let people in.

But the fact remained that he had played her. He'd only ever approached her because of who she was, what she could do for him. She had opened up, shown all her vulnerabilities and fears to a man who had always planned to betray her.

She put her cup down decisively. Enough. Tomorrow was Izzy's birthday and she had promised her friend that she would celebrate. The B&B was only half-full, thanks to the wedding party cancellation, but the café-bar was as busy as ever. There was plenty for her to do to keep her mind off Damir. So she should get up and do it.

'Lily?' Ana was calling and slowly Lily got to her feet. 'Could you get the reception desk? We have some walk-ins asking if we have a room.'

'On my way,' she called back, straightening her shoulders and preparing her best hostess smile. Guests, work, keeping busy. That was the only cure for a broken heart, she knew. She just had to hope it worked.

She entered the villa through the side door, dodging through the hot, busy kitchen, emerging into the bright wide hallway. Three people were waiting by the reception desk and as they turned recognition shot through her, followed by a relief so deep it almost floored her. 'Mum? Josip? Marija? What are you doing here?'

'We didn't want you to spend Izzy's birthday alone and when we realised the cancellation meant you had room for unexpected guests, we decided to come and join you,' her mother said.

'I'll always have room for you,' Lily stepped into her mother's arms and allowed herself to be held for several long minutes before hugging Josip, realising that he had come home after all these years for her. Gratitude filled her as she kissed his cheek.

'Marija's room has been kept clean and ready just

in case she decided to come and check on us, and lucky for you two the best room is still available thanks to our flaky bride. I'll get Luka to take your bags up. Are you hungry? Of course you are. Let's find us all something to eat. I am so grateful you are here.'

They spent the rest of the afternoon catching up and showing Lily's mother around Lokvar, planning a few days of sightseeing for her—and for Josip who had left a very different place all those years ago. The next day, Izzy's birthday, they visited the Old Town. Memories of Damir were around every corner, but Lily resolutely pushed them away, determined to make new memories with her family, not dwell on old painful ones. During the day she tentatively raised her ideas for a foundation in Izzy's memory, grateful for her family's advice and input.

That evening Lily had planned a private dinner, tasking Antun to make a welcome-home feast of Dalmatian classics and setting up a table on the side terrace, away from the crowded and noisy bar. She was the first to change and come back downstairs and, grateful for a moment's reflective solitude, Lily wandered over to the swing seat and rocked gently, trying to absorb all that had happened in the last twenty-four hours, the last few weeks.

'Lily, are you all right?'

She looked up at the sound of Josip's voice and smiled, immediately moving up to make space for him, leaning against his reliable solidness. 'Of course. I am thrilled you are here. Thank you.'

'You needed me,' he said simply. And that right here was Josip distilled, what she and her mother needed, he provided. Somehow, Lily had never really appreciated that for over half her life she'd actually had the stability she craved. Josip had her back, always.

And this weekend he had proved his love by coming back to the country he had fled from all those years ago for her. She squeezed his arm. 'Has it been very hard? It can't be easy, seeing all your old haunts.'

'Haunts is the right word, there are ghosts everywhere.' He sighed, rubbing the dark stubble on his square, capable chin. 'But it has been good for me to come back and face them. I let it go on too long. It's not easy, walking around and listening to people talk about the city as a TV set, discussing fictional violence when last time I was here war was all too real, but the city has healed and moved on. I should too.'

'Easier said than done.'

'Always.' He paused. 'You know I don't like to pry, Lily, your secrets are yours, but is Damir Kozina the reason you've been so quiet, the reason for those shadows under your eyes?'

'There are no secrets on Lokvar,' she said, attempting to make light of the question.

'No secrets between my mother and Ana.'

'I suppose not. We were together and now we're not. These things happen.'

They rocked in silence for a moment before Josip spoke again. 'What's he like, Damir? Last time I saw him he was little more than a baby with determined eyes and a very stubborn will.'

Lily stared out to sea, searching for the right words. 'He's unsettled,' she said at last. 'He thinks the next project, the next deal will make him happy. Of course it won't, but he's too afraid to work out what will. Too afraid of his own feelings to try or to trust.' She smiled then. 'I see it because I was similar once, not that long ago.'

'His dad was the same. But *his* father, Damir's grandfather, drove him hard. He was a difficult, bitter man, always wanted more, to be the best, to be in charge. He coveted this place, made several offers after the war, but it's been in our family for generations. My family would never consider it. In time Damir's papa became the same, obsessed with money and status, forgetting about the things that really matter.'

'When did you stop being friends?' Lily couldn't stop her curious questions, thirsty to know more about the man who somehow had crept into her heart.

Josip rocked the swing a few times before answering. 'We drifted apart rather than any one definitive moment. I wasn't here, of course, that didn't help, no internet or instant messages or texts in those days. And we didn't understand each other. After all, everything that made me want to leave Croatia made him want to stay. I tried to outrun my ghosts, he tried to build over his.'

'Damir may make his father and grandfather's dreams come true yet. You don't want the villa and although I considered buying it, even with Izzy's legacy I wouldn't have enough, and Damir will outbid anyone else. I hope it makes him happy, although I hate the thought of seeing this place pulled down for one of his resorts. I'll have to look for somewhere else to base the foundation if that happens.'

'Would you buy it, if you could? Would you stay?'

'I would.' The words surprised her as she spoke them and she turned to Josip, eyes wide. 'I would! I'd have to diversify to make the villa pay through the off season, and I'd have to learn Croatian and to sail, and to cook a little for emergencies, and to learn to mix more than a gin and tonic, but I would. The last few months I've met such interesting people, it's a lot more fun than legal sub-clauses!

'And most importantly there's the setting. Waking up to this view, walking on the beach has brought me the kind of peace I didn't think existed. I'd love to stay. But it's a dream. I know that. Marija needs to fund her retirement and this is prime real estate, she needs to maximise what she can make from it. I just hope she puts clauses in to limit development. I don't know Croatian planning law but I would try and help if she wanted.'

'What she wants is for the villa to stay in the family, and you *are* her family. You're my daughter, Lily, you have been since the day I collected you from your grandparents to come and live with me and your mother, and I couldn't be prouder of you. I hope you know that. If you want to stay then the villa is yours, we both agreed that it should be. It wouldn't surprise me if this wasn't her plan all along.'

Lily stilled, trying to process his words. 'And you wouldn't mind?'

'Me? Not at all. Although I would have one condition, that you have a room for your mother and me when we need it. Now I've finally come back, I know I can't stay away so long. London is my home now, but Lokvar is part of me.'

'Always,' she promised. 'Always.'

'And Damir?'

Lily looked down at her hands. 'I don't know,' she said honestly. 'I don't know if I can ever trust him. He lied to me, and that's not something I can easily dismiss. It takes a lot for me to trust, and knowing I got him wrong, that's hard for me. But he has his own problems, I don't think I'll be seeing him again. That's okay. I've survived much worse.'

'You were always stronger than you gave yourself credit for. And if Damir doesn't see that then he doesn't deserve you. I just want you to be happy, Lily.'

'I am,' she told him. 'At least, I have the tools to be. I will always miss Izzy, always, and I can't deny that I've been bruised by what happened with Damir, but at least I know I'm capable of wanting a relationship. He gave me that at least.'

Josip smiled and dropped a kiss on top of her head before heading back inside to find her mother. Lily held her smile until he'd gone and then let it slide off her face. She hadn't lied, she was ready to embrace her new life, the opportunities she had been given, the opportunities she wanted to create. But getting over Damir was going to take time. She just had to be patient and hope it didn't hurt for too long.

CHAPTER TWELVE

LILY GOT TO her feet and raised her glass, smiling at her family, her heart filled with love for these people who had travelled over a thousand miles to spend this day with her. Some things in her new life might have gone horribly wrong, but she still had so much to be thankful for.

'I'm not going to make a long speech you'll be glad to hear,' she said. 'But I do want to thank you with all my heart for coming and celebrating Izzy's birthday here with me today. I want to thank you for all the support you've offered in helping me find a way to remember and honour her. I especially want to thank Marija for giving me a chance to start anew and Ana for being so patient while I learned the ropes.' She paused, gathering her thoughts, catching first Josip's, then Marija's eyes, both full of confidence and belief. Belief in her.

'As you know, Lokvar, Fire Cove and this villa are very special places. I came here broken, and they healed me. And that gift is one I want to share with other people who need it, who need a break, to find out who they are and what they're capable of. I'm so happy that I will be able to see that happen.

'I had assumed that my stay would be short, one summer only, but I've been given the opportunity to try and make a home here and that feels more right than I could ever have imagined. Sorry, Ana, but we need to restart those Croatian lessons. Thank you all again, I hope you will visit me here often.' She looked up at the stars. 'Let's raise one final toast to Izzy.'

'To Izzy,' they chorused. Lily looked at each face in turn, her heart twisting with affection. Her mother, at peace after so many troubled years, was gazing at her with pride, Marija's smile was smug as if she had planned this very outcome—and maybe she had—while Josip looked more relaxed than he had in a long time.

There was still a lot to decide, a lot to organise, but she had a way forward. This move was nowhere in her life plans, but it felt right.

As she sank back into her seat, the whole table quietened and everyone stared at something—or someone—behind her. Lily felt his presence before she turned around, every nerve and sinew springing into life. She turned slowly to see Damir leaning against a tree, his hands in his pockets. He was formally dressed in one of his devastating suits, the tailored cut outlining the breadth of his shoulders and the length of his legs, but stubble shadowed his mouth and the hollows under his eyes mirrored hers.

'I'm sorry to interrupt,' he said. He sounded completely at ease, but his jaw was tight and his expression hooded. She swallowed, doing her best to seem as relaxed as him.

'That's okay,' she said. 'Mum, Josip, everyone, this is Damir. He owns the big hotel by the harbour.' She paused, not knowing what to say, what to do. Yell at him, cry, ignore him, throw him out? In the end good manners took over. 'Why don't you join us for a drink?'

She could sense her mother looking at him curiously, almost see Josip's protective hackles rising. Meanwhile Marija was leaning back in her chair, her bright eyes fixed on her neighbour speculatively.

Damir smiled. 'Thank you.' But he made no attempt to join them. 'Actually, there's something I need to say first.'

Lily couldn't read him, he was so rigid, his jaw set and eyes determined. 'Marija, last year I offered you twice what the villa was worth and you turned me down. I'd like to renew that offer today. Here in front of witnesses.'

The disappointment that flooded over Lily almost drowned her. He wasn't here for her, of course he wasn't. He was here for the villa. He knew her thoughts and dreams and yet he had marched in to hijack her remembrance dinner. Her hopes that there was a better man inside the ruthless tycoon were just that. Hopes. She could almost physically feel her heart break, an actual crack so loud she couldn't believe the whole table hadn't reacted. Nothing mattered to him but a deathbed promise and ambition, and woe betide anyone or anything who got in the way.

Her hands clenched on her glass. She shouldn't see it as a personal betrayal, she had known who he was. But like a fool she'd hoped that where she was concerned he could be better. She'd hoped she'd mattered. She'd hoped he'd fallen for her the way she'd fallen for him. But maybe he was incapable of that kind of feeling for anyone or anything that wasn't bricks and mortar.

'Damir...' She trailed off. She wanted to tell him that he was too late, that the villa was being given to her, that some things were more important than money. But it wasn't her place to say it. He was offering Marija a small fortune. Lily had to let her grandmother decide for herself.

'I want to buy the villa,' he repeated. 'For Lily. So that she can help children like her friend, so that she can make a difference.'

Hang on a minute. What had he just said? She was on her feet without realising it. 'You want to do *what*?'

Her family were almost unnaturally silent, as if their volume button had been turned off, looking from her to Damir, like spectators at a tennis match.

Damir took a step closer. 'I want to give the villa to you. I want you to live your dreams, Lily, whatever they may be. I want to help you live your dreams if you'll let me. I'm sorry I'm so late, I know this day is hard for you. But this is my gift to you. In memory of your friend. If you'll take it.'

The whole scenario felt unreal, like she was on stage only she had no idea of her lines or what happened next.

'I...' She had to get them away from their audience. 'Come with me.'

Lily jumped to her feet and marched away from the table and away from Damir towards the gate leading to the beach. She knew he was following her, that he would have followed her even without her instruction.

She didn't speak until they were out of earshot and then she turned. 'What's going on?'

This was it. This was his chance. He'd never felt so nervous in all his life. As if as all his happiness hinged on the next five minutes. And it did.

Damir took a deep breath and looked at Lily. She looked utterly beautiful in a flowery maxi dress, her hair caught up in a loose knot, tendrils caressing her cheeks. His chest ached with all he hadn't said, all he'd repressed. 'I love you.' It wasn't the speech he had prepared, but it was everything, it was all he that he had. Lily took half a step backwards, clasping her hands in front of her.

'I don't understand, where is this coming from?'

'I love you, Lily.' Now he'd finally said it, Damir was more emboldened, the words flowing naturally. 'I know we haven't known each other very long, but I love you. I think I have from the very first. From when I saw you here shouting defiantly at the sea.'

'From when you saw me and tried to figure out a way to use me,' she said, and he nodded.

'I did. And I am sorrier for that than I can say. But underneath the plans and the calculations and deceptions, there was something more, something driving me towards you, and that was terrifying. When you've spent as long as I have trying not to feel, you'll do anything to keep things that way, including lying to yourself.'

'Last time I saw you, you said we were just having fun.'

He grimaced. 'By then I had stopped lying to myself but I lied to you instead. I wanted you to walk away, you deserved so much more than I could give you. I thought that was the right thing to do.'

'And now?' She sounded cool, distant, but her fingers betrayed her emotion, twisting together, her eyes were bright with tears. Damir couldn't hold himself back any longer, couldn't restrain himself from offering her comfort, and he closed the short distance between them to take her hands, tilting her chin so he could look into her face, try and read her thoughts.

'I went to see Kata today. She has a son, another baby on the way, she's living the life she always wanted. And as I stood there, in her house full of toys and love and happiness, I realised that I am richer than even my father dared to dream, but I have nothing. Not if I'm too afraid to let anyone in. But I'm not afraid, not any more. And that's down to you.'

'Me?' Her voice trembled as she spoke the single syllable.

'After Kata left I decided that emotions just mess things up. That I was better concentrating on work, concentrating on things I could control. Then I met you and for the first time in a long time I felt something other than ambition. I lost control. And it terrified me. Feelings I didn't know how to manage threatened to break through and ruin all that hard-won peace.'

He paused, trying to find the words to show her, convince her of his sincerity. 'I recognised something in you from the first. I saw a woman who had experienced real tragedy and used it to move on. That shamed me, Lily. I allowed my past to define me, to hold me back, while you used yours to propel you forward.

'You have been through so much, more than I could ever imagine. Your childhood, the loss of your friend. It could have hardened you, turned you into someone like me, but instead you decided to embrace life, to get as much from it as you could. You make me want to be different, Lily, you make me want to be more. And that terrified me, because if I take away work then what's left? Who am I? Not Damir Kozina, hotelier, developer, investor but just Damir? I didn't know, and I wasn't brave enough to find out.'

'I don't know what to say, what to think,' she said, her fingers tightening around his, looking up at him with a mingled expression of hope and fear. 'You pushed me away so completely. I didn't expect to see you again, not properly. And now you're here and saying all this, trying to buy the villa for me. What about your dreams, your ambitions?'

'I still have them, but they have changed. I don't need to be bound by other people's visions, I need to find my own. I am sorrier than I can say for deceiving you. Although I'm not sorry for getting to know you, the times we spent together were the most special times of my life.'

He ran a finger down her cheek and felt her quiver under the light touch, she felt like coming home. 'You are clever and insightful, you're funny and you're kind and obviously you are insanely gorgeous. Those are the reasons I'm attracted to you, but you're more than that, you're made of steel, you're resilient and strong and you care and that's why I love you.'

That was it. That was all he had. His heart on the line.

Lily stared up at Damir, barely able to process all he had said, let alone believe it. 'But how, why?' she said in the end, inarticulately.

'We were watching the concert,' he said. 'And you'd just told me that you needed my advice. That shook me. I'd been fooling myself that we were just like any other affair, that all we had was attraction. But it wasn't true. You wanted more than my money and my body, you wanted my opinion—I can't tell you how that felt. You saw me, saw behind the mask. Maybe I fell in love with you before that, when you brought cakes on our daytrip to Dubrovnik. You never just took, you always gave.'

'They weren't even very good cakes,' she said, half in shock, and he laughed.

'They were amazing, because they were made with care and generosity. I realised at the concert that I didn't want to let you go, that the man I was when I was with you was a better, a happier man. But the last time I felt like that everything fell apart, my father died, my mother blamed me, my marriage disintegrated. I was terrified of what would happen if I acknowledged my feelings, acted on them. I was already distracted, making mistakes, unfocussed. It felt like history was repeating itself.

'When you discovered the plans, walked away, it felt almost fortuitous, gave me the opportunity I needed to step back, push you away. But that didn't help. And I couldn't help but ask myself who I was doing all this for. I told myself owning the villa, building a resort here would make me happy, but they were hollow lies. Nothing would make me happy if I was too scared to love, to really live.'

'You don't need to woo me with grand gestures, Damir. Buying the villa? It's too much.'

'Is it a grand gesture if I mean it? Your vision is inspired, Lily. I just want to help you achieve it, in any way I can.'

Lily bit her lip. 'Marija has offered to give it to me, if I want to stay and run it. She's got quite a bit put by, so she's thinking of building herself a small home in the garden for when she's here and spending more time with Josip and mum the rest of the time.'

'So my grand gesture was unnecessary?' His smile was rueful and her heart melted.

'No. It was the single most thoughtful thing anyone has ever done for me.'

'I wanted to make a public declaration, I wanted you to know that I meant every word, that I was willing to make a fool of myself for you. Willing to do whatever it takes.' He stopped then and stared at her, eyes full of hope and love. Love for her. Lily's heart thumped almost painfully at the intensity in his dark gaze. 'Wait, Marija has given you the villa. Does that mean you're staying?'

'It does. Does that change things?' Her pulse speeded to rushing point as she waited for him to reply. It was one thing to open up to someone who was leaving, who would always be a romantic fantasy, quite another to do it to someone real, who would be there no matter what happened.

'Change things? I hope so.' He smiled properly then, sweet and sexy and so devastating her insides melted. 'I hope it means I get a chance to put things right, a chance to go back to the beginning and woo you the way you should always have been wooed. To see where this leads when time is on our side, to hope it leads to a home like Kata's, one filled with love and happiness. Is that possible, Lily? Would you be able to give me a second chance?'

Lily didn't answer for a long moment, trying to make sense of her jumbled thoughts. Damir had hurt her and understanding why didn't change that. But understanding him made it easier. 'I didn't come here looking for anything but a way to heal. Meeting you, meeting anyone, wasn't part of the plan.' She reached up and cupped his cheek. 'From the start I suspected you were too good to be true—and then I found out how you planned to use me. Fool me once...' Her voice trailed off.

'I know I made mistakes. Asking you to trust me again is a lot.'

'It is.'

Lily hesitated. The sensible thing would be to say thanks but no thanks. To walk away with her dignity intact if not her heart. But the hope and sincerity blazing out of Damir's face, in his voice, his whole body made her pause and hope, more than his grand gesture to buy the villa.

Go on, she could hear Izzy urge her. *Give him the chance to prove himself to you. Don't be afraid, Lily.*

'It is a lot,' she replied. 'But so is taking on permanent management of a B&B and trying to run it all year round. I suppose it would be useful to have an expert on hand to help me figure it out. And I've heard it can get cold and lonely on Lokvar in the winter months. A local man might be just what I need.'

It took him several incredulous seconds to respond but then Lily found herself swept up and whirled around. 'You won't regret it,' Damir vowed.

'I know,' she said, smiling up at him. 'Because I love you too and I don't give my heart away easily or often, Damir. So I have to trust you to be careful with it.'

'I will. Always.' And then he finally kissed her, a

kiss filled with all the pent-up love and emotion, an almost overwhelming kiss that consumed her entire body. 'Always,' he murmured against her mouth. 'I love you, Lily, and I will spend every day proving it to you, if it takes the rest of my life.'

'I love you too.' And as she kissed him back, Lily knew her heart was safe with this man, in this place, and that hard as the past had been, with Damir by her side her future would be more than she had ever dared dream possible.

One year later

LILY WALKED OUT of the villa, cake in her hands, and paused, taking in the scene below. It was almost as if she had stepped in a time machine and she was back to this point one year ago. The table was set on the private terrace, her mother, Josip, Marija and Ana were sitting around it, the remains of a delicious meal still on their plates.

But this year there were extra guests. Damir was sprawled on one side of the table, gently flirting with Marija and Lily's mother, and Janet, Izzy's foster mother, had come over to celebrate Izzy's birthday, bringing the two teenagers she currently fostered, the first beneficiaries of the Isabella Burton Foundation. They were here for two weeks of rest and relaxation for Janet and activities and sunshine for the kids.

'I hope you'd be happy, Izzy,' she said softly. 'They're having a great time, and Tia is already asking about coming over to work when she's eighteen. She reminds me of you. Lots of drive, lots of ambi-

tion and plenty of brains' She looked up at the stars
for a long moment. 'I miss you. I'll always miss you.'

She blinked back tears, pasting on a smile as she
carefully carried the cake down to the table. Antun
had outdone himself and the lavishly decorated con-
fection deserved all the oohs and aahs that greeted
it, and her smile widened and became genuine as
she set it carefully in front of Ana, who was the best
cake cutter in the villa.

'You look happy, Lily,' Josip said as she took her
seat next to him. 'Happy and well.'

'I am happy,' she told him. 'It was the right decision, to spend the off season in Dubrovnik in Damir's
villa, and the summer here. I still think there are
ways to make the villa productive through the winter
but setting up the foundation, trying to learn Croatian and learning to sail were important too.'

'No regrets?' he asked her, and she smiled, her
gaze settling on Damir, relaxed and at ease, and more
handsome than ever, at least in her totally biased
opinion.

'None at all. This felt like home the day I first
woke up here and now I can't imagine living anywhere else. I'm just glad Marija decided to work
one last season. I'm learning so much from her. I'm
also so happy you and Mum have visited so often.'

'It's taken time but I've found my peace with the
past,' Josip said. 'I'm glad you have as well, Lily.
You deserve all the happiness.'

At that moment Ana passed her a slice of the
chocolate orange cake and Josip's attention turned

to comparing the size of his dessert to Tia's and Leo's, good-naturedly protesting that they had far bigger slices than he did. Lily leaned back and looked around the table, counting all her blessings as she did so. She lived in a place she loved with a man she appreciated more every day, doing a job she found rewarding whilst spending the long off season learning about the culture of the beautiful country in which she now lived. She didn't think she could possibly be happier.

The dinner finally came to an end, and as the teenagers began to help Ana clear the table, Damir slipped his arms around Lily's waist, kissing her neck as he did so, and she leaned gratefully back against him.

'I've missed you,' he said.

'Then you shouldn't take such long business trips,' she said, and felt his laughter rumble through her.

'I hurried home as soon as I could. Walk with me?'

'Of course.' It was their usual custom to walk along Fire Cove after dinner as long as Lily wasn't working. She often thought this moment, hand in hand with the sun setting around them, was her favourite part of the day.

'It's so beautiful here,' she said, as they walked past the last of the tourists onto the quieter part of the beach. 'I know I say it every day, but it's true every day.'

'It is.'

'Glad you didn't turn it into an exclusive resort?' And he smiled.

'I wouldn't go that far, but the area I've found is spectacular. I can't wait for you to see it when it's done.' But he sounded distracted.

Lily squeezed his hand. 'Are you okay?'

He started. 'Yes, fine.'

They carried on until they reached the end of the beach but they didn't stop there, Damir leading her over the rocks until they reached the tiny curve of sand, flanked by rocks and dunes and sea where they had first made love.

'I love it here,' she said softly, looking out at the boats bobbing up and down on the far horizon. 'It's like our own secret beach.'

'Yes.' He sounded distracted again and she turned to look at him. 'Damir?' She faltered to a stop. 'What are you doing?'

He was on one knee, a small velvet box in one hand. 'What does it look like I'm doing? No, ignore that, that wasn't in the script.'

'The script?'

'I wanted this to be perfect.' Damir was usually the most confident-seeming person she knew, but he didn't look confident now, his throat working as he seemed to search for words. 'I want this to be perfect, because you are perfect. Lily, I love you. You brought the sunshine into my life and the hope into my heart and have given me more happiness than I ever thought possible. I want nothing more than to keep loving you, laughing with you and to grow old with you. Would you, Lily Woodhouse, do me the very great honour of becoming my wife?'

He flipped open the box to reveal a beautiful ring, a sapphire flanked by diamonds, and Lily gasped.

'Oh, Damir. Yes, of course I will.'

He smiled then, boyish and so handsome it took her breath away. 'That is good, because there is champagne chilling behind that rock and I asked Josip and your mother's permission this morning...' He paused then. 'I hope you don't mind, I know you don't need anyone's permission to do anything...'

'No, I don't mind.' Her heart turned over with love and thankfulness for his thoughtfulness. 'Thank you for including Josip and showing him how important he is to me. Wait, they both said yes, didn't they?'

'After a very long time,' Damir admitted, getting to his feet and extracting the ring from the box. Lily held out her left hand, feeling unaccountably shy as Damir slid the ring onto her third finger.

'It's perfect,' she said, cupping his cheeks and rising up to kiss him.

'So are you,' he said, looking into her eyes. 'So are you.'

* * * * *

HIS LAST-CHANCE
CHRISTMAS FAMILY

MICHELLE MAJOR

To the Special Edition team.
Thank you for making my books shine.

Chapter One

Brynn Hale glanced at her watch, fifteen minutes late for her lunch date. She checked her cell phone, which still displayed *No Service* in the top left corner of the screen.

Another turn of the key in the car's ignition produced only a hollow click, click, click.

She muttered a curse under her breath and immediately felt guilty. Her mother had taught her from a young age that swearing was unladylike. While Brynn had disappointed her mom in so many ways, at least she kept her language clean. Usually.

Desperate times and all that.

In the distance, she heard the sound of a car

engine, a first since she'd realized her old Toyota sedan wouldn't start on this lonely stretch of mountain highway.

She climbed out of the car, which she'd parked on the shoulder near the sharp curve of Devil's Landing, into the cool mountain air. The location was only about twenty minutes outside the town limits of Starlight, Washington, where she'd lived for her entire twenty-eight years.

It hadn't been her plan to become a townie. Most everything about Brynn's current life hadn't been part of how she'd dreamed things would turn out.

She'd made the best of things, even the events that had rocked her to her core, which was what had prompted her visit to mile marker six on this cold, damp December day.

Easing around her car, she was careful to stay to one side of the white line that bordered the two-lane highway. A lift into town would be good, a trip to the ER because she got herself hit by a passing motorist not so much.

Her stomach dipped as she realized the approaching SUV had police lights on the roof. Not Nick. Let it be anyone but Starlight's police chief.

The urge to return to her car and duck was almost overwhelming, but it wouldn't do any good. The officer was bound to stop. She lifted her arms to wave just as her boot heel caught on a random patch of ice. She lost her balance, dropping to one knee before righting herself.

"Son of a biscuit," she said through clenched teeth. The fall had ripped a hole in her new black tights and tiny pieces of gravel stuck to her palms.

Before she had time to brush them off, the police vehicle had lurched to a stop next to her car, blue and red lights suddenly flashing, beacons of color against the dreary gray of the winter day.

Because that's how her day was going, Nick Dunlap bolted from the car and rushed toward her.

"Brynn, are you okay?"

Her breath caught in her throat as he reached for her, grabbing her wrists and examining her hands before giving her an intense once-over. His honey-brown eyes were filled with worry—panic if she was reading him correctly. The smell of cinnamon gum and spice drifted over her, a potent mix she always associated with Nick.

Brynn hated the flood of memories that scent evoked.

"What's wrong?" he demanded. "Are you hurt? Tell me."

She yanked away from him, frustrated at her visceral reaction to the warmth of his calloused hands on her skin. "What's wrong with you?" she countered. "You're being overdramatic."

"Overdramatic," he repeated, taking a step back, the mask of stalwart police chief falling over his handsome features. Nick had always been too good-looking, with thick hair, chiseled features, an easy grin that showcased the most annoyingly adorable dimples Brynn had ever seen on a person.

He'd been a girl magnet since his family moved to town in third grade, first on the Starlight Elementary playground and then in the hallways of the high school, at the local football field, and behind the bleachers and too many places for Brynn to count. Places she'd never experienced with him.

The most popular boy in school didn't take his best friend and sidekick behind the bleachers. Nick spent time with Brynn in the library and in his mother's cozy kitchen and watching reruns or playing video games in the family's remodeled basement.

Brynn had been the literal girl next door, even though she'd always wanted more from Nick. Things he couldn't—or wouldn't—offer her. Always, until those few minutes peeing on a stick in her pink bathroom just before high school graduation had changed everything.

"Do you know where you are?" he asked, turning his gaze to the valley below them. Their town was down there, under the fog that clung to the mountain today.

She felt her jaw clench. "Of course I know."

"And the date?"

"Yes," she whispered.

"Then why the hell are you here?"

"None of your business."

He scrubbed a hand over his face. "Tell me anyway," he said, his voice calmer. Low and gentle. The little hairs on the back of her neck stood on end. "Please," he added, which was a nice touch. "Because I've got all kinds of bizarre rationales running through my mind at the moment."

"What kind of rationales?"

His gaze flicked to the section of guardrail that was newer than the rest, rebuilt after her late husband's truck had slammed into it before hurtling off the side of the cliff and landing in a fiery crash two hundred feet below.

"Do you think I came out here to follow Daniel into the great beyond?" In the list of life moments that made Brynn feel like swearing a blue streak, this one vaulted to the top. "Are you joking?"

She paced to the edge of the barricade and then back again, hands fisted at her sides, anger and disbelief flooding through her.

"I thought you knew me," she told him tightly.

He blew out a breath. "I do."

"I would never…" She closed her eyes, mentally counted to ten. "I have Tyler to think of. You know that." Her ten-year-old son was everything to her. Even the suggestion that she might risk the chance to raise him, especially from someone like Nick, cut her to the core.

"I know. Brynn, I'm sorry. Seeing you out here on this day and then watching you fall to your knees...it caught me off guard." The emotion in his voice did funny things to her insides. Then he placed a hand on her arm, and she had to force herself not to shift away from him again. "Tell me why you're here."

She looked down, noticing for the first time a tiny spot of blood on her knee where the tights had ripped. "I have a date."

Nick went completely still in front of her, so she continued, "Mara set me up with a guy from Weatherby who came into the coffee shop last week when he drove over on business." Her friend Mara Johnson managed Main Street Perk, Starlight's popular local coffee joint. "I wanted to tell Daniel, and it felt strange to go to his grave site. This was the last place he was alive, so I came here."

"A date?"

Brynn glanced up at Nick, who was now looking at her like she'd sprouted a second head. Although he normally kept his sandy blond hair cut short, it was in need of a trim and a thick lock fell over his forehead. He had broad shoulders and a muscled build that filled out his dark police uniform in a way that would have most women begging him to handcuff them.

Not Brynn.

She wouldn't ask Nick Dunlap for a single thing

if she had any choice in the matter. "You keep repeating what I say," she pointed out.

"I'm trying to process this and also get my heart to slow down. Seriously, you scared the hell out of me."

"I'm not yours to worry about," she reminded him.

A muscle ticked in his jaw. "Duly noted, but friends show concern for each other."

Friends, she thought to herself, trying not to let him see what that word did to her. Brynn and Nick could tell everyone they were friends. But it wasn't like it had been before. She missed those easy days.

He released her arm. "I thought you'd decided against dating."

She crossed her arms over her chest as a brisk gust of air blew up from the valley, whispering through the pine trees that surrounded them. "Can you give me a ride into town, Chief? I'm already late."

"What about your car?"

"It's the alternator. Jimmy warned me it needed to be replaced the last time I had the car into his shop for an oil change, but I never got around to it. Now I will."

"You can't ignore stuff like that."

"Nick, come on. Save the lecture and just give me a ride. I'll call Jimmy after lunch and have him send a tow truck for the car."

"I could take a look at it," he offered.

"Not your problem."

He looked like he wanted to argue but gave a small nod instead. "Grab whatever you need and make sure it's locked."

"Thanks." She turned for the Toyota, then spun back around. "Hey, Nick?"

One side of his mouth curved. "Yeah?"

"What were you doing up here today?"

He shrugged. "It's the five-month anniversary of Daniel's death. Same as you, in a way, minus the dating part. I was visiting my buddy."

"Oh." Emotion tumbled through her like debris coming down the side of a hill after a rockslide. The reminder that Nick was her late husband's friend as much as hers shouldn't hurt her at this point.

But it did.

"Tell me more about dating," Nick said, relieved his voice didn't waver as he made the request. He would never admit how much the thought of Brynn in another man's arms affected him. Hell, he'd been one of the groomsmen in her quickie wedding to Daniel Hale a decade ago and had managed to stay friendly with both of them over the ensuing years.

He'd blown his chance with Brynn back in high school, when he'd been a selfish, egotistical, immature kid. Maybe he'd grown up a little since that time, but he knew he still didn't deserve a woman like her.

Not that Daniel had, either. When he'd told her he'd driven up to Devil's Landing, the picturesque overlook in the hills to the east of town, because of the anniversary of Daniel's death, it hadn't been a lie. But he wasn't there to honor a friend. Nick had so much pent-up anger over the way Daniel had treated Brynn during their marriage, carelessly like she was some sort of old pair of shoes instead of his precious wife.

Whatever friendship he'd had with Daniel had been cut short by the other man's callous actions, the serial cheating and constant disrespect. After the accident, Nick's anger mixed with guilt, an almost untenable brew. What if he had pushed Daniel to give up the women? What if he'd convinced him to try to make his marriage work?

What if Nick had asked Brynn not to marry Daniel in the first place?

He hadn't done any of those things. He'd minded his own business and kept both Daniel and Brynn at a friendly arm's length. Driving through the winding roads of the Cascades' towering pine forests with Brynn next to him somehow calmed Nick. He needed all the calm he could muster to handle what was coming next.

"It's fairly straightforward," Brynn replied, and he noticed the edge in her tone. She tucked a lock of dark hair behind one delicate ear. Everything about Brynn was delicate. Her small frame, pale skin and clear blue eyes framed by thick dark lashes. She looked more like a fairy-tale princess who should be conversing with tiny forest creatures than the over-worked single mom she was. "I'm meeting a guy for lunch. Maybe we'll hit it off. If not—"

"The last I heard, you wanted nothing to do with dating. You were devoted to Tyler."

He heard her soft gasp and realized he'd said the wrong thing. Nothing new where Brynn was concerned, he supposed.

"I mean—"

"I understand what you mean." One finger picked at the edge of the hole in the fabric above her knee. "Mara and Kaitlin are convinced it will be good for me." She turned to him. "Going out to lunch with a stranger has nothing to do with my devo-tion to my son."

"I know. I'm sorry. Really sorry." His fingers tightened around the steering wheel. "I'm still not thinking clearly. You're a great mom. The best. No one compares. If there was an award for—"

"Nick, stop."

He blew out a relieved breath when she laughed. The last thing he wanted to do was hurt Brynn. She'd been through enough already.

"I did say at Mara and Parker's wedding that I wasn't interested in dating, and I'm still not sure I'm doing the right thing. Maybe this is too soon, but it's no secret my marriage wasn't exactly a happy one."

They'd gotten to town and he turned to her at the traffic light at Starlight's main intersection. "You deserve to be happy."

Her lips curved into a genuine smile, and it made his heart sing at the same time his chest squeezed painfully. He didn't want to consider Brynn happy with another man.

"Can you drop me at The Diner?" she asked after a long moment.

The Diner was a popular place in Starlight, one that was sure to have lots of locals happy to gossip about the widow out with a new man.

"Sure." He drummed his fingers on the console between the two seats, trying to appear like he didn't want to follow the man she was meeting out of the restaurant and find some flimsy excuse to pull him over and harass him for the heck of it. Nick wouldn't do that. His personal life might not be much to speak of, but he prided himself on being a good cop and leader for his town.

It had taken a tragedy for him to wise up and make something of himself, but he'd done it. And he had more sense than to mess it up now.

"Mara and Kaitlin are calling their little project the twelve dates of Christmas. They have a whole list of potential men to match me with until I find the right one."

He swallowed back the bile that rose to his throat. "You're going on dates with twelve different guys?"

"Hopefully not. I can barely find time to brush my teeth some days. Wait a minute. Are you slut shaming me, Nick Dunlap?" She unclicked her seat belt as he pulled to the curb in front of the restaurant. "I know you." She wagged a finger in his direction. "Not just Chief Dunlap. I knew Tricky Nicky and your revolving door of girlfriends from high school. You might remember it was my house you sneaked over to the night that half the cheerleading squad showed up on your front lawn so you could vote on which one was the hottest."

He pressed two fingers against the side of his temples. "God, I was an ass."

"You still are from the sound of it."

He almost laughed at the truth in her statement. That was the problem with Brynn, or with his reaction to Brynn. He wanted to be her friend and support her but always managed to say the wrong thing. She was right. She did know him—or at least had known him—better than anyone. He hadn't been alone with her, even for something as straightforward as a car ride, since high school.

It had been easy enough to put her in the category of "might have been" when she was married to Daniel. Nick had locked up any feelings he had for her that went beyond friendship. Up until recently, he'd believed the key to that lock had been thrown away along with so many other childhood dreams.

But now…

He shook his head. No. Daniel's death didn't change anything. Nick knew he wasn't cut out for love. After hurting Brynn once, he wouldn't take the chance of doing it again.

"I want you to be happy," he said again. "I hope this date, and any of your other twelve-men-a-milking or pear-tree-partridge outings go well. Seriously, I do."

"No partridges or milking men," she said with another small laugh. "It's lunch. Not a big deal."

Tell that to his heart.

"If you need anything, or if Tyler needs anything…" He cleared his throat. "Just know I'm still your friend."

Her gaze gentled. Brynn was far stronger than she looked, stronger than most people gave her credit for, including him for too long.

She'd gotten married at eighteen to a boy she barely knew after their first sexual encounter left her pregnant. Ten years later, her husband died in a car crash, but he hadn't been alone in the truck when it careened off that cliff. His mistress had been in the passenger seat, and in a small town like Starlight, that fact was big news.

But he'd never seen Brynn cower from the gossip or do anything but hold her head high and keep moving forward. He guessed her motivation came from Tyler and her desire to be a role model for her son. Either way, he admired her quiet strength.

"That goes both ways," she said quietly. "I know the holidays can be rough for you."

He scoffed even as his gut tightened. "I'm fine. Busy at the station, which is how I like it. December is like any other month to me."

She studied him for a long moment, and his inclination was to fidget like a naughty schoolboy caught with his hand in the cookie jar. But he managed to keep his expression neutral.

"Will you be at the tree lighting tonight?"

"On duty," he confirmed. Every year, the residents of Starlight kicked off the holiday season in front of town hall with the annual lighting of the town's Christmas tree. The women's auxiliary would serve hot cocoa and the local choir led everyone in singing carols to celebrate the countdown to Christmas.

Nick always volunteered to work the event because so many of his deputies had families to attend with. He had…well, his mom. What self-respecting late-twenties bachelor would admit that fact?

"I'll see you there," she said with a final smile.

"You can tell me how your date went," he responded.

Her eyebrows shot up in response, but she nodded. "Sure, Nick. What a funny role reversal for us. Me sharing my dating adventures instead of the other way around."

"Good luck."

He didn't move for almost a full minute after she disappeared into the cheery restaurant. *Funny* was the last word he'd use to describe the thought of listening to Brynn's stories of dating other men.

Friendship. That was all Nick had to offer, he reminded himself. He'd been a lousy friend when they were younger and distant since her marriage. He had a chance to make up for that now. It was December, the month of increased caring and generosity, and he was going to make sure Brynn's Christmas was a merry one.

Chapter Two

Brynn held Tyler's small hand later that night as she scanned the crowd that had already gathered in front of town hall. She'd parked a few blocks away and owed a debt of thanks to Nick. When she'd called Jimmy at the auto shop after the most boring lunch date in the history of the world, he'd informed her Nick had already been by about her car.

According to Jimmy, the chief had insisted that towing Brynn's car needed to be moved to the top of the shop's priority list. They'd dispatched a truck, brought in the vehicle and installed the new alternator.

All Brynn needed to do was bring in her keys

so they could make sure there were no other issues and she'd be all set.

Nick's unexpected thoughtfulness had saved her an entire afternoon, additional time off work and the headache of dealing with the repair. She'd gotten used to handling life's little crises on her own since Daniel's accident, but that didn't mean she liked it. The sense of relief and gratitude at having someone take care of a problem so she didn't have to overwhelmed her. The fact that Nick had been the one to come to her rescue made her stomach flutter in a way she hadn't anticipated.

Brynn had long ago given up her childhood crush on Nick Dunlap. Nothing dampened teenage ardor like a blatant rejection that led to a surprise pregnancy with the boy she'd chosen as her "rebound." Having sex—her first time—with Daniel Hale had possibly been the most spontaneous and rash decision Brynn had ever made in her life.

Lesson learned.

Tyler squeezed her fingers, reminding her that despite the broken promises and unfulfilled dreams she'd endured as a result of those few minutes, it had all been worth it.

"I see Logan and Jake," he told her. He pointed to two boys weaving through the crowd. "Can I go say hi?"

She let go of his hand. "Sure, sweetie, but…"

Tyler didn't wait for her to finish. He dashed toward his friends with all the confidence of a kid who'd been attending the annual holiday event every December he could remember.

"Find me for the lighting," she finished, then bit down on the inside of her cheek. Her son was still young but growing up every day, becoming more independent and sometimes a little sassy. The sass had ramped up a notch since his father's death. The adjustment from being a mother to filling all the parental duties tried the patience of both Brynn and Tyler. Daniel hadn't been the world's best dad, but he'd loved his son. Tyler clearly felt his absence in ways that made him lash out at the one person who would tolerate the emotional roller coaster he often seemed to be riding.

They'd always attended the tree lighting as a family. Most years, Daniel would head to the bar with buddies from work after, but they'd be together as a unit for the ceremony. Tyler loved to perch on his father's shoulders, and the happiness in her son's eyes had made Brynn's heart glad. It had made everything that was wrong with her marriage seem not so important.

Now she was alone. Sure, she had Tyler and told Mara and Kaitlin he was enough. He filled her heart, but she knew she needed more in her life. For Tyler's benefit if no other reason. Brynn had been raised by a single mom and always understood the sacrifices her mother made to raise her.

Her mom had wanted more for Brynn, and Brynn had disappointed her in the most fundamental way possible. She never wanted Tyler to feel like he was a burden or responsible for his mother's happiness. Brynn had to manage that on her own.

"Are you going to join everyone or watch from back here?"

She turned to find Nick standing behind her, still in his dark police uniform, but now with the addition of a canvas jacket to ward off the cold. At six foot three, he towered over her, as he'd done since he hit puberty at the end of seventh grade and shot up seven inches before they got to high school.

Fighting against her innate physical awareness of him, Brynn shrugged. "I'm girding my loins, as the saying goes."

He grimaced. "That always sounded painful to me."

She laughed despite the nerves running through her. "It's our first Christmas without Daniel," she said, suddenly sober.

"Yep." He shifted closer. "You okay?"

The question felt different than when he'd huffed out the words at her on the side of the road. Or she felt different. Not so revved up with anger and bitterness. The start of the holiday season made her wistful, so much potential for kindness and cheer. Over the years, life had given her ample reasons to believe more in the stresses of the season—loneliness, missed opportunities, unrealistic expectations.

But December always gave her hope for something better.

This year she wasn't sure how she felt. *Okay* didn't seem to come anywhere close.

"I want to make the season special for Tyler. Even though they seemed silly at the time, we had traditions that involved his father. Putting up the tree with Daniel cursing a blue streak. The cat knocking ornaments to the floor after it was decorated, which led to more cursing. Pancakes on Christmas morning—"

"Tell me those didn't involve cursing," Nick said with a sigh.

"Not usually." She smiled even as her throat grew tight with the emotion balled there. "Our life wasn't perfect, but it's what Tyler knew. I don't know how to be both Mom and Dad for him. I want him to be happy. I want to be happy, but it's been a long time since I'd describe myself that way. I'm not sure if I know how to get back there." Her voice cracked, and she didn't bother to hide it. She and Nick might not be close any longer, but he was still her first best friend.

The relief that washed over her at not having to pretend to be fine was a shock, but she leaned into it nonetheless, allowing herself to feel everything she'd tamped down for the past five months.

Nick ran a hand through his hair, looking ten kinds of uncomfortable at her confession. "You'll figure it out."

"Definitely don't quit your day job to become a therapist," she advised with an eye roll and an elbow nudge to his ribs.

Nick chuckled, then asked, "Did the date today make you happy?"

"Did you know tapeworms don't have a stomach, so they absorb nutrients from the outside in?"

"Um...no." He turned to her more fully. "Tell me that wasn't part of your conversation over lunch."

"Not just part," she clarified. "Turns out Mara's partridge in a pear tree is a scientist who researches parasites. He teaches at Gonzaga and was on his way to a conference in Seattle when he passed through Starlight last week."

"No wonder he needed to be set up on a blind date. With those kind of skills, he's probably in the longest dating dry spell known to man."

"Ouch," she whispered. "What does it say about me that I needed to be set up?"

His hazel eyes were intense on her. "Your situation is different."

"Right." She threw up her hands. "The poor grieving widow and single mom. Textbook pathetic."

"No one thinks you're pathetic."

"They feel sorry for me," she countered. "Which

might be as bad. It's why you found me standing back here. My circumstances make people uncomfortable."

"Don't say that."

His voice skimmed over her like a cool breeze on a summer day. There was a reason she'd kept her distance from Nick. Her physical reaction to him had been a constant in her life and seemingly out of her control, as if her body came to life when he was around. She should walk away but couldn't—wouldn't was more like it. She'd spent most of her life shifting away from difficulties, glossing over trouble with a smile on her face. Always the good girl, always the person who could be relied on to put those around her at ease.

Where had it gotten her?

No place she'd recommend that anyone visit.

Since Daniel's death, Brynn had begun to change. The parts of her she recognized were quickly disappearing to be replaced with pieces that felt raw and rough. It started at the funeral, where she'd sat in the first pew of the church and fought the urge to scream at the top of her lungs. To shout at her dead husband for the reckless, hurtful choices he'd made and at herself for becoming so small it felt like her entire existence could fit on the sharp tip of a thumbtack.

There had been no outburst, of course. She'd remained calm and composed for her son, who quietly cried next to her. She'd cried for him and for the hand life had dealt her. Then a few days later, when he'd gone back to school, she'd driven up to Devil's Landing, the same stretch of road where Nick had found her today. She'd gotten out of her car, walked to the edge, where bright orange cones and caution tape marked the spot of Daniel's accident.

There, she'd screamed and screamed until her throat burned and her voice gave out. It had been such a relief to release the sound, her wails echoing across the valley.

That moment had freed something in Brynn, and she'd spent the past five months recalibrating her internal life to try to honor the change. It felt monumental. So she wouldn't—couldn't—walk away from a difficult conversation or her latent feelings for Nick. Not anymore.

"I make you uncomfortable," she told him, the words stated as fact rather than opinion.

"No." The denial fell flat, and he blew out a long breath. "I'm your friend, Brynn. I want to be your friend again. I'm simply not sure how to do it anymore. God knows I made a mess of things the first time."

"You did," she agreed, and his eyes widened. "Did I shock you?"

His broad shoulders lifted, then lowered. "A little. You never used to call me out on any of the crap I pulled."

"I'm not the same as I used to be."

"I'm glad."

This time it was her turn for shock. "You used to count on me being your mealymouthed sidekick."

"If I treated you that way, I'm sorry. It's good to know you're taking a stand for yourself." He lifted a hand, as if to reach for her, then lowered it again. *Yes*, her traitorous body screamed. *Please touch me. No*, her mind admonished. *That's a terrible idea.* "I've grown up, too."

Brynn didn't want to notice all the ways Nick had grown up. He'd been boyishly handsome as a teen, all rangy limbs and lean muscles, but had indeed developed into more.

"I should join everyone before they start the ceremony," she told him, needing some space from the rush of emotion this quiet moment with him had unleashed inside her.

He nodded. "I'm going to check around back."

"Do high school students still drink in the shadows behind town hall?" she asked with a smile.

"Some things change in Starlight," he answered. "Some things stay the same."

She thunked the heel of her palm against her forehead. "Oh, my gosh. I almost forgot to thank you for taking care of my car. You didn't need to do that, Nick."

"Not a big deal. Jimmy has a habit of getting rowdy when he's drinking. He owes me for all the rides home from the bar before he could get himself into trouble."

Her instinct was to protest again or make a statement about how she could have handled the car on her own. She didn't like to rely on anyone. Pretty much everyone in town knew her circumstances. The only way she was able to hold her head high was by making it seem like she could take care of anything. But this was Nick, and she didn't have to pretend. "It was a huge help, and I appreciate it."

The look of satisfaction that crossed his face made her breath catch in her throat.

"You're welcome," he told her, and with a final wave, she hurried to join the crowd in front of town hall.

Too much time with Nick wouldn't help her to feel more in control of things.

She caught sight of Tyler at the hot cocoa stand, and he grinned as he held up a handful of marshmallows, then popped the whole bunch into his mouth.

The laugh that escaped her lips felt refreshingly normal. Normal was a balm to her battered soul these days, and she loved seeing her son enjoying the event without the weight of memories she couldn't seem to shake off.

"You're here. We've been looking for you."

She turned toward Kaitlin Carmody and Mara Johnson, her two closest friends in Starlight. Neither of them were natives to the small town, which

Brynn guessed was part of what made her so comfortable with them. Yes, they knew her situation, but there was none of the complicated judgment from either of them that seemed to define most of her longtime friendships in the community.

They both had regrets from their own pasts, and the acceptance they gave her had immediately put her at ease. No preconceived notions of who she was supposed to be or all the ways she hadn't lived up to her potential as she'd tried to make her marriage work and raise her son in a loving home.

Since Daniel died, they'd gotten even closer, and she couldn't imagine life without them.

"I'm so happy you're both here." She hugged each of the women and made certain a smile was fixed on her face. Honesty with Nick was one thing, but she wasn't about to let her tumbling emotions put a damper on the start of the holiday season for Kaitlin and Mara.

"Finn, Parker and Josh are saving a spot near the front so the kids will have an unobstructed view of the tree," Kaitlin told her.

"That's sweet," Brynn murmured. Although she'd been closer with Nick, she'd also been friends with Finn Samuelson and Parker Johnson most of her life. Josh was Parker's younger brother, and his daughter, Anna, had become besties with Mara's little girl, Evie, when Mara moved to Starlight over a year ago. "Tyler is with his buddies right now, so

I need to round him up." She checked her watch. "We have a few minutes before the ceremony is scheduled to start. Why are the two of you looking at me like that?"

"The date," Mara said, pushing a thick strand of bourbon-colored hair behind her ear. "You haven't said anything."

Brynn shrugged. "He's into tapeworms."

"That's not a thing." Kaitlin grimaced. "Tell me that's not a thing."

"It's part of the science curriculum he teaches," Brynn explained. "And he's kind of obsessed. Parasites don't do it for me, so I'm not sure we're a good match."

Her friends stared wide-eyed a moment longer, then both of them dissolved into fits of laughter.

"Gross," Mara said, shaking her head.

"You should add *no parasites* to your online dating profile," Kaitlin advised.

"I don't have a profile," Brynn reminded her. "If you'll remember, I think this whole dating thing is a waste of time."

Kaitlin grew serious as she touched the diamond engagement ring that graced the third finger of her left hand. "Love is never a waste of time."

"She's right," Mara confirmed. "And sometimes you find it in the unlikeliest place. You can't give up. We're committed to this quest."

Brynn's cheeks ached with the effort of keeping

her smile steady. She appreciated her friends and had been glad to watch them find love in Starlight. First Kaitlin with Finn and then Mara and Parker, an unlikely match in so many ways, particularly because he'd represented Mara's ex-husband in their divorce.

Both couples had overcome plenty of difficulties on the road to their happily-ever-after. Brynn wasn't convinced she was on the same path.

"Being set up makes me feel more like a charity case," she admitted.

"Don't say that." Mara reached for her hand, squeezing gently. "Everyone agrees you deserve a great man in your life."

"I have one in Tyler," she replied automatically.

"A man other than your son," Kaitlin clarified.

Brynn groaned. "When you put it like that, it sounds even more desperate than I feel."

"You aren't desperate. You're willing."

"Which makes it seem like I've scrawled my contact info on every bathroom stall this side of the Cascade Mountains."

"Don't be silly. Also, Finn met with the new owner of the hardware store yesterday. He came in to talk about an expansion loan. He's pretty cute and single."

Finn's family owned First Trust, the longest-running local bank in Starlight, since the institution's founding. Finn had returned to Starlight to help his ailing father with the bank this past summer, and although he and Kaitlin had started off more as enemies than friends, they'd quickly discovered love.

Brynn was happy for both of her friends and tried to ignore the sliver of envy that ran through her. "Did he put *single* on his application?" she asked with a raised brow. "Or did you interrogate him?"

Kaitlin headed up customer relations at the bank. The slim blonde sniffed. "*Interrogate* is such a harsh word. We talked and I mentioned I have a gorgeous friend who knows the best places to eat in Starlight."

"There are three restaurants in this town, if you don't count the food trucks at the mill." She nodded. "The food truck variety is awesome, if I do say so myself."

"Then you can take him on a date to the mill."

"I work there. That's weird." Brynn's pregnancy had changed so many things about her future. She'd planned to start her freshman year at Washington State University the fall after graduating high school, but instead had been dealing with swollen ankles and adjusting to marriage with a boy she barely knew. Over the years, she'd worked odd jobs around town, cleaning office buildings at night and doing filing for the local attorney and accountant's office—things that allowed her flexible hours so she didn't have to put her son in day care or rely on anyone to help.

No one had expected Brynn to handle motherhood well, so she'd been determined to prove everyone wrong. Once Tyler started elementary school, she'd worked in the front office and as a substitute teacher. She'd also volunteered for the PTO and in the classroom, her quest to demonstrate her worth never ending.

More recently, Parker and Josh Johnson had redeveloped the Dennison Mill, the town's deserted lumber mill, into a smorgasbord of adaptive-reuse space. There were retail stores, a second location for Main Street Perk, as well as community events. Somehow, Brynn had found the nerve to convince the brothers to hire her as their marketing and events manager. She'd planned to study advertising in college, and although she didn't have a degree, she loved the challenge of coming up with a plan for the mill.

"The mill is awesome," Mara said, "and so is your work there." She turned to Kaitlin. "What's number two's name anyway?"

"Number two?" Brynn questioned.

"Will MacFarlane," Kaitlin answered, then winked at Brynn. "Date number two of twelve."

"Oh, lord. That sounds bad."

"You're getting into the holiday spirit."

"I'm going to need heavy spirits to get through all these dates."

"Not if number two becomes your number one,"

Mara said with a cheeky grin. "Then you can have the rest of the dates with him. Mr. Right."

"I don't believe in Mr. Right," Brynn said, even as an image of Nick flitted across her mind.

"At least be open to Mr. Right Now," Mara urged. "We hung mistletoe at both locations of Perk."

Brynn stumbled a step as Tyler's thin arms wrapped around her legs. "Mom, I almost lost you."

"You didn't lose me, sweetie." She ruffled his hair. "I was waiting for you right here."

"I can't see the tree," he complained, craning his neck to see around the people who surrounded them. "I want to see."

Brynn's heart pinched, knowing that this year was different since her son wouldn't be higher than everyone else on his father's shoulders.

"Then let's go to where you can," Mara told him without missing a beat and led the way toward the front of the crowd.

"You'll have the best view ever," Brynn promised, taking his smaller hand in hers. As she followed her two friends, she vowed that no matter how hard she had to work, this Christmas was going to be the most magical she could make it.

Chapter Three

"Stop lying to yourself," Finn counseled a few nights later over a round of beers at Trophy Room, Starlight's most popular bar.

"And to Brynn," Parker added for good measure.

"Whose side are the two of you on?" Nick demanded, his voice pitched to almost a growl. He was sick of being lectured by his two closest friends. Drinking alone at home was starting to seem like a way better option.

"Hers," Parker said at the same time as Finn's emphatic, "Yours."

Finn immediately swatted Parker on the arm. "Dude."

"Both of yours."

"Said like a true attorney," Nick mumbled.

Parker flashed an unapologetic grin. "I take that as a compliment."

Nick grunted. "Don't." He held up a hand when Finn would have spoken again, took a moment to drain his beer, then returned the empty pilsner glass to the scuffed tabletop with a thud. "I've told you guys a hundred times now. Brynn and I are friends. Nothing more. Nothing less."

"Then you're going to lose her," Parker answered.

"Again," Finn added. "I don't understand why you're being so stubborn about this."

"I hurt her," Nick said as if it explained everything. "I won't take the chance of repeating that."

"You were an idiot." Finn grabbed a chip from the heaping pile of nachos in the middle of the table.

It was a Monday night, and a crowd had gathered in the bar's wood-paneled interior for food, drinks and football. The atmosphere was downright festive, even though neither of the teams playing tonight were located within a thousand miles of Washington State. Ever since he'd joined the force, Nick had gotten into the habit of assessing any space he entered, and he detected only camaraderie in the bar tonight.

"We all did plenty of stupid things back in high school," Parker added before digging into the nachos.

"Like the pact we made," Finn said.

Parker nodded as he shoved a loaded chip into his mouth. "Incredibly stupid."

"You only think that because you're in love." Nick didn't bother to hide the derision in his tone as he emphasized the final two words with air quotes.

"Don't air quote at me," Finn told him. "That vow was made out of fear and immaturity."

Parker nodded. "Apparently some of us haven't grown up."

Nick drew in a deep breath and forced himself not to push back from the table and stalk away from his friends. It annoyed the hell out of him that just because they'd both jumped on the truelove bandwagon he was automatically expected to hitch a ride.

He didn't need or want love in his life, no matter how his body reacted to Brynn. Maybe he couldn't control the beating of his heart, but he damn well had control over whether he gave it away.

Back in high school, Finn and Parker had felt the same. They'd all been hurting in different ways, but one thing the three of them had agreed on was that love wasn't worth the pain it could cause. The night of their high school graduation, after too many swigs of cheap liquor, they'd taken an oath not to fall in love. It might sound silly and they'd been more than a little drunk, but on that night, Finn, Parker and Nick had been serious about honoring the promise they made to each other.

Nick had woken up the next morning, his head pounding under the bright morning sun. Parker and

Finn had still been asleep a few feet from him, both of them snoring loud enough to rival a freight train. He'd felt sick and cotton-mouthed but his heart, for the first time since he'd seen Brynn dancing with Daniel Hale at prom, had been light.

The friends had rarely talked about that oath over the years. All of them had been eager to leave their hometown behind and set out to make their way in the world. Nick had been the first one to return when his mom's health declined after his brother's death in Afghanistan and the subsequent fatal heart attack his father suffered.

In Starlight, people settled down. Plenty of women he'd known growing up—and some new to town— had been interested in enticing him to settle down.

He'd never been the least bit tempted.

The vow, he'd told himself. It was because of the vow.

It had been a shock when Finn and then Parker had thrown aside their oath and fallen in love. He didn't want to resent them for their choices. Hell, Kaitlin and Mara were awesome.

But when Nick made a vow, he kept it. Even if he was the only one. Not that he'd had a reason to break the vow since that night, or a woman who made him want to give up on the promise he'd made.

"Nothing is going to happen between Brynn and me."

"Fine." Finn gave a disgusted sigh. "It's probably better anyway. She needs someone steady in her life. A man she can count on."

"I'm steady as a ro—" Nick clamped shut his mouth. Without a doubt, his friend was trying to bait him. He wouldn't fall for it.

"I met the new owner of the hardware supply company Kaitlin wants to introduce her to," Parker offered. "Seems like a decent guy. Maybe they'll hit it off."

"What's the damn obsession with finding Brynn a boyfriend?" Nick demanded. "Can't you keep your women occupied?"

Finn and Parker stared at him with twin expressions of horror on their faces. "You better not let Mara hear you talk like that," Parker warned.

"Kaitlin would skin you alive for that comment," Finn agreed.

"I know. I know." Nick held up his hands. "I realize I sound like an oaf. It's a new habit."

"*Oaf* is one word for it." Finn pushed the plate of nachos toward him.

"Need anything, fellas?" They all turned as Jordan Schaeffer, the former NFL tight end who'd moved to Starlight after a career-ending injury, approached the table. "Damn, Chief, you look like someone peed in your Wheaties."

"We're talking about the quest to find a guy for Brynn Hale," Finn explained. "It's making him grumpy as hell."

Nick sighed. "Do you really think she'd want us discussing her love life in the middle of a bar?"

"I know all about it." Jordan flipped a towel over one beefy shoulder. "Mara brought me a plate of cinnamon rolls the other day and asked what my idea of a perfect first date would be. Brynn is sure pretty and sweet as can be…"

Nick's gut clenched as he glared at Jordan.

"But not my type," Jordan finished quickly. "Another round?"

"No." Unable to endure this topic any longer, Nick straightened from his chair. "In case any of you are wondering, Brynn's perfect first date would be a hike in the woods, followed by a quiet dinner and watching some late-nineties rom-com to end the evening."

"Not that you're going to do anything with that bit of insider knowledge," Finn said, shaking his head.

"I'm going to go home and take Teddy for a walk." Nick thought of his dopey black Lab and smiled. "He's way better company than any of you."

A chorus of chuckles followed him away from the table, but he ignored his friends. It didn't matter what anyone thought he should do with Brynn. She was strictly relegated to the friend zone.

He walked out into the clear evening and took a breath so deep the cold air burned his lungs. He welcomed the pain, something to focus on other than the ache in his heart. Just as he got to his truck, a woman climbed out of a small hatchback parked behind him at the curb.

"Nick Dunlap?" she asked, voice trembling. "Are you Chief Dunlap?"

"Yes, ma'am." His law-enforcement spidey sense went on high alert. "How can I help you?"

The woman took a step closer and then glanced toward her vehicle. In the glow of the streetlight above it, Nick could see the outline of a baby's car seat in the back.

"Is everything okay, ma'am?"

"Daniel always said good things about you," she said, her hands clenched in front of her. "He said you took care of people."

Nick went still, although a thousand warning bells clanged inside his brain. "How did you know Daniel?"

"I need to talk to his wife," she continued, ignoring his question. "Brynn. Can you take me to Brynn? She'll be more comfortable if you're there. Daniel said you and Brynn were friends. He said you'd look out for her after…"

Her voice trailed off and her thin chest expanded with what looked like a painful breath. She had long brown hair and thin features, pretty in an unconventional way.

"After what?"

"He was going to leave her," she whispered, almost more to herself than him. "For me." Her eyes darted to the car's darkened interior again. "And the baby."

Brynn rubbed absently at her chest as she sat at the dining room table two hours later. Just when she thought her life couldn't turn any further in circles, there it went, spinning and tumbling like an avalanche. She expected to feel more.

She should feel something after receiving the news that her late husband hadn't only had one mistress at the end of his life, the woman who'd died in the accident with him. Apparently, if her late-night visitor was to be believed—and Brynn had no reason not to—Daniel had been planning to divorce Brynn and move on with another girlfriend, the one who had been nine-months pregnant with his baby at the time of his death.

She could feel the steady beat of her heart under her rib cage. Thump, thump, thump. Nothing else. From the moment Nick had called earlier, his voice low and apologetic as he explained the story of the woman who'd approached him in town, Brynn had gone numb. She'd put her son to bed with the same routine they had every night. Tyler had only recently started sleeping in his own bed again. The night his father died, he'd crawled under the covers with Brynn, and she'd allowed him to sleep there until he finally told her he was ready to return to his room.

"Would you like more tea?" she asked the woman sitting across from her.

"If you don't mind," Francesca answered, biting down on her lower lip. "The heat in my car hasn't been working, and it was a slow drive from Seattle. I can't seem to get warm."

Brynn could relate.

"I'll help," Nick offered, pushing back from the table at the same time Brynn straightened. She didn't need assistance pouring hot water from the teakettle but understood that wasn't why Nick wanted time with her in the kitchen alone.

"It's freaking me out how well you're handling this," he told her, as she turned on the gas stove's front burner.

"Would it make you feel better if I burst into tears or threw some plates against the wall?"

"Maybe." He ran a hand through his hair, which was already standing on end in messy tufts. "Hell, Brynn. I'm about to lose my mind over all of this. The woman who'd been with him in the car was bad enough."

"Katie," Brynn murmured, unable to help herself. "Her name was Katie."

She'd met the parents of the woman who had died along with her husband, about a week after Daniel's funeral, for coffee at Main Street Perk. They'd been a regular middle-aged couple, heartbroken over the loss of their only daughter. It had been a strange and surreal conversation. Katie, who lived in a town about thirty minutes from Starlight, had talked to her parents about her new boyfriend, but they hadn't met Daniel.

As far as the couple knew, Katie had been unaware the new man in her life was already married. They'd wanted Brynn to know that. To understand their daughter hadn't been a home-wrecker.

But even with the loss of Daniel so fresh and raw, blame hadn't been important to Brynn. Moving forward and helping Tyler move forward was her focus.

"We don't even know for sure the baby is Daniel's," Nick said, and Brynn could hear the desperation in his voice. The hope that her late husband had been someone different than the serial cheater they all knew him to be.

Brynn had given up hope years ago, and now was embarrassed she'd gone along with the farce instead of walking away.

The kettle whistled, and she poured the steaming water over a fresh tea bag that she'd placed in Francesca's mug, ignoring the way her fingers shook. The porcelain had a cheery band of snowmen circling it. Money had always been tight, and Brynn prided herself on the holiday decorations she'd purchased from thrift stores and garage sales, making their small house festive each season. Making things appear normal, even when they were anything but.

"The baby looks like a girl version of Tyler at four months," she said softly. "Don't pretend like you can't see the resemblance." She forced her gaze to Nick's. "She looks like her daddy."

He blew out an unsteady breath. "I hate this. I hate that he's done this to you. Obviously, Francesca is struggling, but I want to escort her to the town limits and tell her not to come back. I want it all to go away."

"You can't always get what you want," she answered, the decades-old song lyric somehow the story of her life.

"Tell me about it," Nick muttered, and the past curled between them like a plume of smoke, thick enough to choke her.

"She's alone." As Brynn picked up the mug, she concentrated on the warmth that seeped into her fingers. "Alone and scared. I'm not going to ignore her. That baby—Remi—is Tyler's sister."

"You're always a good person," he said, and his tone made the words sound like an accusation.

"I'm as human as everyone else," she told him. "You didn't turn her away, either."

"I wish I had."

"Stop. I know you don't mean it, Nick. You'll help her."

"I'll help you, Brynn. I'm here for you."

Those simple words, more than anything else, made emotion clog her throat, but she pushed it away. If she allowed the vulnerability locked up inside her any room to breathe, it might bloom and grow and crowd out everything else.

She moved toward the hallway that led to the dining room situated at the front of the house. "This mess is on Daniel, but I've got to clean it up."

"We," he corrected. "Even if I wasn't your friend, I have a duty as a public servant to help someone in need."

"Thank you," she said quietly but stopped at the dining room threshold, swallowing back a soft groan of empathy.

Francesca had moved to the wingback chair that sat in the corner of the room. In her arms, baby Remi was noisily slurping down a bottle of formula while her mother dozed. Francesca had propped a pillow underneath the arm that cradled the baby and the tiny girl didn't seem to notice that her exhausted mama had fallen asleep.

"Poor thing," Brynn murmured, remembering countless overnight feedings with Tyler. She'd breastfed, and Tyler hadn't taken a bottle until he was nearly a year old. It had been the two of them in the quiet nights and she'd woken any number of times with her baby in her arms after falling asleep for a few minutes.

"She looks exhausted," Nick said. "I don't think becoming a mother has been easy for her."

Francesca was a couple years younger than Brynn

according to what she'd told them. She worked as a waitress in a chain steak restaurant outside of Seattle. She'd met Daniel on one of his insurance sales trips into the city. He'd gotten a promotion a year and a half ago and those overnight forays to Seattle had become more frequent. Given his history, Brynn probably should have questioned him, but she'd enjoyed the evenings with Tyler when the tension of her marriage wasn't a palpable force in the room.

She placed the mug of tea on the table and approached Francesca and the baby. Remi looked content as she ate, her skin pink and a layer of downy hair covering her small head. She was nearly five months old, born only two weeks after her father's death.

Brynn's heart pinched at the baby's resemblance to her own son. She didn't relish the thought of explaining this situation to Tyler but hoped the idea of having a younger sister would ease the transition. Most people might think she was a fool, but this baby was a part of Daniel and that made her a part of Tyler. Brynn couldn't know whether helping her son to forge a relationship with his half sister would benefit him, but her heart told her it was the right thing to do.

If only Brynn had trusted her heart more often, she might not be in this situation in the first place.

"Hey," she whispered, touching a gentle hand to the woman's knee.

Francesca blinked several times before her gaze met Brynn's, panic and fatigue swirling like a cyclone. She glanced at the baby in her arms, almost as if she were surprised to find the child there.

"I'm sorry," she said. "It's been a day. I should go. I have a long drive back home."

"You can stay here tonight," Brynn offered without thinking about it.

She heard and ignored Nick's sharp intake of breath. "I'll get her a room at the Starlight Inn," he said in his official chief-of-police voice.

His commanding tone might work on some people—Francesca looked vaguely terrified—but it didn't faze Brynn.

"Don't be silly. We have a guest bedroom all made up."

"Are you sure?" Francesca asked, moving the bottle away from little Remi, who whimpered in protest.

Brynn thought about it for a moment, and for the first time since the accident, a sense of peace settled over her. Maybe it was the holiday spirit of generosity, but she knew taking in this lonely, frightened woman and her baby was the right thing to do.

"Yes," she answered.

"Thank you." Francesca's voice shook as she dashed a hand across her cheeks. "Also, I'm sorry

I had to be a part of Daniel hurting you. I'm sorry I believed the things he said."

"It's fine," Brynn assured the woman. "If you'd like, I can hold Remi for a few minutes while you get ready for bed? We could all use a decent night's sleep."

"Okay." Francesca didn't hesitate to hand over her daughter. "She probably needs her diaper changed."

Brynn sighed as the baby curled her hand into the front of Brynn's shirt. "I can handle that."

She purposely didn't look at Nick as she showed Francesca the guest bedroom and the hallway bathroom where she kept extra toiletries. Francesca hadn't brought an overnight bag but insisted she felt more comfortable sleeping in her clothes than borrowing pajamas from Brynn.

She gave the other woman a few minutes of privacy and returned to the dining room for the diaper bag.

Nick was waiting for her. "You can't do this," he said, arms crossed over his chest. "She's a stranger. You don't invite a stranger into your home."

"Thanks for your opinion," she answered, "and your work here is done. I'll call you tomorrow, okay?"

"Brynn, listen to me."

"Nick, look at the baby." She turned toward him fully. "She's Tyler's sister. Her mother is in a bad way, and I didn't get one weird vibe off her other than she was overwhelmed and tired as all get-out.

I remember those feelings. I still feel them most days. I'm not sending her away."

He stared at her so intensely that heat crept into her cheeks. "I'm running a background check on her before I head home, and I'll be back in the morning."

"Unnecessary," she muttered.

"Humor me, Brynn. Please."

Darn him and his manners. "I'll text you when we're awake."

He looked like he wanted to say more, but Remi sniffed and let out a cry. "She needs a diaper change."

"Call me if you need anything. I don't care what time it is."

Brynn nodded and let him out the front door, locking it behind him. After putting a fresh diaper on Remi, she lifted the baby into her arms again and snuggled the child closer. She didn't know what would come next but had no doubt this little girl was about to change everything.

Chapter Four

"Mommy."

Brynn blinked awake at the sound of Tyler's voice. Glancing at the clock on the nightstand, she held out her arms to her son. Just after six in the morning. Too early when it felt like it had taken hours for her to fall asleep last night.

"Did you have a bad dream, buddy?" She scooted over on the mattress to make room, but Tyler didn't climb in with her.

"I think Santa Claus came early," he told her, his voice solemn. He wore a stegosaurus T-shirt and striped pajamas that were too short for him now, although she'd bought them only a couple of months ago at the change of seasons. Often her days seemed interminably long, but time sped by when she marked it by her son's growth. His thick brown hair stuck up in sleep-mottled tufts, as it had almost every morning since he was a toddler.

Brynn commanded her fuzzy, sentimental brain to snap to it as she sat up in the bed. She couldn't imagine Francesca was already awake with how exhausted the woman had appeared last night, but if Remi had woken in the guest room downstairs, Tyler might have heard the baby crying.

This moment was what had kept Brynn awake. How would she tell her son that he had a half sister, let alone that the baby and her mother had ended up in Starlight? But the past five months had taught Brynn she was capable of handling more than she could have ever guessed.

"Did you hear something, Ty? I can explain—"

"Santa left us a baby," her son explained. "Under the tree."

A baby under the tree? Brynn was out of bed in an instant, panic blooming fast and hard in her chest.

"Someone spent the night here," she said, as she took Tyler's hand and tugged him forward. "A… um…friend of your daddy's. She has a baby, so it wasn't Santa. Did you see a grown-up, sweetie? I'm sorry. I thought I'd be awake to introduce you but—"

"Just the baby." Tyler followed her down the stairs, his fingers gripping hers tightly.

"Francesca?" Brynn called, as they got to the bottom of the steps. Silence greeted her. "Maybe she's in the bathroom or she went to her car for something."

"You're the only grown-up here."

Brynn shook her head. That simply wasn't possible.

But there was Remi, under the tree in her infant seat, small feet kicking as she contentedly sucked on two fingers. Brynn's panic morphed into a heavy sense of foreboding when she saw the folded slip of paper tucked into the padding next to the baby girl.

"Francesca?" she called again, even though at this point she didn't expect a response.

She let go of Tyler and dropped to her knees on the carpet in front of the tree. The baby's rosebud mouth curved into a smile when her sweet brown eyes fixed on Brynn. With trembling fingers, Brynn opened the paper and read the message written in a shaky scrawl.

Her lungs constricted as reality wrapped around her in a choke hold. Francesca was gone. According to the note, she'd left in the middle of the night, certain Remi would be better off without her since becoming a mother hadn't been part of Francesca's plan until the pregnancy happened.

"We should get her up," Tyler suggested, nudging Brynn's shoulder. "She's squirming like she wants out."

"That's a good idea, sweetie," Brynn said, trying not to sound as panicked as she felt. Was Francesca a danger to herself? What time had she left the house? How far had she gotten?

The baby gurgled happily as Brynn lifted her from the infant seat, kicking her legs and waving her arms. Brynn's heart felt like it was about to beat out of her rib cage.

"I wonder what her name is," Tyler said, smiling at the baby.

"Remi." Brynn ruffled her son's mop of hair. "Her name is Remi. The note said there are bottles for her on the counter. Let's see if she's hungry, and I'm going to call Nick and ask for his help with finding her mommy."

"Her mommy probably misses her already." Tyler led the way to the kitchen. "Did Daddy know Remi?"

"No," Brynn whispered, then cleared her throat. "She was born after your dad died."

There was so much about this situation she couldn't understand. How on earth would she explain it to a ten-year-old child? Instead of allowing herself to become overwhelmed, she did what she did best and focused on what she could control in the present moment.

Warming a bottle and feeding a hungry baby topped the list. Even as she heated water, Brynn was aware of the seconds ticking by. Every minute that elapsed was more time with Francesca out on her own, either getting farther away or potentially a danger to herself.

Brynn wasn't an expert on postpartum depression, but she certainly understood how it felt to be desperate and afraid of not being able to handle your own life.

When the water was the right temperature, she mixed the formula and moved toward a chair.

"Can I feed her, Mommy?" Tyler asked, still at her side.

"Sure, bud. Let's take her back to the family room because it will be easier for you to hold her on the couch. Babies seem small, but they get heavy in your arms."

"I'm strong." He scratched his belly as he walked next to her.

"Don't I know it," she murmured under her breath.

Brynn snatched her phone from the charger on the counter. Once she had Tyler settled with Remi, who still had yet to fuss, she showed him how to tip up the bottle to prevent pockets of air from forming.

She helped guide the nipple to the baby's mouth, and once Remi had begun to enthusiastically suck, Brynn sat back.

"She's hungry," Tyler said with a smile, as he glanced between Brynn and the baby. "Me, too. Will you make me a waffle?"

"Of course. Let me text Nick first." She figured

texting might be easier at this point because that way Tyler wouldn't hear the thread of alarm she doubted she could keep from her voice.

Forcing her features to remain calm for Tyler, she typed out a series of short messages to Nick that explained the situation and that she didn't want to talk about details in front of Tyler. Then she took a quick photo of Francesca's letter and forwarded it. Almost immediately, three little dots popped up on the screen alerting her Nick was responding.

Brynn could barely contain a relieved sob when the first message came through.

On my way.

She might want to keep her distance from Nick on a personal level, but Brynn knew he was a good police chief and trusted his judgment implicitly.

She placed her phone on the coffee table. Now that Nick was involved, she felt safe to focus her energy entirely on the baby.

"She's taken about half the bottle, so it's time to burp her." She reached for Remi, but Tyler handed her the bottle instead.

"Tell me what to do, Mommy."

Tears stung the corners of Brynn's eyes at how much Tyler seemed to like taking care of the little girl. "Put her over your shoulder while supporting her head and gently tap on her back." Brynn shifted closer, ready to help if the boy needed it.

He did as she said, and a few moments later Remi let out a massive belch that made both of them laugh.

When was the last time she'd heard her son's sweet laugh?

"She puked on me." Tyler made a face as he turned to look at his shoulder.

"Only a little spit up," Brynn assured him. "I'll grab a towel to clean you up."

By the time she returned, Tyler had the baby back on his lap. Remi stared up at him with wide eyes, like she'd never seen anything so fascinating. Then her face lit up with a gummy smile that Tyler returned with a broad grin of his own.

"She's pretty cute, even with the puking."

"You were adorable, too," Brynn told him, wiping the puddle from his shirt. "And you had horrible reflux that made you spit up all the time."

"Do all babies look alike?" His grip was sure as he held on to Remi. Brynn gave him the bottle and he tipped it up so the baby could finish it.

"Not all of them."

"This one looks like I did." He pointed to a framed photo that sat on the bookshelf next to the mantel. He'd been six months old when the picture was taken, only about a month older than Remi.

"She does," Brynn said softly, not sure when or

how to share the reason for the resemblance. This moment felt too soon, too fragile. There was too much unknown to drop a bombshell in the middle of it.

"She smells funny." Tyler wrinkled his nose.

"I'll change her diaper when she's done with the bottle." Brynn winked at him. "Unless you want to try that, as well."

"Nope."

"I don't blame you." She rose from the sofa. "I'm going to get your breakfast ready and then I'll take her from you. Okay?"

Tyler nodded, his attention focused on the child in his arms once again.

Brynn mentally calculated how long until Nick arrived as she toasted a waffle and started the coffeepot. She ran a hand through her hair, irritated that despite the chaos of the morning she still thought about how she must look. Tired, terrified and quite possibly like she'd been dragged to hell and back.

Too bad, she chided herself. She shouldn't— wouldn't—care what Nick thought of her appearance. Caring about Nick could only lead to more pain and she had more than her fill already.

Nick repeated the make and model of Francesca's car to the dispatcher and then disconnected the call as he parked in front of Brynn's house.

The sky was beginning to lighten, with shades of pink and purple stretching above him like slender

fingers. He'd driven his truck instead of the department's Bronco this morning, but didn't doubt for a
second the news of him paying an early-morning
visit to Brynn Hale would be all over town by the
time most people had finished breakfast.

At this point, he couldn't bring himself to care.
He was too busy wishing he'd had a do-over on last
night. One where he would have insisted on staying or making sure Francesca was stable. He would
never have guessed the young mom would do something like this, but now he felt like he'd failed everyone involved, especially Brynn.

He hated that she had to deal with Daniel's baby
with another woman on top of everything else she'd
been through.

Climbing out of the truck, he noticed the curtains in the front window of the house across the
street flutter. Karen Remington lived there, and the
retired nurse was one of Starlight's biggest gossips.

Nick sighed. He hadn't planned to settle in his
hometown, but he'd grown accustomed to it and
his role in Starlight. In truth, he couldn't imagine
living anywhere else. He loved the community and
the sense of purpose it gave him to lead the town
as police chief.

But sometimes a little anonymity wouldn't be
the worst thing he could imagine.

Brynn opened the door as he approached, the
baby cradled in her arms. The sight of her hit him

like a swift punch to the gut, knocking the wind out of him. Brynn looked so damn beautiful standing in the doorway, her hair tucked behind her ears like she used to wear it back in high school. She wore a shapeless T-shirt and loose pajama pants, and somehow the casual intimacy of the outfit only added to the emotions assailing him.

"You look tired," he blurted out, then wanted to kick himself for once again saying the wrong thing to her.

"And panicked and overwhelmed," she added with an eye roll. "Excuse me for not making myself pretty for you, Chief. I was busy taking care of this little one."

"I didn't mean it like that." He shut the front door behind him as he followed her into the house. "You don't need to do anything to make yourself pretty, Brynn. You're already beautiful."

That was better, right?

Maybe not, based on the look she threw him over her shoulder. "Do you have any leads on Francesca?" she asked.

"Not yet. I've called the sheriff's department and state highway patrol. I haven't reached out to social services yet, but if she doesn't resurface soon, I'll need to alert them."

"What will happen to Remi?"

He watched as Brynn took a mug from the cabinet and poured coffee into it. How was she able to function so adeptly while holding the baby in her other arm and the chaos swirling around them? Was this some inherent gift mothers had?

"Thanks." He took the steaming mug she handed to him. "Foster care unless they can find a member of her family to take the baby. First they'll have to track down her records."

"I don't even know her last name." Brynn chewed on her lower lip. "There are so many things about last night I'd do differently if I had the chance."

"You can't change the past," he said after taking a long drink of coffee.

Her sky blue gaze darted to his, and the air grew charged between them.

"Trust me, I get it," she said quietly.

"Hi, Nick."

Nick turned as Tyler entered the kitchen and immediately walked to his mother's side.

"Hey, Ty. How are you doing with all this?"

"I fed her this morning and got her to burp." The boy tickled the baby's tiny foot. "She spit up on me, but it wasn't too gross."

Brynn smiled at her son in a way that made Nick's chest ache.

"That's impressive," he told the kid. "I'm not sure I'd want someone puking on me."

"Mommy said I used to spit up a ton. Way more than Remi. But I don't remember on account of I was little then."

"But you're a big help now." Brynn trailed a finger along her son's cheek.

"Did you find Remi's mommy?" Tyler turned toward Nick, his gaze serious.

"Not yet, but we're working on it."

"She can stay with us until her mom comes back." Tyler glanced up at his mom. "Right?"

"Of course, she's welcome here," Brynn answered without hesitation. "But she might have family or someone who's better suited to take care of her, sweetie."

"She likes me." Tyler's feathery brows furrowed. "And I like her. I didn't even know I liked babies but turns out I do. Colby Myers has a baby brother, but he cries all the time. Remi doesn't cry much."

"Not so far," Brynn agreed, sounding as unsettled as Nick felt.

The baby didn't look anywhere close to tears. She blew a few spit bubbles, then reached for Tyler.

"See, Mommy. She likes me."

"Because you're the best. Let's put her on the floor in the family room and you can play with her for a few more minutes before you head off to school. I think I have some of your old baby stuff in the basement that we can use for her while she's here."

"Cool," Tyler said and led the way from the kitchen around the corner to the family room.

Nick grabbed a fleece blanket from the back of the sofa and spread it on the floor. Brynn knelt down next to him and placed the baby on the soft fabric.

Remi seemed thrilled to have more room to stretch and wiggle. She kicked her legs and babbled when Tyler joined her on the blanket, making faces and grinning.

"She likes me a lot," the boy announced, clearly reveling in the baby's adoration.

"Who can blame her?" Nick asked, as he straightened.

Brynn crossed her arms over her chest as she watched the two children, a wistful smile playing at the corner of her mouth. A few years back Daniel had complained to a group of guys about Brynn wanting another baby. It had been at the bar after a softball game, and Nick had wanted to punch his supposed friend for the way Daniel insinuated that Brynn and Tyler were already too much of an inconvenience without adding another kid into the mix.

Brynn had always been a natural caregiver, sweet and nurturing when other kids—kids like Nick— were totally focused on themselves.

There was so much Brynn had compromised on when she'd married Daniel, and Nick still blamed himself for the turn of events that led to their quickie wedding.

He massaged a hand across the back of his neck, trying to rub away the irritation that pricked at his skin.

Brynn seemed to force her gaze away from Tyler

and Remi to give Nick a weak smile. "Could you help me bring up a couple bins from the basement?"

"Sure." He followed her out of the room and down into the cramped, unfinished space. "I'll call and check in with the station to see if she's gotten word from anyone after we get the stuff upstairs."

"I went through most of Daniel's things a month after the funeral. I don't remember any mention of a Francesca to help figure out her last name, but I can check his emails again." She sighed. "He was pretty good at covering his tracks, or maybe I was willfully ignorant to how unhappy he truly was with me."

Anger coursed through Nick, so hot and bright he was shocked it didn't light up the house's lower level. A few colorful rugs covered the floor and the cement block walls had been painted a cheery yellow. The washer and dryer were positioned on one wall with bins and storage shelves taking up most of the space on the other. Leave it to Brynn to make even a dreary basement look inviting. "Daniel's behavior wasn't your fault."

Her shoulders stiffened. "There's a baby upstairs whose presence in my house—in the world—would refute that statement. My late husband was adamant he didn't want other children. Apparently, the caveat was he didn't want children with me."

"You don't know the details of his relationship

with Francesca or what he thought about her pregnancy."

She exhaled a sharp laugh. "Thank heaven for small favors."

"I need to call child protective services, Brynn. Probably sooner than later for your emotional well-being."

She'd moved to the back corner of the basement, where gray plastic bins were stacked five high. "What does that mean?" she asked, standing on tiptoes to reach for the top container.

He moved behind her, once again wondering how a person who appeared so small and physically fragile could in reality be such an emotional powerhouse. His arms brushed her shoulders and the warm smell of vanilla drifted around him. Brynn's scent. How was it possible she still smelled the same as she had back in high school?

Okay, Nick wasn't an idiot. He understood how fragrance worked. His mom had been using the same brand of lotion since his childhood, and he'd always associate Olay with her. But this was somehow different, as if the scent were a part of her essence. Silly musing for a grown man.

Brynn shifted slightly, and Nick realized he'd gone still while he tried to untangle the reason her scent affected him on such a primal level. Although they didn't touch, his body cocooned hers in the quiet of the basement, the only sound their breathing and the hum of the furnace in the far corner.

"If you grab the top box," she said after a long moment, "I can get the one I need."

He lifted the container and moved away to set it down, filling his lungs with normal air. Damn if he didn't want to bury his face in the crook of her neck and stay there for as long as she'd let him.

"What did you mean about my well-being?" she asked again, as she handed him a heavy bin, twin spots of color flaming on her cheeks.

"We both know what that baby represents," he said, smacked back into reality once more. "You can't want her here."

At Brynn's shocked gasp, guilt assailed him. But he had to say the words. They both needed to deal with the truth of the situation.

"She's an innocent child without a mother at the moment." Brynn shook her head. "None of this is her responsibility. And she's Tyler's half sister. She's welcome here as long as needed."

"Are you going to tell him?"

She chewed on her bottom lip. "Yes. No. Once we have more clarity about what happens next."

They walked back to the stairs, and Nick stopped before climbing. He placed the bin on the bottom step and turned to face Brynn. She held another container, one labeled *unisex clothes*, as if she'd been anticipating what might come next. He took that tub from her and put it on the cement floor.

"What do you want to happen?" He used one finger to tip her chin toward him when she looked away. "Tell me, Brynn, and I swear I'll do everything in my power to make it come to pass. Anything."

There was a second of vulnerability that flashed in her gaze, like she might truly let him in to help. As if he might finally get a chance to make up for some of the mistakes he'd made in the past. He'd do anything for that chance.

Then she blinked and her gaze shuttered. She elbowed him out of the way and hefted the bin he'd left on the step into her arms. "I want what's best for Tyler and for the baby. It's all that matters."

Chapter Five

Three hours later, Brynn walked into her office at the Dennison Mill with an infant seat hooked on her arm. She'd been working full-time at the shopping area and community gathering place for only a couple of months but already felt a deep commitment to the project's success.

She'd grown up with Josh and Parker Johnson, the two brothers who'd bought and redeveloped the former lumber mill and turned it into a mixed-use space.

Brynn's unplanned pregnancy and subsequent wedding had derailed her plans to go to college like so many of her high school classmates. Daniel had gotten a job working for a local insurance agency while he went to school part-time. Brynn had stayed home with the baby, many hours on her own, and done her best to pick up odd jobs around town. Anything to feel like she was contributing.

She'd thought that would make Daniel happy. For the past decade, she'd worked her butt off to make her marriage a happy one, mostly for Tyler's sake. Still, she wouldn't deny she'd wanted more from her life and her relationship with her husband.

More than he could give apparently.

As much as she'd loved the kids and the staff at the school, it hadn't felt like enough. Certainly not enough to support herself and her son as a single mom.

She wanted something for herself.

Something more.

The job at the mill checked all the boxes, and she'd already planned a makers' market craft fair, a holiday wish list shopping event and a series of concerts by local performers. This holiday season was going to be the most successful she could make it. Josh, who was her primary boss now that construction was mainly complete, seemed to be satisfied with whatever she planned. Brynn wanted more than satisfied. She wanted to prove she could make the mill—and herself—successful.

A lot of her work could be done at home, but she liked to be on-site in order to talk to shop owners and customers. Little Remi stared up at her as she contentedly sucked on her pacifier. Did the baby realize her life had been turned upside down?

Of course not, but Brynn couldn't stop her eyes from pricking with tears every time she looked at the child. What was going to happen to her?

Nick had called a friend at the department of child welfare before leaving her house this morning. He'd convinced the social worker to drag her feet in processing the case, giving them at least the rest of the day to track down Francesca.

There had been no new leads on the missing mom, and Brynn wondered how hard to push to find her. As much as she hated to admit it, Brynn understood Francesca's need to flee. Being a new mother was overwhelming in the best circumstances, but to feel alone and scared could only magnify the anxiety. If Francesca hadn't wanted the baby in the first place, would she truly be able to give Remi the love and devotion she needed?

Brynn set the carrier beside the chair, then sat down at her desk and powered up her computer, forcing herself to put aside thoughts of the uncertain future. She was only going to stay at the office for a few hours, if Remi cooperated, and needed to get as much done as she could.

She logged on to her work email and her gaze immediately snagged on a message that was timestamped an hour earlier. The subject line read *Remi*.

Heart hammering in her chest, she clicked on the

message. It was from Francesca, as she expected. The note explained Daniel's death had left a gaping hole in her heart and she couldn't imagine raising his baby on her own. She wrote that she needed time to gather her emotions, but in her current state of mind, she believed it would be better for Remi to be raised by people who could truly devote themselves to her.

Brynn forwarded the message to Nick's work email account and then pulled out her phone and texted him to let him know she'd sent it and that Francesca specifically asked for privacy to make a final decision in her own time.

Tyler's sister had been orphaned by her mother.

It wasn't a shock. Brynn had known deep in her heart Francesca wasn't going to come back and claim her baby. But she hadn't wanted to believe it, refused to consider what this meant going forward. Before she could truly process the ramifications of the inevitable truth of the situation, there was a knock on her office door.

She glanced up to find Mara Johnson waving from the doorway. Mara's hazel eyes widened, and her smile disappeared.

"What's wrong?" she asked, as she let herself into Brynn's office and closed the door behind her. "Has something else happened? Did they find Francesca?"

"I read an email she sent early this morning."

Brynn swiped at her cheeks even as she glanced at the little girl. "She's adamant about giving up the baby. I don't think it's postpartum depression. The email... She sounds resolute but sad and asks for time to contemplate the future. How can she feel resolved around something like this, Mara?"

"I don't know, hon." Mara came forward and gave Brynn a tight hug. "I can't imagine it, but know we're all here to help you and Tyler with whatever you need."

"Oh, lord," Brynn said with a laugh. "I must be a bigger mess than I thought if you're hugging me."

Mara stepped back. "I hug people. I'm warm and caring. A regular Mother Teresa." One corner of her mouth twitched because they both knew that, although Mara had a huge heart, her outer layer was as prickly as a porcupine. "Okay, the truth is you look like hell. Desperate times and all that."

"I appreciate the hug." Brynn gestured to the baby. "Look at her. She's so innocent and now so alone. I don't even know how to process any of this, and I've become quite the expert on handling untenable situations."

Remi was currently occupied with the toys that hung from the handle of her infant carrier. She swatted at a colorful butterfly, totally unaware of her circumstances.

It broke Brynn's heart.

"She's not alone. She has you." Mara handed

Brynn the brown bag she held. "I'm guessing you haven't eaten this morning. I brought blueberry muffins. You need food."

"Thanks." Brynn opened the bag and inhaled the delicious scent of Mara's freshly baked treats. The other woman might have a tough exterior, but she put heaps of love into every homemade goody she baked for Main Street Perk's two locations—both popular coffee shops owned by her aunt Nanci and Dennison Mill.

Mara had come to Starlight almost two years ago, emotionally scarred from her divorce but determined to make a new life for herself and her five-year-old daughter, Evie.

It probably seemed strange to some of the locals that Brynn's two best friends in town were Mara and Kaitlin Carmody, both women who were newer to Starlight. Being the girl who got pregnant in high school had changed more than Brynn's own life. It shifted how people in town saw her and treated her. Mara and Kaitlin didn't judge her for what had happened a decade earlier, and she need to create relationships with people based on the person she was now instead of who they wanted or expected her to be.

It was a little strange that her two friends had fallen in love with men Brynn had known since elementary school. Finn and Parker also happened to be Nick's two best friends, which made get-togethers with everyone sort of awkward. Good thing Brynn had become accustomed to awkward over the years.

For most of her adult life, Brynn handled things on her own. Daniel hadn't wanted to be bothered with mundane details and she'd had no desire to give her mom any more reason to judge her for the mistakes she'd made. Even after Daniel's death, she'd soldiered on, refusing to admit, even to herself, how his lies and callous treatment of her had worn away at her confidence until she was a shell of the woman she wanted to be. She'd become friends with Mara and Kaitlin over the summer, during an ill-fated stint as a coffee barista at Perk. The job hadn't been a fit, but she treasured her two friends and the unwavering support they gave her.

As she considered what to do next, Brynn broke off a piece of muffin. The sweet and tangy blueberries burst on her tongue, a tiny reminder that as numb as she felt, she was still capable of recognizing the good in life, even if it came in the simple form of a perfect muffin.

"Do you really believe Daniel was planning to leave you for Francesca and the baby?" Mara sniffed. "Your late husband was the worst kind of jerk, but I can't imagine even him leaving behind one family to commit to a new one."

"I don't know," Brynn answered honestly. "I turned a blind eye to rumors of Daniel's infidelity, and that's on me. But the story Francesca told, the way she seemed to love him, I'm not sure what to think at this point."

"You don't know her," Mara commented. "You don't know for certain she and Daniel were exclusive. I hate to say it, but without a DNA test, it's impossible to know whether Remi—"

"She's his." Brynn unbuckled the baby and lifted her out of the carrier. "She looks like him and almost exactly like Tyler did as a baby."

"That isn't a guarantee."

Brynn shrugged. "I'm not sure I can explain it to you, but there's not a shred of doubt in my mind this little girl is Tyler's sister."

"She's certainly a cutie." Mara's frown morphed into a smile as Remi gave her a wide grin. The pacifier dropped from her mouth, and Brynn reached out to catch it before it hit the floor. "I know this is a difficult situation, but it will work out. Once Francesca's parental rights are terminated, a wonderful family will come forward to adopt her. Or maybe there's someone in her family who—"

"I'm keeping her," Brynn whispered, then bit down on her lower lip. The thought had been ricocheting around her brain since she'd seen Tyler holding his sister. This baby was her son's family, and if her mother couldn't take care of her, Brynn would step in to be the mother she needed.

"You can't mean that." Mara blew out an unsteady breath. "Come on, Brynn. I know you have a huge heart, but it wouldn't be right."

Resolve made Brynn's shoulders stiffen. "Why not?"

"She's the baby of your late husband's mistress. A different woman than the one who was in the car when he died. How are you going to explain it?"

"I can't explain most of what I've experienced since the night of the accident."

Remi let out a small cry of distress, and Brynn loosened her hold on the baby. "Great. I'm starting out by squeezing her too tight. That will look amazing in my home study. Not." She patted Remi's back and cooed softly to her.

"Home study," Mara repeated, sounding dazed. "Have you thought about this?"

"I don't need to think. I know it's the right thing." She touched two fingers to her chest. "In here." The baby rested her head against Brynn's shoulder, and she took it as a sign. "I can do this. Tyler and Remi are siblings. It might be unorthodox, but I can give her a good life for as long as she needs me."

Mara shook her head. "I'm still not convinced, but you know I'll support you in whatever you need."

Glancing at her watch, Brynn let out a soft yelp. "Right now I need to get to the meeting about the wish list shopping event with the retail shop owners. I owe them an update on the marketing efforts."

"Let me watch Remi for you." Mara held out her hands. "I have some time before I need to get back downtown. I'll start calling people who might be able to help with baby supplies."

"I don't want to put you out," Brynn protested.

"Don't be ridiculous. I love babies."

Brynn chuckled.

"Okay, the only baby I've loved so far in my life is Evie, but I can handle this little one."

"Thank you." Brynn transferred Remi to Mara's arms. "Things are going great with the holiday campaign, so hopefully I won't be long. There are diapers and formula in the bag if she needs anything."

"Go," Mara urged, as she scrunched up her nose. "So you can get back soon."

Brynn took a deep breath as she grabbed a notebook and headed out of her office toward the banquet space at the end of the hall that also served as a meeting room. She glanced at her phone when it dinged to see a reminder pop up for the date she had tomorrow night. A date she'd no doubt cancel at this point.

If her dating profile had been pathetic before, this morning's turn of events pretty much sealed the deal on the coffin of her love life. Single working mom of a ten-year-old boy in a job she desperately wanted to be good at but felt underqualified for and overwhelmed by most days, plus an orphaned baby added to the mix.

Oh, yes. She was quite the catch. One most men in their right mind would throw back without a moment's hesitation thanks to all of the baggage that came with her.

"You can't be serious."

Nick's glare only intensified when Brynn shoved a microfiber rag and bottle of furniture polish into his hands.

"Be a friend and dust the bookshelves. The social worker will be here in a few minutes. I want her to see this place shine." Brynn glanced around the rarely used formal living room and grimaced. "Or at least I want it to smell shiny."

She'd always had plans to turn this cramped room into something besides the place where her mother's cast-off furniture went to die. The rest of the house reflected her tastes, but this room had been a forgotten item on her to-do list. At least now she had someplace to talk with the caseworker assigned to Remi that was out of earshot of Tyler.

The first thing her son had done when he arrived home from school that afternoon was place a gentle kiss on the baby's forehead. The gesture strengthened Brynn's resolve to become Remi's adoptive mother. She still hadn't told Tyler about his connection to the babe. She had no reason to believe she wouldn't qualify as a potential parent, but until it was more certain, she didn't want to say anything too revealing to her son.

"Your house is fine," Nick told her through clenched teeth. "It's your brain that's out of whack."

"Don't be rude."

"You can't adopt Daniel's mistress's baby." He shook his head. "Listen to how that sounds, Brynn."

She turned to him, hands on hips. "What do I care at this point?" After darting a glance toward the back of the house to make sure Tyler was still engrossed in his video game, she took a step closer to the police chief, who hadn't taken her announcement about her plans to make Remi part of their lives permanently half as well as Mara had.

"Do you know how many awful, pathetic stories around town of wasted potential and stupid choices involve me?" She lifted her hand to tick off her list. "The dumb girl who got knocked up her first time and forced unfortunate, noble Daniel Hale into marriage. Brynn, the pathetic young mom who spent every late night for years scrubbing toilets just to have enough money for her kid's birthday parties and new clothes at the beginning of each school year. Brynn Hale, the wife whose cheating husband was the worst-kept secret in all of Starlight." She leaned in, narrowing her eyes. "And there are heaps of badly kept secrets in this town."

"No one thought poorly of you," Nick insisted.

"Your right eyebrow is twitching."

He lifted a finger to his face. "What does that mean?"

"It's your tell, Nick. It always has been. When you lie, you get twitchy."

They were standing only inches apart, so close Brynn could see the flecks of gold in his brown eyes. His breath smelled like cinnamon gum, and it was like they were swapping childhood secrets all over again.

"I'm not lying." His strong jaw was set as if that could keep the rest of his face in line. "No one who means anything thought less of you because of Tyler."

"Then those same people won't find any fault with my decision about Remi."

"Point taken." His gaze stayed on hers as he reached out and touched the tip of one finger to the back of her hand. The touch was featherlight, but Brynn felt it like a missile had been launched within her body. He spoke the next words in hushed tones. "You've been through a lot this year."

"So has Tyler," she reminded him, trying to ignore his effect on her. "Do you know what having a sister would mean to him?"

"I'm thinking more about what it might do to you. I'm worried about you."

"That's not your job." She took a step away, but he grabbed her hand.

"We're friends. I care about you. I'm going to worry."

Her gaze dropped to their linked fingers. It felt strange—and somehow right—for Nick to be holding her hand. It felt good to be touched by a man, his calloused palm both rough and gentle against her skin.

She looked at him again, only to find his gaze trained on her mouth. The look in his eyes—longing if she had to guess—terrified and thrilled her.

Then the doorbell rang.

The social worker who stood on the other side, Jennifer Ryan, appeared to be in her midforties, a no-nonsense woman with a blunt bob and sharp features. She greeted Nick warmly and then he moved to the far side of the room to give Brynn some privacy with her.

Nerves fluttered through Brynn as she answered the woman's questions about Francesca and her late husband, as well as her current life as a single mom. The baby dozed in her arms, her grounding weight and the warmth of her small body a comfort to Brynn's frazzled nerves. When Brynn explained that she wanted to adopt Remi if Francesca didn't return in order for her to grow up with her half brother, the social worker blinked several times before answering.

"This is a unique situation, but I appreciate your willingness to step in. At this point, you're not approved as a foster parent." Jennifer flipped through the file she held on her lap. "We can begin the application paperwork, but it will take a couple of weeks for everything to be processed. Maybe longer at this time of year."

"But I can keep her in the meantime?" Brynn asked. A thread of panic snaked through her and she hugged Remi more closely. "You can talk to anyone in town about me or go through my closets. Whatever you need to do to put your mind at ease."

"I'm sure Nick would give you a reference, but it's not quite so simple." Jennifer's voice was gentle but firm. "The child must be placed with an approved foster parent. We'd like to keep her in this county, but the closest family available is in Pullman."

"No." Brynn swallowed back her emotions as she looked from the woman sitting across from her to Nick, who had moved to the edge of the sofa. "That's an hour away. We need Remi here with us. With me." Brynn couldn't explain her connection to the baby. She understood it made no sense, but much of her life hadn't since Daniel's death. All she knew was her heart told her keeping this child close was the right thing to do. For all of them.

Nick looked at her with a tortured expression, as if he could feel her pain. "There has to be another way," she said, as much to him as to the social worker.

"I'm sorry." The woman shook her head. "Unless there's an approved—"

"I'll take her." Nick massaged two fingers against his right temple. "I'm a licensed foster parent. Everything is up-to-date."

"Well, then." Jennifer gave a small smile. "Thank you, Chief Dunlap. I'll get the paperwork started and—"

"No." The word escaped Brynn's lips before she could stop it.

Both Nick and the social worker stared at her. "You have an objection to the police chief?"

Wasn't that question more loaded than a dirty diaper? Brynn shook her head. "Not to Nick but..." She turned to him. "You don't want to do this."

Although tension lines bracketed his mouth, he flashed a smile. "I told you I'd do anything to help you." He took the baby from her arms, balancing her far more naturally than Brynn would have guessed. "Remi and I will manage for a few weeks until you're approved." He leaned in. "No twitching at the moment, you'll notice. I want this, Brynn."

"Mrs. Hale?"

Brynn turned to the social worker, her mind dazed by a turn of events that she couldn't have expected even in the midst of so much emotional chaos.

"If there are no issues, I'm going to head out. I'll need you to come into the office for fingerprints.

A background check is standard, as well as an official home visit."

Issues. Yes. She had a million of them, but how could she give voice to a coherent thought when her mind refused to stop spinning?

"Fine," Brynn murmured.

"Thanks for stepping up, Nick." Jennifer stood and patted the baby's back. "I'll email the insurance information to you so you can schedule a routine checkup with a local pediatrician. You have my cell number if there are any problems."

"Appreciate it," Nick replied. "Say hi to your husband for me. I owe him a day of fishing come spring."

"He'll take you up on that."

Nick saw the social worker to the front door while Brynn stood rooted to the spot in the formal living room. She was afraid to move for fear she'd crumble to the ground.

As the door closed, Nick turned to face her again. "That went better than expected."

"Are you joking?" She felt her jaw drop and snapped it shut again.

"We can do this." He bounced the baby in his arms. "It will mean a lot of time together over the holidays, but that's not the worst thing in the world."

She continued to stare. Spending the next few weeks in close proximity to Nick might not be the worst thing, but it might take her down all the same.

Chapter Six

"She's precious, but are you sure you know what you're doing?"

Nick took a long pull off the beer he'd just opened.

"I have no idea what I'm doing, Mom. That's why I called you."

Alice Dunlap frowned, her thin brows pulling together as she glanced around the open-concept living area of his craftsman-style house. "The place will need to be babyproofed," she told him.

"She's five months old. I think the outlets are safe for now."

Alice sniffed. "Better to be safe than sorry."

The overarching mantra of his mother's life had

been choosing safe over sorry. But Nick had so many regrets from his choices, and not only the ones that concerned Brynn.

Top on the list was his brother's death eight years ago from a roadside bomb during his first tour in Afghanistan. Two years older, Jack had been serious and studious as a kid. Nothing like Nick who, much to the consternation of his physician father and town matron mother, hadn't taken anything seriously. Jack had gone off to Georgetown for college but dropped out after his junior year to enlist in the army. It hadn't made sense to anyone back in Starlight, but his brother had claimed that being in DC made him want to do his duty for the country.

Jack had been a true hero and look where that had gotten him. The opposite of safe and leaving everyone sorry in the wake of his death.

Nick had left college to return to Starlight six months later, when a heart attack stole his father's life. All desire to mess around had been obliterated in the wake of the pain he'd caused Brynn followed by the sorrow he felt after losing Jack. He knew he was at best a sloppy second for the role of good son, but he tried. All he could do was try.

"Right." Nick placed the beer on the counter. No sense finishing even one when he had no idea what the rest of the night would bring. "Thanks for rallying your knitting group to gather baby supplies." He gave his mom a genuine smile. "If those ladies were in charge of the world, it would be a much more efficiently run planet."

He'd called his mother from Brynn's house, without giving many details other than he would be fostering a baby girl and needed any type of clothing or furniture items she could round up. His relationship with his mom might not be the closest, but he knew he could depend on her and her network within the community.

"They were happy to help their favorite police chief," she said with a wave of her hand. "Although I'm going to hear about my lie of omission when the truth finally comes out about that baby."

"I appreciate that, as well." He moved toward the table and took the seat across from his mom. Teddy, snored softly on the dog bed situated under the window. "It's not exactly a secret, but I want to give Brynn the chance to tell Tyler the details before it hits the town phone tree."

His mother chuckled. "We text now or use the Starlight Facebook page."

"Even scarier," Nick muttered.

"Brynn is sure about adopting the baby?"

"As sure as I've ever seen her."

"That girl has always been stronger than people give her credit for. She's special."

"Are we talking people in general or someone in particular?"

Alice tapped a finger on the table. "The two of

you were so close growing up. I can remember all the time she spent at our house with you. She followed you around like you walked on water."

"Someone should have told me I couldn't. It would have saved me a lot of time trying not to drown."

His mother's eyes gentled. "You're doing okay."

Okay. Not exactly a ringing endorsement, but he'd take it.

"We both are."

"And Brynn," Alice added. "Especially given all she's been through. What does she think about you fostering the child?"

"She's not thrilled, but it's better than Remi being taken out of Starlight. I don't think she has a lot of faith in me."

Alice raised a brow.

"I'm not the same as I used to be, Mom. Hell, you said yourself, town residents respect the job I do. I'm working my butt off. Why can't people let go of judging me by my past?"

"Are we talking about people in general?"

He shook his head, amused and irritated at his earlier question being posed to him. "I want to help her."

"And you are. You will." Alice reached across the table and covered his hand with hers. She'd turned sixty last year, and while her hands were still delicate, with long graceful fingers and manicured nails, there were also subtle age spots and obvious veins covering the backs of them. Time didn't stop for anyone, even those rooted in the past.

"What are you going to do with Remi while you work?"

"I've called Mimi Briggs to see if she has room in her day care. A couple of the women from the department used her when their kids were little. I trust her." He glanced toward the baby monitor as it crackled on the counter.

"It's a shame to have another disruption for the child." Alice patted his hand. "Why don't I come over during the day and take care of her? At least for the first week."

Nick's heart slammed against his chest. He never would have expected his mom to make that kind of offer. "It's a big imposition."

"It will give me something to do—a good distraction. The holidays aren't my favorite time of year anymore."

Nick nodded. He struggled every year to make sure his mom didn't slip into a pre-Christmas depression. There were so many reminders of his dad and his brother and the traditions they'd had as a family.

A sharp cry sounded through the monitor, and he immediately stood. "I'd appreciate that, Mom." He leaned over and gave her an awkward hug. Nick still found himself unable to release the thought that she'd lost the wrong son. Nick's guilt and his mother's grief had coalesced to form an invisible barrier between the two of them. He loved her, of course, but recognized his love would never be enough to truly help her heal from the losses she'd suffered. "I need to go check on her."

She nodded. "I'll head home unless there's anything else?"

"You've done so much already. Thank you again."

"Nick, you're my son. I'd do anything for you."

Breathing through the rubber band that tightened around his chest, he nodded, then started for the stairs.

Remi was crying in earnest by the time he walked into the spare bedroom where he'd set up the crib his mom borrowed. The tiny wails cut through him, and he wondered at the wisdom of allowing his mom to leave.

What the hell did he know about taking care of a baby? He'd signed up for the foster program after his second year on the job, mostly so he could work with and mentor older kids and teens who might not have another positive role model in their lives. Despite his training, he'd never expected to be called on to serve in this way.

In theory, he knew what he was doing. In reality...

Alone in the quiet of his house, with only a dim night-light illuminating the room...he was as lost as if he'd been dropped into an unfamiliar forest in the dead of night.

He scooped her up and ignored the fact that his hands trembled. Of course, he'd seen friends and coworkers who were parents hold babies. He supported her head with one hand and her body with the other.

There was no funky smell like she had a dirty diaper or another sign of obvious distress. He'd fed her recently, a full bottle. But even as he cradled her close, her squalls became louder and more insistent.

"I wish I spoke baby," he murmured, racking his brain for any random baby-care tips he might have inadvertently picked up. As a single guy, Nick had never paid much attention to babies. He was going to be renting *Mr. Mom* and *Three Men and a Baby* as soon as he had a moment to spare.

Which might not be anytime soon if Remi didn't stop crying. He walked in a circle around the small space in front of the crib, jiggling her the way he'd seen his deputies do with their babies. "Please stop crying. Please stop crying." He said the words over and over and then put them to a melody. His own little desperate lullaby.

Oddly enough, as soon as he started singing, Remi's cries lessened. Nick was so shocked that he stopped, sending her into another fit of wailing.

Could singing be the secret sauce to settling her? He didn't know any kid songs or real lullabies so he launched into a version of his favorite Johnny Cash tune.

Remi continued to whimper for the first verse but by the time he got to the chorus about a burning ring of fire, she'd relaxed against him. Her breath came out in ragged sniffles as if she'd exhausted herself.

Did babies this young have nightmares? Or had she been roused by something—the sound of the old radiator or the house settling—and gotten spooked at being in a strange room.

He couldn't blame her, nor did he have any illusions he was some kind of talented baby whisperer. His voice was gravelly and off-key on certain notes, but the little girl in his arms didn't seem to care.

And all he cared about was the fact that she seemed to be falling back asleep. Not taking any chances, he sang about a fever hotter than a pepper sprout next. At the end, he glanced down and found her sleeping soundly, one small hand curled into the fabric of his flannel shirt.

As gently as possible, he lowered her into the crib once again. He stood watching for almost a minute, until he was certain she would stay asleep.

Then he turned to leave, only to stop in his tracks. His heart beat a wild rhythm against his rib cage as he realized that he and Remi weren't alone.

Brynn stood in the doorway of the bedroom, watching Nick like she was as spellbound by his singing as little Remi.

* * *

Brynn's breath caught in her throat as Nick walked toward her. Emotions assailed her from all directions, but even more powerful was the deep feeling of need that invaded every part of her body.

Without thinking, she reached for him, wrapping her arms around his neck and pulling him close. His hands splayed across her back, their strength and warmth an unexpected comfort. She rested her head on his shoulder and exhaled. The tension that filled her released its hold, and even if it was only for this moment, she appreciated any reprieve.

"Thank you," she whispered, although the words felt like a paltry choice to express how she felt.

She'd gotten to Nick's door as his mother was leaving. Although Alice Dunlap was one of the leaders in what passed for society circles in Starlight, she'd also been one of the few people in town who hadn't seemed to judge Brynn for her unplanned pregnancy. Brynn's mother had deemed Alice a snob and maintained that Nick's mom and her friends looked down their noses at women who weren't part of the town's "in crowd." Unlike her mother, Brynn had always admired Alice's grace and composure, even after enduring the back-to-back deaths of her older son and her husband.

"You're doing the right thing by that child," she'd said, as she gestured Brynn into Nick's house. "Don't let anyone tell you different."

"Nick is the one who saved the day," Brynn had responded and then jolted when she heard Remi's loud crying from upstairs.

Alice had given her a small smile. "He might need a bit of saving himself," she'd said before closing the front door.

Brynn had hurried up the stairs, more concerned for Nick than the baby. Babies cried and a tiny part of her envied Remi the freedom she possessed to let the world know her feelings. But Brynn didn't want Nick to regret his seemingly unplanned offer of help. This wasn't going to be an easy journey for anyone, and she would do everything she could to mitigate any difficulties.

If Nick had doubts about handling a baby, he was keeping them to himself. By the time she got to the small bedroom, he was singing quietly and Remi's cries had subsided. Brynn had stood transfixed by the scene in front of her.

The broad-shouldered, handsome-as-sin police chief crooning to the tiny babe in his arms. Was it possible for a heart—along with ovaries—to actually melt? If so, Brynn's would be in a sloppy puddle around her feet.

They stood together for several minutes, and Brynn drew comfort from Nick's big body and his heat. He felt both familiar and totally new. They'd spent so much time together as kids and teenagers, and she'd been half in love with him for most of her youth. She knew his scent and the way he took a longer inhale then exhale. But their bodies pressed together was a different sensation all together.

She tried to ignore her reaction, the way every inch of her skin tingled. It had been so long since she'd felt this way—if she'd ever felt this way.

On a shuttering sigh, she pulled back, afraid if she let herself stay with him for one more second, she might not have the strength to let go.

Nick didn't release her. Instead, he lifted one hand and smoothed his thumb across her cheek. "Your freckles have faded."

She opened her mouth to answer, but all that came out was a soft puff of air, so she gave a shaky nod.

"Brynn?"

Still no words, so another nod.

"I'm going to kiss you."

At those whispered words, she couldn't even manage a nod. Her body went on high alert. Involuntarily, she licked her lips, drawing a sexy half smile from Nick.

He leaned in, his breath fanning her mouth. "Was that a yes?"

She didn't respond, couldn't make a sound. Instead, she pressed her lips to his, a gentle touch that reverberated through her like a fanfare of fireworks.

A low groan sounded in the silence, and she realized it was Nick and not her. His palm cupped her cheek in the way of kissing scenes from every romantic movie she'd ever watched. She should have guessed that Nick Dunlap would kiss like a movie star.

His mouth grew more insistent, and she gladly opened, inviting him in deeper, caught up in the taste of him and the way the kiss made her come alive.

She'd felt numb for the longest time.

How was it possible to be in her twenties and feel like her lady parts had already shriveled up? Now everything inside her seemed to bloom like desert flowers after a heavy rain.

She wanted this. This moment. This man. So much more.

The thought of more in her already complicated life made warning bells go off in her fuzzy brain. Then Remi let out a small cry in her sleep, which had Brynn yanking away. Nick wasn't for her. She'd learned that lesson years ago and couldn't afford to repeat her past mistakes.

Especially not when the baby sleeping a few feet away needed her. Needed both of them.

He released her without hesitation, color high on his cheeks and his chest rising and falling like he couldn't quite catch his breath.

At least Brynn wasn't the only one affected.

She gave a wan smile and turned for the stairs, hoping he believed her fast retreat was so they didn't wake the baby by speaking.

In truth, she needed time, even a few seconds, to gather her wits. What the heck had she been thinking kissing Nick?

Where could that lead? No place good for her heart or her peace of mind.

When she got to the kitchen, she stopped, then pivoted toward him.

"That can't happen again," she said at the same time he blurted out, "I've wanted that for so long."

Brynn swallowed when it felt like her heart leaped into her chest. "Excuse me?"

"Never mind." Nick dipped his chin and gave a small shake of his head. "You're right. It was a mistake. Forget about it."

He'd wanted to kiss her? That didn't make sense. Nick had barely spoken more than few a pleasantries to her since high school. Of course, their paths crossed in a town the size of Starlight. He'd been one of Daniel's friends. Brynn's friend. But despite the crush on him that had felt so overpowering when she was younger, he'd never looked at her in that way. Or so she'd thought.

She didn't want to forget even if she didn't believe it could go anywhere. Her body hummed with awareness, but she ignored it. If nothing else, Brynn was a master of ignoring what didn't serve her. "Our focus needs to be on Remi," she said, careful to keep the emotion out of her voice.

"Yep," he agreed, his lips barely moving.

"I came over to check on her," she continued. "On both of you. Not for..." She waved her arm between the two of them and then quickly realized it looked like some sort of spastic bird, wing flapping, and pulled it down to her side.

"Understood."

"Your mom let me in."

"I figured."

"And I heard Remi crying so I came upstairs." She forced her lips together. Nick wasn't an idiot so he didn't need her stilted play-by-play.

"I hated hearing her cry that way."

"You comforted her," she reminded him, then exhaled a laugh. "I forgot how much you love Johnny Cash."

"The man in black never fails." One side of Nick's mouth quirked. "Unlike some of us."

"I'm glad your mom was able to help round up supplies."

"She's going to watch the baby while I'm at work." He ran a hand through his hair. "At least until I can arrange other childcare."

"I'll help, too. Of course." She nodded, more to herself than him. "I can't tell you how much I appreciate you fostering her until I can be approved."

"It's not a big deal."

"It's huge." She stepped forward, reached out an arm, then drew it back into her body. Touching him would get her nowhere.

"Have you told Tyler?" he asked quietly.

She shook her head. "I meant to tonight, but every time I opened my mouth, I started to cry. It's ridiculous. I've cried more in the past twenty-four hours than I did after Daniel died."

"It's been a lot to process."

"We both know how things work in Starlight. I have to talk to my son before word gets out about Remi."

"That's part of why my mom is going to stay with her during my shifts," he replied. "She won't say a word to anyone."

"Your mom looks good. Are things okay between the two of you?"

The question felt inadequate given all she knew about Nick's family history. His older brother had been the golden child, leaving Nick in the role of family clown. Brynn had always known there was more to him, deeper wells of emotion and ambition, but he refused to shake his devil-may-care personality. Then Jack was killed and Nick's father had a massive heart attack six months later. Alice sank into a deep depression that was spoken of in hushed tones in grocery store aisles and after Sunday service.

Nick returned to Starlight and became a deputy, quickly earning a promotion when the longtime police chief retired. At the time, Brynn had been busy with a toddler and trying to make something of the cards life had dealt her.

Their paths had gone in different directions, and she'd forced herself to disregard how important he'd been in her life. Her best friend.

At the moment, memories assailed her from every side, especially when he shrugged and offered her the self-deprecating smile he'd perfected at a young age.

"I think so. I'll never be Jack, but no matter how much we both want him to still be here, I think she's come to terms with that. I have."

"You're a good man, Nick. You always have been."

His gaze grew more intense as he studied her. "Not always."

Heat flushed along Brynn's skin. She'd spent a decade believing she was over her feelings for this man, only to discover how quickly they could blossom again.

"Close enough," she muttered, then took a step away. Needing to get out of the house before she did something stupid like launch herself at him. "Mara is at my house, so I should go. Like I said, I wanted to stop by and make sure you didn't need help. Clearly, you're doing fine without me."

"I wouldn't exactly say that." Nick's voice was a low rumble.

"Then neither of us should say anything more."

His expression went blank, as if he understood her meaning but didn't like it. But he followed her to the front door without speaking.

"I'll check in tomorrow," she said at the edge of the porch. "I'd like to spend time with Remi while my foster application is in process so it's not such a big transition for her. If that's okay?"

"That would be good," he said.

"Good night, then." She lifted a hand and he waved in response.

Hurrying down the walk toward her car, Brynn was grateful for the cool night air surrounding her. She needed all the help she could get so she didn't overheat from the desire that stretched like an electric charge between them.

Chapter Seven

"Why can't we keep her now?"

Brynn placed a plate with grapes and a peanut-butter sandwich in front of Tyler, then took the seat across from him at the kitchen table.

"Because the state has a process for approving foster families. She's going to stay with Nick until my application goes through. Are you sure you're okay with this, bud? I know it's a big shock. If you have questions…"

"Would Remi still come to live with us if Dad was alive?"

The possibilities of what the future might have held if Daniel hadn't died ricocheted through Brynn like a bullet, tearing flesh and wreaking havoc on her insides. She kept her features neutral as she met her son's open gaze.

There was no anger or bitterness in his dark eyes. Only curiosity, as if they were riddling out a puzzle together.

"I'm not sure what would have happened, but she's your half sister. That wouldn't have changed."

"Mike DeMarco has a little sister. She's three and always messes with his Legos. She destroyed the Millenium Falcon he built, and it took him like a gazillion hours to finish it."

"We've got some time before Remi could get into your toys, and we'll make sure to put up anything that's special to you, so she knows not to play with it."

Tyler's mouth dropped open and he sat up straighter. "Oh, no, Mommy. We have a big problem."

Brynn braced herself. She suspected Tyler's easy acceptance of the news that Remi was his sister might have been initial shock and not his true reaction to a massive shift in both of their lives.

"Tell me." She nodded. "You can talk to me about any problem."

"Will Santa Claus know to find her here?"

Brynn blinked, then blew out a surprised huff of laughter. "Yes," she assured him. "Santa Claus will know."

Tyler took a big bite of his sandwich and asked around a mouthful of food, "How?"

"Um…" Brynn's gaze caught on Santa's jolly face grinning at her from the dish towel that hung over the handle of the oven. She decorated for the holidays in every room and had probably gone overboard this year, wanting their house to be festive and happy no matter how she felt on the inside.

"The elves will update him," she said finally. "They keep track of all the children around the world."

"Do you think Remi has sent him a letter?"

Brynn shook her head. "I don't think babies send letters to Santa."

"Then how will he know what to bring her on Christmas? Like he's going to know that I want Legos and a remote control race car and a microscope."

"Hold on." Brynn held up a hand. "I don't remember seeing a microscope on your list for Santa." They had a tradition of writing the letter on the day after Thanksgiving. This year it felt like Tyler had taken an especially long time to come up with his list and asked her several times if she thought the items on it might be too expensive.

His concern just about broke Brynn's heart. She'd assured him that the gifts on his list were well within Santa's capabilities and the look of relief on his face was both comical and disturbing. She knew it was only a matter of time before he stopped believing in that particular part of the magic of Christmas. And while it would be a relief not to go through the trouble of hiding gifts and secretly shopping, she wasn't quite ready to check that childhood milestone off the list.

"I added it at the last second before we sealed the envelope and mailed it." He looked embarrassed and a little concerned. "Max stood up in math a couple of weeks ago and yelled out that there's no such thing as Santa. He made Juliana Dalton cry."

"That wasn't very nice." Brynn felt her eyes narrow. She'd like to have a word with Max. "What did you think when he said that?"

"I thought he was a big fat liar," Tyler confided, tearing the crust off the end of his sandwich before taking a final bite. "I told him so, too."

"No name-calling," Brynn reminded him.

"Yeah, I know." Tyler gulped down half his glass of milk, then wiped his sleeve across his upper lip. Good thing Brynn had placed the napkin next to his snack plate. "I thought if I sneaked something on my list that you didn't know about, I could prove Santa was real."

"Well…yes, that would work." Brynn racked her brain for where she'd hidden Tyler's letter when he gave it to her to mail. Normally, she read over it several times during the weeks leading up to Christmas to make sure she didn't miss anything. This year, she was operating on autopilot in most areas of her life, trying to balance her new job with single motherhood and not reveal any of the massive cracks in her armor to the outside world. How many other little things had she missed or overlooked in her need to keep up the facade of normal?

The possibilities were endless.

"Remember, bud, Santa lives in your heart. It's the spirit of Christmas that allows people to believe in him." She stood from the table and moved to give her son's small shoulders a squeeze. "I don't know why Max doesn't believe, but Christmas isn't about proving the truth beyond a shadow of doubt. It's about faith."

She smoothed the hair out of Tyler's eyes as she gazed down at him. "Does that make sense to you?"

"I guess." He pushed back his chair and grabbed his plate off the table. "Can we still write a letter for Remi?"

"Sure."

"Can we go visit her now?"

"Visit?" Brynn swallowed. Nick would be at work and his mom at the house, so maybe this was the right time to go over. In all honesty, she hadn't expected her son to take all of the impending changes to their lives in stride.

"If you bring your laptop, I can show her some toys for babies. Maybe she'll kick her feet or something to tell me what she wants on her list."

"Maybe," Brynn agreed. "You do homework, and I'll call Nick's mom and ask if it's okay that we stop by."

Tyler placed his plate and glass in the sink. "Does Grandma know about Remi?"

"No one does yet." Brynn kept her tone light even when panic flooded her. "But I'm sure people will find out soon, and I'll call your grandma tonight. I wanted you to be the first to know."

Tyler nodded and Brynn appreciated his easy manner, even though she knew he didn't understand the full impact one small baby would have on their lives. Brynn did her best to put aside some money toward Tyler's college fund every month. Now, in addition to providing for Remi, she figured she should start a new fund for both of the children to use for therapy later in life. She couldn't believe things could be this easy. Nothing in her life up until this moment had been.

"I always wanted a little brother or sister," Tyler told her.

A lump formed in her throat. "I didn't know that, bud."

"I have one now, and I'm going to teach her all the things about being a kid." He drew in a deep breath, swallowed, then opened his mouth and let out a loud series of belches. "Like how to burp the ABCs. I got up to *G* the other day at recess."

"Nice work," Brynn told him with a grin. Her mother would tell her to try to curb that kind of behavior, but Brynn figured Tyler had enough of his childhood stolen from him with his father's death.

Why sanction a bit of silly fun? "But stop delaying on the homework."

He groaned. "We're doing times tables in math. I hate multiplication."

She lifted a brow. "It doesn't get done if you don't do it."

"Fine," he grumbled. "I'm going, but you can't make me not hate it."

"I'd never try," she promised. When he'd disappeared up the stairs, she grabbed her phone and sent off a quick text to her mother, asking for Alice Dunlap's cell number.

Within seconds, her mother replied, sending the number with the question WHY? in all caps. Whitney Roberts did a lot of screaming via text. Unlike Brynn, her mother had a big blustery personality and had no problem expressing her emotions. Too bad most of them were judgmental and negative when it came to Brynn.

She responded she had a quick question about the local church choir's Christmas concert. That seemed like an easy enough answer. Alice had been in charge of the concert for ages, and this year the event was being held at the Dennison Mill.

She waited for her mother to reply, to ask about Brynn's job or how she could help with the event. Or to ask about her only grandson or...

The screen remained empty and Brynn cursed the disappointment that crested inside her. She should be used to her mother's disinterest in her life. That didn't make the indifference hurt any less, even after so many years.

With a sigh, she touched her thumb to the hyperlink of Alice's number and lifted the phone to her ear.

The smell of garlic and tomato sauce enveloped Nick the second he opened the door from the garage into his small laundry room. His stomach grumbled in response, a sharp reminder of the chaotic day he'd had and the fact that there hadn't been a minute to stop for a bite to eat since he arrived at the station that morning.

Teddy padded into the room, tail wagging, and nudged Nick's leg, then went to sit by his dog bowl. Nick wasn't the only hungry guy in the house.

In addition to responding to a car crash out on the main highway and a possible burglary at a farm outside town, he'd had meetings with the chamber of commerce and the mayor's communications director. In fact, Nick might still be at work if one of his deputies hadn't agreed to come in early.

Nick hated asking for help, but he also didn't want to burn out his mom on her first day watching Remi. The baby had been asleep when Nick left for work, and the truth was he wanted to see her. Yes, he trusted his mother, but the baby was his responsibility and he was well past the age of shirking his duties.

He walked into the kitchen, but instead of his mother, Brynn stood at the stove, stirring something in a large pot that he assumed was the source of the amazing scent permeating his home.

She wore a Starlight High School sweatshirt and jeans that hugged her curves. Her hair was loose and her feet bare. She looked casual and comfortable and the scene in front of him was the sexiest thing Nick had ever seen.

Damn, he must be getting old if domestication was a turn-on. Although in his heart, he knew the reaction had more to do with Brynn being at the center of it than anything else.

A few feet away, Remi sat in the high chair his mother had procured, contentedly gnawing on some kind of toy.

"Hi, Nick," Tyler called, waving to him from where he was coloring at the table. "Mom's making spaghetti."

Brynn spun toward him, yanking the wooden spoon to her chest like a shield.

Nick cringed as red sauce splattered down the front of her sweatshirt. "Sorry." He held up his hands, palms out. "Didn't mean to startle you."

"I didn't hear you come in." She pointed to Teddy, who'd followed Nick into the main house. "He seems to be a barker when people come to the door."

"He knows the sound of my car." Nick bent and scratched between the dog's ears. "Is my mom here?"

"Not anymore." A blush staining her cheeks, Brynn placed the spoon on a plate next to the stove and grabbed a paper towel, blotting at her sweatshirt. "Tyler and I stopped by to see Remi and while we were here, your mom got a call from Jolie Patterson. Dave fell off a ladder while putting up Christmas lights and Jolie was afraid he broke his hip. Your mom asked if I could stay so she could meet them at the hospital and sit with her."

Nick frowned. "I drove by the Pattersons' a few days ago. They've already got so many lights on the house you could practically see it from space."

"You know how Jolie likes to decorate and Dave likes to make Jolie happy. I'm sorry I didn't think to warn you we'd be here."

"Making dinner," he added, as he moved toward her. He took a clean dishrag from a drawer, wet it under the faucet and handed it to Brynn. "This might work better than paper towels."

"Thanks." She concentrated on the stains on her sweatshirt instead of meeting his gaze. "I'm sorry if making myself at home is a problem. Tyler and I always eat at six, so I thought…"

"It's fine." Nick reached out a hand and tipped up her chin. "My house hasn't smelled this good… well…ever. I love spaghetti."

She chuckled, and the sound reverberated through

him like music. "That was obvious since jarred sauce and frozen meatballs seemed to be the only thing other than condiments in your pantry and fridge."

"Is it almost time to eat?" Tyler asked from the table.

"Yes." Brynn turned to the boy. "Wash your hands and you can help set the table."

"What's sweet Remi doing?" Nick looked more closely at the baby. She was chomping on the plastic toy she held with surprising gusto.

"It's a silicone teething ring that I put in the freezer for a few minutes so it would be cold on her gums."

"Mom said I could help feed her dinner," Tyler announced, as he walked by on his way to the sink. "Since she's my sister and all."

Nick felt the boy's gaze on him, primed for a reaction.

"She's a lucky kid to have you for a big brother, Ty."

That earned a cheeky grin. "Yeah, I know."

"I'm going to change clothes and wash up, too." Nick moved to the high chair and bent to place a soft kiss on the top of Remi's head. She smiled and held out her toy to him. "You keep that, sweetheart. Looks like you're having a grand time with it."

"Any chance I could borrow a shirt?" Brynn asked. "I'm kind of a mess with sauce all down the front of me." Her tone was casual, but Nick could hear something in it. A thread of sensuality that had awareness alighting through him.

"Sure. I'll grab something upstairs for you." He avoided looking directly at her. Despite the shapeless sweatshirt, he had no problem envisioning the curves it covered. Imagining those curves covered by something he wore made his blood run hot. Could he be more pathetic? "Be down in a few."

In his bedroom, he changed out of his uniform and into a T-shirt and jeans. He washed his hands in the bathroom sink and splashed water on his face. A cold shower wouldn't be out of the question at the moment. *Get a hold of yourself,* he chided. There was nothing about this situation that would appear the least bit seductive to an outside observer.

And everyone knew Nick was a committed bachelor. Hell, even the town cronies, who loved to matchmake as much as they loved a rousing night of bunco, had given up on him. One pseudo-family dinner with people who didn't even belong to him would change nothing.

Flannel shirt in hand, he reentered the kitchen, and his breath caught in his throat. All coherent thought dissolved at the sight of Brynn in a thin white tank top, placing plates on the table while Tyler trailed behind her with forks and knives.

Was this how Ward Cleaver felt every time he walked into the house and found June engaged in some mindless domestic task? No wonder the man had seemed so happy during all those late-night kid channel reruns Nick watched with his brother when they were kids.

As if sensing the weight of his stare, Brynn turned and offered a tentative smile. "I hope you're hungry," she said, then bit down on her lower lip. "We really have invaded your space."

"I appreciate the meal." His voice sounded too gravelly, even to his own ears, and he cleared his throat. "Here's a shirt."

Her fingers brushed his as she took it, and he wished he knew if the blush that stained her cheeks was from her reaction to him or strictly a result of working in the kitchen.

"What's your wee sister having for dinner?" he asked Tyler, needing to get his mind off Brynn's body.

"Green beans and rice cereal," the boy answered with a grimace. "So yucky."

"Not to a baby." Brynn put a hand on her son's shoulder. "Concentrate on your food first and then you can feed Remi."

"What can I do?" Nick's stomach rumbled as he took in the inviting spread of food on his normally barren table. A big bowl of noodles, meatballs and sauce sat in the center with a salad and a basket of garlic bread flanking it on either side.

"Do you have salad tongs?" Brynn asked.

"How about two forks?"

She grinned. "Perfect."

He grabbed the utensils and raised a brow in Tyler's direction. "One scoop of salad or two?"

The boy climbed up onto his chair across the table. "None."

"One," Brynn corrected.

Tyler rolled his eyes. "A tiny scoop."

Nick dished out salad to each of them while Brynn filled bowls with the pasta and passed around the bread basket.

"I can't believe you came up with a dinner this good from stuff I had in the house. I didn't realize I'd bought lettuce."

"Your mom told me it was in the fridge. She brought veggies over this morning because she guessed you wouldn't have any."

"Because vegetables are nasty," Tyler offered.

"Amen, little dude." Nick grunted when Brynn's toe connected with his shin. "I mean, not all of them. And they're good for you, so we all need to eat at least one scoop."

He looked at her across the table for confirmation he'd redeemed himself.

Brynn shook her head, but her lips twitched and somehow that felt like a win. He wanted her to smile more, and he wanted to be the man who made her smile.

"Where'd these place mats come from?" He ran a finger along the edge of the woven fabric.

"I found them in one of the drawers."

"Huh." He owned place mats. Who knew?

Remi let out a cry of delight when Brynn dipped a spoon into the small cereal bowl and offered her a bite.

They'd gone over her feeding schedule and the variety of foods she could have at five months with the social worker, but Nick was still relieved to have an actual mother here to oversee the baby's first dinner in his house.

"You like it," Brynn told the girl. "Remi is such a good baby. You're going to grow big and strong like your brother."

"She's even messier than me," Tyler said with a laugh, then shoved half a piece of garlic bread into his mouth.

"Slow down," Brynn admonished gently.

"I want to finish so I can feed her."

"You'll have plenty of opportunities to feed her." Brynn wiggled her eyebrows. "Don't forget diaper duty."

Tyler made a face. "Gross."

"I can confirm gross," Nick told him with a wink. "Last night she had a blowout."

"A blowout," the boy repeated, sounding mesmerized.

"Poop halfway up her back."

"Seriously? Mom, did I ever have a blowout?"

"You were legendary," Brynn answered, laughing. "And your timing was impeccable. Something about the car seat got you moving like nothing else. I can't tell you how many times we'd pull out of the driveway only to pull right back in."

"She gets her blowout talent from me."

Brynn wrinkled her nose. "I'm not sure that's a talent."

"She still takes after me." Tyler shoved a final meatball into his mouth, wiped his hands on a napkin, then pushed back from the table. "Can I have a turn feeding her? I even ate the salad scoop." He darted a wicked side glare toward Nick. "Which wasn't small at all."

"Nice work with the salad," Nick said and Tyler nodded, seemingly mollified by the praise.

Nick ate his dinner and watched as Brynn instructed her son on feeding the baby. As soon as Tyler moved into Remi's line of sight, she squealed with delight and pumped her whole body back and forth, as if a current of electricity coursed through her. It was hard to believe the two of them could have formed a bond in such a short time, but the connection was undeniable.

In the space of one day, Nick's life had been turned upside down. Wednesdays normally meant dart night at Trophy Room. He'd begged off tonight without explaining his reason. Remi's presence would be public knowledge soon enough, but he wasn't up for fielding questions he didn't have the answers to. No one would believe he'd willingly become the foster parent to an orphaned baby.

But no one understood what Brynn meant to him.

He'd denied the feelings for so many years that even he couldn't quite comprehend how quickly she'd once again become essential to him.

It was different than it used to be, and not just because of the divergent paths their lives had taken. He'd been a young, stupid, selfish kid back in high school, his ego preventing him from believing that his life would ever be anything but perfect.

Brynn had been a steady presence in his life, and he'd been an idiot to believe that would never change.

His heart clenched as Tyler dissolved into a fit of giggles when Remi took a bite, then let it dribble out of her mouth.

The baby grinned and smacked her hands against the top of the high chair table.

"I think she's had enough," Brynn said, humor lacing her tone, when Remi repeated the action two more times.

"She's funny," Tyler observed. "Was I a funny baby?"

Brynn gave his cheek a quick kiss. "You could make me laugh harder than anything."

The boy shrugged away from his mom's embrace even though it was clear he enjoyed the attention. "Did I make Dad laugh, too?"

The band around Nick's chest tightened for an entirely different reason as Brynn's smile turned wistful.

"All the time," she answered. "Your dad thought you were the funniest, smartest, cutest baby in the whole world."

"I wish he was here to meet Remi."

"Me, too, sweetie," Brynn whispered, reminding Nick that as perfect as this night felt, this wasn't his family. They didn't belong to him.

In a few weeks, when Brynn's application was approved, Remi would be gone from his home and Brynn would continue building a life with her two children. And Nick would be alone again.

Chapter Eight

Nick looked up from his computer two days later as the door to his office opened. "I'll be done in a…"

He swallowed back a groan as Finn and Parker shot him twin death glares. Finn closed the door, giving Nick the briefest glimpse of the curious stares from his assistant and the deputies in the station's outer office.

"It's not a big deal," he said, pushing the chair away from the desk. No point bothering to pretend he didn't understand why his two friends had cornered him at the station. "I was going to tell you when the time was right."

"There is no right time for you to be fostering

Daniel Hale's illegitimate baby." Parker crossed his arms over his chest, the tie knotted at his neck shifting in the process. Parker's big-city style had relaxed since he'd returned to Starlight, but he still favored tailored suits during the workweek.

"It's not her fault her dad was a two-timing loser." Nick shook his head. "I'm doing this as much for Brynn as for the baby."

"You don't have any experience with babies," Finn reminded him.

"Neither do you," Nick shot back.

Finn handed Nick and then Parker a wrapped sandwich from the brown bag he carried. "Which is why I didn't agree to foster one. Eat the chicken salad and come to your senses, man."

"If you're aware I've got her, then I'm sure you've also heard that Brynn is planning to adopt her if the mother doesn't return."

"Also irrational," Finn said.

"Don't call Brynn irrational," Nick warned. "She's the most levelheaded person any of us know."

"She wants to raise her cheating husband's—"

"Stop." Nick stood. "We all understand the situation. Brynn is doing what she thinks is right for Remi and for Tyler. It's not anyone's place to judge. We need to support her, to support all three of them."

"Did you give that line to Mara?" Parker asked,

shaking his head. "She said almost the exact same thing to me this morning."

"Kaitlin, too." Finn scrubbed a hand over his jaw. "I admire Brynn's devotion to mothering an orphaned child, but I don't like that you're involved."

"Why not?" Nick demanded. "I'm the police chief. My job is to take care of the community."

"Which has nothing to do with it." Parker pointed a finger at him. "She's a baby, Nick. A human being. Someone you have committed to keeping alive for the indefinite future in order to impress a woman."

Irritation made his skin flush hot. "That's offensive to both me and Brynn."

"Not our intention," Finn insisted. "At least where Brynn is concerned. But you, my friend, are not equipped to be responsible for a baby. You know nothing about babies."

"As a matter of fact…" Nick jabbed his finger into the air. "I watched *Three Men and a Baby* last night. Even I know you don't dry a kid's bottom by lifting them over a blower in a public bathroom. Those things spew a crap ton of bacteria into the air."

Parker swatted Finn's arm. "We may have underestimated the severity of the situation. He's talking about germs in public restrooms."

"What the hell is the problem?" Nick demanded.

"Just tell Brynn you're in love with her," Finn shouted.

Nick cursed and stalked around the side of his desk. "Keep it down. The last thing I need is that hitting the gossip train in town, especially when it's not true."

"Come on," Parker urged, running a hand through his thick blond hair. "It's been the same way since high school."

"I feel it necessary to point out that you both spent the better part of the last decade away from this town. Neither one of you know everything that went on with Brynn or with me during that time."

Finn and Parker both had issues with their respective fathers while growing up and had left their hometown for college without looking back. Nick had done the same thing—or at least that had been his plan until his brother died. His two friends hadn't returned to Starlight until this past summer to attend Daniel's funeral. It had been easy to slip back into friendship, but there was no denying all of them had changed in the intervening years.

"Besides, I'm keeping our pact even if I'm the only man standing." He ignored how foolish the words sounded, as if anything could block his feelings for Brynn.

"It's not a pact if there's only one person upholding it," Finn pointed out. He straightened the cuffs of his crisp white button-down. Although Finn had taken over the running of the bank his family owned in Starlight, like Parker, he still dressed the part of a big-city executive with tailored suits and expensive Italian loafers.

But there was no denying his dedication to the town. In the same way, Parker had partnered with Starlight's most accomplished attorney, who'd been waiting for the right moment to transition out of his practice.

Nick couldn't help but feel a tiny bit jealous of his friends. They'd gotten to leave town, experience the world and return on their own terms. It might not have felt like it to them when they first arrived back, but he'd never had the choice to make something of himself outside of who people knew him to be.

He'd changed, and it was more than the uniform he wore or the outward appearance of honor. His role in town wasn't just a job to him, although it had started that way when he'd first come back and joined the department.

He'd come to care, more than he ever thought possible, about the town, its history and future. It got under his skin that his friends didn't think he was capable of taking care of Remi.

Never mind that he would have said the same thing back in the day. "I'm not telling Brynn anything. She's got enough to deal with, and I won't be a complication she doesn't need. What she does need is for me to be her friend. She needs support, and I'm going to give her that."

"You have a second chance with her," Finn urged. "Baby or no."

"No." Nick crossed his arms over his chest and refused to think about what it had felt like to kiss Brynn. The taste of her and her inherent softness. He wouldn't let his own selfish desires eclipse his intention to help her.

His two friends shared a look. "What can we do?" Parker asked after a moment.

He stared at them.

"To help with the baby," Finn clarified.

"To help with whatever you need," Parker added around a bite of sandwich. "We may not agree, but we're here for you."

The band choking his gut eased and he blew out an unsteady breath. "You're probably right about me," he admitted. "I got certified as a foster parent so I could help older kids. I'm unqualified to have a baby in my care."

"So are most new parents." Parker shrugged. "We came in here to give you grief."

"Mainly to see how you'd react," Finn said. "This new, responsible, town golden boy Nick takes some getting used to. We remember the Nick who didn't give a care about anything or anyone."

"A test?" Nick rolled his eyes. "You two weren't the only ones who grew up over the past ten years. I know that a baby is different. You should have seen Brynn's face when she thought they were going to take Remi away from Starlight, even for a few weeks. I owe her after how I treated her in high school."

"She might disagree," Finn said quietly. "Have you talked to her about what happened back then?"

"There's nothing to talk about." Nick couldn't imagine revisiting that time or the pain he'd caused both of them with his selfishness. "I'm going to do my best with Remi until Francesca returns or until Brynn's foster application is approved. She shouldn't be punished for the fact that her father was a jerk."

"You're not alone," Parker reminded him. "You've got Brynn and you've got us. Even Mara was charmed by that little girl, and she's a hard sell when it comes to small creatures."

"But you should still," Finn said with a raised brow, "talk to Brynn about your feelings."

"Hard pass," Nick muttered. "I can't even believe you spoke the words *talk about your feelings*. Hello, Pot. This is Kettle calling."

Finn grinned. "What can I say? I'm a changed man. The love of an amazing woman will do that to you."

"Pass me a barf bag," Nick told his friend, ignoring the stab of jealousy piercing his chest.

"When do we get to meet her?" Parker asked with a grin.

"Brynn asked if I'd bring her to the holiday concert at the mill tonight."

"She's doing a hell of a job with marketing the events. Josh said they've exceeded projections for revenue the past two months and the holiday season is going to be even bigger than expected."

While Parker and his brother, Josh, had worked on getting the mill up and running together, Parker had turned his attention to establishing his law practice in Starlight once they'd had the grand opening. Josh still focused on his construction company but also retained his ownership in the mill.

"It's given her a shot in the arm of confidence. I hope taking on a baby won't deter that."

"You know Josh will give her a flexible schedule. She's not alone and neither are you."

Finn leaned in. "Is this the part where we talk about the fact that Kaitlin and Mara haven't given up on finding Mr. Right for Brynn?"

"She won't have time for dating," Nick observed. "Not with Remi in the picture."

"Are you sure about that?" his friend asked.

"I'm sure." In truth, Nick wasn't sure at all. He assumed Remi's arrival would put everything else on the back burner, but he hadn't actually discussed Brynn's love life with her.

"My wife is determined that Brynn gets another chance at love." Parker popped the final bite of sandwich into his mouth and balled up the paper it had been wrapped in. "When Mara sets her mind on something, look out, world."

A knock sounded at his office door, and Marianne peeked her head in, looking like she wished she'd been a fly on the wall for the past twenty minutes. "Your appointment is here."

"Lunch break is over," Nick announced, tossing the sandwich wrapper into the trash can next to his desk. This conversation had unsettled him more than he cared to admit.

His two friends did the same. "We'll see you tonight," Finn told him. "I don't want to make you all squeamish with talk of emotions or friendship, but know we've got your back."

Parker nodded. "Always."

Anxiety skittered down Brynn's spine as she watched the Starlight residents filing into the open space in the center of the mill. Skittered like a million arachnids tap dancing along her nerve endings. She couldn't tell which she was more nervous about—the first in a series of weekly holiday performances she'd arranged or the thought of Nick bringing baby Remi to the mill and the knowledge of Brynn's plan to adopt her late husband's illegitimate child becoming public.

It was bound to happen sooner or later, and with how small towns worked, she understood that she needed to control the narrative before the gossips got a hold of it.

She'd met her mom early that morning, before Whitney's daily water aerobics class at the community center's indoor pool.

Brynn's mom had taken the news about as well as Brynn expected. She'd stomped around the small kitchen, railing about Brynn's life being dictated by mistakes and Daniel topping the list even after his death.

Then she'd predictably gone down the path of how the news would affect her and the nosy neighbors she'd have to deal with and the judgment she was sure to get from people she counted as friends in the community.

Not once in her ten-minute tirade had Whitney asked about Brynn or Tyler and how they were dealing with this latest revelation of a husband and father's betrayal.

Par for the course, but it still hurt. Brynn wished she could turn that part of herself off. The part that still cared about her mother's disappointment in her.

As she'd done a decade earlier, she would put on her blinders and move forward. Tyler and Remi were her priorities, and she could take comfort in the fact that she was stronger now. She had friends, a support system and proof that she was a survivor.

The trick now was switching from survival mode to flourishing in life.

She waved to Mara, who walked in with Parker, her daughter, Evie, as well as Josh and his daughter, Anna.

Josh, who was both a few inches taller and broader than his older brother Parker, gave her two big thumbs-up, and pride chased away some of her nervous energy.

The interior of the mill had been transformed into a winter wonderland, with strands of twinkling lights, ribbons and fresh greenery from a local nursery. Although the temperature was cold, lines had formed at the three different food trucks parked in front of the main building.

She'd checked and double-checked with Martin Nielsen, the director of the high school honor choir. He displayed a calm disposition and had been the choir and theater director at the school since Brynn was a student there. He'd always encouraged her to participate in extracurricular activities, but she'd been too shy to do anything more than volunteer for the stage crew.

She was about to go look into things with the various shop owners when she caught sight of Nick walking toward the entrance from the parking lot, Remi's infant seat hooked on one arm. From where she stood, it was easy to watch people staring at Nick. If he felt the attention, he did a great job of ignoring it.

Brynn had kept herself mostly hidden. She preferred to work behind the scenes normally, but tonight in particular she relished her role out of the spotlight.

Ignoring her anxiety, she moved toward Nick. The crowd in front of her seemed to part as if people could sense her focus like a palpable force. A few called out greetings, but most simply watched her, curiosity burning in their gazes.

She didn't relish the thought of being the topic of conversation throughout every holiday event scheduled in Starlight over the next few weeks. As much as she knew she shouldn't rely on him, having Nick in this with her did make the whole situation a bit easier.

"Thanks for bringing her," she said, her heart filling as she gazed down at Remi, who was sucking on her pacifier. Nick had covered her with a blanket and put a knit cap on her head so only her face was visible. "How was today?"

"Mom said she slept and ate like a champ. She really is an easy baby."

"You better knock on wood," she told him with a laugh. "Tyler is getting dessert with friends. Let's bring her to my office until the show starts. I told him I'd meet him in front of the stage. He's curious as to what Remi's favorite song will be."

"Can a five-month-old baby have that kind of preference?"

She flashed a smile, still aware of the myriad of gazes on them. "I have no idea."

"Everyone is watching," Nick murmured, his thick brows drawing together. "I know you don't like to be scrutinized. I'd like to tell them to—"

"It's okay." She placed a hand on his arm, squeezing gently. "I'm learning not to care what other people think. It's a lesson I wish I'd mastered a long time ago."

He looked like he wanted to say something more but only nodded and followed her as she made her way through the people gathered.

"Stop glaring," she commanded, glancing over her shoulder. "People are starting to look more afraid than curious."

"Good," he muttered. "Maybe that will stop them from asking stupid questions."

Brynn appreciated the sentiment even if she knew he couldn't stop the curiosity. She unlocked the door that led to the mill's private rooms. At the moment, Josh was basing his construction business out of the location, so in addition to her small office, there were several rooms dedicated to his general contracting company.

Wanting the spirit of the holidays to permeate every inch of the mill, she'd decorated with fresh wreaths and more bows and greenery, so the sweet smell of pine filled the air.

She led Nick into her office and flipped on the

light. He set the infant carrier on the ground, and she immediately bent to unbuckle the baby.

"Hello, sweet girl," she said, kissing Remi's soft forehead. "I missed you today. What a pretty outfit." She'd dropped off the red velvet dress to Nick's mom, along with a dozen other pieces of clothing she'd bought. She knew Francesca could return, and nothing was certain, but Brynn already felt like the baby belonged to her. "I want to hear all about your adventures."

Remi gurgled in response, then grinned as the pacifier dropped into her lap. "Did you really? And then what did she say?" Brynn asked, lifting the girl into her arms.

"Um…did you actually understand her babbling?" Nick asked, sounding astonished.

Brynn shook her head as she held the baby close. "I used to talk to Tyler the same way. For some reason, it felt like asking him questions made him more vocal."

"You're a regular Dr. Spock," Nick murmured.

She chuckled. "What do you know about Dr. Spock?"

"My mom left the book on my nightstand. I'm not sure she took into consideration that between my normal work schedule, the extra shifts I volunteer for the weeks leading up to Christmas and taking care of a baby, my only choice might be winging it."

"I'm sorry," Brynn said automatically. "I know this is a lot for you and you volunteered because—"

"Because I wanted to help." He reached out a finger and pressed it to her lips. She felt the touch all the way to her toes. "There's nothing you need to apologize for, Brynn. Ever."

"I'm not perfect, Nick."

"Damn close," he whispered, then looked genuinely surprised when she narrowed her eyes. "Um… that was a compliment."

"I've made mistakes," she said, shifting the baby to her other arm and popping the pacifier into Remi's mouth. "I can be selfish and petty. A lot of times I make decisions based on avoiding conflict instead of taking a stand. My marriage was a perfect example of that."

"You can't blame yourself for anything that happened with Daniel."

"I can blame myself for being a doormat," she countered, then raised a hand when he would have protested. "I don't want to be on anyone's pedestal, either."

A muscle ticked in his jaw as he stepped closer. "What do you want?"

You, her body screamed. If only she had a roll of duct tape, she'd use it on her traitorous lady parts. Where the heck was a self-preservation instinct when she needed it?

"I want to be seen for who I am, flaws and all."

Before he could answer, she stepped around him.

"I need to get back out there before Tyler starts looking for me. Thank you, Nick. Thank you for everything."

Chapter Nine

If ever Brynn needed a reminder that her life had turned out exactly how it was meant to, the holiday concert served that purpose.

Not only had she been surrounded by friends the moment she and Remi walked back into the throng of people, but Mara and Kaitlin had stayed at her side the entire night. They were like two sentry guards, ready to attack if anyone dared come forward to give her grief for wanting to take in the baby her late husband had fathered with one of his mistresses.

Tyler had bounced up to her before the start of the concert, seemingly unaware people might have a reason to frown on her decision to keep Remi. He'd proudly introduced his two best friends to his new sister.

To Brynn's surprise, several parents she knew from the elementary school also approached to coo and fuss over the baby. Remi preened under the attention, offering charming baby smiles, then tucking her head against Brynn's shoulder when she felt shy. By the time the music started with "Santa Claus Is Comin' To Town," she felt far more relaxed than she had in a long time.

She purposely didn't look around to make eye contact with anyone who might not approve of her decision. Instead, the knowledge that she had a core group of people to support her bolstered her confidence. In addition to Mara and Kaitlin, Parker and Finn stayed close. She could feel Nick behind her even though she didn't turn around.

As the popular holiday songs and carols continued, she could sense the audience was totally enamored with the performance. Although the show was free, they were accepting donations to go toward a spring break trip for the honor choir. After three songs, Martin paused to introduce the soloists and give background on the choir, including a plug for donations.

Then Josh took the makeshift stage to thank everyone for coming and for the support of Dennison Mill. As Brynn had worked out with the business owners, he announced a calendar of daily discounts for the different shops and explained that the mill would be donating to various local charities as a thank-you to each group performing throughout the holiday season, including five-hundred dollars toward the choir's spring break trip.

Brynn smiled as the students on stage cheered and the crowd applauded. This was exactly the reaction she'd wanted. Part of her plan to make the Dennison Mill project a success was positioning them as a community partner.

"I'd also like to give a special shout-out to the person whose tireless work has made all of this holiday hoopla possible."

"Oh, no," Brynn whispered, starting to take a step away.

"You can't run away," Nick said, his breath warm against her ear. He placed a steadying hand on her lower back. "You've earned this."

Blood pounded in her head as Brynn listened to Josh's praise. She knew she was doing a good job, or at least trying her best. But Brynn wasn't used to being singled out in this manner.

If people weren't looking at her before, she was the center of attention now. Tyler stepped closer and even Remi seemed to notice, pausing as she sucked on her pacifier.

When Josh finished, the thunderous round of applause had tears pricking the backs of her eyes. Yet, she could also imagine the comments and questions that would come as she stood there holding a baby who didn't yet belong to her.

"Keep smiling," Mara told her, as if sensing her nerves.

Kaitlin wrapped an arm around Brynn's shoulder. "We're all so proud of you."

Brynn mouthed a thank-you to Josh and then the concert continued. She felt both proud and overwhelmed.

"Let me take her for a minute," Nick said when Remi began to squirm. Mara was watching as Parker danced with Evie and Anna, and Finn had wrapped his arms around Kaitlin, gently swaying to a holiday classic.

She forced herself to meet his gaze as he lifted the baby from her arms. "Everyone is going to be talking about me."

"Because you kicked butt here tonight."

"That's not the reason, and we both know it."

His gaze gentled and he quickly squeezed her fingers. Subtly, so no one watching would notice. "I thought you were done caring about what other people thought about you."

"I was at the moment we discussed it." She rolled her eyes. "I wish it were so easy to stay strong."

"I know," he said quietly, and the understanding in his tone was a bigger comfort than she could have guessed. "I also know you're not perfect. Remember, I was the one who watched you fling boogers across the room while we played video games."

"Oh. My. God. I never flung boogers." Brynn shoved him, but it was like trying to move a mountain. His strength reminded her he'd changed as much as she had over the years.

"If only we'd had camera phones back in the day."

At that moment, the choir began a rousing rendition of "All I Want for Christmas." Remi let out a squeal of delight, pumping her arms and legs.

Tyler grinned at the baby. "Is this one your favorite, Remi?" he asked in a singsong voice.

More squealing and toothless grins came from the girl.

Tyler smiled at Brynn. "I knew she'd tell us her favorite."

"Wow." Brynn placed a hand on her son's head. "You know her well, bud." She shared a look with Nick, who appeared as flabbergasted as she felt that Remi indeed seemed to have an opinion on a favorite Christmas song.

The baby giggled as Nick began to sing along with the choir, sliding back and forth as he danced with her.

Tyler and his friends sang, too, along with Anna and Evie.

Brynn's breath caught because she was happy in a way she hadn't been for as long as she could remember. She knew things wouldn't always feel as easy as they did at this moment. The push and pull of disappointment and joy were familiar companions to her, both of them a comfort in their own way.

But she'd also been through enough to grasp on to pure happiness when it offered itself up like the bloom of a Christmas cactus, a wonderful surprise after so many months of lying dormant. Instead of worrying about what tomorrow might bring, she began to sing along, letting the words of the song remind her of the magic of the season.

The clock on the nightstand read 4:30 a.m. when Nick woke Monday morning to the sound of his cell phone's insistent ringing.

Groggy with sleep, he picked up the device, his gut clenching when he read the name of the incoming caller.

"Barrett," he said, as he accepted the call from Starlight's fire chief. "What happened?"

"She's okay," Kellen Barrett answered, then coughed as if he'd inhaled smoke. "They're both okay, Nick."

Nick's mind raced with the possibilities of what the other man wasn't telling him. "Who?" he demanded. "What the hell is going on, Chief?"

"There was a fire at Brynn Hale's house tonight. We think it started when a faulty strand of lights overloaded an electrical socket."

Nick let out a stream of curses so colorful it would have made a hardened sailor blush.

"I'm going to need you to keep it together," Kel said on a sigh. "You two are close—or whatever you'd call it—so I thought you'd want to know."

"Yeah." Nick was out of the bed and pulling on a pair of jeans. "I'll get over there as soon as I can. You're sure Brynn and Tyler—"

"Shell-shocked but fine. The fire spread to the kitchen before we could contain it, so the main floor of the house is a mess, but no one was hurt."

"Thanks for the call, Kel," Nick said. "I'm on my way."

He grabbed a sweatshirt from the chair next to his dresser and was halfway down the hall when he realized he couldn't go anywhere without Remi.

He blew out a shaky breath and thumped his fist against his forehead. In his panic over Brynn, he'd almost forgotten the baby in his care.

What kind of an idiot forgot a baby?

Brynn would have his head if he disturbed the girl's sleep, so he punched in Finn's number. He and Kaitlin lived closer to town than Parker, so they could be at Nick's house sooner.

His friend picked up on the third ring, sounding as sleepy as Nick had felt a few minutes earlier. Like Nick, Finn woke up immediately as he explained the situation in succinct sentences. They disconnected, and Nick paced the length of his first floor, imagining the fear that Brynn and Tyler must have felt to wake up to their house in flames. His heart twisted as a thousand horrible might-have-beens raced through his mind.

He tried calling her twice, but both times it went straight to voice mail. For all he knew, her phone was still inside the house. Kel wouldn't lie about her being fine, but Nick would only feel secure when he saw her for himself.

It felt like hours before he heard Finn's car pull up to his house, but in reality only eight minutes had passed.

Finn and Kaitlin rushed toward the front of the house as Nick opened the door. "I'll try to be back before she wakes up. In case I'm not, there's formula in the fridge, and I put the dry rice cereal she has for breakfast in a bowl on the counter. Just add water to that and heat the bottle—"

"I've got it," Kaitlin interrupted, placing a hand on Nick's arm. "Go."

With a terse nod, he headed for the garage.

"Give us any updates you can," Finn called after him.

"Take care of her," Kaitlin added.

With my life, he promised silently.

The few minutes it took to get to her house felt like an eternity. He drummed his fingers on the steering wheel and glanced at his phone every few seconds. Maybe a text would come through. Another call. He needed to hear her voice.

As he drove through Starlight's darkened streets, Nick noticed how many houses had left their lights on overnight. Plastic holiday figures still glowed in the night, and he could see a number of Christmas trees shining from front windows. He'd need to talk to Kel about posting to the town's social media accounts about holiday-decorating safety.

As he rounded the corner to the block on Maple Lane where Brynn lived, the glow of a fire truck's lights flashed ahead of him. His heart stuttered at the sight of an ambulance parked at the curb. He parked directly behind the emergency vehicle, then jumped out of the truck.

"Sir?" A young man, who Nick didn't recognize, wearing a firefighter's uniform approached him. "You can't be—"

"It's fine, Jacob. Chief Dunlap belongs here."

The firefighter enthusiastically nodded. "Sorry, Chief."

Nick nodded to the young man and then turned his attention to Kel. "Where is she?"

"Tyler wanted to check out the control panel on the ladder truck. They're on the far side."

Nick stared at the house as he moved past the two firefighters. It looked normal from the exterior, other than the firefighters moving in and out.

He walked around the front of the fire truck, his

heart hammering, then stopped in his tracks. Brynn stood next to the truck with a blanket wrapped around her shoulders. Her hair was tucked behind her ears and she had a gray smudge of soot across one cheek. And she was smiling. Not a fake stiff grin like she was struggling to hold it together.

He took another step forward and saw Tyler flipping instrument levers while two firefighters stood nearby.

"Brynn."

She turned at the sound of his voice and for a brief instant the emotion that appeared in her gaze overwhelmed him. He saw fear and vulnerability and she swiped at the corner of one eye even as she forced a smile back into place.

"I'm okay," she whispered.

He walked forward, laughing that he'd thought it would be enough to see that she was fine and hear her voice. He needed more. He needed to—

She met him halfway. The blanket fell to the ground as he gathered her close. Once again, she fit perfectly in his arms.

"You're okay," he said into her hair, which smelled like smoke.

"I just said that," she told him with a shaky laugh.

He leaned back, cupping her hand between his palms. "Don't scare me again."

He saw her throat work as she swallowed. "I woke up and smelled smoke. It was heavy, Nick, like sand in the air. The smoke alarms went off a moment later. I don't know what took so long. Tyler was still asleep. I had to pull him from the bed."

"You did a good job, honey."

She shook her head. "The flames were everywhere. Or at least that's what it seemed like. There was heat and smoke, and I didn't know if we'd make it out." Her body went stiff in his arms. "Maybe I'm exaggerating, but that's what it felt like to me. It felt so hot, Nick. And I'd done it."

"You didn't set fire to your house, Brynn. You can't blame yourself."

"Of course I can." Her eyes went even wider. "I was the one who left the lights on and plugged so many of them into one outlet. Lights that shouldn't have been strung up in the first place."

"You have a Christmas tree with lights. So does most of the town, and I can tell you that a lot more people than you keep them on overnight."

"You don't understand."

"Nick, look at me!"

Nick turned as Tyler waved from the side of the truck. Brynn pulled away, crossing her arms over her chest. He felt the loss of her all the way to his bones.

"Hey, buddy."

"I got to turn the lights on and off." He ran forward. "But the Christmas tree blew up, and now we're going to have to live with Grandma." He made a face. "Her house smells like old socks."

"Your mom told me you were very brave."

He heard Brynn draw in a sharp breath. "You were very brave," she repeated, her voice trembling.

Without thinking, he moved closer to her, hoping to offer whatever comfort he could. "You were both brave." He turned toward Brynn. "Why would you have to live with your mother?"

"Nick, look at the house. Kel says—"

"The kitchen and family room will need to be restored." The fire chief approached from the back of the truck.

Tyler, who'd moved next to Brynn, didn't look quite as jubilant as when he'd been on the side of the truck. "Do you think my Legos survived?" he asked, a catch in his voice. "I finished building the space station yesterday."

"Maybe," Kel offered. "Things need to cool off a bit and then we can assess."

"Hey, Kel, has Tyler been up to the top of the truck?" Nick gave the fire chief a pointed look.

"Would you like to climb up?" The other man placed a hand on Tyler's shoulder. "I'll even let you."

Tyler sniffed and glanced at his mom for approval.

To her credit, Brynn's smile was genuine. "That's a great idea, bud." She bent and hugged her son. "I know it will be a huge bummer if your stuff got damaged, but stuff is replaceable. You're not. All that matters to me is we made it out safely. We also need to thank Chief Barrett and the rest of the fire crew for getting here so quickly. Things could have been a lot worse."

"Thanks," Tyler dutifully told the chief.

"My pleasure, son." Kel led the boy around the truck, the word *son* reverberating through Nick's chest.

Tyler had no father.

"Have you talked to your mom yet?" He bent his knees so he was at eye level with Brynn.

She shook her head.

"I know you don't want to move back in that house."

"What choice do I have?"

"Mara and Kaitlin—"

"Have lives of their own. I won't be a burden to them."

"Neither of them would consider you a burden."

"We'll be fine at my mom's," she insisted even as she cringed. "Hopefully Josh will have a crew over here quickly. Maybe we'll be back in by Christmas?"

"Stay with me," he said on a rush of breath.

Her lips parted. "You don't mean that."

He shouldn't make the offer. Not with how being near Brynn affected him. It was hard enough planning to see her regularly because of Remi. Having her under his roof would be like slow torture. Reminding him of all the things he didn't—couldn't— have in his life.

"I do," he said because clearly he had an emotional death wish. "I have the extra rooms and it will be good for Remi. You won't have to go back and forth between my house and yours to see her. Tyler would love it."

She shook her head. "I'm not sure, Nick. What will people think?"

"Who cares? It's the right thing." Now that the idea had taken root, he couldn't seem to shake it. He knew this rediscovered closeness with Brynn would most likely stop when her foster application went through. The built-in end date made the whole thing almost irresistible. "No one can deny the connection Tyler has with Remi but visiting a baby for an hour or so is different than having one move into your house. This will get him used to the day-to-day business of sharing you and his home in a place that's neutral for him."

"You sound like a counselor." The barest glimmer of a smile played around the edges of her mouth. "When did you get so smart, Chief Dunlap?"

"I was born this way. You never noticed before now because you were too dazzled by my good looks."

Her eyes went wide for a moment, and he wondered if he'd overstepped with the teasing. "I was dazzled by you. That part is true." She rolled her eyes. "But I guarantee you didn't show this kind of insight when we were younger."

He should make some funny comment back to

her, keep the moment light. Instead, he let his gaze lower to her mouth as he took the soft ends of her hair between his fingers. "I might not have messed things up so badly if I had."

She drew in a sharp breath and he stepped away. This was not the time to spook her. "Come on, Brynn," he coaxed. "We both know it's not going to be good for anyone if you stay with your mom."

"She doesn't even want to meet Remi," Brynn told him, her full lips pressing into a thin line.

"Her loss," he said quietly. "All along it's been her loss. Say yes. Please."

She shifted and looked to where Tyler had disappeared with Kel. Without turning back to Nick, she nodded. "Yes," she said finally. "Thank you for the offer. I appreciate it and promise we won't disrupt your life." Now she did turn to him. "Very much anyway," she added with a smile.

"Easy as pie," he said, ignoring the fact that his heart was beating as fast as if he'd just finished running a marathon.

Chapter Ten

"It's no big deal," Nick told Remi later that morning. "She's a friend, and I'm doing her a favor. Nothing more."

The baby hopped up and down in the jumping seat he'd affixed in a doorway. She chewed on her fist, drool pooling around her chubby fingers.

"No one believes me," he continued, taking her silence for agreement. "This isn't about my feelings for Brynn. I'd make the offer for anyone."

Remi gurgled and bounced with enthusiasm.

"Okay, maybe not for Cyndi Jennings." He stared at the baby, hands on hips. "When the candle burned down her living room, I wasn't about to offer to move her into my house. She kept telling me how limber she was because of her gymnast history."

When the baby continued to bounce, her attention now focused on the ceiling, Nick let out a sigh. He'd thought it strange when Brynn talked to Remi like she could understand, but he found himself having one-sided conversations more often than not.

Remi might not be able to respond with words, but it still felt like she was a good listener.

Voices at the front of his house had him moving toward the door. Teddy barked and trotted along at his side. "Best behavior," he warned the dog. "We're both going to be on our best behavior while they're here."

The black Lab whined low in his throat.

"No matter how hard it is for either of us."

He opened the door as Kaitlin walked up the porch steps followed by Tyler holding a pillow tight between his arms and carrying a backpack that looked like it weighed about as much as he did.

"Can I help?"

"Is Remi awake or napping?" Tyler asked, scratching Teddy's soft head.

"In her jumper seat in the kitchen. If you want to go check on her, I'll help your mom unload the car."

"There's not much," Kaitlin told him. "She only packed enough for a few days. I think she's still hoping that Josh will perform some renovation miracle."

"If anyone can, it would be Josh, but I doubt it."

"It was nice of you to let her stay here." Kaitlin looked over her shoulder. "Finn and I would have been happy to have them but…"

"She has a hard time accepting help." Nick sighed. "I've known her long enough that I could get away with bullying her into it."

"I doubt you bullied her," Kaitlin said with a laugh.

"I think Remi being here sealed the deal. You can put the suitcases at the bottom of the staircase. I'll get the rest."

She nodded but her brows drew together as if she wanted to say more. Whatever it was, Nick didn't want to hear it, so he jogged down the front walk to Brynn's compact Toyota.

The sun was just rising, and a light wind had picked up, reminding him that although it didn't snow often in this part of the state, winter was fully on its way.

"You travel light," he said, offering her a smile, which he noticed she didn't return.

"I ruined it." She tugged her lower lip between her front teeth. "A few weeks before Christmas and I've ruined everything."

The pain in her voice made his heart hurt. He grasped her arms and squeezed. "Nothing is ruined, Brynn."

"Tyler's already been through so much this year and now we're going to be displaced for Christmas."

She tried to laugh but it came out sounding more like a sob. "Imagine the years of therapy he's going to need to process all of this. I'm the worst moth—"

"Don't say that." He placed a finger to her mouth. "You're a fantastic mom. Yes, he's had trauma, but you're seeing him through it. If he needs counseling when he's older, you'll support him through that, as well. Hell, I see enough people in my job that could use someone to talk to. There's no shame."

She swiped at her cheeks. "I'd never make him feel ashamed. Unfortunately, I'm another story."

He could see the dark circles under her eyes and the sharp pull of worry at the corners of her mouth. "You're exhausted, sweetheart."

"Great. On top everything else, I look like crap."

"I didn't say that." Nick let her go and picked up a duffel bag as she closed the trunk. "You're always beautiful. But a fire is upsetting for anyone. Let's go inside, have something to eat and then you and Tyler can get some rest."

"Nick."

"Yes?"

"You don't have to do that."

"What?"

"Call me beautiful." She strapped her purse to one shoulder and began to wheel her suitcase up the walk. "It's the second time you've made the comment in the past week. I've never been beautiful, and at this point in my life, I don't care. You don't have to try to placate me."

"I'm a lot of things," he told her, as he followed. "But I don't lie, and I won't blow sunshine up anyone's skirt. Even yours. I'm telling you you're beautiful because it's true, Brynn. Whether you choose to believe me is on you."

They got to the porch and he grabbed the suitcase's handle when she would have lifted it. "Let me get that. You and Tyler will be staying upstairs. I moved Remi to the sitting room so Ty can have the spare bedroom and she'll be across the hall. You'll have the master."

"I can't take your bedroom," she said, sounding shocked that he'd made the suggestion.

"It's already done." He entered the house and gave Teddy a quick scratch between the ears. "I've moved my things to the office on the first floor. It has a pullout couch."

"Nick, no."

"Mom, come and watch Remi jump," Tyler hollered from the kitchen.

"Go ahead," Nick said with a smile. "I'll bring the bags upstairs."

"Leave mine down here," she told him. "I don't mind the pullout."

Like hell he was going to put her on a lumpy sofa-bed mattress. Nick could sleep wherever, so the arrangement suited him fine.

"Mom!"

"Coming," she called. "We're not done with this discussion," she said to Nick's back.

She could discuss it until the cows came home. Nick wasn't going to change his mind. It took two trips to transfer all of the luggage upstairs. He deposited it in their respective bedrooms, replacing the pillow in the spare room with the one Tyler brought. He wished the boy had more things to make him feel at home.

He made his way back downstairs as Kaitlin was leaving.

"Thanks for your help," he told her. Her car was parked at the curb in front of Brynn's.

"If this doesn't work out, she's welcome with us." She gave him an expectant look. "I know Mara and Parker feel the same."

"She's fine here."

The blonde didn't look convinced. "Finn says you're in love with her," she said in a hushed tone. Her hand tightened on the doorknob.

"Finn talks too much," Nick grumbled. "Brynn and I are friends, and I haven't been a very good one. I'm making up for lost time."

"She needs someone who will put her first in his life." She studied Nick. "Mara and I still have a number of potential suitors in mind."

"Suitors?" Nick choked out a laugh to hide the irritation that flamed in his chest. "Is this the eighteenth century? I'm sure Brynn is plenty capable of finding herself a date if she wants one."

"She wants one." Kaitlin clearly wasn't going to argue the point. "We promised her twelve dates before Christmas."

"I heard," he muttered.

"She's been on two so far."

He wondered if the pretty blonde could hear his teeth grinding. "I know."

"We discussed the number of dates but not who she'd go out with. The point isn't for her to meet a dozen different men. I'll admit Mara and I hoped she'd meet a nice man and have multiple dates with him." Kaitlin leaned in closer like she was telling him a secret. "With her Mr. Right. Any ideas of whom that might be?"

Nick's breath stuttered to a halt in his lungs. He couldn't imagine Brynn's friends would think he'd make a good match. Not when Finn and Parker understood how badly he'd treated her in high school. And they knew about his vow regarding love. Dating and a moratorium on love didn't exactly go hand in hand.

"I'm not right for her." The words sounded rough as they rolled off his tongue.

"She's got a lot going on right now," Kaitlin said as if he hadn't spoken. "It would be nice if someone she trusted could help her enjoy the next few weeks. She deserves a special Christmas. She and Tyler both."

He nodded. "Yeah, they do." Maybe he wasn't perfect or right for her, but he'd vowed to himself to help her through this Christmas. Maybe the fact that her friend seemed to support the idea meant he wasn't so ill-fitted for the role, after all. At least temporarily. "I'll do my best."

Kaitlin gave him a slow smile. "That's all anyone can do."

Brynn stared at the ceiling of Nick's bedroom late that night, wishing she could fall asleep. She was afraid to nod off to dreams of Nick and then wake in the morning alone in his bed.

She was lying in Nick's bed. They'd argued about where she should sleep, but in the end, it had been Tyler who'd convinced her to give up the fight. As the boy's bedtime had drawn closer, he'd gotten an almost haunted look on his face. The same look she remembered from the weeks after Daniel's death. He'd taken her hand and asked how far her bedroom was from the one he was staying in.

The vulnerability in his eyes had torn her heart open all over again. She'd offered that he could sleep in the bed with her, but her sweet, brave son had insisted that he'd be fine in his own bed.

Nick had told the boy they were safe, and that Nick would be right there if anything happened or if Brynn, Tyler or Remi needed him. Tyler had listened intently and then let out a heavy sigh, his shoulders deflating as if they'd been carrying a heavy weight.

He'd put on a brave face when she picked him up from school earlier that afternoon to pack his bag and move what was salvageable from the family room. Tears had lodged in her throat as she'd taken in the damage from the soggy carpet to the smoke-stained furniture.

After meeting with the insurance agent, she'd spoken with Josh at the mill and he'd promised to start the restoration work as soon as possible and that his crew would make the house even better than it had been.

Better was good but with all of the changes pummeling them, Brynn could have done without updated appliances if it meant a little consistency in her world.

She threw back the covers and placed her feet on the thick rug that took up most of the floor. How in the world was she supposed to sleep with Nick's scent surrounding her all night? He'd told her the sheets were clean, but under the freshness of laundry detergent was his smell. She'd hung her clothes next to his in the closet, and it had taken a monumental effort to resist burying her face in his shirts.

Her body felt charged with electricity, and tonight was only the beginning.

No, she scolded herself. She would not freak out about Nick's smell or the way his laugh rumbled through her when he reacted to the jokes Tyler liked to tell.

But she appreciated being able to put Remi down for bed and then tuck in her son without having to get in her car and drive to a different house.

Nick had been right that being together would make them feel like a family. Remi was a great distraction for Tyler, a silver lining in the dark cloud of the fire damage. If only Brynn didn't notice how well Nick fit into their little family.

She straightened from the bed and slipped across the hall, quietly opening the door to Tyler's bedroom. Her son was sprawled across the mattress, the raggedy stuffed bear he'd packed clasped in his arms. Cleo had been his favorite lovey since he was a baby, although now the well-worn bear spent most of its time on the bookshelf of his bedroom.

Watching him sleep with Cleo tonight made Brynn nostalgic for the passage of time.

After shutting the door again, she went to check on Remi, who was also sleeping soundly. Then Brynn padded down the stairs and headed for the kitchen. Maybe a glass of milk would settle her nerves.

A light glowed from the partially open doorway of Nick's office. Her breath felt like it was coming out in strangled puffs as she moved toward it, drawn forward even though her rational mind warned she should run back up the stairs and not come out of the bedroom again until morning.

She knocked lightly and heard his answered greeting like she were listening from under a wave, his voice muffled from the pounding between her ears.

The office had an oversize cherry desk situated in front of the window and bookshelves lined one wall. On the wall to the other side of the door was the sofa bed. It looked to be at least full-size and not as uncomfortable as she'd imagined.

Nothing prepared her for the sight of a shirtless Nick propped against several fluffy pillows, a laptop open in front of him with a screen displaying...

"Is that the Lego website?" She stepped into the small room, still reeling from half-naked Nick but also confused and touched at what his browsing selection might mean.

"Tyler said the set he'd been working on in the family room melted." He shrugged, one big shoulder lifting, then lowering. Her attention focused on his body once again.

She'd seen Nick shirtless plenty of times when they were younger. The two of them would swim at the lake or run through the sprinklers in his family's backyard. And then in high school when it seemed like the entire football team took pains to parade around shirtless after practice.

But being with him in this cozy room reminded her how much had changed. Nick was a man in his prime and she was a late-twenties single mom of soon-to-be two kids with stretch marks on her breasts and hips.

If the rest of their differences didn't make clear why she was not a good match for Nick, the physical comparison—and there was no comparison—certainly would. Still, she wanted to beg him like some kind of obsessed fan girl to always walk around with no shirt while she was in the house.

"You don't have to do that," she said. "I have a plan for Christmas."

"I want to help," he answered simply. "Are you having trouble sleeping?"

She nodded. "On my way to the kitchen for a glass of milk."

He flipped back the covers to reveal a pair of loose gym shorts. "I can get it for you," he said, reaching for a T-shirt on the floor next to the bed.

"Don't."

The word came out sharper than she'd expected, and Nick paused and glanced at up her. His brows furrowed like her outburst didn't make sense, but his eyes darkened as if he could read her mind. "Don't go to the kitchen?"

"Don't put on the shirt."

She stepped closer. Her body hummed with awareness. She should back away, walk out of the office and shut the door behind her. What was she doing in here?

There were so many reasons this was a mistake, but at the moment Brynn didn't care about any of them. The sensations rolling through her were both unfamiliar and not. Worry and anxiety were constant companions, but they took a back seat to her visceral desire.

Would it be so bad to give in to it? Even for one night.

It had been so long since she'd done something for herself. Oh, her friends had talked to her about "self-care" after Daniel's death. She'd read plenty of articles that said a mom had to be good to herself in order to take care of her kids.

No at-home spa treatement or binge-worthy series in the world would compare to touching Nick.

He didn't speak as she took his hand and then sat down next to him, the thin mattress depressing under their combined weight. His chest rose and fell in ragged breaths and his gaze was intense on her, filled with so much need it was difficult to believe this was the same man who'd kept his distance from her this past decade.

With trembling fingers, she reached out and placed her hand on his shoulder. She traced a line along his collarbone, need pooling low in her belly at the heat and softness of his skin.

There was a scar just below his biceps, a tiny

mark she wasn't familiar with, which meant it had happened when he was an adult. She knew the dot of graphite from where Tommy Lencner had poked Nick with a pencil during a fifth-grade sword fight. One that had landed both of them with detention.

"What is it?" she whispered, fascinated by the raised skin.

"Knife wound," he said, his voice gruff.

She sucked in a breath.

"Not a big deal. It was my first year on the force and I was careless during a meth-lab bust. Surface wound. That's all, Brynn."

"Why didn't I know about this?"

What else didn't she know?

"Not many people did." He covered her hand with his. "I made a rookie mistake, so the fewer people who knew the better, as far as I was concerned."

"You could have been killed." She raised her gaze to his. "Any day you could be killed."

"That's not going to happen." He flashed a cocky smile. "I'm smarter now."

"Your job is dangerous." She flattened her palm on his chest. His heart raced. "You risk your life to serve the town."

He stiffened, as if a cold burst of air chased across the space between them. "Don't make me into something I'm not."

"What kind of something?"

He laughed without humor. "A hero."

"I don't need a hero." She licked her lips, swayed closer to him.

"What do you need, Brynn?"

Color stained his cheeks and a muscle ticked in his jaw, like it was taking every inch of strength he had to control his reaction to her.

Suddenly, Brynn was filled with the need to lose control and take Nick Dunlap along with her.

Without letting rational thought have a vote in the decision, she pressed her mouth to his.

Chapter Eleven

It only took a moment for the kiss to turn from exploring to demanding. Nick pulled her closer, almost into his lap, and her senses reeled as he moved his hands up and under her pajama top.

His rough palms on her heated skin were heaven. She opened for him as their kiss deepened.

He lowered himself back against the sheets, taking her with him. She straddled him as he continued to kiss her and wondered if she could ever get enough of this. He inched the baggy shirt up and over her head with one hand while the other unclasped her bra hook. Should she be alarmed at his dexterity? Even she couldn't unhook a bra that easily.

Brynn had the fleeting thought she should have

packed the lacy lingerie her friends had encouraged her to buy. Then they were skin to skin, and it didn't matter. Nothing mattered except this man and this moment.

"How are you this soft?" he whispered against her mouth, as his hands cupped the weight of her breasts. "So damn beautiful."

A denial bubbled into her mouth, but she swallowed it back. She might not have much experience with men, but she knew better than to reject a compliment, especially when it came from a man looking at her as if she were Christmas morning, the Fourth of July and his favorite team winning the Super Bowl all wrapped into one.

He lifted his head and covered one taut nipple with his mouth. Brynn moaned and braced her hands on either side of his broad shoulders. She was once again in jeopardy of spontaneously combusting from the desire swirling through her.

Nick seemed in no hurry to move things along. He took his sweet time giving attention to her sensitive breasts, and Brynn ground her hips into his.

She could feel how much he wanted her, and that knowledge inflamed her need. His hands settled on her hips, and his thumbs traced the edge of her pajama shorts. Goose bumps erupted along her skin as he continued to move higher on her upper thigh.

Just when she thought she couldn't hold herself upright from the pleasure, he flipped her onto her back, staring down at her like she was the most precious thing he'd ever seen.

But something else flashed in his gaze. A hint of trepidation, and she was terrified he'd stop touching her. Brynn wasn't sure if she'd make it through the night if he stopped now.

"I want you," she told him, lifting a palm to cup his rigid jaw. "I want this."

"Brynn." Her name on his lips sounded like a prayer. A plea.

"Please, Nick." She didn't care if she had to beg. There was nothing else that could fill the void inside her. Not at the moment. "I need—" she wrapped her arms around his neck and drew him down toward her "—you," she finished, then traced the tip of her tongue along the seam of his lips.

"Then I'm yours."

He slipped his hand into the waistband of her pajama shorts and panties, finding the spot that craved his touch. Her hips arched off the bed when he skimmed a finger along her center and bright spots of color flashed behind her closed eyes.

How was it possible he could make her feel so much with a simple touch?

"Open your eyes," he told her before sucking her earlobe into his mouth. He nuzzled her neck, then raised his head to gaze down at her as his fingers continued to work their magic. "I want to see you."

The look in his eyes was enough to push her over

the edge. She cried out, spiraling through the air like she was riding on a thousand points of light.

Nick bent his head again, whispering sweet things into her ear and placing gentle kisses along the column of her throat.

She waited for what came next, the feel of his body over hers, and swallowed back her shock when he moved to one side with a final kiss.

"We're not…" She sat up at the same time he did. "You didn't…"

He handed her top to her and shrugged into his shirt without making eye contact. "It's late," he said, his voice at once gruff and tender. "And you've had a traumatic day. I don't want to take advantage of you."

"What if you're not?" she said, pulling her shirt on over her head even as her body continued to tingle in the afterglow of her release. "What if I want—"

"I'm trying to be a friend," he said, running a hand through his hair.

A terrifying thought crawled into her still-fuzzy brain. "Oh, no." She shook her head. "Was that a pity…interlude?" Her cheeks flamed with embarrassment.

"No." Nick muttered a curse and then grabbed her hands, lifting them to his mouth. He grazed a kiss across her knuckles. "Of course not. Brynn, you have to know I want you. That watching you come apart in my arms was the best thing that's happened to me in forever. It was a dream come true."

She frowned. "Then why stop? I'm a big girl, Nick. I don't need you to worry about taking advantage of me. I'm capable of making my own decisions, and I know the difference between sex and love. Trust me. I know all about that."

"I'm not trying to make you mad." He squeezed her hands, then released her, standing to pace to the bookshelf. "I can't seem to do anything right where you're concerned."

Brynn couldn't help the laugh that escaped her lips. "You definitely did some things right."

He glanced at her, and some of the tension in his shoulders eased. "I want you, Brynn," he repeated. "I can barely control myself around you. That can't come as a surprise. But you had one hell of day. If we're going to be together, it will be the right time."

"Most of my life is based on timing that's been horribly wrong," she said quietly, straightening from the bed. "Why should this be any different?"

"Because you deserve better," he said tightly.

She wasn't sure whether she felt grateful or offended that he assumed he knew what she wanted or deserved. But she couldn't deny her body was way more relaxed than it had been when she'd knocked on his office door.

She should take that as a win at least.

"Good night, Nick," she said, knowing there was no point in arguing any more tonight.

"Sweet dreams," he told her, and she let herself out of his office.

By the end of the week, Nick felt like he might actually be going crazy with frustration. After her late-night trip to his office, Brynn hadn't spoken to him other than to discuss Remi's schedule or make meaningless small talk over dinner with Tyler.

He hated the distance that had emerged between them, when holding her in his arms had been the best feeling he'd had in ages. But he didn't regret not going further that night, despite how much his body continued to protest. As much as he wanted Brynn in his bed, his priority was being a good friend to her. To his mind, a decent guy wouldn't be selfish enough to be intimate with a woman who was traumatized by having half her house go up in flames.

He knew she'd met with Josh and his crew. According to the bits she'd told him, they were going to begin the project early next week and Josh hoped to have her back home by Christmas Eve. Nick found it hard to believe they could accomplish so much so quickly, and he'd been looking forward to waking up to watch Tyler open his presents on Christmas morning.

But it was important to Brynn that Tyler spend

the night before Christmas in his own bed and Nick would be a supportive friend, even if it killed him.

He walked into Trophy Room at five o'clock on Friday, forcing smiles for the locals who greeted him by name. Jordan Schaeffer, the bar's former-NFL-playing owner, waved from behind the bar, which was currently lined with customers. Nick knew it would only get more crowded as the night wore on, but he'd be long gone.

In fact, he didn't even want to be there at the moment, but Brynn was hosting some sort of annual cookie-baking party at his house. Kaitlin, Mara, Evie and Anna, along with Mara's aunt, his mom and two of her book-club friends were currently gathered in his kitchen.

Kaitlin and Mara had both offered to have the gathering at their houses, but he'd insisted Brynn invite everyone to his place. She'd put on such a brave face about the damage and the challenge of reconstruction, but the change in plans for her annual event had seemed to affect her like a physical blow.

He would not have her losing it over a few dozen cookies.

He headed for the table at the back, where Finn, Parker and Josh were waiting.

"I thought you'd be home rolling out fondant," Josh said with a laugh, moving over to make room for Nick.

The rest of them stared at the single dad, and

Nick was gratified to see his confusion was mirrored on his friends' faces. "What the hell is fondant?" Finn asked after a moment.

"Icing," Josh said, frowning. "You use it to decorate cakes and cookies."

Parker looked even more befuddled at his brother's familiarity with the details of pastry decorating. "Why do you know that?"

"Give me a break," Josh muttered. "Anna likes baking shows, and I watch with her. It's not like the man-card police are going to hunt me down for discussing the virtues of fondant or buttercream."

"There's more than one type of icing?" Nick grabbed a wing from the basket in the center of the table. "I thought it was all frosting."

They all turned as the waitress approached the table.

"The usual?" she asked, placing a cardboard coaster down in front of Nick.

"Please," he answered. "Jocelyn, have you heard of fondant?"

"It's the icing that tastes like crap, right?" She wrinkled her nose. "I like the spreadable stuff better."

Josh nodded. "Buttercream."

"Sure," Jocelyn agreed, then walked away.

"Do you wear a ruffled apron?" Parker asked his younger brother with a laugh.

Without hesitation, Josh flipped a one-fingered

salute. "Mara texted me the pic of you with a bubble mask when you did the spa night with Evie. Don't make me post it on the town Instagram account."

"I don't know anything about a bubble mask." Finn shook his head. "But does the fact that we're having a conversation that involves televised baking shows and spa nights mean we're officially lame?"

"I'm not lame," Nick protested, then thanked Jocelyn when she brought his beer to the table.

"You have dried spit-up on your shoulder," Josh told him.

"Fine." Nick took a long drink of beer to avoid checking his sweater. "I guess I'm lame along with the rest of you all."

"How's it going with your full house?" Finn asked, as he grabbed a wing and dipped it in blue cheese dressing. In addition to the basket of wings, they had a bowl of smoked cheese dip and the best jalapeño poppers Nick had ever tasted. Trophy Room was a throwback as far as decor, with its paneled walls and neon beer signs, but Jordan had hired a classically trained chef to update the bar's menu after he took over. She focused on classic bar food with a twist, so the wings were basted in a sesame soy glaze and a simple cheese dip had layers of flavors that even a big-city food snob would appreciate.

The bar had earned a reputation for serving the best selection of regional brews outside of Seattle and offering the most scrumptious menu items to go with them.

Nick normally wouldn't walk into the place on weekends, when tourists and visitors swarmed the valley. Despite the crowds, Jordan still managed to attract plenty of locals, so Nick always knew at least half the patrons by name.

"It's fine," he said, keeping his tone casual, almost flippant. "I like having the help with Remi at night. Makes me feel less like I'm going to make some kind of colossal mistake on my own."

"I think he was asking about Brynn." Parker raised a brow. "How's it going being so close to her again?"

"Fine," Nick repeated.

"That's the third time you've said *fine* since you sat down," Josh pointed out, none too helpfully. "You're not very convincing."

"What do you expect?"

The three men stared at him so long that he felt a bead of sweat drip down between his shoulder blades.

"I'm not going to have a relationship with her."

"Why are you being so stubborn?" Finn demanded. "Kaitlin and Mara are determined to find a man for Brynn, and we all know you never got over her."

"I was friends with her dead husband." Nick

shook his head. "Hell, I set them up in the first place."

"In high school," Parker reminded him. "A lot has changed since then."

Josh nodded and then waved a hand between Finn and Parker. "These two yahoos were gone for most of that time, but I've been here. I can vouch you were nothing but respectful toward Daniel and Brynn's marriage. I don't think anyone outside of your close circle of friends even knew you had feelings for her."

"Because it wasn't my place to have feelings for her." Nick took another long drink of beer. "I lost that right when I hurt her."

"You're different now," Finn said quietly.

"In a lot of ways," Nick agreed. "But I don't do relationships."

"You haven't done relationships," Parker corrected. "That doesn't mean you're incapable of it."

Josh chuckled and elbowed his brother. "If this one can take the plunge, I'd bet money anyone could."

"What about you?" Nick pointed a chicken wing in Josh's direction. "I'm not the only one who's single at this table. Maybe we could work on matchmaking for you, and I could get a damn break around here."

Josh sighed. "I'd love to find a nice, even-tempered woman to date."

"That sounds boring as hell," Finn said on a choked laugh.

"I've had the exciting whirlwind," Josh responded. "It didn't work out so well for me. Boring is right up my alley."

Nick hadn't known Josh's ex-wife well but he didn't think much of her. After a swift courtship and quickie wedding in Las Vegas, Josh and his bride had returned to Starlight, but as far as Nick could tell, Jenn had never been happy. The timing of their separation had been particularly brutal. Jenn left town shortly after their daughter, Anna, who was not even in kindergarten, had been diagnosed with cancer, leaving Josh on his own to handle the girl's treatments, as well as try to explain the breakup of their family.

Josh didn't talk much about the past, but it had been a dark time, and he deserved to find a good woman as much as Brynn did a good man.

"Boring is underrated," Parker agreed. "I never thought I could be entertained watching princess movies, but an evening on the couch with Mara and Evie beats a late night out at the bar any day."

Nick felt irritation prick his skin. He knew exactly what Parker was talking about and it annoyed the hell out of him. He'd ordered a Lego set from the internet and couldn't wait to put it together with Tyler when it arrived. What kind of grown-ass man was excited about overpriced plastic toys?

"Maybe you should date Brynn," he muttered to Josh.

"Because she's boring?" the other man asked with a frown.

"Hell, no, she's not boring." Nick wiped his fingers on a napkin and focused his gaze on his beer. "But she's nice, even-tempered and damn near perfect."

Josh shifted closer. "And you're okay with me asking her out?"

Nick ground his teeth. He opened his mouth to give his blessing, but the words refused to pass his lips. He should encourage the match. Kaitlin had told him that she and Mara weren't giving up on their stupid plan for twelve dates. Josh had been through the wringer with his divorce. Brynn's marriage had left her with far too many emotional scars. Maybe they'd be the perfect salve for each other.

The thought made Nick want to puke.

"No," he breathed out finally, then finished the rest of his beer. "Not even a little."

Finn patted him on the back. "Nice to see you can pull your head out for a few seconds. We can build on that."

"I don't deserve her," he said, needing his friends to understand. "She's too good for me."

"Duh." Parker threw up his hands. "You just hit on the magic, buddy. We're with these amazing women who are so far above us and somehow they love us anyway. Here's a little secret…" He leaned across the table. "You're a fool if you don't take the opportunity."

"I'll think about it," he said through clenched teeth. "But can you all stop Dear Abby-ing my life for a few minutes so I can enjoy the wings in peace."

"Speaking of peace…" Finn made a face. "Or more likely a disturbance in the peace… Ella gets to town tomorrow. I mentioned Remi to her and she's up for nannying for a few weeks until she figures out her next steps."

Finn's younger sister, Ella, had been a wild child back in the day. She hadn't been on Nick's radar much, since she was a couple years younger. She'd gone out of her way to antagonize their rigid father, especially after their mom died while the kids were in high school. She'd left Starlight and gone to school to become a nurse.

Nick knew from Finn that she'd spent the past several years all over the globe as a travel nurse.

"How long has it been since you've seen her?" Parker asked gently.

"Too long." Finn's mouth pressed into a thin line. "She had a layover in San Fran a couple of years ago, so I flew down for lunch. I still don't understand why she's coming back right now. She'd always wanted to stay as far away from Starlight as possible."

"I never understood you people being so determined to leave this town behind," Josh said around a bite of popper. "I couldn't imagine living anywhere else."

Nick could. He'd had the same driving need to escape the confines of small-town life and his role in it that his friends did. The need had been even stronger once Brynn and Daniel married. Out of sight, out of mind and all that.

Now he wondered if returning to Starlight contributed to his commitment issues. How was he supposed to risk hurting another woman with the regular reminder of what his selfishness had done to Brynn?

It was a big part of why he'd stopped before things had gone too far with her. Too far when he knew they weren't meant to be.

"Tell her to call me when she's ready to meet Remi." He nodded at Finn. "My mom has been uncharacteristically great in this situation, but I can see that it tires her out."

"Kids are exhausting," Josh said with a laugh. "It's why they're made so cute."

Chapter Twelve

"This is irregular to say the least."

Brynn swallowed and gave Jennifer her brightest smile. "Nick and I have been friends since we were kids, and I appreciate that he's letting Tyler and me stay here. It's unconventional, but on the plus side, Remi is getting to know both me and her new brother more than she would have if we'd been only able to visit. When she's part of our family—"

"Nothing has been approved yet," Jennifer reminded her gently.

"But there's been no word from Francesca?" Nick prompted.

The social worker's mouth thinned as she shook her head. "Not yet."

A sliver of worry sliced through Brynn's chest. "Do you think she might return to claim Remi?" Brynn had set her mind and her heart on the idea that Remi would become her daughter.

She had so much love to give.

"She still has time before her parental rights are permanently terminated."

"She abandoned her baby." The note of panic must have been clear in Brynn's tone because Nick shifted closer to her on the sofa so he could cover her hand with his. Her gaze strayed to the baby, who was contentedly sucking on her pacifier in the social worker's arms.

"The law is clear that the priority needs to be reunification with the biological parent. We discussed that in our first meeting."

"Yes, but…" Brynn trailed off. Of course, she'd heard the social worker's words, but she hadn't been able to process them through her shock. A thousand regrets rushed through her, and she suddenly felt like the most foolish mother that ever lived. What if Francesca returned? That would be enough of a blow, but what if the other woman was unwilling to forge a relationship between Tyler and his sister?

The boy had dealt with so much loss. They might have taken things slower, but Francesca leaving the baby with Brynn had given her no choice. He'd already formed a bond with his sister. Brynn refused to consider the possibility he might lose that, too.

"We'll cross that bridge if we come to it." Nick squeezed her hand. "We need to focus on Remi being safe and loved now. Brynn's reconstruction is on-track according to the contractor, so our living arrangement is only until Christmas. You can see the baby is thriving, Jennifer. Surely that's what the state wants."

Brynn forced herself to breathe at a normal rate. Nothing would be served by coming off as an emotional basket case in front of Remi's social worker. Nick was right. She'd faced challenges she would have never expected and overcome them. She would make sure things worked out the right way with Remi.

"True." Jennifer smiled down at the baby. "And right now, the system is flooded with kids who need homes."

"Right before Christmas?" Brynn's heart broke for those children. "That's so unfair."

The social worker laughed without humor. "This job is a continual lesson in the unfairness of life. But Nick's right about this little sweetheart. She's doing great."

She'd held her breath when going over the details of the house fire, afraid it would be a strike against her. But the social worker had been surprisingly understanding about the entire situation.

Brynn straightened and took the baby from the woman. Remi immediately placed her head on

Brynn's shoulder and yawned. "Our sweetheart is tired and in need of a nap. If you don't need me for anything else, I'm going to take her upstairs."

Jennifer nodded. "Nick and I can finish up. Good luck with your house, Brynn. Call me when you're moved back in and we'll schedule a follow-up home visit. That will be the final step in the process of approving your foster application."

Brynn blinked, then nodded, taking care not to make eye contact with Nick. She'd almost forgotten this setup was temporary. Once she was approved, Nick wouldn't be a daily part of their lives anymore. It had only been a week since they'd been living under the same roof, but co-parenting with Nick felt as natural as slipping on a comfortable pair of shoes. Well, other than the part where she wanted to jump his hot body.

It would be a big adjustment to go back to the way things were before. One she didn't relish.

"I'll definitely call," she told the woman, then carried Remi up the stairs, still unwilling to meet Nick's gaze, although she felt him watching her.

She would deal with her emotions in private—wrestle them down to something less humiliating—before she faced him. Because if Nick looked in her eyes right now, he'd know. He'd know that she was ignoring the reality that Francesca might return. Brynn had pressed forward, making plans in her mind, carving out a future for herself and her two—definitely two—children. It was easier to ignore the past than admit how its shadow loomed across her life.

She'd scheduled herself to work from home today in order to meet with the social worker. Now she wondered if Jennifer assumed she was playing house with Nick, allowing herself to be caught up in a fantasy that would never materialize. Her face burned with embarrassment, like she'd been caught in class writing *Mrs. Nick Dunlap* in a notebook over and over. Like she'd once again reached above herself, wanting a man and a future she was never meant to have.

But she refused to believe Remi wasn't meant to be part of her family. The baby was already in her heart. Blinking away tears, she sang "Have Yourself a Merry Little Christmas" as she changed the girl's diaper and dimmed the lights in her room. The sweet, sad lyrics fit Brynn's mood, and Remi didn't seem to notice her melancholy.

The girl sighed as Brynn lay her on her back on the soft sheet, her eyes heavy with sleep. Brynn stood watching her for several minutes more. There was no way she wanted to go back downstairs if the social worker was still in the house.

In fact, she was half tempted to hide out in Nick's master bedroom until he left for work again. Give herself more time to regain her composure. It was amazing how much she'd made it through without falling apart, when now every tiny bump in the road seemed to send the apple cart of her emotions nearly tumbling to the ground.

She took a deep breath and let herself out of the room, closing the door behind her.

Nick stood across the hall in the doorway of his bedroom. He wore his dark uniform and looked like every fantasy she'd ever had come to life.

"I'm fine," she lied.

He held out a hand. "Come here."

Brynn felt like an emotional kamikaze as she moved forward, but right now she didn't have the strength to say no. The truth was she wanted the comfort. She wanted someone to tell her things would turn out all right because she desperately needed to believe it.

Christmas was in a couple of weeks. If ever there were a season for a miracle, Brynn could use one.

Nick drew her into the room, then wrapped her in his warm embrace. "I use the word *fine* when I mean the opposite," he said against the top of her head.

She breathed in the scent of him. "You never were great at grammar."

His laugh rumbled through her, loosening some of her anxiety.

"I feel so stupid," she admitted. "It isn't as if I don't know that Francesca could return and claim her baby. Honest to goodness, sometimes I log on to my email with my breath held and one eye squeezed shut. But every day, I believe more surely that Remi is supposed to be mine." She lifted her gaze to Nick's. "I'm broken, and it feels like that little girl is what's going to put me back together."

"You aren't broken," he said, smoothing a hand over her face. "You're totally together."

"That's what I want people to see." She bit down on her lower lip. "It's the role I play for Tyler. But inside I'm like a pile of smoldering ash. A shadow of who I want to be."

His brows drew together. "I don't believe it. Look at what you've done with your life since the summer. The job at the mill and going on dates."

"I bought new underwear," she said with a sniff.

"Right. Lots of changes."

"But something was missing…"

"Your old granny panties?"

Brynn choked out a laugh. "I never wore granny panties, just the regular five-pack of cotton bikinis."

He grinned, then blew out a strangled breath. "We need to stop talking about your undergarments. Tell me what was missing."

"Remi," Brynn answered simply. "As soon as I read Francesca's note, I knew that baby belonged with Tyler and me."

"There's no reason to believe she won't end up with you. No one has heard from Francesca. Based on how she seemed that first night at your house and her letter, she knows she isn't capable of raising a child."

Brynn nodded, wanting to believe him. "I know I'm borrowing trouble, but Remi already feels like mine. I don't know how to turn off my feelings for her, and yet if things don't turn out…"

"Then we'll get through it. Remember, you're not alone."

"I've always felt alone." She swallowed. "It still boggles my mind that I was married to a man for ten years and yet feel like I spent the past decade on my own."

"Brynn, I know I've said it before, but I'm sorry I pushed you toward Daniel back in high school. I have a stockpile of regrets in my life, but none as big as that one."

"It's not your regret to have." She could see the guilt in his gaze. She didn't want that. "I made the choice. No one forced me into it."

"There are so many things about that time I'd change. How I treated you." He sighed. "The way I acted with my family, especially Jack. If I hadn't been such a joker, maybe he wouldn't have felt like he had to be the perfect son to make up for it. Maybe he wouldn't have enlisted and then—"

"Hush." She hugged him closer. "You can't take responsibility for the choices your brother made any more than mine. We're quite a pair at the moment, both of us repenting for things we had no control over."

He turned his head into hers, and she felt more than heard his deep inhale, his face pressed against her skin. Then his lips touched the sensitive place behind her ear, and goose bumps erupted along her neck.

"Nick," she whispered, half moan and half plea.

"We're a pair," he repeated, his mouth moving along her jaw.

Then it was fused to hers and she lost herself in the feel of him, the barrage of sensations.

"I'm not going alone this time," she told him, as she broke the embrace. "Together or it stops now."

He raised a brow. "You'd say no to that kind of pleasure?"

"I want that." She exhaled a shaky breath. "Definitely. But I want it with you, Nick. I don't want you to worry about hurting me or to consider what's going to happen after Christmas. I want—need—to feel something."

"Me, too," he said softly and her heart, along with other parts of her body, leaped with joy.

Brynn's teenage crush on Nick seemed like a million years in the past. So much had happened to both of them, and right now she was grateful for the passing of time.

Because Brynn was no longer the infatuated schoolgirl who got tongue-tied and flustered at the drop of a hat. She was a woman, a mother, and she had enough experience in life to appreciate a moment like this without reservation.

They tugged on each other's clothes, the sensations swirling through her both familiar and new. She loved the feel of his skin against hers and the way he lowered her to the bed with the gentlest movement. He lavished attention on every part of her body until she trembled with need.

"I want you so badly," Nick whispered.

"I'm...right here," she said, even though what she meant was *I'm yours*. For as long as it lasted, she belonged to this man.

He looked deep into her eyes as he settled between her legs, and when he entered her, it was like coming home.

Brynn closed her eyes and let the pleasure of their joining carry her away. Nick covered her mouth with deep kisses. In truth, she was afraid to look at him, afraid of what she might reveal.

This was about now, and she wouldn't ruin it for either of them by second-guessing. Not that the force of their mutual desire could be derailed. Their bodies fell into a rhythm, and Brynn wondered if she'd been specifically made to be loved by this man.

It wasn't long before pressure began to build, driving her higher until she broke apart. Her body shattered with the pleasure of it and a sensation of completeness filled her as he found his own release. She held on to him, wanting nothing more than to savor this moment as long as possible.

He shifted to lie beside her, the quiet punctuated only by the sound of their breaths.

Brynn stretched out her toes and wiggled her fingers, surprised to find that her body looked the same as it had this morning. The last few minutes had changed everything about her. After a moment, Nick turned to her.

"Should we talk?" he asked, reluctance clear in his tone.

"Definitely not," she answered with a laugh, surprising both of them based on his sharp inhale.

She glanced over to find him staring at her with an inscrutable expression. "I mean it, Nick. My plate is spilling over with worries at the moment. I need something easy and fun. Something casual."

"And you and I are casual?"

"In this way." She nodded. "You like your women uncomplicated. I'm a tangled mess, but we can make this part of it straightforward."

He traced a fingertip along the ridge of her nose. "That's what you want?"

Her stomach clenched, but she nodded again. "It's what I need. What we both need."

"Okay, then," he agreed, although his tone had become strained. He was up and out of the bed an instant later. Her heart tripped in response to how easily he went along with her suggestion. As the door to the adjoining bathroom closed behind him, Brynn pulled off the covers and dressed.

Naked under a sheet was one thing, but now she needed the armor that clothes provided.

Nick didn't seem to share her modesty as he re-appeared in all his naked glory. Her knees shud-dered in response and she forced herself to look away. She walked to the mirror that hung above the dresser on the far wall and straightened both her hair and outfit.

Nothing good would come of anyone knowing that she and Nick had been together in this way.

"I need to get back to work," he said, and she could hear the frown in his voice.

"Sure. I've got a call scheduled in thirty minutes with Nanci and Mara to discuss a cupcake order for the next concert." She plastered on a bright smile. "If Remi doesn't take a long nap, I'll have time to run to the grocery before Tyler gets home from school."

Good lord. She wanted to slap herself. What kind of pathetically boring woman went from the best sex of her life to talking about groceries?

Nick was probably already regretting what they'd done, although he'd had a good enough time during the act based on his reaction.

"Not that you're under pressure to have dinner with us," she quickly added, unable to stem the tide of verbal diarrhea spewing from her mouth. "Having Remi, Tyler and me here must be disrupting your life." When he didn't respond, she continued, "Cramping your style."

From the reflection in the mirror, she could see he'd pulled on his boxers and uniform trousers, so Brynn felt it safe to turn around.

"What style?" he asked as he buttoned his dark navy department-issued shirt. His jaw was tight, his gaze hard.

"You know..." She laughed nervously. "Dates or whatever it is you do."

"Do you think I'm planning to go from sex with you to a date with another woman?" He made a noise that sounded suspiciously like a growl. "Like I'm trying to set some kind of land-speed record for being a heel."

"It's not like that," she protested. "*We're* not like that."

He tugged on his shirt cuffs and ran a hand through his hair, once again the tough law officer he'd matured into. "Are you still planning on finishing your twelve dates of Christmas?"

"The dates were a stupid joke from the start." She crossed her arms over her chest.

"Which doesn't answer the question."

"How would I have time to date between work, Tyler and adding Remi and the renovation in the mix? I barely managed it before all the changes to my life."

"Still not an answer."

"No." She rolled her eyes. "Not before this Christmas anyway. What man would want me given my current situation?"

"Any man in his right mind."

"Oh." Although he sounded angry—or at least frustrated—that was one of the nicest things someone had said to her. "Well, I'm putting the dating plan on hold. That doesn't mean you have to."

"Good to know," he ground out, then turned for the door before spinning back to face her. "Don't go to the grocery store."

Brynn inclined her head. She knew so much about Nick but could not begin to guess what he was thinking at this moment or why he seemed so irritated with her. Wasn't it every man's dream to have permission to date around? That's what ten years of marriage to a serial cheater had taught her.

"Why?"

"The holiday performance is tonight," he said. "I thought we could go out before heading over."

"You're going to the school?" She couldn't mask her surprise.

He tugged at the collar of his shirt like it was suddenly too tight. "Tyler invited me, so I planned on it. Unless that's a problem."

"I'm sure it would mean a lot to him to have you

there." She shrugged. "I figured I could take Remi and give you a night off from—" she waved her hands in the air like spastic birds "—all of this."

He closed his eyes for several seconds, and she could almost imagine him silently counting to ten. What was the problem?

"What time does he have to be at the school?" he asked instead of responding to her comment.

"Six."

He nodded. "I'll pick you up here at five, and we can get something at the downtown diner. Tyler mentioned he likes the fries."

"They're his favorite."

"Great." Nick's shoulders relaxed slightly. "If there's time, we could grab ice cream and drive around to look at lights after the performance."

Brynn felt her mouth drop open and snapped it shut. "Sure. That would be great."

"Great," he repeated.

"Does *great* mean the opposite in the way *fine* does?" she asked, referring to his earlier comment.

He shook his head and his mouth lifted into a half smile. "It means we're going to have a great time tonight."

"Okay," she agreed, wondering why she was suddenly breathless again. "We'll see you at five."

His grin widened. Had they just made progress on some problem she wasn't even aware of? "It's a date," he said softly, then disappeared into the hall.

A date?

Alone in the room, Brynn sank down to the edge of the bed. *Could this day get any stranger?* she thought, as she smoothed a hand over the comforter. The best sex of her life and now a date—a date— with Nick Dunlap. Talk about checking off the list of Christmas miracles.

Chapter Thirteen

Nick walked toward his front door just before five o'clock, nerves dancing through his stomach. His friends would get a laugh out of that, and he couldn't blame them.

Who got nervous approaching the house they'd lived in for the past five years?

Night was descending over the town, and already Christmas lights glowed from the homes around him. Starlight might not get much snow or below-freezing temperatures, but its residents still went all out for the holiday like they were living at the North Pole.

"I'm hungry for fries." Tyler opened the door as

Nick got to the top step. The boy zipped out past him before Nick had a chance to respond.

"You're not wearing your uniform."

He glanced up to find Brynn standing in the doorway. Remi's infant seat was on the floor next to her.

"I keep a change of clothes at the office," he explained, suddenly self-conscious and not sure why. Instead of his uniform, he'd put on a pair of khaki pants and a button-down shirt. Nothing special, but Brynn stared at him like he'd shown up in a tux and tails. "It's easier that way."

She licked her lips, and awareness zinged across his skin in response.

"These are for you." He shoved the bouquet of daisies he'd bought from the local florist toward her.

Her brows puckered. "Why?"

Nick scratched his jaw. "I thought you'd like them. I remember that yellow was your favorite. Or used to be. I guess I don't know—"

"It's still my favorite." She took the flowers from him, almost reluctantly, and lifted them to her nose. "Thank you. They're beautiful."

"Come on," Tyler called from the driveway. "I'm starving."

"I'll get Remi and Ty settled if you want to put them in water."

"Okay," she whispered, still staring at the flowers.

"Is something wrong?" he asked. "Did I mess up again?"

"Not at all." She flashed a watery smile. "Pay no attention to me."

"I don't think that's possible. Brynn, what's going on?"

"The flowers are beautiful," she repeated with a small shake of her head. "I love them."

She turned for the kitchen. Still puzzled at her response, he picked up the car seat and headed for his truck. Tyler climbed into the back seat, talking about the perfect ketchup-to-fry ratio as Nick clipped Remi into the seat's base.

He wasn't sure what the hell had happened on his porch, but he decided the best course of action was to press forward. Nick had done a lot of thinking during his shift today, about Brynn giving up on dating—which he was all for—and what Parker and Finn had told him about her friends wanting to find a man for her.

He'd made a vow to himself the night of the tree lighting that he would give Brynn the Christmas she deserved. If that included finishing the ridiculous commitment to twelve dates, he'd give her those dates.

Even if he couldn't give her more. Even if he refused to admit to himself he wanted more.

He adjusted the radio to a station playing holiday classics as she got into the truck a few minutes later.

"All set?" he asked, glancing at her and relieved to see she looked less astonished and more like her normal, controlled self.

She nodded. "I'm excited for the winter concert." She looked over her shoulder toward Tyler in the back seat. "You're going to be the best narrator Starlight has ever seen."

Each year, the elementary school children performed skits and songs around the theme of winter and peace on earth. Nick knew Brynn was grateful Tyler seemed happy about his expanded role in the production and that he wasn't focusing on the fact that his father wasn't there to see him perform.

"Remember last year I had to be one of the sheeps," Tyler answered. "That's what the little kids have to be, but now I'm a big kid so I get actual lines. Someday Remi will be a sheep."

"She's got a few years before that happens," Brynn answered with a tight laugh.

He had a feeling she was thinking about the potential of Francesca returning. He wished he could take the worry from her mind, but even he couldn't predict the future.

"Remind me to show you the scar I've got on the back of my head," he said, meeting Tyler's gaze in the rearview mirror. "When your mom and I were in third grade, we had to do this holiday concert, and it was so hot in the gymnasium that I passed out. Fell right off the bleachers and knocked my head on one corner. I ended up with twelve stitches."

"Seriously?" Ty sounded awestruck.

"Not only did Nick pass out," Brynn added, "but two other girls in the class followed suit when they saw the blood. It was a gruesome ending to the concert."

The boy laughed. "That sounds awesome."

"Other than Nick getting hurt," Brynn said, her tone gently chiding. "It was scary."

"I milked the attention for all I could," Nick told the boy. "Your mom brought over chocolate chip cookies to make me feel better."

"She makes the best cookies," Tyler confirmed, then began to sing along with Bing Crosby as a popular holiday tune filled the cab's interior.

Brynn joined her son, and Nick thought about all the times the woman next to him had been a good friend to him. She'd been his biggest cheerleader for sports, tutored him in every core subject and been the one person in his life to make him believe he didn't come up short in comparison to his brother. In return, he'd alternately taken her for granted and ignored her outright.

Nick knew he had to stop dwelling on what an idiot he'd been in the past. It would do no good and the best he could hope for was to change going forward.

He pulled into the parking lot of the popular local

restaurant, unsurprised to see that it was already nearly filled.

"Oh, no." Brynn sucked in a breath. "It looks like there's a wait. We might not have time—"

"I called ahead," Nick told her with a smile.

She frowned. "Stan doesn't take reservations."

"Your friendly neighborhood police chief might have helped his son out of a bind a few years back." Nick winked. "I've got connections."

"Lucky you," she murmured, grinning at him.

Lucky indeed, Nick thought, as they walked toward the entrance. He placed a hand on the small of Brynn's back as Stan showed them to a table near the front of the restaurant. He couldn't help his need to claim her, at least temporarily.

Nick had always thought he was fine on his own, the stereotypical "lone wolf" lawman. He'd figured it was his destiny. But the more time he spent with Brynn, the more he wanted something different. The more he believed he might be able to claim a future he'd never expected.

"People are staring," she said under her breath, as she shrugged out of her wool coat.

"It's because you look so pretty tonight." Affection bloomed in his chest as color stained her cheeks.

"I doubt that." She pulled a plastic spinning wheel with a suction on the bottom out of the diaper bag and stuck it to the table in front of Remi's high chair. "The town gossips are going to have a field day seeing us like this."

"Like what?" He shrugged. "We've been friends most of our lives, and now we have Remi as a connection between us."

"For now," she said.

He nodded, although he didn't want to consider the temporary nature of their arrangement. "I'm not worried about what other people think." He ruffled Tyler's thick mop of hair. "I'm too busy plotting how I'm going to steal this guy's fries."

"No way," the boy said, then his eyes went wide as a waitress put down a big plate of the restaurant's famous french fries in the middle of the table.

"Stan sent these over for you to enjoy before your food comes." The waitress was in her midfifties with her hair pulled back into a low ponytail. "Are you ready to order or do you need a few minutes?"

"Ready," Tyler answered and rattled off his order, adding a *please* at the end, then grinning at his mother.

Brynn and Nick ordered as well, and Remi smiled at the waitress.

"Your daughter is adorable," the woman said to Brynn. "She's a perfect mix between you and your husband."

Nick felt a combination of happiness and unease rush through him. It made sense that a stranger would assume he was the baby's father. They were out for what looked like a perfectly normal family dinner. But he didn't want the presumption to add to Brynn's anxiety.

He kept his features neutral as he glanced toward Brynn. Her smile looked forced but didn't waver. "She's a sweet girl."

Remi babbled excitedly as if to verify that assessment.

"She sure is. I'll get those orders right in," the waitress said.

"Will you pass me the crayons?" Tyler asked, seemingly unaware of the awkward tension that had descended over their group. He gestured to the plastic cup in the center of the table.

Nick reached for it, his fingers grazing Brynn's as she did the same. She immediately drew back as if his touch was electric. Nick handed the cup to the boy, who began to complete a word search printed on the paper kids' menu.

"It's crowded for a weeknight," Brynn said, as she glanced around the restaurant.

He nodded. "There aren't a lot of options for casual dinners in Starlight."

She blew out a shaky laugh, then visibly relaxed her shoulders. "What the waitress said wasn't a big deal."

Nick couldn't decide which one of them she was trying to convince.

"It's an obvious assumption if you don't know us."

It was his turn to laugh. "I'm not used to someone in town not being able to identify me. I kind of liked it."

Her eyes widened a fraction, and he wondered if she thought he was referring to being unrecognized or someone mistaking him for her husband. Honestly, it was a little of both, but he had no intention of admitting that.

"It's good to have new people come to town." She drew one finger around the rim of her water glass. "Josh and I are working on plans for an addition to the mill that would include a sit-down restaurant. I think it would attract more locals as well as out-of-town visitors."

"That's a great idea," he told her. "Although some of the food-truck owners might be disappointed. I heard you have a waiting list for trucks on-site during weekends."

Her grin was natural now. "We still want to utilize the trucks. The response to our theme nights has been overwhelming."

"You're doing a great job with the marketing. Everyone says so."

"I don't know about everyone." She rolled her eyes. "There are a number of old-timers around who aren't thrilled about the town's new growth. But even they can't deny the refreshed energy of the community. It feels good to be a part of it, and

I'm so grateful to Josh and Parker for giving me a chance."

They continued to talk about her work and his job. Nick appreciated that the tension from earlier had disappeared, even when the waitress brought their food and Stan stopped by the table. The older man commented on how pretty Brynn and Remi looked, but Brynn only blushed and thanked him for the compliment.

By the time they got to the school, Nick felt calmer than he had in days. Maybe they could forge ahead with a fresh start, after all.

Brynn looked at her reflection in the hazy mirror above the girls' bathroom sink down the hall from the school's auditorium. Nick had dropped her off with Tyler so she could walk him to his classroom, where the students were meeting before the start of the performance.

She'd gotten waylaid talking to the teacher she'd subbed for the previous semester, when the young mom had been on maternity leave, and then made a quick stop at the bathroom because she needed a quiet minute to herself. Nick texted that he'd gotten seats near the aisle in case Remi needed to be whisked out midperformance.

Brynn didn't want to compare tonight to the years she and Daniel had attended the school performances together. He'd never been all that interested in young kids doing their thing on stage, and she'd had to cajole and threaten him into coming with her every year, making sure she showed enough enthusiasm before and after the performance that Tyler wouldn't notice his father's lack of interest.

Nick acted like he was going to a Broadway play, and his excitement—even if it was all for Ty's benefit—melted her heart. As if she needed another reason to fall for Nick Dunlap.

The door to the restroom opened, and she turned as Cassie Monaghan entered. Cassie had been in the same graduating class as Brynn, although they hadn't run in anywhere near the same circles. Brynn had stuck with the misfits other than when she was trailing around after Nick and his buddies like some kind of worshipful sidekick.

Cassie, on the other hand, had been one of the "it" girls. She and her friends had run the school, from the cheer team to homecoming and prom courts. In fact, Cassie had been Nick's date to senior prom. The memory burned like acid in Brynn's gut even now. There were plenty of good things about living in a small town, but she didn't consider unwanted reminders of the past part of that.

"Hey, Cass." Brynn smiled as she tugged a paper towel from the dispenser. "I didn't know you were back in town."

"Just until after Christmas." The other woman

smirked. "I got hired at a new salon in Portland, so I took a week off to recharge."

"That's great." Somewhere in the back of her mind, Brynn knew Cassie was a hairdresser. She certainly had a beautiful mane of thick, perfectly curled blond hair. In fact, the woman was perfectly turned out from the top of her shiny hair to her shapely legs tucked into red cowboy boots. She looked as polished and intimidating as she had a decade earlier.

Brynn shifted when Cassie continued to block her way to the door and resisted the urge to scratch at her lace bra, which suddenly felt itchy in all the wrong places. She glanced down at the simple black shift she wore with colorful patterned clogs. She might not work at the elementary school any longer, but she still dressed the part. Maybe it was time for an update of more than just her undergarments.

"It's nice of you to come to the performance. I'm sure Gillian is glad to have you here. She'll do great." Cassie's niece, Gillian, one of Tyler's classmates, was the star of the show this year.

When Cassie didn't respond, Brynn made to move past her. The other woman grabbed her arm. "He's not going to fall for you," she said, her voice barely above a whisper. "You weren't his type in high school, and you aren't now."

Brynn's stomach dipped. "I don't know what

you're talking about." She managed to keep her voice steady.

"Nick," Cassie clarified, although she must know Brynn wasn't that dense. "We've stayed in contact over the years, you know."

"Yeah," Brynn answered, even though she'd known nothing of the sort. But Starlight was a small town with one popular bar for locals and tourists alike. She'd seen Cassie around during holidays and breaks, so it shouldn't surprise her that Nick had, as well. Heck, Daniel had even mentioned running into her at Trophy Room a few times over the years. The sick pit in Brynn's stomach gaped wider. For all she knew, her husband had cheated on her with this woman.

"We get together when I come back." She leaned in closer. "You know what I mean by together, right?"

Brynn didn't bother to answer.

"This week I text him and he tells me he's too busy for a drink."

"Maybe he's too busy," Brynn said through clenched teeth. "Or maybe you should take a hint."

"Nick and I are cut from the same cloth." Cassie's fingers dug into Brynn's skin, and she yanked away from the painful grasp. "We like our relationships straightforward, no-strings-attached. You're the biggest ball of tangled yarn I've ever seen, Brynn Hale. Between getting yourself knocked up, a husband who couldn't keep it in his pants and now taking on one of his bastards, you're a bigger mess now than you ever were. You should have stayed the mousy wallflower. Nick will never let himself be saddled with you and your two sad-sack children and if you think—"

Brynn's arm shot out and before she knew what she was doing, Cassie's back was up against the cold tile wall of the bathroom with Brynn's forearm pinning her so she couldn't move. Rage bubbled up inside Brynn, hot and fiery, in a way she barely recognized. It coursed through her like molten lava, giving her a ferocity she hadn't known she possessed.

She'd taken a lot of grief, pity and judgment over the years. She could deal with it, but there was no way she would let anyone disparage either of her children.

And they were both hers. No matter what the future held for Remi, Brynn knew without a shadow of a doubt that she would always love that girl with her entire heart.

"You don't know Nick, and you never have." She leaned in, satisfied when Cassie's heavily mascaraed eyes widened in shock. "And you definitely don't know me or my children. Let me tell you that I'm proud of the life I've made for myself and them."

"That baby isn't even yours," the other woman said on a hiss of breath.

"She needs a mother, and I'm honored to fill that

role. I don't care what you or anyone else thinks about it." She released Cassie and stepped back. "Your opinion means nothing to me. I have a feeling you mean less than nothing to Nick." She smiled broadly. "Merry Christmas, Cassie," she said and walked out of the bathroom.

She walked to the auditorium with her head held high, greeting the people she passed in the hall by name or smiling at the ones she didn't recognize. The rows of chairs were half-full, and she quickly found Nick and took a seat next to him.

"What's wrong?" he asked immediately, concern filling his gaze. He held Remi on his lap, and to Brynn's great joy, the baby reached for her.

"Everything's fine," she said, lifting the girl into her arms. "I ran into Cassie Monaghan in the bathroom."

Nick muttered a curse.

Brynn kept the smile on her face as she snuggled the baby to her chest. To anyone watching her—and she could feel the weight of multiple stares—there was no outward sign of the turmoil racing through her body.

"If you want to go out with her, or hook up, or whatever it is you two do over the holidays, don't let me or Remi stop you."

She heard his sharp intake of breath.

"I haven't gone out with Cassie in years," he said, voice tight. "I have no plan to start now."

"Anyone," Brynn modified. "If you want to go out with anyone, it's—"

"No." He placed a heavy hand on her leg, and she wished she could stop her reaction to his touch, but it felt too good. Too right. "How many times do I have to say it before you'll believe me, Brynn? I don't want anyone else. I'm happy with you. I know that it's not permanent, that you don't think of me in that way. I'm not going to push you away. But I've missed you. If nothing else, believe that."

She gave a shaky nod, grateful when the elementary school's principal took the stage to begin the show. Her mind spun at the sincerity in Nick's tone. Was he trying to placate her, or had he spoken the truth? How could he think she wouldn't see him as someone who could be a permanent part of her life?

Was it possible that he doubted her commitment to him as much as she doubted his? In her wildest fantasies, she'd never considered a world where Nick Dunlap could be hurt by her. Brynn didn't hurt people. She was on the receiving end of emotional suffering and had gotten used to laughing it off. Anything else was like the world tilting in a way she couldn't understand.

She might not be able to comprehend this new revelation, but her heart stammered at the simple idea that Nick could want her in the same way she wanted him. He squeezed her leg, and she flashed a quick smile in return, careful not to make eye contact with him. The lights went down in the auditorium and she focused on the students filing out onto the stage. Once again, Nick had changed everything for her.

Chapter Fourteen

Nick sat on the edge of the mattress later that night, elbows on his knees and head in his hands. His mind raced in a million different directions, but at the end, all of them led back to the same place.

Brynn.

He'd thought he left his stupid ego moves behind years ago but realized now that he was still an idiot. His big plan to give her some sort of magical Christmas and the dates she seemed to want had blown up in his face. Not that she realized it. No one would because Nick was too good at keeping his feelings hidden.

Well, his friends had an inkling, but that stemmed

more from the way he'd decided he felt about her too late in high school than anything now. Back then, she'd been the one that got away. The one he'd pushed away.

He'd assumed his inability to get over Brynn had more to do with a mix of his competitive nature and the fact that he'd gotten used to her constant presence than true heartbreak. It didn't matter that his chest had ached every time he saw her in town, either with Daniel and Tyler or on her own. He'd taken to avoiding her over the years because that helped dull the pain. Pain he attributed to guilt.

Daniel Hale had been a horrible husband, and Nick knew Brynn would have never ended up with the man if Nick hadn't arranged that fateful prom date.

Despite everything, he'd always assumed he was in control. But it didn't matter how high he built his defenses. They were nothing Brynn couldn't scale. Hell, she didn't even have to work at it. In truth, she held the key to his heart and always had.

Where did that leave him?

He looked up at the knock on the door and his heart stammered against his ribs as the woman who consumed his thoughts beyond all reason stepped into his office.

"I wanted to thank you again for tonight," she said, her tone soft, hesitant. Her hair was down, tucked back behind her ears, and she wore the thickest, fuzziest robe he'd ever seen. The robe was so big and bulky it almost swallowed her whole. Even with the shapeless fabric engulfing her, his body immediately sprang to life. Her scent floated to him, and his fingers itched to pull her close. He tucked his hands under his thighs and nodded.

"It was fun," he said, laughing at the unbelieving lift of her brow. "I mean it. I haven't been to a school event since we were that age. Watching the kids do their thing reminded me of the real meaning of the holidays. People get so worked up about presents and the commercial stuff, but it's most important to make time for those kinds of moments."

"Tell that to all the parents scrambling to finish Christmas shopping."

"Yeah." He shrugged. "I guess I don't understand what it's like."

"You understand plenty," she said and took a step forward. "You've made this past week bearable. I'm not sure Tyler will want to go home when the renovations are complete. He's having too much fun with you."

"It's Remi. He likes being around her." Nick ignored the ping in his heart at the thought he might be important to the boy. "Once she's with you, he won't even think about me."

"I'll think about you," she said, her voice low. She gave a strangled laugh. "I think about you far too much for my own good."

"Brynn." He wanted to give her some reassurance, to explain he was the one in danger of losing his heart and maybe his mind. That she held more sway over him than he ever could have imagined. But the words caught in his throat when she locked the door to his office and then untied the belt of her robe.

The fuzzy material opened, revealing a red slip made of silk and lace. He made a sound—nothing coherent—a guttural noise somewhere between a groan and a growl.

"I bought this a while ago," she said when she stood directly in front of him. "After…this summer… I made a whole list of things I wanted to do and try."

"And killing me was at the top?" he managed to choke out.

She grinned, and the knowing and utterly feminine smile did wicked things to his body.

"I don't want to kill you," she assured him, as she shifted so that the robe fell to the floor at her feet.

The air whooshed out of Nick's lungs.

"But I wanted to make sure you'd notice."

He laughed. "I thought you were the sexiest thing I'd ever seen wearing a fuzzy robe. I'm not sure I'm equipped to handle you like this."

"And yet you'll try?" She raised a brow. "Because if I went to the trouble for nothing, it's going to make me so sad."

The small smile that played around the corners

of her mouth belied her words. She looked anything but sad. She was beautiful and radiant and absolutely irresistible. He reached for her and tugged her between his legs. His hands splayed across the silky fabric that covered her hips.

"For as long as you'll let me," he promised.

She bent her head and their mouths fused together as his hands slid over the satiny fabric. He pulled the slip over her head, then covered the tight peak of her breast with his mouth, and the soft needy sound she made almost undid him. He pulled her with him onto the mattress, and they were a tangle of limbs—kissing and touching until he lost track of where he ended and she began.

When he couldn't wait any longer, Nick grabbed a condom wrapper and sheathed himself, then entered her in one long slow stroke. It felt different than before. Brynn didn't hold anything back, and the way she allowed herself to be exposed—both physically and emotionally—rocked him to his core. He couldn't imagine a time in his life when he wouldn't want this. Wouldn't want her.

He tried to hold back even as his desire surged forward. Physical need and emotion didn't meld for him. They'd always been separate, easy for him to keep different parts of his life in segregated boxes. But the way he felt with Brynn knocked away everything he'd known before. His control. His boundaries. There was nothing between them. She knew him better than anyone ever had, and she chose him anyway.

And he knew her—wanted to know her more. To understand every nook and cranny of her soul. Something both sharp and sweet blossomed in his chest as the physical pressure built, so much more than he expected when she shuddered and cried out beneath him. It was all he needed to push him over the edge of release. How was it possible he'd gone all these years without this kind of soul-baring intimacy?

Maybe because it made him vulnerable. He was like a lovesick puppy, ready to turn over and expose all his soft bits to this woman. Nick would rather go out on a million life-threatening calls at the station than set himself up for the kind of potential pain he risked if things didn't work out. And it wasn't only his heart. Now that Brynn was back in his life, he realized how he'd missed her friendship. He'd missed talking to her and hearing her take on every slight detail of their lives.

He didn't want to lose any of it.

That line of thinking got him nowhere, especially when he'd just had the best damn sex of his life. What was wrong with him, to go looking for trouble before it even showed up on his doorstep?

He lifted his head and her eyes fluttered open, half-dazed but filled with the affection he craved.

"Hi," she whispered.

"Hi, yourself." He dropped a kiss on the tip of her nose.

She smiled at him, almost shyly. "I'm going to say my lingerie worked."

"The slip was sexy as hell, but you're all I need. Silk or a fuzzy bathrobe. Either works for me, Brynn. As long as it's you."

"You make me feel good," she told him.

"That's my pl—"

"Hey." Panic gripped him when a tear slid from the corner of her eye. "What's wrong?"

She shook her head and laughed. "I didn't expect... This wasn't what... I'm happy."

Those two words made him feel ten feet tall. "Me, too," he told her, then excused himself to the bathroom. He climbed back into the bed with her, pulling her close. Her leg wrapped around his hip and her delicate fingers curled over his chest.

"I'm happy you're happy," he said, breathing in her sweetness.

They were silent for several moments and then she said quietly, "I don't trust happiness."

"Oh, honey." He squeezed her shoulder. "Do you trust me?"

He didn't like how long it took her to answer. "I want to."

"I'm going to give you every reason to trust me. To believe your happiness is my top priority."

"You have," she said, propping herself on an

elbow. "You've been amazing, Nick. I don't know how I'll ever repay you for your generosity."

He frowned. Something about her words made it sound like she'd need to repay him because he was doing her a favor. That once this ended she could bake a cake or bring over dinner and a bottle of wine as a thank-you and they'd be done.

Nick didn't like that thought, but he was still afraid to push her. Afraid to reveal he might need her more than she needed him.

"I care about you, Brynn." He smoothed a lock of dark hair away from her face. "About Tyler and Remi, too. No repayment needed."

She smiled again and then yawned. "I should go back upstairs. Tyler is a sound sleeper now, but I'd hate for him to wake up and not find me across the hall."

It was difficult to let her go, but Nick forced himself to release her. "Close your eyes," she told him, as she scooted to the far edge of the foam mattress.

His brows furrowed and amusement spiked in his chest. "I've seen you naked," he reminded her. "In fact, I've kissed about every inch of your body."

"It's different." She leveled him with a steely stare. "Eyes closed. I mean it, Nick."

"Fine," he answered with an amused sigh.

"No peeking," she commanded, and he felt the lift of the mattress when she got up. It only took a few seconds before she gave him the go ahead to open his eyes again.

Once again, she was bundled up in the fluffy robe. A strip of red lace peeked out from the pocket, sending his body into overdrive once again at the memory of his hands and mouth all over her body.

"Good night, Nick," she said, bending to kiss his cheek. "Thank you for a lovely evening."

He almost laughed at the simple statement. Leave it to Brynn to be unfailingly polite after raking her fingernails across his back minutes earlier.

When he was alone again, he closed his eyes and drifted off to sleep with every hope he'd find a way to dream about the woman sleeping upstairs.

"She's adorable."

Brynn watched as Ella Samuelson, Finn's younger sister, lifted Remi into her arms. The woman, who was a year or so younger than Brynn, looked comfortable with the baby, which Brynn appreciated.

"That's the consensus." Brynn smiled. She continued wrapping presents as they spoke. "I appreciate you agreeing to start right away. I'm sure you have a lot of catching up to do with your family now that you're back."

Ella shrugged and kept her attention focused on Remi. "I need a little distraction in my life right now." She had the same blue eyes as her brother, but her hair was several shades lighter and she had the kind of loose-limbed grace Brynn could only dream about possessing. "Starlight has changed since I left, but my feelings about the town haven't caught up. Coming home felt like the right decision when I was sitting in a hut in a Brazilian rain forest. The reality of being here is almost as foreign as any of the places I've traveled to in the past few years."

"It must have been exciting to see so much of the world." Brynn sighed. She'd been as far as Chicago for a high school choir trip but hadn't traveled out of the country once in her life. When her friends had been off to college and life adventures, she'd been busy raising Tyler.

"I loved getting to experience different cultures and meet people from all kinds of backgrounds." Ella bit down on her lower lip. "After a while, living out of a duffel bag gets old, even with a spectacular view."

"Can I ask you a personal question?" Brynn paused with a roll of tape in her hand and studied the other woman.

"Sure," Ella agreed readily despite the hesitation in her tone. "I appreciate that we skipped over the formal interview for the nanny position but I expected you to have questions about me and my qualifications."

"You're a pediatric nurse," Brynn said with a laugh. "You're overqualified to be a nanny. Which leads to my question. Why?" She shook her head.

"I'm sure you could get hired immediately at the local hospital. Why do you want to be a nanny with your impressive résumé?"

Ella handed Remi a plastic giraffe. The girl kicked her feet and shoved the toy into her mouth to investigate. "Because I don't want to be impressive right now," Ella answered. "I want to be happy." She met Brynn's gaze and her gaze softened. "I haven't stayed in the same place for more than six months in the past five years. I'm not expecting my return to Starlight to be permanent. I need a break, but I also want to stay busy. Taking care of this little cutie will allow me to do both."

"Something happened to you," Brynn said quietly.

Ella's smile was forced. "Lots of things happened to me. I'm not special, and my story isn't unique. Maybe it's burnout at twenty-seven, which sounds pathetic. Still, I need a break."

"I appreciate you taking that break with Remi. Finn and Kaitlin are so glad you're here," Brynn told her.

"I never expected to see my brother settled down and ready to get married. He really loves her."

"She's an amazing person. Kaitlin is devoted to both Finn and your father. She's helped them get close again."

Ella made a face. "I'm still having trouble wrapping my mind around the fact that my dad and my brother are close." She blew out a sharp laugh. "This is going to sound awful, but it feels like Finn is being disloyal. The one thing that bonded us was always mutual disdain for our father. Now I'm the one on the outside, and they're all chummy. I can't get over it."

"You're not on the outside," Brynn said, hearing the pain in the other woman's voice. "It means a lot to both of them that you're here."

"I'm not staying," Ella said suddenly. "Two months at the most and then I might travel a bit on my own before the new contract with Traveling Nurses starts again. I took a six-month leave."

"It's amazing that you have so many options."

"It's kind of amazing that you have so many presents to wrap," Ella replied with a laugh.

"I want this to be Tyler's best Christmas ever." Brynn wrapped a swath of colorful paper around a microscope box. "I know I went overboard. I'm like most people around the holidays. I can talk a good game about the point of the season not being materialistic, but I get sucked right down the consumer rabbit hole." She eyed the pile of gifts she'd stacked on the far end of the table. "Are you disgusted by my rampant consumerism? It probably looks like gluttony to you."

"It looks like you're overcompensating for sure."

Brynn winced at Ella's honesty. "Well, you aren't wrong."

Ella grinned at Remi. "I remember when you got pregnant," she said suddenly. "I was a junior, and it was all anyone could talk about."

"A cautionary tale," Brynn murmured with a dry laugh. "I'm sure my story was used as an example of the importance of abstinence for parents around here for years. The best birth control money couldn't buy."

"I never thought about it that way," Ella said softly. "I thought it was amazing you kept your head held high and did what needed to get done. Back in high school, I liked to rebel for the sake of rebelling. But it was stupid. You made decisions about what was going to happen with your life, and you didn't care what anyone else thought. You were a true maverick."

"I cared," Brynn whispered. "I just cared about my son more."

"Like you care about Remi."

"My mother is certain I'm trying to ruin her life."

Ella sucked in a breath. "By adopting a baby?"

"She doesn't think I can handle another child, and she definitely objects to the circumstances of Remi's birth."

"You don't have your mother's support?" Ella sounded genuinely shocked.

Brynn shook her head, trying to ignore the ache in her chest. "She's also angry that Nick is involved and that his mom has been helping with her. We were neighbors growing up, and my mom always felt like his mom judged her for being a single parent. She hated that and didn't want it for me. When I got pregnant, she made sure I knew getting Daniel to marry me was the highest priority." She rolled her eyes. "That didn't work out the way she expected and, of course, it had to be my fault. She's never really gotten over her anger at how my life turned out, and Remi adds to it. It makes me a topic for gossips in town, and my mother hates feeling like she's associated with gossip."

"Those people are jerks," Ella said. "And stupid. Stupid jerks."

"I've gotten used to people not expecting much of me," Brynn said with a quiet laugh.

"No one should get used to that," Ella countered.

"Maybe, but it's what I know."

"How did Nick get involved in this?" Ella asked, glancing around the living room. "I had such a little-sister crush on both him and Parker when I was in high school. He was hot as a five-alarm fire but kind of a selfish prick, you know?"

Brynn grinned. "Trust me, I know. And I know all about crushing on him. He's grown up a lot since then. I need to be approved as a foster parent, so he agreed to take in Remi so I could be close to her."

"You two were besties back in the day, right?"

"Something like that."

"He seems different now." Ella tapped a finger

against her chin. "Not just grown up like Finn and Parker. He's more serious. He used to crack jokes and prank people all the time. Now he's almost subdued."

"His brother died in combat while Nick was away at college," Brynn explained. "His dad had a fatal heart attack shortly after. Coming back to Starlight to help his mom changed him."

"I get that," Ella murmured.

"You were a teenager when your mom died." Brynn turned fully to face the other woman. Ella's rosy complexion had gone pale as if the memory still caused her physical pain. "That's a hard age to lose a parent."

Ella flashed a tight smile. "Especially when the one who's left doesn't like you very much."

"Are things still rough with your dad? Is that why you've come home? I heard he's starting another round of cancer treatment."

Remi let out a small cry, and Ella picked her up, then began to sway back and forth as she rubbed the baby's back. She kept her head down for several long seconds, and when she finally looked up, Brynn saw tears swimming in her eyes.

"Oh, I'm sorry." Brynn immediately stood and reached for the baby. "I didn't mean to upset you. We've been talking so freely. I've told you more about my emotional scars in one conversation than most of my friends know. If I crossed a line…"

"You didn't." Ella swiped at her cheeks. "It's so strange, this business of bursting into tears at the drop of a hat. I spent years working with struggling populations. I've held children when they've taken their last breath and comforted mothers who've lost their babies to disease and illness. I managed all of it with a professionalism that sometimes worried the people I worked with. Apparently, I was compartmentalizing my feelings. As of six months ago, all of the compartments were full. Everything that happens affects me until I feel like I'm being crushed under the emotional weight of it."

"Oh, Ella. I can only imagine how tough that is."

Ella sniffed. "I wish I could say I came back to patch things up with my dad. It would be the noble thing to do. I bet it would be how you'd handle it. Mainly, I ran away from my life with my tail between my legs. Starlight was the only place I could think of going where I might distract myself from everything I can't stop feeling. But I've been here three days and I've barely spoken to my dad. I'm staying in his guesthouse and I'm still so damn angry at how he treated Finn and me after my mom died that I don't know what to say."

"That's understandable," Brynn said, even though she didn't understand it. She couldn't imagine having that sort of anger at anyone. Maybe it's why she'd been such a pushover in her marriage.

"I'm angry with Finn, too," Ella admitted on a

rush of air. "The biggest bond we had was our animosity toward Dad. Now I'm this lonely, angry woman who can't seem to stop crying." She gave a watery laugh. "I bet you wish you'd known all this before you hired me to take care of Remi."

"It wouldn't have changed anything," Brynn told her.

"You're too nice of a person."

"I get that a lot."

"I'm not nearly nice enough."

Brynn kissed Remi's cheek when the little girl snuggled against her. "You have a big heart, Ella. I can tell. It might feel a bit bruised right now, but hearts can heal. Trust me. I'm an expert."

"This may be none of my business, but are you and Nick an item?"

Brynn wasn't sure how to explain what was between her and Nick, but the word *item* didn't begin to do her emotions justice.

"*Complicated* is the best way to describe it," she said with a laugh. Remi fussed and wiggled in her arms. She checked her watch. "Time for a diaper change and a nap," she told the girl with another soft kiss to the head.

"I'll take her up," Ella offered. "It will be good to see if she'll go down for me without a fuss."

Brynn gave Remi to the other woman reluctantly. It was difficult to let the baby go, but she knew Remi was in good hands with Finn's sister.

She checked the messages on her phone after Ella headed upstairs. Josh had texted to tell her they were still planning to finish the work as promised, so she could prepare to return to her house on Christmas Eve.

A flood of conflicting emotions washed through her. On one hand, she was grateful Josh's crew had stayed on schedule, a rarity in the world of construction. On the other, she felt a pang of sadness about not being with Nick on Christmas morning. Over the past few days, his house had come to feel like home.

She'd talked to Jennifer at social services, and as soon as the background check came back, Brynn would be approved as Remi's foster parent.

And Nick would be free of her.

A thought that pained her more than anything else.

Chapter Fifteen

"I mean it, Marianne. Go take care of your yule log."

The station's longtime receptionist chuckled as she straightened from her desk and began to load her tote bag. "That sounds kind of dirty, Chief," she told him with a wink. "I'm going to have to tell Daryll you were talking about my yule log."

Nick rolled his eyes even as he felt a blush rise to his cheeks. Marianne had a bawdy sense of humor for a woman pushing seventy and took great pleasure in embarrassing Nick and his deputies. She'd been a fixture at the department since way before Nick's time, and normally was the calmest, most easygoing woman on the planet.

But it was three days before Christmas, and something had gone wrong with the recipe she'd made for a family dinner tonight.

"In all seriousness," she said, patting his hand. "I appreciate it. Daryll hasn't been doing too well, and it means a lot that all our kids are coming back to celebrate Christmas with us a couple days early. It's different when they have kids of their own, so I don't take it for granted," she sniffed. "That dessert has been my tradition since they were toddlers baking in the kitchen with me. It has to be right."

"Then go make it right," he told her. The station was quiet, with only a few of his staff out on calls.

Just as he turned to head back to his office, the door opened and Jennifer Ryan walked in. Nick's stomach dropped as the social worker gave him a wan smile.

"Did we have an appointment?" he asked, an uncomfortable shiver passing through him.

"No. Can we talk in your office?"

Her tone did nothing to ease his growing panic, but he didn't want to alert Marianne or any of the deputies still in the station that something might be wrong.

"Remi's mother contacted the department this morning," Jennifer said as soon as the door clicked shut.

Nick's hand squeezed the knob as he forced his breath to stay even.

"What did she say?"

Jennifer shook her head. "She wouldn't tell us exactly where she was or if she had a plan for returning."

"She reached out with no details?" He released the knob and stalked to the edge of the desk. How was he supposed to feel about this development? Of course, Nick wanted what was best for Remi, but he knew in his heart Brynn was meant to be the baby's mother.

"I'd left messages," Jennifer said softly, then shrugged when he gave her a quelling glance. "You know how this goes, Chief. We can't terminate parental rights until we do our best to reunite the mother and child. The state has a duty to contact the parent."

"She abandoned her baby," he reminded the social worker.

"I know." Jennifer sighed. "Brynn is close to being approved, but if Francesca returns to claim Remi within the allotted time frame, we have to try to make things work with the biological parent."

"It doesn't take a rocket scientist to see she isn't equipped to care for that baby. She should have no claim to Remi now."

"Stop. You don't mean what you're suggesting. It was clear that young woman was hurting, and we all need to support her if she wants to be a mother to her daughter. It's the right thing to do."

For a moment, he wished he could be old Nick—selfish Nick—the one who didn't care about doing the right thing. Instead, he gritted his teeth and nodded. "Why does doing the right thing sometimes feel like crap?"

"I wish I knew," the social worker murmured. "I convinced Francesca to schedule an appointment with me to discuss the future. We're supposed to meet a couple of days after Christmas when the office reopens. I encouraged her to tell me her plans over the phone or come in earlier, but she's visiting friends in Arizona and was adamant about the timing."

"So now we wait."

Jennifer nodded. "Do you want to tell Brynn?"

"Um, no." Nick shook his head. "Not at all."

"I'll call her, then."

"No."

The social worker blinked like she was having trouble understanding him. Nick knew he was taking a risk, but the fear of losing Remi would overshadow everything about Christmas for Brynn. He'd vowed to make her holiday happy, and he was determined to see that through.

"You want to keep this from her?" Jennifer made a tsking noise like a disappointed schoolteacher. "She has a right to know. It affects her the most."

"I get that," Nick agreed. "I just want to wait until after Christmas to tell her. She and Tyler have been through so much this year. They deserve a happy holiday, and the thought of Francesca returning would cast a shadow over everything."

"It's a real possibility that she'll want another chance with her baby."

"Yes, but not a guarantee." Nick ran a hand through his hair, wishing he could come up with a better plan. A way to tell Brynn everything now without hurting her. But he couldn't, so he'd protect her the only way he knew how.

"You said she won't be back until after the holiday anyway. I'll tell Brynn then, so she can prepare for what might happen. In the meantime, I'm holding out hope for a Christmas miracle."

Jennifer closed her eyes briefly. "I don't like this, but you know Brynn better than me. If you think the news would be too hard before Christmas, then we wait. But she has to know, Nick. Not dealing with it won't make the situation go away."

"I understand. Thanks, Jen. I promise I'll fill her in on everything. You'll call if you hear anything more from Francesca?"

"Yeah." She inclined her head as she studied him. "I'm surprised at how easily you've adjusted to taking care of a baby."

"I watched *Mr. Mom* at least half a dozen times," he said with a laugh. He needed to keep the conversation light so that he wouldn't blurt out how much Remi had come to mean to him in the past couple of weeks. Brynn wasn't the only one who'd be distraught if the baby's mother returned. He'd never admit it out loud—at least not yet—but Nick had started fantasizing about the future and what it would look like if he, Brynn, Tyler and Remi became a real family. If he claimed them as his own.

It was the future he'd never expected but one that called to his heart.

"You're doing a good job," Jennifer said. "I wish all of our foster family situations went this smoothly."

He walked her to the entrance of the station and watched as she got into her dark blue sedan and drove away. The morning had started out sunny and mild, but in the past hour the wind had picked up and gray clouds were moving in. He tried not to see the changing weather as a harbinger of things to come.

Instead, he focused on the positive. Maybe the falling temperatures and overcast skies would mean snow for the valley. A white Christmas in Starlight and a happy holiday for Brynn no matter what Nick had to do to make it so.

"You're welcome to stay a couple more days. It's not a big deal and that way Tyler and Remi could wake up together on Christmas morning."

Brynn waited until Nick turned around from loading the final suitcase into her trunk, then lifted onto her toes and brushed a kiss across his mouth. "Thank you for everything," she said, splaying her hand over his chest. They were loading her car while Remi stayed inside with Nick's mom, and Tyler had gone on a quick playdate to Max's house. "As tempted as I am by your offer, it's important for Tyler to sleep in his own bed on Christmas Eve. We have a tradition with cookies for Santa and carrots for the reindeer."

"I heard reindeer like cupcakes," Nick said, one side of his mouth curving.

"Only Rudolph." She winked. "I'm going to get us settled at the house and then we'll see you later at Parker's."

He kissed her again. "I'll miss you."

"We're talking a few hours, Chief."

"Doesn't matter." He pulled her in for a hug and she wrapped her arms around his waist.

"I wonder how many of your neighbors are watching us," she murmured.

"That doesn't matter, either." He leaned back, tipping up her chin until she met his gaze. "I don't want to hide what's going on between us."

She chewed on her bottom lip. His words sent a combination of trepidation and delight spiraling through her. She didn't want to hide, either, but a part of her still didn't trust that Nick Dunlap would be truly interested in her. So much had changed from those years of unrequited love back in high school, but her heart still bore the scars of his tacit rejection.

She'd felt like she was getting her life back on track after Daniel's death. Could she risk opening her heart to Nick again? What if he hadn't changed as much as she thought? What if he hurt her and this time she didn't recover?

"You're thinking too hard," he said, tapping her forehead with one gentle finger.

"What's going on between us?" she blurted.

He looked confused. "We're together." He said the words like they were obvious.

"But what does that mean?" She narrowed her eyes. "To you."

His chest rose and fell as he drew in a long breath, then glanced at a spot over her shoulder. Maybe she shouldn't push him. Maybe she should enjoy the way he made her feel and not worry about anything more.

But Brynn had become too good at ignoring things over the years. As much as she loved—yes, loved—Nick, she was learning that loving herself was just as important. Part of that meant not settling. She wasn't willing to simply wait to see what bone he'd throw her. The new Brynn would fight for what she wanted, but first she needed to know where they stood. If a future was even a possibility.

"It means I don't want to hide. I want to take you

on dates—more than twelve—and be a part of your life, of Tyler's and Remi's lives."

"Okay," she said slowly. It wasn't exactly the grand declaration of love she might have wanted, but it was a start. "I do have some dates to make up for."

"You've already met your dozen quota," he told her proudly. "But you can tell your friends that I've got plans for more."

She released him and took a step back. "Wait." She thought back to the past couple of weeks. "The picnic, lunch dates, candlelight dinners after the kids went to bed? Those were official dates?"

Nick looked affronted. "You couldn't tell?"

The laughter bubbled up inside her, unbidden, spilling out until she was doubled over, her shoulders shaking.

"My attempts at dating are funny to you?"

"Yes," she managed between fits of laughter.

"What did you think was happening?"

She straightened, wiping tears from the corners of her eyes, and then dissolved into another fit of giggles at the way Nick was glaring at her. "I thought you were distracting me."

"Brynn." He threw up his hands. "I'm courting you."

"No one courts anyone these days," she said, still smiling at the sweet sentiment. "We've been living together, Nick. That horse kind of left the barn already."

He shook his head. "Then it's a good thing you're moving back to your own house, because we're courting. I'm going to take you out on dates and show you off to the whole town. Heck, I might even post a selfie of the two of us to the official Facebook page." He stepped closer, cupped her cheeks between his warm palms.

The way he held her face made her feel special, cherished. And she realized that's what he'd been doing the past several weeks. No wonder she'd fallen for him all over again. He might not be the gregarious charmer of their teenage years, but his appeal as a grown man was even more devastating.

At least for her.

"You mean the world to me," he said, and her heart thumped against her chest. "I missed my chance ten years ago, but I'm going to make up for lost time."

"I like the sound of that," she said softly but pulled away when he would have kissed her again. "Right now, though, I need to unload the car before Max's mom drops off Tyler. This might be the last year he believes in Santa. I need to hide the presents while I still have time."

"Are you sure I can't pick you up tonight?" He held her hand as she moved around the car to the driver's-side door, then lifted her fingers for a soft kiss.

"I told Mara I'd get there early to help with dinner preparations. We'll see you and Remi later. Tell Ella we expect to see her there, as well."

He seemed reluctant to let her go, which made butterflies flit across her stomach all over again.

She waved in the rearview mirror and smiled at the thought that she was about to have her best Christmas ever.

"Tyler, we're leaving in ten minutes," Brynn called up the stairs a few hours later.

"I'm almost done arranging Legos," he shouted from his bedroom.

Happiness bloomed in her chest at how elated he sounded. Although she already missed being under the same roof with Nick and Remi, it was good to be back in her own house.

Her house…only better. Josh and his crew had done an amazing job with the renovation. The carpet and tile were both new, and he'd managed to find maple cabinets at a great price, so the insurance money covered all of the updates.

The first floor had received a new coat of paint, a cheery sage green that Daniel would have hated. She pressed a hand to her stomach as she thought about her late husband and the years they'd muddled along together, neither one of them anywhere near happy in their marriage.

Brynn had been so determined not to raise her

son on her own. All of her life, she'd watched and listened to her mother's subtle and obvious complaints about single parenthood. Although Brynn had never known any different, her mom seemed to believe their lives would have been so much better if Brynn's father hadn't left when she was a baby.

Her mom had always told her fatherhood was too much for some men and had encouraged her to make sure Daniel didn't see Tyler as a burden.

The implication, of course, being that Brynn had been exactly that to the man who'd left both her and her mom.

She wondered what would have happened if she or Daniel had voiced their dissatisfaction with their marriage. Obviously, her late husband found outlets for his unhappiness. Brynn had thrown herself into being the perfect mom and the most upbeat, helpful version of herself that she could.

She'd never complained. Never asked for anything for herself. Mainly because she didn't want her son to feel the guilt she'd grown up with—guilt for being born and changing her own mother's life.

But she'd been a shadow of a person and had come to not like or respect herself very much. And if she didn't respect herself, how could she expect anyone else to?

That was changing. She'd changed, and she liked the new version of herself.

She walked toward the kitchen to pull the potato

and-fennel gratin she'd made from the oven. Mara was the best baker Brynn had ever met, so they left the fancy desserts to her and the rest of the group was bringing side dishes for the meat Parker was planning to smoke. This marked the first year their group of friends was getting together for a big Christmas Eve celebration.

In the past, Daniel watched football while Brynn and Tyler binged on holiday movies in the bedroom. She'd always envied close-knit families with boisterous celebrations. Brynn's mom had left for winter in Florida and would stay there until spring.

A sound at the back door had her glancing around. She gasped and rushed forward, her heart suddenly thumping hard against her rib cage.

"Francesca," she breathed, as she threw open the door.

The petite brunette stood outside in the cold air, her hair pulled back in a low ponytail. She wore a light jacket that wasn't nearly enough protection from the wintry wind blowing. It was almost five o'clock and shadows blanketed the backyard, which was covered with a fine dusting of snow. Not enough for sledding or snowball fights but enough that they'd have a white Christmas, which had made Tyler inordinately happy.

"Merry Christmas," the other woman said, almost shyly. "I know I shouldn't be here."

"It's fine." A cacophony of emotions clamored

through her—fear, anxiety, resentment, guilt. Brynn gave herself a mental shake and stepped back into the house. "Please come in. Come out of the cold."

Francesca frowned as if she wanted to refuse but then stepped into the house. "It smells nice in here. Like garlic."

"It's a potato casserole." Brynn smiled, although the muscles of her face felt stiff. She wanted to be kind, but panic clawed at her chest. Had Francesca returned for Remi? "Can I get you a glass of water or tea?"

"No." Francesca glanced around the kitchen. "It's not the same."

"There was a fire," Brynn answered with a grimace. "Nothing serious. Faulty lights on the Christmas tree. But we had to move out for a couple of weeks. In fact, this is our first night back in the house. My son wanted to wake up here on Christmas morning. Santa Claus and all that."

"Tyler," Francesca whispered. "Daniel spoke about him often."

Resentment made Brynn's chest tighten and she resisted the urge to curl her lip. As much as she wanted to show kindness to a woman who needed it, she didn't appreciate the reminder of Francesca's relationship with Daniel. Who knew if he really had been planning to leave Brynn for this woman standing in her kitchen once again? Knowing Daniel, he could have been playing them both.

"How's Remi?" Francesca asked, her gaze darting past Brynn.

"She's good." Brynn managed another smile. "Healthy. She rolled from her back to her tummy." She pulled the phone from her back pocket. "I have a video. Would you like to see?"

"No." The word came out on a sharp exhalation of breath. "It's not a good idea. I hadn't planned on coming here." Her fingers picked at one of the buttons on her jacket.

"I'm glad you did," Brynn told her. "We were worried about you. How have you been?"

More fidgeting. "I'm staying with my cousin in Arizona, and I've been offered a job in one of the local school districts. I know the official meeting with the social worker isn't until after Christmas, but the decision about the future and Remi—it's all I can think about."

"You have a meeting scheduled with Jennifer?" Brynn frowned.

"She said she'd talk to the police chief because he's Remi's foster parent right now." She held up her hands when Brynn gaped at her, obviously misunderstanding Brynn's reaction. "I'm sure you'll be approved. Daniel told me all you cared about was being a mom. He said you probably wouldn't even notice when he left."

Brynn had trouble processing Francesca's words

over the pounding in her head. "Nick knew you were coming back?" she whispered, her voice hoarse.

"That's what the caseworker told me. But don't worry. I'm going to sign the papers to terminate my parental rights." Her voice cracked on the last words. "I want what's best for my baby, and I believe you're it. I've had a lot of time to think over the past few weeks." She laughed softly. "I've done very little except think. Can I admit something to you?"

Brynn nodded, still trying to wrap her mind around this latest turn of events.

"I didn't miss her." Francesca swiped at her cheeks and Brynn's heart ached for the pain in the woman's voice. "Does that make me a horrible person? I'm her mom, and I didn't miss her. I liked being able to sleep in and only worry about my schedule. I love her, but I don't want to be her mother."

"That's not horrible." Brynn reached out and squeezed Francesca's trembling hand. "It takes courage to do what's right for your child even when society makes you think you're wrong for that decision. I know what it's like to be judged, and I believe you're doing the right thing. I promise Remi will always know you loved her. Your daughter will grow up understanding both of her mothers loved her in the best way they could."

"Thank you," Francesca said with a sniff. "I want to tell you how sorry I am again that I believed the things Daniel said about you. That you were weak and boring. He didn't know you at all."

Brynn offered the other woman a shaky smile. "Apparently, he's not the only one. Would you like me to be there when you meet with Jennifer to sign the papers? I understand what it's like to feel alone."

"Yeah." Francesca nodded, then offered the time of the appointment. Brynn put the date into her calendar and walked Remi's biological mother to her car.

She'd offered Francesca to stay the night with them, but the woman seemed eager to be on her way.

Relief should be her overwhelming sensation. She knew that. Her mind understood it and her heart felt it, but the joy at knowing Remi would be hers was tempered by the disappointment and humiliation that Nick had kept the knowledge of Francesca's return from her.

He'd talked a good game about believing she was strong and able to handle anything, but when it mattered, he'd hidden something from her because he obviously hadn't thought she could handle it.

Like everyone else who mattered, he didn't believe in her. The question was, what was she willing to do to prove she believed in herself?

Chapter Sixteen

It was nearly ten o'clock when Nick knocked on Brynn's back door. Worry clawed at him and had been since he'd arrived at Parker and Mara's house only to be told Brynn wasn't feeling well so had decided to skip the big Christmas Eve dinner.

He'd texted her and called but gotten no response. Both Mara and Kaitlin had been acting strange, although they'd assured him that Brynn needed a quiet night to rest.

It didn't make any sense because he knew how much she'd been looking forward to the evening.

His mom had accompanied him to the dinner, so he hadn't wanted to make a scene and leave midmeal. Even Ella seemed to notice how odd it was that Brynn wasn't part of the festivities. She'd pulled him aside as he was strapping Remi into her infant seat and told him she'd stop by after the party to stay with Remi so he could check on Brynn.

His first inclination had been to refuse the offer of help, not wanting to admit there was an issue. But he still hadn't received any responses to his texts and couldn't stop the feeling that something was really wrong.

The back-porch light flicked on and a moment later Brynn appeared, a glass of wine in her hand. She wore a bulky sweatshirt and leggings with her hair pulled back into a messy bun.

"Are you sick?" he asked, noticing the high color on her cheeks and the almost wild look in her eyes.

She scrunched up her nose. "I've eaten what feels like my weight in potato casserole and nearly finished a bottle of pinot grigio. I'm not sick yet, but the night it still young. Santa and I are getting our party on."

He didn't like the edge to her voice.

"I was worried when you and Tyler didn't make it to the dinner and you never responded to my texts."

"I'm not your concern," she said, and the chill in her tone made the little hairs on the back of his neck stand on end. "Despite what you seem to think, I can handle my life."

"I know you can," he agreed, trying to figure out what the hell was wrong. "Could I come in?"

She drained her glass and then shrugged. "You're going to do whatever you want anyway. Let's not pretend you care about my thoughts or feelings."

"I care." Despite her flippant attitude, he could almost feel the pain radiating from her. He didn't understand it, but it sliced across his heart like a razor. "Brynn, what the hell is the problem?"

"No problem. In fact, I'm celebrating. Making spirits bright and all that." Without warning, she turned and stalked toward the counter, pouring another large glass of wine for herself.

Nick followed her and closed the door to the winter air, which did nothing for the chill that settled in his chest. Something was very off with the woman he loved. He knew how hard the holidays were after the death of someone close. As troubled as their marriage had been, Daniel had been Brynn's husband for a decade. It was a lot of time to spend with a person. A lot of making Christmas joyous for their son. She'd been so strong these past few weeks—months, even—maybe the pressure had finally become too much for her.

What would it take for her to reach out and let him support her? How could he prove he was a man she could depend on?

"I love you," he blurted out, watching as if in slow motion as she whirled toward him, her eyes wide with shock and something that looked like rage. No, he had to be mistaken. Rage didn't make a bit of sense.

Wine sloshed over the side of her glass, and she placed it on the counter, then stalked toward him, finger wagging. "Don't say that to me. Don't you dare."

"It's true," he whispered, palms up like he could diffuse her anger somehow. "Brynn, please. Tell me what's wrong. I can't stand to see you like this."

"Francesca came to see me today."

Nick blinked. "No. She's not supposed to be in town until…"

The words tapered off when Brynn's gaze narrowed. "I wanted you to enjoy Christmas without worrying about losing Remi," he said, not bothering to pretend he no longer understood her anger. "I was trying to protect you. Don't be mad."

"I can feel however I want to feel," she said, enunciating each word. "I'm not a delicate flower, Nick. I don't need to be sheltered. I won't fall apart at the first hint of something difficult. Do you know how many difficult things I've dealt with over the years?"

"Yes." He nodded. "I do, and I know you can handle anything."

"But you didn't trust me to handle the idea of losing Remi."

"I was going to tell you after Christmas. We don't even know exactly what she's thinking."

"I know," Brynn said through clenched teeth. "I know because my late husband's mistress is the only person who seems to think I can manage the truth. My own mother didn't think I could handle becoming a mom and taking care of a baby. Daniel was afraid to leave me because he thought I'd fall apart." She laughed. "Heck, even my friends don't trust that I can find a man on my own, so they have to concoct some sort of dating game for me. And you're the worst of the lot."

His heart twisted at the accusation. "I promise I was trying to protect you. Nothing more."

"I thought you understood I don't need protection. I need someone to believe in me, to support me in standing on my own two feet. I want a partner, not a protector."

Nick ran a hand over his face, took a step toward her, then stopped when she crossed her arms over her chest. "Brynn, I failed you in high school. I failed my brother and my family. I was selfish and self-centered. This is me trying to do the right thing."

"It's you trying to control every aspect of the situation because you're afraid of what might happen if you don't," she countered.

Yes. Yes, he wanted control. He'd purposely shirked responsibility for most of his youth, and in doing so had hurt the people he loved. Brynn most of all.

"I didn't want you to be hurt."

"You need to learn that I can handle being hurt, Nick." She shook her head. "I'm practically a damn expert at it."

"Does she want to be reunited with the baby?" he asked quietly. "Why did she come to see you and not me?"

She stared at him for several long moments and then answered, "Nick, I fell in love with you before I even understood what love was. But I know now. I know what I want from love. It's more than having someone take care of me. I need a man who will be at my side to support me taking care of myself, as well. Someone who will trust me with their weaknesses and fears as much as I trust them."

She pressed a hand to her stomach. "For years, I made myself small because it's what I thought was the right thing to have a happy marriage. But neither one of us was the least bit happy. I owe it to my son and my soon-to-be daughter to be a role model."

"You are a role model to so many people," he agreed.

Her gaze had gone from angry to sad, which scared him even more. "I thought we might have another chance, but I can't be with a man who doesn't believe in me."

"I do, Brynn. So much."

"No. There's a difference between caring and coddling." She reached out a hand and gripped the edge of the counter with her fingers like she needed the support. "I think you should go now," she said without the barest hint of emotion in her voice.

He wanted to rail and argue. This wasn't how it was supposed to go. Tonight was Christmas Eve. He'd planned to spend the evening celebrating with their friends and then tomorrow morning enjoy the holiday together as a family.

But once again, he'd failed someone he loved. It didn't matter that his own heart was breaking in the process. He knew he wasn't cut out for relationships. Hell, he had a string of ex-girlfriends who could attest to that.

Tears shone in Brynn's blue eyes, and he hated himself for putting them there. He hadn't trusted her. He was afraid without Remi to bind them she'd realize she deserved better than he could give her. He'd lied to her for reasons he thought were valid, but he'd been a coward. Now he had to deal with the consequences.

"I'm sorry," he said, and the words had never sounded lamer.

She gave a tight nod. "Me, too."

It felt like slogging through mud, but he forced himself to turn around and walk away, knowing he was leaving behind his best chance at happiness.

* * *

"The Roman Colosseum," Tyler shouted, as he held up the box for his mom to see. "Can I put it together now, Mom?"

"Sure, sweetie." Brynn bounced Remi on her knee and tried to make her smile seem normal.

"Should I wait for Nick to come over so he can help?"

The innocent question was like a dagger to her heart.

Ella set a plate of cookies on the coffee table. "Nick ended up having to work today, bud. Official police chief business. I'm sure he'd want you to go ahead with the Lego set."

Tyler snagged a cookie and nodded. "Maybe he'll come by when he gets off. Mom, can I use your phone to FaceTime Max? I want to see what he got for Christmas and then I'll start."

"Five minutes, Ty." She handed him the phone, and he grabbed the gifts he'd just opened, kissed Remi's cheek and headed upstairs to his room.

"Thank you," Brynn said to Ella when they were alone with Remi. "I'm going to have to get better at answering questions about Nick. It's funny because I'm so used to talking about Daniel with Tyler. Now to have another man disappear from his life…" She swallowed back a sob. "It's too much, you know?"

Ella sat down on the chair across from Brynn and broke off a bite of cookie. It was a few minutes past noon on Christmas, and Brynn had expected to have a quiet day with Tyler until Ella texted and told her she was bringing over Remi for a visit.

Apparently, Nick had asked his temporary nanny to bring Remi for a holiday visit with Brynn and Tyler. It made her so happy to hold the sweet baby, although she could faintly make out Nick's scent when she snuggled the girl to her chest. The wave of longing that rose inside her threatened to take her under.

"He's still there," Ella said softly. "It's none of my business, but the guy is beside himself broken up about what happened."

"It wasn't just that something happened." Brynn shook her head. "He lied to me. He didn't trust me to handle the truth."

Ella sighed. "I have control issues, too. Blame it on my job or all the years of living out of a suitcase."

"I haven't left Starlight beyond a couple of weeks of vacation for over a decade," Brynn told her. "What's my excuse?"

"You don't need an excuse, but you might want to think about giving Nick another chance."

"I don't even know that he wants one. Our deal was not for anything long-term. We both knew it would end when Remi came to live with me."

Her brain might have been muddled last night by the wine, but one thing stayed clear. She and Nick had been a temporary thing. If he'd really known her, he would have trusted her with the truth of Francesca's upcoming visit.

"Did you, though?"

Brynn lifted Remi above her head and kissed the tip of the baby's nose when she giggled. "I'm a mom. That's my deal."

Ella rolled her eyes. "News flash. Women who are mothers are also human. You're allowed to have needs beyond your kids."

"Easy for you to say."

"Doesn't make it less true." Ella leaned forward and pushed the plate of cookies toward Brynn. "You need a cookie and you need a man. Nick specifically."

"I need a bunch of cookies." Brynn plucked one from the tray. "And a decent night's sleep and a million dollars and fresh highlights in my hair." She took a big bite and said around a mouthful of chocolate-chip goodness, "But not a man."

Ella laughed. "Not convincing at all."

Remi let out a wide yawn. "You should take her back to Nick's," Brynn said as emotion welled up inside her. "She's getting tired."

"I'm sorry for all of this." Ella watched with sympathetic eyes as Brynn lowered Remi into the infant seat and fastened the straps.

"None of it is your fault." Brynn swiped at her cheeks. "I have so much to be happy about and crying on Christmas is ridiculous."

"I won't judge you for being ridiculous." Ella winked. "But for the love of everything holy, enough with the waterworks."

Brynn gasped, and Ella gave her shoulder a gentle nudge. "Just kidding, but I snapped you out of the crying, right?"

"Actually, yes." Brynn had never met anyone like Ella Samuelson. She appreciated how the woman had assumed the role of friend without hesitation. Brynn had a habit of second-guessing every minute detail of her life. The relationship with Nick being a prime example.

But before she could deal with him, she had to get the rest of her emotional life in order. Tyler and Remi deserved that.

"I almost forgot." Ella slipped an envelope out of her purse as she hooked the infant seat over her arm. "Nick asked me to give this to you. He said it's a copy of the letter he submitted to social services."

Brynn frowned. "About me?"

"I guess they asked him for a reference letter. I don't know if it's because you two are friends or in his capacity as police chief. It's still strange that never-serious Nick is the law around here now, you know?"

"Yeah," Brynn breathed, her fingers numb as she took the envelope from Ella.

She gave Remi a last snuggle and then walked them to Ella's Jeep. After they drove away, she checked on Tyler, who was engrossed in his latest Lego set. With nothing else to act as a distraction, she sat down on the edge of her bed, holding the letter between two fingers. Her heart pounded as she contemplated whether to even open it.

Did she want to see what Nick had written about her? Did it matter?

"Stop pretending," she muttered to herself after a few moments. It mattered. She ripped open the seal and began to read.

Chapter Seventeen

"She's yours." Kaitlin smoothed a finger over Remi's soft hair and grinned at Brynn. "For always."

"Not yet." Brynn held up a hand. "Don't jinx it. I have at least a couple more months until the adoption is finalized."

"But she's here." Mara joined them as they stood behind the kitchen island, looking out to the friends who had gathered in Brynn's renovated kitchen and family room.

The party to celebrate Remi becoming her official foster daughter, along with the New Year, had been Kaitlin's idea. Although Brynn often wasn't comfortable being the center of attention, she'd agreed.

She wanted to celebrate this milestone. She was choosing to become the baby's mother and she didn't care what anyone else thought of her decision. It was so different than how she'd felt as a pregnant high school graduate, embarrassed and frightened about what the future might hold.

"How's Nick?" she asked suddenly, unable to keep her curiosity at bay one moment longer.

Both of her friends focused on the baby.

"Come on," she urged. "I'm going to see him eventually, and I know Finn and Parker have been talking to him. I still care about him even if it didn't work out between us. Again."

"You know he really does love you?" Kaitlin glanced from Remi to Brynn.

She met her friend's concerned gaze. "I think he wanted to love me," she answered, allowing Kaitlin to take the baby from her arms. "But not in the way I want to be loved. I'm not the timid girl I used to be," she said, more to herself than her friends. "I thought Nick and I could make a fresh start, but maybe there's too much past between us. Maybe he's still trying to make up for setting me up with Daniel."

"That was an unfortunate move," Mara said with a small laugh.

"But the choice to go out with Daniel and sleep with him and to marry him after I ended up pregnant were mine. I spent a long time making excuses for not taking responsibility in my life. Things happened to me," Brynn said, sighing, "but I let them. I controlled my reaction."

Kaitlin arched a brow. "And now you've cut Nick out of your life to prove you're in control."

Brynn let out a gasp of surprise. "That makes me sound foolish and petty."

Kaitlin feigned surprise. "Does it now?"

"And you're an expert on relationships?" Brynn asked.

"Before Finn, I was an expert on screwing up relationships," Kaitlin clarified. "My baggage had baggage, but I can still see when two people were meant for each other. Everyone can see what's between you."

"It's true," Mara confirmed.

Brynn sighed and turned to the counter to refill her coffee mug. "I gave up everything to make a go at marriage with a man I didn't love. I thought it was the right thing to do. I'm finally coming into my own, but it's not going to work if I'm with a man who tries to shelter me from anything bad. I want someone who will walk through fire with me, not for me."

"Oh, honey." Mara placed a hand on Brynn's arm. "Trust me, you want both."

Brynn blinked as her brain scrambled for purchase with that thought taking hold. Maybe she'd gone too far with her need to stand on her own two feet. Too many years of being brushed aside or underestimated had definitely made the pendulum swing in the other direction when it came to her desire to feel independent and in control.

"It's too late now," she whispered.

"He's miserable," Mara blurted out, then threw up her hands when Kaitlin gave her a quelling look. "What? It's true."

"We weren't supposed to say that out loud." Kaitlin turned to Brynn, shifting Remi in her arms as she did. "This hasn't been easy for Nick, either. To everyone's surprise—including his own, I imagine—he liked having a baby in the house. And you and Tyler, too, of course. But he wants you to be happy."

"We all do," Mara added.

"He's going to give you the time and distance you need, and he's telling Finn and Parker that all he wants is to be your friend again if you'll give him a chance."

"Do you think that's true?" Brynn drew in a shaky breath.

"I think you need to decide what you want from him and then be brave enough to ask for it." Kaitlin dropped a kiss on the top of Remi's head, then smiled. "To get what you want, sometimes you have to risk being hurt."

"I'm not great at asking for what I want," Brynn said with a shake of her head. "I'm more the take-the-lemons-life-hands-me-and-try-to-make-a-whole-meal-out-of-them type of person."

"Remember—" Mara leaned in "—this is new Brynn. Brynn 2.0."

Brynn held up a hand. "Fine. But no more talk about a dozen dates. I'm done with playing games, even well-intentioned ones."

"I thought you'd been on your twelve dates," Kaitlin said softly.

With Nick. A slow ache expanded in Brynn's chest but before she could respond to her friend, Tyler came running up to her. "Mom, you need to get Evie and Anna out of my room. They keep trying to touch my Lego sets. Anna wants to turn the fire station into a beauty salon." He threw up his hands in obvious disgust. "Like where girls get their hair cut."

Remi began to cry.

"She's probably hungry," Brynn said to Kaitlin. "Let me take her."

"Mom, you've got to make them leave." Tyler crossed his arms over his thin chest. "I want everyone to leave."

"Ty, be nice." Brynn bounced Remi in an attempt to quiet her, but the baby was having none of it. She smiled as several guests looked over toward them, familiar embarrassment causing heat to creep along the back of her neck. She didn't need a baby and a boy meltdown at the moment. "Everyone is here to celebrate your sister."

"I'll handle the girls," Mara said, reaching out to pat Tyler's shoulder. He yanked away with narrowed eyes.

"They're stupid," he muttered.

"Tyler." Frustration made Brynn's tone sharper than she'd meant.

"It's fine." Mara headed for the stairs with Tyler stalking after her.

"I think it's also time for the celebration to wrap up," Kaitlin said.

Remi's cries grew louder. "I need to get her fed." Brynn took a premixed bottle of formula from the refrigerator and popped it into the bottle warmer Ella had brought over along with the other supplies from Nick's house.

"Don't worry about any of us," Kaitlin told her.

But Brynn did worry. Once the bottle heated, she moved to the kitchen table and sat down with Remi. The baby sucked hungrily but remained uncharacteristically fussy. Her friends cleaned up the food and paper products, talking in hushed tones as if that would help Remi feel better.

Maybe it would. Maybe, like Brynn, the baby was overwhelmed. Mara reappeared with Anna and Evie, both looking irritated, and threw Brynn an apologetic glance.

Parker and Josh hustled the girls out of the house,

and Mara walked toward the table. "Evie accidentally knocked down one of the completed sets. I helped gather as many of the scattered bricks as I could find, but Tyler's pretty upset."

"Thank you. He'll be fine. I'll check on him as soon as Remi finishes."

She accepted hugs from both Mara and Kaitlin, and after another round of thanking them for their help and support, her friends left.

Brynn blinked away tears. Not because she was overwhelmed at this moment. She'd had plenty of struggles as a mom and knew she could deal with cranky babies and angry ten-year-olds. But she couldn't help but wonder if she'd done the right thing for all of them. Tyler, Remi and her. Was this new normal—the bumpy road of being a single mother to two children—the best future she could offer?

She couldn't imagine loving another man besides Nick, and now she'd pushed him away because of her anger and pride. What kind of example did that set for her children?

Remi continued to fuss as Brynn patted the baby's back to elicit a burp. After she'd taken the bottle, Brynn headed upstairs with the girl still crying. A nap was definitely in order, maybe for all of them at this point.

She knocked on Tyler's door and was greeted with a firm, "Go away."

"I'm sorry about your Legos," she said through the door. "Do you want help?"

"I want Remi to be quiet," he shouted back.

"Working on that, bud," she told him. "I'm going to put her down for a nap and then we can spend some time together."

She took his silence for agreement and turned on the night-light and sound machine in Remi's bedroom. The room was small and still held the bed and dresser from its previous use as a guest bedroom.

Brynn changed the baby's diaper while Remi fussed and then sang her several lullabies before placing her on her back on the gingham sheet.

Remi continued to wail, so Brynn lay down on the bed, planning to watch the baby for a few minutes until she settled. She had a feeling Remi was simply overstimulated after so much attention at the party. Since it was out of character for the little one to cry this way, Brynn didn't want to take any chances.

Once she made sure Remi was okay, she needed to spend some quality time with Tyler. He'd been a trouper with all the changes, but she knew this transition would have a few bumps, and she needed to take care of her first baby as well as the new one.

"Your mom is going to be really worried," Nick said, glancing into the rearview mirror as he drove the short distance between his house and Brynn's.

"All she cares about is Remi," Tyler muttered. He used one finger to draw patterns on the misty window. "It's exactly what Max said would happen. I hate Remi." The last three words came out on a choked sob, and Nick immediately pulled over and shifted the car into Park.

He undid his seat belt and turned to face Tyler, who looked as miserable as a grubby-faced boy could manage. Tyler had shown up at Nick's house on his bicycle, winded and spewing a convoluted story about how Mara's and Josh's respective daughters ruined his most recently completed Lego set, the one Nick had given him for Christmas. He hated girls and he hated his new sister and he wanted to come and live with Nick where there were no females in the house.

The boy had been brimming with frustration, and it took Nick a full five minutes to understand that Tyler had left the house without telling his mom where he was going. Nick had tried calling and texting Brynn but had gotten no answer. Once Tyler calmed down, Nick explained they had to return to his mom's house so she wouldn't panic when she realized he was gone.

"Is that true?" Nick asked gently.

The kid's jaw worked for several seconds before he gave a sharp shake of his head. "No, but it's her fault that Evie broke my Lego set. And Mom loves Remi better than me now."

"I know that's not true." Nick's heart melted for the boy. Tyler had been a pint-size emotional rock during these past few weeks and in the months after his father's death. Nick knew it couldn't be easy to deal with all of the changes, especially when Tyler obviously felt like he had to be strong for his mom. "She loves you more than anything in the world, and she has since the day you were born. Even before. I was the first person she told she was having a baby."

"Even before my dad?" Tyler's feathery brows drew together.

"Your mom was my best friend back in high school," Nick said instead of answering the question directly. "We told each other everything. She was nervous like young mothers are, but I could see in her eyes how happy the thought of you made her. I knew she'd be an amazing mom."

"I don't want to hate Remi," Tyler said. "I want her to be my sister, but I'm so mad."

"You're allowed to be mad at your sister," Nick assured him.

"But she's a baby."

"I know." Nick smiled. "It's still okay. It doesn't mean you don't love her. You do."

The boy drew in a shaky breath. "Yeah."

"I guarantee she'll make you mad about a million more times in your life, but you'll still love her. That's how it is with brothers and sisters."

"Do you have a sister?"

"No." Nick shook his head. "I had a brother, but he died. I miss him every day. He was a way nicer person than I am."

"You're nice to me," Tyler told him with a sniff. "And to Mom. Are you guys still friends?"

"I'll always be your mom's friend. She needed some time to adjust to the changes when Remi came to live with you, so I probably won't get to see you as much now. Babies take a lot of attention, but she still loves you as much as she did before."

"You and I can still hang out, right?"

Pain sliced across Nick's chest at the expectation in the boy's gaze.

"I hope so," he whispered, then turned back around and fastened his seat belt. "Right now, we need get you home."

A profusion of thoughts cascaded through his mind as he turned onto Brynn's street. He'd hated everything about the past week and blamed himself for making her believe he didn't have faith in her. If he'd only told the damn truth in the first place, maybe they wouldn't be here right now.

Or maybe they would. He still struggled to believe he could be the man Brynn deserved. But damn if he wasn't going to give it his best shot. Not just because he loved her, though he knew no one would ever have the hold on his heart that she did. It was more than just their connection. He loved Tyler and Remi and the thought of the three of them becoming his family made a peace descend over him that felt like coming home.

Now he needed to convince Brynn he could be her home, as well.

His phone beeped as he parked in her driveway. "Brynn?"

"Oh, my God, Nick." He hated the panic in her voice. "Do you have him? Tell me you have him. I fell asleep and—"

"We're here, Brynn. He's home." He turned off the engine.

She made a noise somewhere between a sob and a cheer and he heard a sound like she'd dropped the phone to the floor.

Tyler was already climbing out of the back seat and looked over his shoulder. He flashed a sheepish grin. "I guess you were right. She missed me."

Nick didn't have time to answer before they both turned when Brynn shouted for her son. Nick's chest tightened as he watched Brynn tear across the front lawn and scoop Tyler into her arms, hugging him tight until the boy squirmed.

"You're squishing me," the boy complained.

"You scared me half to death." Brynn drew back, holding Tyler's thin arms. "I couldn't find you, sweetie. I didn't know what to think. Please don't ever leave without telling me."

"You were asleep," he said, and she frowned at the soft admonishment in his tone.

"I'm sorry, Ty. But you can wake me. Please. I always have time for you."

"Don't cry." The boy wiped her cheeks with the sleeve of his striped sweater. "I was mad. Nick hadn't been over to see the Colosseum since I finished it, and I wanted to tell him."

"I'm glad you had a friend to go to." She bit down on her lower lip as she offered Nick a watery smile.

"He told me you love me best of all," Tyler said.

Brynn's gaze filled with gratitude before she returned her attention to her son, and Nick felt his heart stammer in response.

"I will always love you with my whole heart," she told her son, giving him another hug.

"But now you love Remi, too." Tyler pulled away.

"There's room in my heart for both of you," she promised. "When Remi came into our lives, Ty, my heart grew with love. So much."

Nick stepped closer as the boy seemed to mull this over. "I guess that makes sense. But she's annoying when she cries."

"There will be plenty of things your sister does over the years that annoy you."

"Nick told me that, too." Tyler nodded. "He said I'll love her anyway."

"Yeah," Brynn whispered.

"Mom, can Nick come in and help me start putting the Colosseum back together?"

The way Brynn frowned made Nick's stomach

clench. *Please don't say no*, he thought. "If he has time, it's okay with me."

They both turned their attention to Nick, and he nodded, trying not to look like a lovesick puppy.

"Maybe you can stay for dinner so you can visit with Remi, too?" Brynn straightened and a blush crept up her cheeks. "If you aren't too busy?"

"I'd love that," he said, grateful when he managed to get the words out with a steady voice.

Tyler grinned, then tugged on his mom's hand. "Let's go."

"You head in," she told him and dropped a kiss on the top of his head. "Nick and I will be there in a minute."

"I'll bring everything downstairs," he told Nick, then looked toward his mom. "And I'll be quiet, so I don't wake Remi."

"Thanks, sweetie."

They both watched him walk away, and an awkward silence descended between them. Nick hated the damn silence. This was Brynn. His best friend. The love of his life, even if it had taken him far too long to realize it.

"I'm sorry," he said at the same time as her.

His eyes widened as she offered a small smile. "Jinx," she murmured.

"Brynn, no." His hands itched to reach for her, but he wouldn't yet. If he touched her, he'd lose all ability for coherent thought and this part was important. "You have nothing to apologize for. I'm sorry I didn't tell you about Francesca. It was stupid and selfish, which should come as no surprise from me."

"You aren't stupid or selfish."

"Always so kind."

"Not always," she reminded him.

He nodded. "You were right to call me out on what I did, but I need you to know I have all the faith in the world in you. Just not in myself. Or in the fact that you would actually choose me if there was nothing to keep us apart."

"Nick." She took a step closer.

He lifted his hand, then ran it through his hair instead of pulling her to him. "I can't promise I won't keep screwing up, Brynn. I'll probably be annoying and stupid and a huge idiot for the rest of my life."

She chuckled. "Is this the part where you're pumping yourself up?"

He dropped down to one knee. "This is the part where I ask you to love me anyway."

Her mouth formed a small o.

"Please give me another chance and I promise I won't waste it. Brynn, I want to spend the rest of our lives trying to do better. Trying to be the kind of man that deserves you."

"Silly," she whispered and cupped his face with her palms. The warmth and softness of her skin against his made his whole body tingle with longing. "It's always been you, Nick. I will always choose you. I pushed you away because I was scared, not because I can't handle mistakes or missteps. We're both going to make those. But I want to make them together."

It felt like a firework display erupted in his heart, and he could lose himself in the bright intensity of it. "Will you marry me, Brynn Hale? Will you make me the happiest man in the world?"

She leaned in and whispered against his lips, "Yes."

And Nick knew, with every ounce of his being, that he'd truly found his home.

* * * * *

MILLS & BOON

Coming next month

TEMPTED BY THE TYCOON'S PROPOSAL
Rachael Stewart

'Come with us, Sophia—come with us to Iceland.'

Her eyes shot open and she gazed down at him, hardly daring to believe the question and knowing at the same time that she couldn't. The thought, the idea of being surrounded by her fear, by the past, by the snow... She shook her head and shifted beneath him to remind him of her body, of what she wanted in that moment. What he so wanted too.

'You can't ask me that, Jack. Don't ask me that.'

He raised himself up over her, his elbows planted either side of her body to bear his weight. 'Why not?'

'Because I can't. We can't.'

He kissed her until she was breathless, panting. 'Why?'

'We don't even know they'll be available for Lily's birthday yet.'

'That doesn't matter. They will be available at some point and I want you to come.'

She shook her head, the emotions clawing at her throat and her chest, making it hard to breathe. 'We both know this has to end and that the longer we spend together with Lily, the more likely it is that she will become attached too.'

His eyes were so serious now as they blazed into

hers. The 'too' spoke volumes; it told him that fear protected her own heart, but did it protect his as well?

'That's not the whole truth, is it?' he pressed, probing for more, probing for her to admit that she feared being faced with her past. All it took was one harmless-looking snowflake, the ice forming over her windshield, and the shivers would start.

'It's enough.'

He shook his head, one hand stroking her cheek and catching a tear she hadn't known was there. 'You need to stop living in fear of your past, Sophia.'

He kissed her to soften his words and she clamped her eyes shut over the rising swell of emotion within. 'You've taught me that; you've made me realise that avoiding a base, avoiding London, is running from it. And by doing it, Lily has suffered.'

She kept her eyes closed as the tears refused to stop. He was right. She'd been a hypocrite to tell him the same and not realise it was exactly how she'd been behaving all along.

'Come with us. Not because I ask you, not because it would make Lily happy to have you there… Come because you want to. Come because you are ready to move on from it.'

Continue reading
TEMPTED BY THE TYCOON'S PROPOSAL
Rachael Stewart

Available next month
www.millsandboon.co.uk

COMING SOON!

We really hope you enjoyed reading this book. If you're looking for more romance, be sure to head to the shops when new books are available on

Thursday 24th December

LET'S TALK
Romance

For exclusive extracts, competitions
and special offers, find us online:

f facebook.com/millsandboon

🐦 @MillsandBoon

📷 @MillsandBoonUK

Get in touch on 01413 063232

For all the latest titles coming soon, visit
millsandboon.co.uk/nextmonth

MILLS & BOON

THE HEART OF ROMANCE

A ROMANCE FOR EVERY KIND OF READER

MODERN
Prepare to be swept off your feet by sophisticated, sexy and seductive heroes, in some of the world's most glamourous and romantic locations, where power and passion collide.
8 stories per month.

HISTORICAL
Escape with historical heroes from time gone by. Whether your passion is for wicked Regency Rakes, muscled Vikings or rugge Highlanders, awaken the romance of the past.
6 stories per month.

MEDICAL
Set your pulse racing with dedicated, delectable doctors in the high-pressure world of medicine, where emotions run high an passion, comfort and love are the best medicine.
6 stories per month.

True Love
Celebrate true love with tender stories of heartfelt romance, fr the rush of falling in love to the joy a new baby can bring, and focus on the emotional heart of a relationship.
8 stories per month.

Desire
Indulge in secrets and scandal, intense drama and plenty of si hot action with powerful and passionate heroes who have it all wealth, status, good looks…everything but the right woman.
6 stories per month.

HEROES
Experience all the excitement of a gripping thriller, with an ir romance at its heart. Resourceful, true-to-life women and stro fearless men face danger and desire - a killer combination!
8 stories per month.

DARE
Sensual love stories featuring smart, sassy heroines you'd wan best friend, and compelling intense heroes who are worthy of
4 stories per month.

To see which titles are coming soon, please visit

millsandboon.co.uk/nextmonth

might just be true love...

MILLS & BOON

HISTORICAL

Awaken the romance of the past

Escape with historical heroes from time gone by. Whether your passion is for wicked Regency Rakes, muscled Viking warriors or rugged Highlanders, indulge your fantasies and awaken the romance of the past.

MILLS & BOON
MEDICAL
Pulse-Racing Passion

Set your pulse racing with dedicated, delectable doctors in the high-pressure world of medicine, where emotions run high and passion, comfort and love are the best medicine.